Hearts Restored

Prue Phillipson

KNOX ROBINSON
PUBLISHING
London • New York

KNOX ROBINSON
PUBLISHING

1205 London Road
London, SW16 4UY
&
244 5th Avenue, Suite 1861
New York, NY 10001

Knox Robinson Publishing is a specialist, international publisher of historical fiction, historical romance and medieval fantasy.

A CIP catalogue record for this book is available from the British Library.

ISBN 978-1-90848313-3

Manufactured in the United States of America, Australia and the United Kingdom.

www.knoxrobinsonpublishing.com

Printed and bound in Great Britain by
Marston Book Services Limited, Didcot

To Alan, my help and support
always.

Also by Prue Phillipson

Vengeance Thwarted

CHAPTER 1

29th May 1660

THERE was nothing now in Daniel Horden's mind but the unplanned wondrous coincidence of this present moment.

The immediate past had fallen away. His seasickness had vanished. His embarrassment at slipping on the slime at the landing stage was forgotten. He was indifferent to his soiled cloak and breeches, though he must soon appear in them before a gaggle of unknown relations. Even the certainty that the three young ladies among them would eye him as an uncouth country boy had vanished from his thoughts. That terror of an imminent future was lost in the brilliance of now.

He was about to see the King.

His mother had opened her letter before the fireplace in the small parlour back home at Horden Hall in the county of Northumberland.

"Well! I am to see my mother and sister after twenty years. They have learnt that we are to get a King again and they feel safe to come." She had turned to Daniel's Father. "Nat, we must go to London to meet them. They expect it. They will stay with the London Hordens and then travel back here with us. What say you?"

Daniel had not waited for his father to speak. "London! Go to London. Oh wonderful. I have never been further than Durham."

It had not occurred to any of them that they might see the new King Charles with their own eyes. Nathaniel Horden's verdict, when he had a chance to speak, was: "We might afford it if we go by sea."

So they had made their preparations and embarked from Newcastle on a day towards the end of May sure that the King would be well established in his chosen palace long before they reached London. But they were no sooner landed than they learnt of his stately royal progress from Dover to Canterbury, on to Rochester where he reviewed the army, and, continuing on horseback, now this very day, would make his entry into his capital.

So here they were in sight of London Bridge, their legs aching from long standing but their bodies held up by the press of people which, impossibly, seemed to be still growing. Surely the King must come soon.

Despite his impatience Daniel kept breaking into laughter at the battering of his senses that London was hurling at him. The noise was the most overwhelming for one raised in remote Northumberland. Cannons thundered, church bells clanged ceaselessly, horses' hooves rang on the paving stones as more troops and great personages passed by but still the main procession was not yet in sight on the bridge.

His eyes ached too with the brilliance of colour and so

much shimmering of silver and gold. Never in his life had he seen such richness of robes and uniforms. Even the thousands of ordinary people had brought out their brightest caps and scarves to wave. Thank God the years of black and drab were being wiped away!

The smells were just as overpowering. While he laughed at the attack on his sight and hearing he held his nose against the stench of the river and the sweat of the crowd. He turned to look down from his six-foot-two-inches at his father and mother standing on tiptoe beside him.

"The Thames stinks worse than the Tyne. And can you see from down there that there are houses on the bridge just like Newcastle's? How will he get through? The people have been allowed to crowd on."

"Who could stop them?" His mother was laughing too at the fantastic madness of it all. She struggled to cover her ears when the guns bellowed, but one hand was pinned to her sides by the vast hips of a washerwoman.

"Tell us," said his father, "the moment that you see him. As he rides by I have vowed to pray rather than cheer. I will thank God for his restoration but pray above all things for peace and freedom of worship under his rule."

Daniel nodded and turned back, sensing a shiver of excitement stirring the sea of people. There was a leaning forward, a craning upward like a wave, as soldiers, glittering with cloth of silver sleeves, tried to make a passage on the bridge. Horsemen in scarlet cloaks appeared and clattered by.

Then there came a universal in-drawing of breath. He was

coming – only one among many riders clad in doublets of silver, but unmistakeable, a towering figure of majesty.

Daniel nudged his father whose lips at once began moving silently.

"He's bareheaded," Daniel hissed and snatched off his own hat. I am in the presence of my King, he told himself, scarce believing it.

As the principal three shimmering figures drew nearer he could see the central one graciously waving his large feathered hat in a gesture of love to his people. A great deep-throated roar of cheering rose from the thousands crushed around them.

Daniel felt a lump rise in his throat. He hadn't lived till this moment. To be here in his own body in London, gazing upon his restored King and all the world rejoicing at the opening of a new age – it was a miracle.

He swallowed hard as the slow-treading horses came alongside. His eyes were riveted on the benign eyes, the dark brows, the curled moustache, the full, smiling lips, and as the procession moved past he burst into a yell with all the rest, "Hurray, hurray! God save the King!"

He felt the royal eyes turn and look upon him. He was unaware how he stood out from the crowd, flourishing his hat far above the massed heads, his long flaxen hair catching the sunlight, but he received a smile and a wave all for himself and his tears spurted up and overflowed.

"He looked at me. He waved to me."

His mother managed to free her arms to clutch him round

the waist.

"Remember this, Dan," she murmured. "Oh, Dan, we will all remember this."

"It came upon me what they did to his father," he choked out.

"A different age," she said. "We must believe that."

I will, he told himself. The new King is a great man and he looked full at me. I am truly alive. On a high peak in the history of England.

Again there was a mass movement as heads turned to stare after the glinting procession till the very last velvet-clad page-boy had disappeared.

Then a great clamour of talk broke out as he heard neighbour telling neighbour how the King had looked. Was he not noble? Was he not head and shoulders above the rest? Who was that by him? Why it was the two dukes, his brothers, don't you know? And those in the red cloaks were the Sheriff's men and did you ever see so much silver lace on ordinary soldiers?

Daniel and his parents gazed at each other, Daniel still on his mountain top of ecstasy. He saw his mother looking about at the people beginning to shake themselves and take reluctant steps – where? he wondered. Home or the ale houses or their work places in this vast city? Surely little work would be done on this momentous day. He heard his mother fetch a deep sigh and grin ruefully at his father.

"That's over then, Nat. We didn't expect to see that. Well, there will be no hackney carriages to be had even if we could afford the fare. My legs are one great ache from three hours' standing. But I wager we can find our way to the Strand on foot. My relations – all your new relations, you men of mine – are expecting us."

Daniel plummeted from his moment of glory. The dread of the encounter to come was back with a vengeance.

"Oh Mother, can we not put it off? Tomorrow perhaps?"

She laughed aloud, reached up her hands to his face and pulled him down and planted a kiss on his nose. "And where would we sleep tonight with scarce the price of a hired bed between us?"

He straightened, glancing about shame-faced. She can smell my fear. Curse her for always knowing. What did my ignorance and inexperience matter just now while I was caught up in great events? Now she knows I am to be painfully exposed before unknown cousins, a fearsome mix of wealthy London merchants and French nobility and me in grubby old clothes.

"Come, come," she chuckled, "you go to them as Sir Daniel Wilson Horden of Horden Hall in the county of Northumberland. Hold your head high. And if it's of any comfort to you the three girls will certainly be hoping to marry you."

"Oh Bel, you should not say that," cried his father.

"Why not? It will give him confidence."

Daniel stared at her. He was used to his mother saying outrageous things that shocked his steady, quiet father. That was Mother Bel – she scorned Arabella – blunt, unconventional, a wild taker of risks, her own woman. She stood there looking up at him, her green eyes mischievous, her square jaw jutted forward. The shawl she had drawn over her head to protect her from the hot sun had slipped to her shoulders. Her cheeks were bronzed from the outdoor life she had led all his childhood riding about the Horden land trying to restore the war-ravaged fields. He loved her with a passion. Yet he must break away soon or she would dominate him and Horden for ever. But marriage! Not yet. Not for a long time. He had to live first.

"You've *frightened* him," his father said with a twinkle in his eye. "I would rather encourage him with the thought of his superior learning. Theology, Greek, Latin, mathematics. I doubt if any of these girls can do more than sing a little and play on the virginals and for all we know they may have many suitors already."

"Nay, I could swear my sister Henrietta wants the baronetcy of Horden for one of her girls. I know her, Nat, though it is twenty years since I set eyes on her. As for the London Hordens they were for Parliament but I am sure old Clifford Horden would like to wed his granddaughter to a baronet. He wanted *me* to marry his boy William when I was Dan's age but backed out quick enough when misfortune fell on us – so stand your ground, Dan. *I* did and picked your father *myself* on a happy day." She gave his father a public hug as she said it. Then laughed aloud again. "Mind, I won't deny we could make good use of the London Hordens' wealth – but I wouldn't have Dan marry for it without love."

She shook out her crushed skirt. "Enough. Let us move. At least we are sure the Strand is west of London Bridge and we only have to keep the river in sight to find it."

It was not so easy to move at all with the crowds still milling about. Boys were already piling up sticks and debris to make bonfires at the corners of every street. The maypoles newly erected since Cromwell's ban were being hung with bunting. The bells were still ringing, the people cheering, sellers of nose-gays, sweetmeats, oranges were shouting their wares and blocking the way. Daniel, his long legs accustomed to taking great strides along country lanes or over the Horden land, was reduced to stuttering along.

His thoughts, though, were at a canter. There was some shame at his father's estimation of his learning. What he knew was due less to his own application than his father's extreme patience. Two of the cousins would be fluent in French and though his mother had tried to improve his, he would be halting sadly if they babbled to him in their native language. And what would they care for his Greek and Latin?

There would be Aunt Henrietta too, married to a vicomte, but thank heaven *he* was not coming. And his grandmother, Lady Maria Horden, exiled all these years for her Roman faith. He peered at his mother's face. Was she longing to greet her mother and sister again? He wanted to ask but suspected she was holding back her deepest emotions. This was a day for new experiences joyfully embraced.

She had spoken lightly of the old merchant Clifford Horden, a cousin of her father. It seemed she disliked him for the episode with his son William. And William must be the father of the English girl cousin. What a tangle!

Now his terror of the young ladies was back a hundredfold. When his mother had first mentioned – so casually – that she would be meeting two nieces for the first time, he had been startled. Were they just little girls? No, they were around his age, one older, one younger if she remembered rightly. And there would also be an English cousin whom she had never met. "She may be grown into a young woman too. So at last, Dan, you will have some elegant female companionship. Just what you need." Of course she was laughing when she said it. And now to throw out, so lightly again, that they would all be expecting to marry him! Did that make it easier for him or a thousand times worse?

What they would be like? He repeated their names in his head as he had done ceaselessly on the sea passage. Madeline and Diana Rombeau, dark French beauties perhaps, and Eunice Horden, a lovely English rose? But how did you begin to talk to such females? What subjects would excite them? He guessed they had not ventured into the thronged streets today so he could speak of that – but, no, that moment when the King smiled upon him was too special, sacred almost. It was not to be the stuff of social chatter.

"I think I will be very cold and aloof," he said now out loud, breaking into his parents' comments on the mass of craft on the river.

His father looked startled. "Nay, Daniel, be courteous above all things."

His mother said, "Just show them your own pleasant nature." But what, he wondered, at the raw, unshaped age of fifteen and a half years, did that amount to?

They had followed Thames Street and here many warehouses obscured the view of the river. Now they had to go inland a little to cross the Fleet, a dirty, stinking stream running down into the Thames. Daniel with his extra height could look above the thronging people and glimpsed up one of the lanes a massive building on the rising ground above them.

"What is that?" he asked his father, the only one of them who had visited London before.

"Ah yes, St Paul's Cathedral. Look, Bel, the biggest church in London." As they emerged onto Ludgate Hill they could see it in all its splendour.

His mother said, "We must visit it while we are here but we had better not stop now. I am parched and weary and this is taking longer than I thought."

Daniel could see that his father's excitement was growing. "We are not far away. We should pass the Branford's place where a friend from my days at Queen's College lives. I must certainly call upon him. He has inherited the title now."

Daniel had heard this friend mentioned. He was an earl now. Father has moved in exalted company, he remembered. Why should I be so diffident before these French connections?

They had made their way from Fleet Street into the Strand at last.

"There," cried his father, "that is the Branford's town house."

It had no land in front but was set back with a paved area and stone steps and a pillared entrance and heavy polished oak door.

"Very grand," Bel said, "but it looks as if they are from home. The shutters are all closed. Oh come, let us get on. I long to sit down."

Nathaniel mumbled something about it being odd if a loyal nobleman was away on such a day as this but he followed Bel. Daniel lingered a moment looking up at the house. Horden Hall was larger and with acres of land about it but of course, he remembered, the Branfords have an estate in Hertfordshire. We are pretty small beer after all.

He soon caught up his father and mother. There were more big houses, some set so far back they were partly screened by the blossom in their gardens. His mother was now looking up at more modest ones whose front doors were visible from the road. They were elegant dwellings of three storeys with attics. In gaps between Daniel could glimpse the river which here looked bluer than the grimy current next to London Bridge.

"Celia, Clifford's wife, wrote that their house has CC with an H below carved above the door frame," his mother was saying, "Dan, your young eyes will pick it out if the house is set far back from the road. There is a walnut tree in front too, she wrote."

They must be getting close. Daniel's heart was pounding now. He brushed vainly at his soiled breeches. His buff cloak with the merest wisp of lace at the neck was too short to cover the stain and the cloak too was marked where he had tumbled against the slime-covered wall of the jetty. The tide had been low and the boatman – curse him! – had not thought a lad like him needed the steadying arm he had given to his parents.

"Is not that a walnut tree?" his father said suddenly. "What grand gates and gravelled carriage-way!"

Daniel narrowed his eyes. Yes, carved into the stone lintel were the initials CC with the H below and above it, incised much earlier, the date the house was built –1620. They had arrived. Clifford and Celia and all the other unknown relations must be lurking behind that handsome façade, while his little family approached, shabby and footsore, from the street like beggars.

"You will be able to change your clothes," his mother said, boldly pushing open the gate. "Our travelling chests we sent ahead from the boat must have arrived long since."

"But to greet them like this!"

His father drew him forward as he hung back. "Daniel, it is the inner man that counts." It was a favourite theme of his father's but here, Daniel was sure, it would carry no weight with ladies familiar with the French court.

But now the door was being opened by a footman and behind him in an oak-panelled hall a thin grey man and a round pudding of a woman were hastening to greet them.

"Cousins Clifford and Celia," his mother whispered to him. "Not royalists, so keep silent about the King."

"We were listening for a carriage, dear Arabella. What! You have been caught in all the crush? We dare not venture out ourselves but we saw from the windows when the procession passed to Westminster. And these are your menfolk. Greetings, Cousin Nathaniel, and you, young man. My, what a height you are! Come come, your family are all agog to meet you," and she led the way up the wide staircase.

He was not to have time to make himself presentable and behind that door where Cousin Celia's hand was reaching to the handle were Madeline, Diana and Eunice, one of whom, if he was not very careful, he might be obliged to marry.

CHAPTER 2

THERE were too many people rising to greet them. At first Daniel's bewildered ears could take in only that they were all female by the massed rustling of skirts. He ought to look at faces. He ought to sort them calmly into young and old but he could hear only exclamations puncturing the air.

"My dear little sister – so long – and how handsome she has grown, Mamma!"

"Arabella, my child, my dear child – such cruel years apart!" An older deeper voice.

Then shriller squeaks. "But he's so tall and not yet sixteen!"

"*Sacre Dieu*! He will be through the roof when he's a man."

Daniel was only aware of the two delicate hands that were being thrust towards him. He glimpsed glossy petticoats as he grabbed the hands one after the other and planted hasty kisses without lifting his eyes.

The older deeper voice was saying, "So I meet my grandson at last. He has the Horden height and slenderness but the flaxen hair is his father's."

Daniel kissed heavily-ringed, wrinkled fingers.

Another cultured voice. "Well, nephew, this is a pleasure." A smooth hand. More rings, more shimmering silk. He was taller than everyone here so it was hard to keep looking down and avoiding faces. He straightened and looked over the heads.

The sun was shining full in his face through an open door onto a balcony. There was the opposite bank of the Thames. He was staring south across London. He could see fields beyond crowded houses.

The narrow shape of Clifford Horden interposed between himself and the scene.

"And this is my granddaughter, your Cousin Eunice."

Daniel looked down. A small, piquant face was looking up at him. Gracious, she was a mere child. He grinned at her and then saw she was also holding out her hand to be kissed. As he took it she lowered her eyes and something about the movement and the sight of her hair coiled tightly up at the back of her head made him doubt that she was a child. She was wearing a white collar over a plain grey dress which hung to the floor.

He kissed the hand and it was swiftly withdrawn as she scurried back to whatever corner she had been lurking in.

He could no longer avoid the other two girls who seized him from both sides and propelled him out onto the balcony. He had no idea which was which. Both had glossy black ringlets and surprised blue-black eyes with long lashes and arched eye-brows. One was in a rose-pink gown and the other in forget-me-not blue. Both had well-formed bosoms that looked ready to escape their bodices, which he thought extraordinary in day-dresses but perhaps that was the French way. Neither was beautiful, their noses too long and their mouths too wide. He was absolutely sure that he didn't want to marry either of them.

What irritated him most was that they persisted in speaking of him to each other in the third person. He felt like an exhibit that an explorer had brought back from foreign parts.

"How did he come in such a state?"

"Do *les jeunes hommes* wear their hair so long where he comes from?"

"And are they all outgrowing their clothes so fast!"

"If he sends his breeches to a *blanchisseur* they will be too short when they come back."

"Did you ever see hair so fair? It is made of straw, *n'est ce pas*?"

Their cackles of mirth brought their grandmother to the balcony.

"Madeline! You should know better. You should restrain your sister. Such unseemly noise. This is a sober, quiet house. Young man, pray come inside. Your hostess is inviting you to see your chamber and refresh yourself from your journey."

Daniel gave the girls a brief bow and his grandmother stood aside to reveal the round shape of Celia Horden beckoning to him. His father and mother had already disappeared. As he passed through the room his eyes sought the silent English girl, Eunice Horden. There she was in a corner, hands folded in her lap, eyes cast down.

Daniel hurried after Celia to a higher landing and was thankful to be shown a small chamber, evidently partitioned from a larger one where his parents were to sleep. His mother had unpacked fresh linen for him and his one fine doublet and breeches with clean white stockings. There was an ewer and basin and silver backed hair brushes laid out.

"What think you of the young ladies?" she asked him when they were all ready to proceed to the dining-room.

"I think nothing of their manners."

"And your Cousin Eunice?"

"She has not so much as opened her mouth but I am determined to hold talk with her soon."

"She reminds me of her father William who was courting me but had not a word to say. Of course she is overwhelmed by the French cousins. My sister tells me they took ship from France as soon as they heard King Charles had sailed and though they landed after the King they hired a coach and four and drove straight here to seek their English relations. Eunice only came this morning so she has had no time to get used to them. Come, we must go down. Cousin Celia says there are oysters, salmon, roasted pigeons, a haunch of venison and three sorts of tarts and they have brought up their best wine from the cellar for this happy reunion."

"I think I might manage most of that." Daniel was aware that he had felt hungry for some hours. He rushed down the oak staircase and found everyone heading for a long dining room which must be below the drawing room as it had windows giving onto the terrace above the river.

In the pause of conversation while they were settling themselves and a maid was carrying in a tray Daniel heard his mother say, looking around the company, "But where is William, my one time suitor? Was he afraid to meet me after all this time?"

She addressed Clifford Horden. Daniel studied him for the first time and saw a grey, grim-faced man with close set-eyes and thin cheeks, the antithesis of the florid genial figure Daniel expected in a highly successful London merchant. At the question the man's teeth clenched and a jerk of his head dismissed the maid.

"William is unable to be with us, Arabella," came the answer from tight lips.

Daniel took a quick glance at Eunice who had been placed beside him. He sensed her embarrassment though she made no movement. There is some secret about her father that shames her.

He realised the French girls were tittering and looking at their mother and grandmother with knowing eyes. He had sorted the older women out by now. Aunt Henrietta *was* beautiful, with the same shaped face as her daughters but just that difference in the proportion of her features that made her lovely to look at. Her mother too, Lady Maria Horden, had been a beauty, but was heavily wrinkled now. It was she of the deep, censorious voice who felt compelled to speak.

"Arabella," she said, addressing his mother, "you are the same bold girl you always were. If you must know it is our presence here that has disposed Cousin William to stay away. He has embraced Puritanism in its most extreme form and we Roman she-devils would contaminate him. We are grateful to Cousin Clifford and Cousin Celia that they are happy to accommodate us until we come back with you to Horden Hall."

Yet the rabid Puritan has allowed his daughter to be here, Daniel thought. Is that because he wants her to meet and captivate *me*? She will do no captivating while she sits as still as a frightened bird.

There were the new fangled forks laid as well as knives so Daniel supposed they were not meant to use fingers. He glanced at Eunice to see how she – an experienced Londoner – managed. She seemed unaware of him as she concentrated on eating quickly but delicately with tiny mouthfuls. Now he couldn't help watching her. She was so small and slight. Almost sallow in complexion she was no English rose but there was something appealing in the way her face tapered to a tiny chin and her hair, mouse-brown, was drawn tightly back from it. He felt an uncomfortable urge to stroke her neck where a bone made a small protuberance above the white collar of her dress.

I suppose I'm sorry for her, he was thinking, having to sit by her cousins with their shining ringlets and flouncing petticoats. And I was told her mother died a while ago and now I know her father has become a little mad. She has only her grandparents – Clifford who is a grumpy old man and Celia – he looked at her – a round doughy-faced woman, frumpish beside the French ladies.

He dragged his eyes away and attacked the food himself. When the fork became too slow and awkward to keep pace with his appetite he resorted to his fingers. His mother was doing the same although *her* stately mother was frowning down her nose.

Cousin Celia was urging them all to try everything, carving extra slices of venison as soon as she saw an empty plate. It seemed to Daniel that the old history of his mother and her son was unimportant to her now. All she wanted was to show off their wealth and be a cheery hostess, but she was not a presence in the room in the way that the French grandmother was.

The conversation turned, with no cooling of the atmosphere, to the day's events. Daniel kept quiet about his own part till his mother looked across at him and said, "Our Dan had a special wave and smile from his majesty all to himself."

The French girls laughed at his blushes and the one in blue, whom he now believed was the elder, Madeline, exclaimed, "How could the King miss him? He is a beanpole and with that light hair he would stand out from the crowd."

"Perchance he can present us at court then," squealed Diana in the pink.

They both dissolved into giggles. Eunice did not even look up.

There was talk too of Horden Hall. Old Lady Maria began asking after places and people that she remembered. She was still upright and strong of voice and Daniel found it strange to picture her as the mistress of the Hall so many years ago, the wife of his grandfather who had died before his parents were married.

"Ah, my dear Arabella," she said, "you can have no idea how much I wanted your father to come with me to France and see his dear Henrietta married. I pined for him when I knew he was ill and my heart bled for you when he died and you were left alone facing so much hardship in the horrible war."

Daniel studied his mother's face. She had told him how her mother had always loved her sister Henrietta more than her. But she answered readily enough.

"I was not bereft long for when the Scots seized the Hall to billet their officers I went to seek the man who loved me." She beamed across the table at his father.

Daniel saw he had flushed up but that was nothing new. Bel Horden would tell all and sundry that their marriage had been one of passionate love from the moment they had set eyes on each other.

I cannot imagine, he reflected, ever falling in love like that. These three girls now. I could go home to Northumberland tomorrow with no desire to see any of them again. I detest Madeline and Diana already and Eunice has spoken not one word to me during the meal. True I have not spoken to her but I will make myself say something before the day is out.

His chance came when it was proposed that they should walk out on the terrace after dinner, the June afternoon being so warm.

Screwing up his courage he elbowed the slight figure into a corner and demanded, "If you have a voice, Cousin Eunice, let me hear it."

She lifted her eyes to his for one searching second. There was emotion there – alarm, confusion, wariness – all three? He couldn't tell, but next moment she had turned her gaze on the river with apparent indifference.

He grabbed at her hand. "What ails you? What have they all been saying about me? I don't care for the lot of them. Believe me I never wanted to travel all this way from Northumberland to meet a brood of French relations. They are coming to stay for I know not how long at Horden Hall after this. I could have waited."

She lifted her thin shoulders and addressed the river. "You saw the King."

"Ay, indeed, I saw the King." He burned with pride, recalling the smile and wave for himself alone.

Then he realised she had spoken. He must keep this alive but why would she not turn and look at him?

"Have *you* ever seen the King?"

"How could I? He only reached London today."

"Of course." He was a fool. "But now that he is in his capital you will have many chances."

"I have been taught that he is a fiend like his father." She let the words drop out as if they were no more than a comment on the weather.

He was aghast. But this was her Puritan father speaking. "You have been *taught*? What say you yourself?"

She began to brush past him and when he would have held her arm she shook off his hand.

"Who am I to speak about anything?"

He caught the words as she moved away and re-entered the house.

He was peeved and intrigued but when he would have followed her he was engulfed by the French girls.

"Cousin Daniel! Come, tell us about this wild border land where you live. We long to see it. Do you have *formidable* Scots warriors descending the hills to steal your cattle? Have you a moat and a drawbridge and armed troops to defend yourselves?"

Daniel shook his head. "No, we have a groom and two housemaids and my old nurse Ursula but she is one of the family. Horden Hall is an ordinary house. It's on a flat plain north of Newcastle. If we see any Scots they are Presbyterian preachers who I wager will creep home now we have a King again."

The girls burst into a gale of giggles. "Is he not droll?"

"He has never been to court."

"The plain north-countryman!"

"Oh if we could show him Paris!"

Madeline, who was taller than her sister, tried to copy her grandmother's stately posture and the way she flourished her fan. She fluttered it now and protested that in Paris they would never stand out in the afternoon sun like this.

Diana, the more exuberant, giggled without restraint.

"*He* will take no harm. He is as brown as a peasant."

Daniel shrugged his shoulders. "Go in then and talk to your cousin Eunice."

The girls pulled grotesque faces. "*C'est impossible*! She say nothing. *Pas un mot*! Are they all like her, the English girls? What say you, *mon cousin*?"

Daniel shrugged again. "I know no girls. I have been at the Grammar School in Newcastle and my father intends me for Cambridge University. I never meet girls."

"*Oh la la, le pauvre home*! But you have society – the Hordens are titled people. This place – Newcastle – it is a big city? There are balls? Theatres?"

Daniel gave a snort of a laugh. "We have a title and no money. And Newcastle is a small town – though it's the biggest in the north. And don't you know we have been allowed no dancing or play-going for many years under the Lord Protector?"

"But now your theatres will reopen and your Assembly Rooms."

"We have no such places. I've been told travelling players came to the town in days gone by. Maybe they will again. But at Horden we are a country place. Once there was dancing round the Maypole on the village green till the Puritans stopped it."

They looked at each other. Diana was open-mouthed. "What will we *do* there?" she asked her sister.

Madeline again made much play with her fan. "Indeed, we should stay in London. This Horden Hall is so far away and if we could ever get there it will be so quiet."

"But *Maman* wishes to see her birthplace."

Daniel beamed at them both.

"Aunt Henrietta and our grandmother could come home with us and you could stay here with Cousin Clifford and Cousin Celia and help to liven up Eunice."

Madeline clasped her hands in mock reproach. "Oh you dreadful boy. You do not *wish* us to visit you."

"But you say you want to stay in London. If you don't care for Eunice *she* could visit us instead. She has no fear of being too quiet." At least, he was thinking, I am curious about *her*. Of these two I already know all I want to know.

The deep voice of the French grandmother broke in on their talk. "What is the argument, *mes enfants*?"

"Eh, it is Daniel," cried Diana, winking at him. "He loves Eunice and wants nothing to do with us."

Daniel felt his cheeks flame up as his grandmother cocked her head and squinted up at him.

"Ah," she tapped his hand with her folded fan, "I believe you have your mother's mischievous spirit. She always spoke her mind in season and out of season. What have you been saying now that has caused offence to these young ladies?"

"Nothing, on my word, Madam, but answer their questions."

"And you tell them you love that mouse Eunice when you have scarce spoken two words with her! Is there some prior *arrangement* – from your cradles?"

Daniel looked desperately past her to see if Clifford or Celia or his mother or father were within earshot to come to his rescue and deny this. No, they were on the lower terrace above the river. He looked back at the French girls who were giggling behind their fans at his discomfiture.

He had had enough of their little games. "I never spoke one word about loving anybody. I certainly have no *arrangement* with Eunice as you put it, Madam, and as for *loving* her the idea is preposterous."

The old lady turned her frown on the girls and Madeline blurted out, "*Mais vraiment*, he said he wanted her at Horden Hall rather than us." As she said it Daniel saw something that sickened him. The little pointed face of Eunice had peeped around the door from the dining room and looked straight at him. When she met his eyes she vanished again.

What had she heard? Oh how he longed to be back at home and free of all his new relations! He might even have given up the King's gracious wave to escape these entanglements with females.

He looked back at the dragon that was his grandmother and the evil pixies that were his cousins. He was sure none of them had noticed Eunice's brief appearance.

Copying his mother's straight talking he addressed Madeline, "You made it plain enough you don't want to come to Northumberland. Why not admit it?"

Madeline gave him a haughty stare over her fan. Then in a wheedling tone she turned to her grandmother.

"Is it so very dreadful, *Grandmere*, as he suggests? You were the grand lady of Horden Hall for many years. Could you have endured it if it had been so *dull*?"

Lady Maria straightened up and looked away into the distant past before she answered.

"I was a few months younger than you, Madeline. I came as a new bride from the Chateau Rombeau. Sir John Horden was a good man and loved me. He also loved the Horden lands. He loved the Hall where Hordens had lived for generations. I lived many years there until the count wanted his grandson to marry my Henrietta. Then I returned to France with your mother and for our faith we were forbidden to return. Now I am back. I wish to see the place again. My son Robert died there – thrown from his horse. I have never seen his grave or my husband's. I should see them before I go to my own." She turned and swept down the terrace steps to join the others.

Daniel almost laughed aloud at the girls' faces.

"So you are to be dragged there," he teased them, "because our grandmother wants to look at two graves. I have seen them often. The Hordens have an old moss-grown stone between carved pillars above a vault in the churchyard at Nether Horden. My Uncle Robert's name and Sir John's are the most recent. Maybe if the journey on our rough roads proves too much for her, our grandmother can be buried with her husband and son."

Madeline slapped his arm. "Why, Daniel, you delight in tormenting us. I thought we could teach you courtly manners – such as we are used to – but I believe there is no hope of that. You are a brute."

"Very well. I am a brute. And you are charming young ladies. I think we'll leave it at that." He bowed and left them and re-entered the house with an idea of seeing Eunice but she was not in the dining room nor, when he ran upstairs, was she in the drawing room. Exploring the upper landing he opened a door and saw another stair but when he descended it he found himself outside a kitchen with servants staring at him. A footman pointed him to a passage which led back to the front hall at the very moment that there came a loud banging at the outer door. The same footman darted past him with, "Excuse me, sir," and Daniel paused in the hall out of curiosity.

A black-coated figure with a tall hat stood outside and, ignoring the footman's bow and indication that he should enter, he stared straight at Daniel.

"You must be Arabella's son!" The voice was harsh and angry.

"And you are?" Daniel demanded, half-guessing.

"William Horden. I have come for my daughter."

CHAPTER 3

A GREAT commotion followed, drawing everyone from the terrace through the dining room into the hallway.

Celia, her cheeks wobbling and her little eyes wide with fright, was defending herself to her ferocious son.

“She said you gave her permission. I would never have kept her if I’d known she’d run away. I was sure you knew she was here for she sent back her maid to tell you she had arrived safely.”

“Maid!” cried William. “She has no maid. Do you suppose we pay anyone for work we can do ourselves?”

Celia absolutely wrung her hands. “There was a girl with her whom she dismissed when we let her in.”

“She has been lying to you then, Mother, for which as her father I am deeply ashamed. Fetch her hither that she may show her contrition.”

Celia looked desperately about her and, seeing the French girls with their surprised eyes riveted on the newcomer, murmured, “Dear souls, run up to that little room next to yours. She must be there.”

Daniel was aware of his father’s distress at the scene, while his mother’s face showed only amusement at the transformation of her one-time silent suitor. Daniel studied the man who had once been betrothed to her. He had the thin Horden face like Clifford's and like the portraits of Daniel's grandfather and ancestors before him that decorated the walls of the Hall. His hair must be very close cropped because it scarcely showed under his hat which he had kept on. His eyebrows made a thick dark line above his eyes. The whole effect with his black clothing and tall hat was of a doom-laden statue, so rigidly did he stand with his eyes fixed upon his cowering mother.

Daniel was seized by an urge to play the knight in defence of a maiden in distress. If that poor little girl has run away from this sinister figure she shall not, he resolved, be dragged away again.

He bit his lip and kept glancing up the stairs as Celia tentatively laid a hand on her son's arm and pleaded, "William, be calm. Madeline and Diana have gone to seek Eunice in the room we gave her. I wanted her to stay for a change while they were here. They are all of an age and I thought a little female com –"

Clifford, who had taken no part so far, pushed her aside. "Be silent, wife, or you provoke him further."

William's face had indeed gone from unhealthy pallor to fiery red. "You would company her with Daughters of Satan?"

"Celia, pray take our guests up to the drawing room." Clifford brought the words out of the corner of his tight lips. "This is a most unfortunate family matter."

But Daniel could tell that both his grandmother and his

Aunt Henrietta were eager to see the end of the dispute and remained with their backs to the panelling, ignoring Celia's gesture towards the stairs.

Now his mother actually stepped forward with her hand outstretched to the black pillar. *She* was not going to be intimidated.

"Come Cousin William, will you not greet me? *I* cannot be a daughter of Satan for you were willing to marry me less than twenty years ago."

He turned his eyes on her with obvious reluctance.

"You were a rebellious child, Arabella, and I – I had scarce begun to live at all. My eyes have been opened since and I have found the way to the strait gate. You have no part in my life." He glared round at them all. "None of you. Take your fine raiment and your jewels out of my sight and bring me my daughter or I will have to invade this house of riches and drag her forth myself."

Madeline and Diana were now hovering in their blue and pink silks and abundant lace on the upper landing tittering behind their fans.

"Maman, elle ne veux pas venir."

"The Lord has set me over her," William roared. "She shall obey me."

No one notices me now, Daniel thought. Here is my chance. He slipped along the passage and found the back stair again. He sensed clustering servants agog to hear all but he darted up two flights, his ears alert to any noise of crying. There was none but, obeying his sense of direction out of the servants' quarters, he opened the door onto the landing. He recognised the door of his own front bedchamber because there was a Chinese vase in an alcove next to it. The young ladies' rooms must be overlooking the river so he began trying doors at random until he heard a small shriek and darting in he closed the door behind him and called out, "Don't be afraid. It is I, Daniel."

Eunice's little face, all puckered up, peeped round the bed curtain.

"Get out. I can't be alone with you."

Daniel pressed his back against the door which he saw had no bolt. He spread his arms out across it to bar her way. "It's your father you're afraid of. You don't need to fear me. I'll save you if I can. He shan't take you home against your will."

She pushed open the curtain and set her feet to the ground. She had already wrapped herself in a grey cloak as if ready to leave but she stayed seated. He thought of a bird perched on a twig. You watched it wondering if it would stay or fly. She let her eyes gaze upward at his with a look of wonder for what seemed like a whole minute. Then all at once that gave way to a violent head-shaking, a frown of anger and at last hopelessness.

She stood abruptly and stepping forward made to thrust him out of her way. He moved of course. What could he do?

There was a small cloth bag down by the wall next to the door. She snatched it up and went out. Above the main staircase she turned and met his eyes again.

"Cousin Daniel, can you not see? I am his possession."

She had addressed him. She had used his name. He was her knight. He must save her.

She was already descending.

"Eunice, stop. You are no one's possession."

She made a dismissive backward gesture with her free hand and carried on to the next floor where the gallery before the drawing room looked over into the hall. She was now visible to all the upturned faces below. Daniel realised he had already been sighted following close behind as if he had driven her back to her father. Ashamed and angry he wanted to sink through the floor.

She walked steadily down as they all watched, seeming to hold their breaths. They parted to let her walk up to her father. Oh if I could rush between them, he thought, if I could be a wall about her, if I had a sword to draw! But the days of chivalry were gone. He saw her hold up her bag towards her father.

"I was putting my things together. I hoped to stay with Grandfather and Grandmother but I am here now."

William drew his brows together and his eyes were like steel points.

"You have been telling lies. What you have just said to excuse your dilatoriness is also a lie. All your lies proceeded from your first evil thought that you would leave our home without permission and proceed to a forbidden place. First you will turn around to your grandmother and ask forgiveness for lying to her."

Eunice turned and sought Celia's face where tears were

running down her podgy cheeks.

"I am sorry for lying to you, Grandmother." It was said in a flat voice as if repeated by rote.

"Oh my poor little cherub." Celia made a movement as if to clasp Eunice in her arms, but checked herself. She is terrified of her son, Daniel thought.

William took hold of Eunice's upper arm. "Now we will remove ourselves." He turned to the door.

Daniel took a step forward. "Will no one speak up for Eunice? Do we stand by and let her be taken back to prison?"

Eunice stiffened and then rounded on him. "Keep out of this. You don't know what you are saying."

Her father had opened the door himself, the footman having discreetly retired at the beginning of the scene. She frowned at Daniel, yet he was sure he saw a pleading in her eyes. But in a moment they were outside and the door was closed on them. He ground his teeth. He had failed miserably and made himself look a fool.

"Well," cried old Lady Horden as everyone drew breath and the tension subsided. "I grieve with you, Cousin Celia, that your son has become a monster."

Clifford flashed back at her. "I beg your pardon, my lady, but the child had been disobedient and deceptive. A father is no monster who reproves conduct like that. I do however apologise to you all that this should have occurred during your stay with us."

"Ah but you requested us to withdraw." Lady Horden gave a short laugh. "And we too were disobedient. *We* apologise to *you*." And she inclined her head and began to mount the stairs to the drawing room as if the whole matter was finished and forgotten. Henrietta and her daughters followed. Celia looked divided over which of their guests needed their company, but a glance at the Northumbrian family huddling together decided her and she and Clifford climbed the stairs.

Daniel exchanged glances with his father and mother.

"None of *them* care a whit for that poor girl. Surely *you* do?"

His father sighed. "Unfortunately what William said was true. As soon as one wrong is thought or committed many others – especially lies – follow, compounding the first error."

"Oh Nat," said his mother, "if I had been in her shoes I would have run away long before."

"I wanted her to," Daniel cried. "I tried to stop her but she said she was his possession."

"Do not mistake me," his father said gravely. "I have great compassion for the poor girl and she is not William's *possession*. She is entrusted to him to be guided and watched over with love but she also has a duty of obedience to him."

"Even if he commands her to do what is wrong, Father? For how can it be right to forbid her to visit her grandparents?"

"He has a fear of Catholic influence from her French cousins and also it seems of the corrupting power of wealth."

Bel stamped her foot. "It is an insane fear. I looked into his eyes. Twenty years ago they were almost without expression and now they are quite mad. She should be relieved of any duty to obey him. I tell you, Nat, you can be too – what shall I say – conforming. But come, we mustn't lurk down here. They will think it discourteous."

She picked up her skirts and scurried up the stairs.

Differences of opinion like that between his parents were common enough and went no deeper than the moment, but Daniel stored away in his memory that William had said his mother was a rebellious child. She was my age when the betrothal was made between them, he remembered her saying. I have her rebel blood but I am not a *child*. I am a man and want action. I will rebel and not go to the University. I have seen my King and I will serve him. I could join the army or better still the navy.

He had no wish to fight fellow Englishmen and the army had so lately been engaged in that horrible thing, a civil war. But it was a different matter at sea. The navy had fought for England against the Dutch.

If I didn't go back to Horden, he was thinking, when the French family go with Father and Mother I could stay in London. Maybe Lord Branford, Father's friend, could present me at court. Ah if I could see the King again and offer him my undying service, and I might contrive to do something for that poor little thing, Eunice Horden. Not *marry* her, God forbid. But rescue her to a life of her own choosing. I swear that for a moment she saw me as her champion knight. There are great things to be done in life and sticking my head in Greek texts is not for Sir Daniel Wilson Horden.

Reluctantly he followed his mother and father to the drawing room to face the French girls again. At least, he thought happily, I am not afraid of them any more.

CHAPTER 4

EUNICE Horden had to scurry to keep up with her father's long angry strides. He had let go of her the moment they were outside her grandfather's door. He almost never touched her but his mental hold was so great that to attempt to run away now never crossed her mind. He was saying nothing so she guessed he was deciding which passage of Scripture she would have to learn by heart before she was allowed any supper.

I had a dinner with more meat in it than I usually have in a month, she recalled. If I am forbidden supper altogether I can last till morning. All I want now is to be alone in my little closet to think about Daniel Horden.

She would not torment herself with recalling every word *she* had said to *him*. They were a matter of indifference for she was unlikely ever to see him again. And she would not remember the awful hurt when he said, "As for loving Eunice the idea is preposterous." No, the pleasure would be in dwelling on that moment when he stood with his back to her door.

He was like a Norse God with his bronzed face and flaxen hair. He stood so straight, taller than the door itself. He had stretched out his arms as though to bar anyone else from entering. His feet were planted solidly. His whole being breathed determination. He was as strong as an angel and as beautiful.

But of course he would have had his evil way with her if she had not escaped. That was why he had tried to stop her going. He would have come to her later – in the night perhaps – the door of that little room had no lock – and he would have had his evil way with her because that was what men did as her father had often told her.

"Never allow yourself to be alone with a man," he warned, "and for the same reason never go out alone because men are lurking for that very purpose and they are stronger than you."

When she had slipped out that morning she had taken with her a sixpence from his poor box and offered it to the first serving-maid she had seen in the street if she would accompany her to the Strand. The maid had objected she would be in trouble for being too long on her errand but the sixpence had tempted her.

She chatted to Eunice all the way there. Yes, she often ran errands alone for her mistress. Oh she would scream very loud if a man grabbed her but it didn't happen in daylight. There were always people about.

Eunice stored these things in her mind and found links with the far off days when her mother was still alive. They had walked together alone, Eunice trotting fearlessly as long as she clutched her mother's hand. No wicked men had seized her or tried to have their evil way with her mother, but she was never afraid.

Her world had closed down around her after her mother's death in childbirth, bringing forth a dead baby boy. She could see plainly the coffins side by side and her broken father prostrated in grief.

Now he was unlocking their front door and motioning her ahead of him. The room they entered occupied all the ground floor. She was seeing it now in contrast to the house in the Strand. It was about the same size as the small room she had been allocated there and was quite crowded with a plain deal table and two benches, a fireplace on the right hand wall and a steep stair going up in the left hand corner. Along the opposite wall were shelves and hooks for a few pots and pans, a bread crock, a wooden cheese dish, a sack of turnips and onions and – she was pleased to see – a parcel of fish. He had been preaching early at Billingsgate when she had slipped out and that must be his reward. If she was contrite enough for her sins she might be allowed a baked fish for supper.

Remembering the feel of the velvet bed hangings in her room in the Strand she cast a sidelong glance at the piece of sacking that hung at the one small window next to the front door. Where there had been a volume of plays by Beaumont and Fletcher at her bedside there was nothing here but a Bible on the table and writing materials for her father's notes.

She knew that this house – off Cheapside in a narrow lane between Milk Street and St Lawrence Lane – had been built by her father's own hands. She remembered seeing the square of trodden earth between a leather-worker's and a baker's and her father saying, "The Lord has led me here. Here we will build."

With the money from the sale of her mother's few jewels he had bought the waste ground from the baker and some bricks and sheets of weather-boarding. The leather-worker had lent his man to help and the little two-storey house had risen between the wooden walls of the two shops. The bricks had made the chimney and hearth, the flue passing through the wall to link up with the baker's substantial one. Both Giles Fletcher, the leather-worker and Luke Thomson, the baker were happy to be repaid with her father's literary skills. He was teaching the leather-worker's youngest boy to read and write and for the baker he wrote excellent letters to the many wealthy customers who ignored their bakery bills. He also sent Eunice to sweep up the leather workshop and the bakery floor at the end of each day.

Small amounts of money came in too from his open-air preaching where he had a bowl for coppers at his side. "A labourer is worthy of his hire," he would quote but he would always place a tithe of his earnings in the poor box he kept on the mantelshelf above the fireplace. This was what she had daringly raided that morning.

Now he took off his hat, pointed her to one of the benches and faced her across the table. His gaunt face with the eyes close together like his father, Clifford's, was thrust towards her. She lowered hers and gazed at a mark in the wood that was like a letter s. S for sin.

"No, you will look at me, Eunice, and tell the truth as we examine every sin you have committed today from the first thought coming into your head that you would go to the house in the Strand."

So it is to be one of these long inquisitions, she told herself, and he will know if I deviate one iota from the truth.

She lifted her eyes to his and began in a small bodiless voice.

"Last week you showed me a letter from my Grandmother inviting me to come to meet my cousins. You said I was not to go."

"What was my reason?" he snapped.

"Because the French relations are Catholic and the family from the north includes a young man."

"And why did you conceive of disobeying me."

"I was curious. You went out early to preach in Billingsgate and I took my chance."

"What else did you take?"

"Sixpence from the poor box to pay a maid to accompany me." She rushed on now, the words tumbling out. "That meant I had to lie to Grandmother that it was my own maid and that I had your permission and when she seemed pleased and asked if I was allowed to stay a few days I said, Yes. When you came for me I hid in the room and when Madeline and Diana sought me I refused at first. Then I knew I must come so I put on my cloak and came down."

He pounced as she expected.

"The young man, Arabella's son, came down with you. Explain this."

She hesitated for a fatal second.

"Tell me not that he had his evil way with you!" His eyes were like flames.

She shook her head. "He came into the room and I told him to get out."

"How did he know which was your room? He had been there before?"

"Never. He tried other doors. I heard him."

"Was there no lock that you could have barricaded yourself from him?"

"No, I believe it was what they call a dressing-room to the larger one where the French young ladies were staying."

"Did he leave you when you rightly ordered him out?"

"I pushed past him and picked up my bag and went out."

"He *said* nothing?"

"He said he wanted to save me."

"Save! He would have sent you to the deepest abyss of Hell." He flung back his head and looked with despair at the ceiling. "Oh Eunice, Eunice! Has all my guidance been in vain?"

"No, I came away with you."

He shook his head, his eyes again probing hers. "But that you should ever have thought of putting yourself in such danger! Have I not striven night and day since your poor mother died to keep you from sin and the wiles of the devil?"

At the mention of her mother she was impelled to get up abruptly and pace about the room. He rose too in alarm.

"An evil spirit has hold of you. Let me pray it from you."

"No," she cried. "God is telling me to ask you a question." She stood still and faced him. "I was five years old when my mother died but I saw how you were stricken with grief. You loved her. *That* was not evil. Am I then never to know a man's love and bear children? *She* did."

He thrust his hands into his short cropped hair as if he would tear it out.

"Oh name her not. She died bearing a child. Would I not spare you that? And other babes died barely out of the cradle. I begged her to abstain. I couldn't bear to see her agony. But love – oh it is not evil but the act itself brings such suffering – even when it is lawful. No, my child, spare yourself. And oh when it is unlawful – when it catches you unawares – then there is terrible retribution. Even if there is abject repentance there must still be lifelong punishment on earth if one is to escape the fires of hell. Would I not strive to keep you from that? And you had a man in your room in that house of sin? You were so close to danger. I can hardly breathe for thinking of it."

She was pleased to have moved him so much. She must pursue this.

"You say Mother suffered. But there was happiness too. I remember a summer's day when you had returned from your Father's business and we walked through streets to some fields. Then we saw people practising archery. I was excited because Mother begged sixpence from you to try her hand. The man who let her have a bow said she should go nearer to the target but she wouldn't and she hit it right in the middle. We were happy and laughing all the way home."

He sank down onto the bench. "Moorfields. We left the

city wall by the Moorgate." He looked at her. "You remember that? All the City amusements had been suppressed, the playgoing, cockfighting, bear-baiting, dancing, singing, but the archery was still going. She was so beautiful, drawing on a bow, so strong. I hadn't the heart to stop her." He bent his head and she looked for rare tears but he fought them fiercely.

She reached both hands towards him. "Oh Father. It wasn't evil. Why can we not be happy again?"

"Because she is dead. She was taken away from us." He lifted his head and looked her in the eye and she saw he was back in the old groove. "Eunice, I have found the strait gate as I told those silk-clad Jezebels hung about with jewels. What did our Lord say? 'Sell all thou hast and give to the poor.' My father made much money buying and selling under the Lord Protector and when he moved into that house in the Strand I knew it was the temptation of riches and fame. Lords and ladies inhabit those places. He has grown proud. Now he will court the new King and flaunt his titled French cousins among his neighbours of the aristocracy. I was glad to be free of his business. I was glad to come here and create this little dwelling for me and thee. But I must know that you will never leave me again. You speak of happiness. Happiness comes from trust. If I say I am walking to Billingsgate to preach there you know that is where I will be. Now that you have broken trust and lied to cover it up can I trust you again? Must I take you with me wherever I go? When you go next door to sweep the shop am I to be racked with doubt that you will run away?"

"I won't run away." They were just words and she spoke

them to see the end of this.

But now he lifted up the great Bible and placed it before her.

"Lay your hand on it and make a vow."

Sickness gripped her stomach. "Oh Father, does not the good book say 'Swear not at all'?"

His brows came together and his eyes pierced her. "Are you being defiant? I call not this swearing. You are making a vow before God. If you doubt yourself, if you doubt that you will keep it you must be mewed up here for always."

Her spirit quailed before him.

"I do not doubt." She laid her right hand on the Bible. "I promise I will never run away again."

"And you repent of your sins?"

"I repent of my sins."

She sank down onto the bench at her side of the table. Well, she was purged, purified. The day of her wickedness was over and she must never have another day like this. It would be wrong ever to think about how Daniel Horden had looked standing against her door or when he shouted out that she was being sent back to prison. Even thoughts must be controlled.

He opened the Bible at the Book of Revelation. "Before you have any supper learn by heart the final chapter and meditate on whether you wish to stand upon Mount Zion or be cast into the lake of fire."

He got up and began setting a fire in the hearth so that he could cook the fish. She watched him for a moment and then turned her eyes to the book.

CHAPTER 5

CLIFFORD Horden had set up his own coach when he moved into the house in the Strand and for Daniel the next few days were a blur of visits with the ladies sitting in the coach and the gentlemen escorting them on horseback. Daniel was a skilled horseman and eagerly boasted to Diana and Madeline that at the age of three he had taken a stool to the Horden stables and climbed onto his first pony bareback. They giggled but had the grace to appear a little impressed.

He was pleased to see that they were impressed too with the open spaces where they could take the air on these occasions, particularly the vast acres of Hyde Park. Their disparaging comparisons of London with Paris became less frequent.

He was himself breathless with the life of London and a little envious of his father's prior knowledge. It was disappointing, though, to learn that his father's friend the Earl of Branford was resting in the country after a fall from his horse. He made sure the French girls heard that his father had a close friend in the aristocracy from his Cambridge days and noticed that they began to treat him with more respect. One day they visited Westminster and Whitehall and Daniel was pleased to hear his father tell them that he had been among the crowds on the street the very day that Charles the First had ridden by at the head of a troop of soldiers to make his rash attempt to arrest the five members of Parliament.

"I fear that was the beginning of the end for him," he commented. "It was a slight that Parliament was reluctant to forgive."

Clifford interposed quickly, "We are all very ready now to accept a King who honours the great institution of Parliament. The nation is united as never before."

Mother Bel whispered to Daniel, "This merchant knows which side his bread is buttered."

Daniel grinned back but he was thinking, Clifford can speak of unity but has a rift within his own family as wide as an ocean. Why does he not strive to heal that and make life comfortable for his one granddaughter?

Clifford was keen to show them the Royal Exchange where much of his business was conducted and the headquarters of the Merchant Companies. Each of these was like a small village in itself, the central meeting hall being only the largest of many ornate structures. Separate buildings housed the treasury and the exchequer, and, for the lavish dinners served there, the buttery, the pantry and the kitchens.

Daniel couldn't help thinking about Eunice in these amazing places that flaunted their wealth so ostentatiously. Her father had worked for Clifford before he turned impossibly puritanical. Had he and his wife ever taken Eunice as a small child to show her this world in which her grandfather had accumulated his riches? Was she too young to remember? He wasn't sure how old she was at the death of her mother but surely she had had the beginnings of a comfortable childhood. How could she bear the restriction of her life now?

They were visiting the Baker's Hall when this thought came to him and for the first time ever he gave thanks for his own parents. He looked at his father, head courteously bent to Clifford who was pointing out the carvings over the grand entrance, and compared him to the forbidding figure of William Horden. Nathaniel's mild eyes and gentle features breathed good humour. He wore his own rather unruly hair not as flaxen now as Daniel's but touched with the red of his mother, Grandmother Wilson. Beside the neatly bewigged Clifford with his thin, hard-lined face he looked pleasantly boyish.

Daniel switched his gaze to his mother who with Aunt Henrietta was watching Madeline and Diana disporting themselves at the bowling alley beyond the main courtyard. Bel was laughing at their antics with her usual exuberance. She looked a different breed from her tall stately sister, not as classically beautiful certainly but her square face had fine bone structure and her dark curls shone in the sunlight. Surely Eunice must have envied me parents like mine, Daniel thought, when that ghastly black pillar appeared to claim her?

Thinking of Eunice had made him weary of the French girls' chatter and in this reflective mood he was content to stand near the older members of their little party and listen to their comments. Celia was enthusing about the gardens to Lady Horden.

"Clifford and I must visit Paris soon if you say there are

gardens like these there but Clifford finds it hard to take even these few days from his business."

Nathaniel was now asking Clifford, "And what are those low buildings over there?"

Clifford almost purred with pride. "Ah those are the almshouses. All the big companies care for their own members when they are sick or old. London is the best organised and most charitable city in the world."

Daniel noticed that he curled his lip provocatively at Lady Horden but she did not rise to the defence of Paris in this category. His mother had heard the remark and stepping close to Daniel whispered, "All the same, we have seen many miserable streets where people live who have not the benefit of belonging to a great company. I wager William has immured poor little Eunice in one of those."

Hearing her name spoken aloud released Daniel's pent-up thoughts. He drew Bel aside ostensibly to admire a grapevine growing on a south-facing wall.

"Mother, I think of her so much. She reminds me of when I was a schoolboy and caught a moth in a little box. I thought I could keep it as a pet and I heard it flapping inside but I forgot about it and when I next looked it was dead. Could we not visit her before we leave for Northumberland?"

Bel looked up into his face. "Do you, son, think of her so much? Well, we *are* to visit her. Clifford and Celia wish us to and say they will send us in the coach to the house where they live. They believe it would be right to bid them goodbye before we leave for Northumberland."

Daniel bit his lip. “Will that not inflame Cousin William?”

“That is what I said to Celia on her own, for I find she is more at ease when her husband is not by. But she believes that whatever William does or says the only way for her poor granddaughter to be rescued is through marriage.”

“Marriage!” Daniel struck one fist into the other. “Not with me I trust!”

Bel laughed. “Ah, I wondered. Your kindly soul is moved but there are limits drawn. Celia hinted of course that Clifford would give a substantial dowry.”

“And is that to move me further, Mother? You said you want me to marry for true love.”

“I do, I do, but you spoke up so in the child’s defence I thought you had come to some understanding that first day upstairs.”

“Nonsense. I had had scarce a word out of her.”

“That was enough for me with your father. When I saw him I knew if I ever married he was the one. You said just now you think of Eunice all the time. That was how I was. I couldn’t get your father out of my mind.”

The others were now beckoning to them. Daniel frowned down at his mother.

“It is to get Eunice *out* of my mind that I’d like to see where and how she lives. If it is not as bad as I fear I can forget all about her.” When he said it he was certain that was the truth. Forgetting Eunice and ignoring Madeline and Diana would allow him freedom to enjoy London and banish his fears of looming matrimony.

They began to drift towards the rest of the party.

"And if her life and her home are worse than you suppose what follows? An urge to rescue her?" Bel gave him her comical grin but seeing his frown deepen she quickened her pace and took her husband's arm. "Dan showed me such a beautiful grapevine, Nat. I wish we could grow one at Horden Hall! I love grapes."

"You shall taste the wine from the vineyards of Chateau Rombeau, sister," Henrietta said. "There are two cases among our luggage. One we have already presented to Cousins Clifford and Celia and the other is to travel north with us to cheer you in the chill air of Horden."

Daniel saw Madeline and Diana, who had abandoned their bowls, pulling faces at each other. They are determined to dread Northumberland, he chuckled to himself. I hope it is cold and wet and they beg to go home as quickly as possible. For himself, he realised, he was in no hurry to be back at Horden Hall while there was so much of London still to see.

The only part of every day he did not enjoy were the evenings. If they stayed in there was music or card games. Madeline and Diana sang and played, as Nathaniel had foreseen, on the virginals. Daniel would have been content to sit in a corner and listen if the sound had been pleasant but Diana's voice was thin and squeaky and Madeline's stronger but harsh. What was worse they kept begging him to sing with them and then teasing him when he wouldn't. At Nether Horden church he sang out happily with the congregation now that his voice had broken and settled down a little but he had no intention of making an exhibition of himself as a soloist.

Then there were the card games. Clifford and Celia sometimes entertained friends with games of cribbage but the French family had brought with them cards for a variety of games which the girls explained more boisterously than clearly, contradicting each other frequently about the rules. While the older members of the party could sit and chat it was always assumed that Daniel would want to play.

On the whole though he feared the going out evenings more than the ones at home. Celia was eager to show off her visitors to friends and neighbours so several invitations had already been accepted which involved suppers followed by dancing.

"He has no sense of rhythm," Diana and Madeline agreed after the first time he was compelled to stand up with each in turn. "He has the grace of an elephant."

At least he had new clothes for these occasions and so had his parents. Lady Horden had ordered them early in their visit, saying she could not bring such presents from France. "You all had to be measured for them. I would never have guessed the height of this young man!"

Securing an invitation to a ball given by an earl and countess was Celia's greatest triumph. Bel came into Daniel's room that evening when he was struggling into his new shirt with sleeves more full and flouncy than he had ever worn before.

She looked at him with fond pride, then sat herself on

the bed and declared with a mischievous gleam in her eye, "I think I should warn you that Henrietta has told me Diana is more in love with you than Madeline is. There is a possible French husband hovering back home for Madeline but we will see."

Daniel was just going to blurt out that that was ridiculous as both girls treated him as a joke. Then it occurred to him that he might sound childish. As befitted his superior clothes he would be cool and indifferent.

He drew on his new doublet before he answered. "Oh yes I recall, you said all three girls would want to marry me. I wondered when something would be said about those two."

His mother chuckled, not in the least taken in by this new pose. She smoothed out her dress of oyster silk, her fingers obviously delighting in its richness. "Well, you see, my dear mother had to make sure we would not disgrace her, since she used to call me a hoyden when I was a girl. I think she was relieved to find I had married so respectable a man as your father and produced a not unpresentable boy. Henrietta, whose under-garments I once chopped up with scissors, has also been pleasantly surprised."

Daniel grunted as his bitten finger nails refused to tie the buttons of his doublet. Diana in love with him! He had seen no such signs.

"You can tell Aunt if you like that I am not interested in her daughters but I would still like to visit Cousin William before we go."

"Of course. You want to see Eunice again, don't you? You

know you can tell me all, Dan?" She got up and fastened his buttons and peered into his face.

He shrugged his shoulders. Joining the navy was suddenly more appealing than ever. "Nothing to tell," he said.

The ball did not break up till two in the morning by which time Daniel was already nodding on a velvet couch in the corner of the ballroom. Madeline and Diana had not required more than one dance each from him but were never without other partners. When his mother joined him he said, "You see, the French cousins have not pestered me for dances."

"I would say Diana at least is hoping to make you jealous."

He snorted. "She is no different from Madeline. All they both want is endless pleasure and I cannot give them that as a dancing partner." He yawned and sat up. "How will they endure our quiet evenings at Horden Hall? I suggest we plague them with boredom till they plead to go home. Aunt will soon see that Northumberland is no place for either of them."

With a small pang he thought he could have had some pleasure in walking or riding about the grounds and the village with Eunice, showing her a countryside which she could hardly know existed.

His mother's head drooped against his shoulder. He looked down at her and grinned. "What, you are sleepy too?"

"Thinking of the Hall makes me long for our early nights and bright mornings and I'm missing Ursula. I've never been away from her so long since the day she came to live with us."

Daniel realised he had hardly given his old Nanny a thought and yet she had been a vital figure all childhood.

"Well, how many more days are we to stay in London? What are they planning for us tomorrow?"

"I think Clifford is impatient to get back to business but I heard them speak of a river trip tomorrow, perhaps up to Richmond. It is pretty country they say."

Daniel was suddenly wide awake. "Could we not go *down* river? There would be more to see and I was too seasick when we came to take much notice."

Ships, he was thinking. The fleet may be in.

"We can ask," his mother said and closed her eyes.

CHAPTER 6

CLIFFORD was very ready to go downstream and his word prevailed. The wherry on which they took seats left from Milford Steps and on an ebb tide with a west wind made good speed under London Bridge.

With mounting excitement Daniel could see ahead of them a good part of the fleet at anchor in the Pool. Most were awaiting repairs, the waterman told them, but two he pointed out had their great guns run out and the sailors exercising.

"Can you read the name on her?" he said to Daniel sensing his interest.

It was a massive three-decker they were approaching. They would pass close under the bows.

"The *Royal Charles*," he breathed and gazed up in wonder as they scuttled by. He was especially struck by the sight of a few officers, handsomely dressed, watching the scurrying activity of dozens of men.

He didn't want to share his delight with anyone, certainly not Madeline or Diana, but he told himself that is where I should be, not translating Greek texts or discoursing on the nicer points of theology. I am a man of action. Oh to serve my King in a great fleet battle!

He thought back to his boyhood when he had read in the

newspapers – which eventually found their way to Horden Hall – vivid accounts of the sea-battles between the Dutch and the English in the days of Cromwell. It hadn't bothered him then that it was not the *King's* navy, as long as the English were winning.

"She was called *Naseby* when she was launched in '55," the waterman said, "but all them Commonwealth names went, painted out the day they brought the King from Holland. She's a fine vessel. Upward of a hundred guns."

Recalling his boyhood Daniel realised that he had been fascinated by the navy even then. He could picture a day when he was eight and enacted the Battle of Scheveningen with toy boats he fashioned himself, making the Dutch warships half the size of the English ones and concluding with a little stick man representing the famous Admiral Tromp shot on the deck of his ship. He had triumphantly thrown his dead body overboard and watched it float away down the Horden Burn.

The waterman continued free with his comments as they came past a two-decker, the *Elizabeth* and the *Royal James,* another towering three-decker.

"Ay, they look powerful and people think they could put to sea at any moment if the Dutch gets up to their old tricks – indeed the word is the Dutch fleet are within sight of our coast now, somewheres near Boulogne, but bless your hearts our ships are not fit for the high seas. I know a man has worked on them, says they're short of men and gear, and the men they've got never gets their pay regular."

"Short of men, are they? Not ready for action?" Daniel was

somewhat daunted by this comment. But secretly he thought, the King needs me.

"Let's hope we are not attacked then," Daniel heard his father say to Clifford. "Long may we stay at peace. That's what I have prayed for under our new King."

Clifford nodded vigorously. "Amen to that, I say. War is bad for trade. Ah, now *there's* a sight." He turned and grabbed Daniel's arm and pointed downriver. "That's what you want to be looking at, young man." A merchant vessel was heading for the docks. "See that. She has on board cotton, indigo and ginger from the West Indies. They are destined for *my* warehouses. I have buyers waiting for my goods from all over Europe. Trade is a wonderful thing." He slapped Daniel on the back. "This evening I will show you and your father my office and warehouses. The ladies will not care for that."

That's why he was keen to come downriver, Daniel thought. He has been expecting this vessel to come in and he is mighty relieved to see it with his own eyes sailing up the Thames after such a long voyage. I have never seen him so genial.

"It's a fine, proud ship, sir," he said and Clifford actually beamed at him.

Having discharged some passengers at Woolwich and taken some more on board they made the return journey and Daniel studied every vessel of the fleet again, making notes of their names and what rates they were from the informative waterman.

That evening Clifford could hardly wait to summon the coach and take him and Nathaniel to his office by the river in a building between two of his vast warehouses.

Here he opened up his great ledgers and pointed to the listing of every piece of merchandise, its quantity, price, origin and destination.

Daniel politely remarked that it was a splendid piece of organisation to know where everything was at any time of the day or night.

"That it is," Clifford said and then laid his hand on Daniel's arm and looked him in the eye. "Well, young cousin, would you not like to come in with me in this great work?"

Daniel stared back, open-mouthed. "What! You mean, sir, be employed by you?"

Clifford switched his gaze impatiently to Nathaniel. "It's a fair offer. He would inherit the business. He'll make more money than he ever will from an impoverished Northumbrian estate. Of course he'd have to learn from the ground up but he's the age my William began and if *he* hadn't gone down his own crazy path he would have been ready to ease into full control now and take the weight off my shoulders. But I am in good health, thank God, and can carry on another ten years by which time your lad here will be fit to take over."

Daniel could see his father struggling to think of a diplomatic answer.

"Has this just occurred to you, Cousin Clifford?"

"Not at all. I've been observing the lad. He is not frivolous. He pays no attention to those silly young French girls. He has shown an intelligent interest in all we have shown him about London."

"But I'm afraid his destiny lies another way. He is heir through his mother to the Horden estates, indeed at his majority title and land are solely his. Before that he will take his degree at Cambridge so that he will be a fit person to make his mark in the capacity of magistrate as his grandfather was and be a respected figure in the community."

Clifford snorted and turned back to Daniel. "What say you, young man? They may hang a Bachelor's gown on your shoulders but you'll never be a respected figure – as your father puts it – if your estates are loaded with debt. I needed no University years. Indeed, my fortune was not built upon the Latin and Greek I learnt at school, so I see not that a heavier dose of the same would have made me any richer. But I am respected. I dine with Lords and Ladies. I have influence in the City."

And yet, Daniel was thinking, watching the workings of the old merchant's lined face, you are not inwardly content in the way my father is.

He smiled down at the close-set eyes. "Well, sir, I thank you for your offer but my father wishes me to go to Cambridge after the summer." It would not be wise to mention the King's navy at this point.

Clifford shook his head as if he could scarcely believe such folly.

"We all have our different destinies," Nat put in mildly and Daniel thought, at least I have pleased my father with my answer. He grinned to himself at Clifford's sour expression. I would be suffocated sitting in an office like this one staring at entries in these close-written ledgers. It could be worse even than the University.

But the time must come when he would break his ambition to his father. One day he would stand on a deck and give orders and sailors would jump to his bidding. He would never be seasick on great vessels like the *Royal Charles*. They couldn't be tossed about like the little collier which had brought them from Newcastle.

It was a disappointed, grumpy Clifford who carried them back home in his coach.

Before he went to bed his mother came in to say goodnight. With much laughter she told him that Clifford had been very disenchanted with him and his father after the rejection of his offer. "So he is going to make arrangements for our departure on the stage coach in three days' time. Celia has just told me that if you had consented to join the business he would have formally proposed a marriage between you and Eunice. Did I not tell you he would be after you for her? Celia doesn't see why it shouldn't still happen. If you whisked Eunice off to Horden it would keep her well away from her father. Of course Clifford's plan was to keep all the wealth in the Horden name."

That night in bed staring up at the ornate tester and its lavish hangings Daniel began to wonder how his parents would respond if he volunteered now for the navy. That day when he was eight and had played out the Battle of Scheveningen they had found him just as he was finishing his game and gleefully throwing away the Dutch Admiral Tromp.

His father had crouched down by him. "Why do you find delight in war and death and destruction? Your Uncle Daniel and I were once persuaded to join the army but it was a horrible mistake. Neither of us could have used our pikes in anger for there was no sense in the cause for which we were fighting. I fell ill and the army moved on. My dear twin brother stayed with me and we neither of us ever joined our troop again. You have been told what happened to him later so you know the whole venture was a disaster. Even when a cause seems just I have ever since felt that war and violence produce no lasting good."

Mother Bel had sat herself down on the bank the other side of him. "Oh Nat, Dan is too young for a sermon. Boys will always play war-games. I acted the Battle of Newburn on this very spot with Sam Turner, and had sticks for the Scots and English soldiers. It ended in complete massacre on all sides. Of course at that time I was still more boy than girl."

Daniel had been surprised because Sam Turner was a tenant farmer on the Horden land. It was odd to think of him as a boy playing games with Mother Bel.

Lying stretched out in bed now Daniel probed those early memories. Would his mother object to the navy now that he was a man? It would grieve his father but he was more afraid of grieving her. She loved the three of them being together at Horden Hall and had freely admitted she would weep when he went to Cambridge. So strong a character, so free, so happy as she was she had carried a dreadful cloud about her for much of her youth.

She had become very quiet later that day when he was eight. He had demanded to know why and as always she answered him honestly. "The day I acted the battle with Sam Turner was the same day I caused the fire in the Turner's haystack for which your father's twin, the Daniel after whom you were named, was hung like a felon. Grandmother Wilson has told you how it was."

"Too many times," he had squeaked out.

"Well, you playing at battles with stick soldiers made me remember and when I do I go quiet."

"You shouldn't think about it because it was an accident."

Then she had laughed and hugged him. "I know but I felt like a killer for a long time. You will never have such a cloud. Always bring your worries into the open, Dan. I had no one to tell and even my dearest friend I couldn't tell because I thought she would hate me."

"Who was that?"

"Why, Ursula, your Nana Sula of course."

"She could never hate anyone."

"I know. I was a silly lost soul to think so. So Dan, hide nothing away inside you like a canker. I tell you everything about my past. I tell you how I love your father and you. Be the same with us. We are all open books together."

He could hear her saying the words that day, such aeons ago it seemed. But now he had reached the uncomfortable point in his life when too much openness was an embarrassment. There were tumbled emotions inside him that could not be laid bare because he hardly knew what they were.

He had found he liked looking at the flaunted bosoms of his French cousins though he was sure he disliked the girls themselves, while little mysterious Eunice tiptoed about in his thoughts till he longed to be free of her. His parents should not expect to know his secret hopes and plans. Nor should the things they had suffered in their past lives have any sway over what he did with his. He didn't want to cause them fresh pain but they had each other. That should be enough.

He turned over seeking a cooler place in the bed. London nights were too warm in June. He was now impossibly wakeful. Recalling that conversation with his mother had set him thinking of home which the whirl of London scenes had thrust far from his mind. How remote it all was! He had hardly given a thought to Nana Sula. Now it hit him hard that Madeline and Diana would see her bustling about the Hall, never without a task in her hands, from polishing silver to weeding the vegetable garden. Yet she ate dinner and supper with the family. How would it be when his cousins were seated around the table too? In *this* house there was complete separation of the two worlds of family and servants. But Nana Sula was no servant. She was in a saintly world of her own.

Thinking of her he found himself clenching his fists. He would struggle not to slap the girls across their impudent faces if they dared to laugh at her. The sad thing about Nana Sula was that her face was terribly deformed. Her mouth was twisted so that some words were hard for her to say, her chin was practically non-existent and her nose crooked. None of this mattered in the least to those who knew her. They saw nothing but her brilliant blue laughing eyes which spoke love to all humankind. Her real name was Ursula and he had been taught she was his Nanny which in his first speech had become Nana Sula. Without any shame he still called her that. Running in on his Saturday afternoons home from the Grammar School his first words had always been, "Nana Sula, I'm back." What would *she* say to him joining the navy?

Quite unable to sleep now his thoughts turned to other facets of his home life. There were his other grandparents, Joseph and Anne Wilson who always dined with them after Sunday service. They didn't live in the Hall but in the vicarage at Nether Horden where the Reverend Joseph had quietly stepped into the empty benefice, laid aside his surplice for the Puritan times and would perhaps be wearing it again now the King was back.

It was a relief to remember that his French grandmother, Lady Maria Horden, Aunt Henrietta and the girls were all Catholic and would perhaps find a clandestine Mass somewhere in Newcastle. Nana Sula was Catholic too and was encouraged to attend from time to time though she did not demand the privilege often. At least she would know where a Mass could be had if they were keen to find one, though he had seen no great eagerness yet on his cousins' part to flaunt their religion. But they would not attend the Nether Horden church and Daniel would not have to be embarrassed at the brief simplicity of his Grandfather Wilson's sermons, always on the theme of love and peace. It was easy to see how his father had absorbed that message all his childhood.

What he did wonder was how his Grandmother Wilson

would tolerate Lady Horden. Grandmother Wilson despised all airs and graces and believed every woman however high borne should be devoted to good works. Shattered in her mind for a while by the terrible fate of her son Daniel, most loved because he was weak in the head, she was still liable to changes of mood and all too outspoken at times. Sunday lunches, her grandson Daniel foresaw, would be very uncomfortable.

He wished he had not been named after his uncle. Grandmother Wilson was sparked into recollections of that unfortunate young man whenever she heard his name spoken. Would she recount the terrible injustice of his hanging on the very first occasion that she met the newcomers? Although she had managed to accept the innocence of his mother's tragic part she could never forget that Grandfather Horden was the magistrate and his son, Robert, the one who had stirred the crowd to the lynching. Being under the roof of Horden Hall was liable to bring on one of her reminiscences and meeting Lady Horden, the widow of Sir John and mother of no-good Robert could be a harrowing experience.

Daniel, tossing and turning, finally pulled off his nightshirt and slid his naked body between the sheets. Had his parents considered what a hornet's nest they might be creating by mixing up the two families for an indefinite period?

Of course he wanted to see them all at home again but if he volunteered for the navy now he would be spared the unpleasantness of seeing two incompatible worlds collided. Boys became midshipmen younger than he . . . .With that thought he finally fell asleep

CHAPTER 7

DAYLIGHT the next morning showed him that his dream of entering the navy now would have to wait. Everything the French family said about their forthcoming visit to Horden included him. His parents spoke of hiring extra horses for Madeline and Diana so they could ride with him as he showed them the farms and woods on the estate. He was still viewed as a boy and the family's plans were his plans.

It was the same with the proposed visit to William and Eunice.

His mother said, "Your father and I have decided against accepting Cousin Celia's offer of the coach to visit William and Eunice. We will go on foot in our plainest garments. Put on the clothes you came in and be ready to go immediately after breakfast."

Celia told then William went out in summer very early to preach in the markets but would be back for some breakfast. "He's at it most mornings though he has no licence to preach. If he is stopped he tells them he must obey God rather than man. Mostly they tolerate him because he keeps himself clean and speaks politely. Besides they know he helps the poor and thinks nothing of giving his last crust to a beggar. Mind, you will be appalled where they live but our man knows the house and will guide you. I dare not come with you. It distresses me too much to see what my son has come to, the dear compliant boy that he always was. But I have writ him a letter which you may give him."

Daniel was both excited and apprehensive. Eunice had said so little to him but every word was clear in his memory. He could not forget the intense look she had given him before suddenly deciding to go with her father. Was there a second or two when she might have rushed into his arms and said, "Save me from him"?

Perhaps he would find out very soon.

Nat said as they left the house, "We are going to see a man who is trying to serve God. Let us not forget that."

They were guided by Clifford's serving-man, walking ahead of them and turning constantly to point out foul places. From the Strand they passed into Fleet Street and the City by Ludgate Hill. This was retracing the way they had come the first day and since then they had visited St Paul's with Madeline and Diana who were rightly shocked, Nat observed, at the noise and bustle of traders in the very nave. So they did not stop today but skirted the great sprawling edifice, surrounded outside too by many stalls, and so up to Cheapside. Daniel noted the way so that he could find it again. When they turned up Milk Street the man pointed along a narrow alleyway off it and indicated a tiny house between a leather-worker's and a baker's. It seemed to embarrass him that his master's son should live in such a place.

"That is their abode, sir." He addressed Nathaniel. "Do you

wish me to wait outside?"

"No. We thank you for coming and will find our own way back."

The man bowed and scurried off.

Bel looked at the house and then at Nat and Dan. "It is not so far in distance but the gulf between the dwellings is immense. What will our reception be? If we are thrown out at once it is but a morning's walk."

Looking about him, Daniel was overwhelmed by a sense of darkness and oppression. The street was so narrow that the overhanging upper storeys shut out the sunlight. Only the house they were looking at did not protrude over the street. While some were three storeys high this had two levels with its steeply sloping roof many feet below the roof lines of the adjoining houses. Obviously built to fill in the gap between them it was almost a toy house with its narrow front door and small window across which a piece of canvas was hanging for privacy.

Nat put his ear to the door. "I can hear William's voice so they are within."

He lifted his hand and knocked.

There was a silence and then a few more sonorous words and a loud "Amen."

They waited as a bolt was being thrust back and the door opened a crack. Eunice's little pointed face peeped out. Her eyes opened wide in astonishment, she uttered an exclamation of dismay and closed the door.

Daniel looked sadly from his mother to his father but

only for a moment as the door was pulled wide and William stood there. He bowed so low that the crown of his cropped head was level with Daniel's chest. Then he straightened and addressed them collectively.

"The child did not understand. If visitors come to our door they are to be welcomed. We were at our prayers. That is good. You find us at one with the Lord. Pray enter and be seated." He stood aside and bowed them in. "Eunice, uncover the window to let in more light."

Daniel stepped to help her. The wooden rod slotted through the sack was only just within her reach but when he held up his hands to it she shrank back so that he wouldn't touch her. He lifted it off its hooks and held it out to know where it was to go. Keeping her eyes down she took it quickly, rolled it up and stood it in the corner beyond the window. Then she retreated to the dark nook under the stair and taking a small brush, swept the top of a wooden box there and sat down on it.

Daniel, looking about in exasperation, saw his father and mother seating themselves on the bench at one side of the table where there was room for him too. William having blown out the candle which stood beside the open Bible placed himself opposite them and gravely laid the palms of his hands together.

Daniel wanted to pick Eunice up and shake her. Why will she not look at me? Why will she sit in the corner when there is room beside her father at the table?

Nathaniel had handed over Celia's letter. "Your mother

asked us to give you this and suggested you read it while we are here."

William took it and stood up. "I will take it to the door for the daylight but first I must offer you what refreshment we have. This morning at five of the clock I was in Covent Garden preaching and the basket of fruit you see on that shelf was my reward. Pray help yourselves from it. I can offer no strong drink but this jug contains milk from the dairy nearby."

"Oh William," Bel exclaimed. "We haven't come to eat and drink. We have had more than enough of that in The Strand. We wanted to see you and Eunice before we return home the day after tomorrow. We had hoped to get to know you a little in our time here."

William merely inclined his head and stepped to the door with the letter.

Bel said, "Will you not come nearer, Eunice?"

When she still sat with her head bent Bel got up and went over to her and held out both her hands.

"I am not a monster, little Cousin, please can we not be friends?"

Daniel watched for a reaction in the small hunched figure. Was she so ashamed of their poverty that she could not speak? He had never seen so cramped a living space and with the same area above, presumably divided into two smaller chambers, this was the whole house. She knows we have come from that mansion in The Strand and she simply cannot bear us to see how they live.

But at that moment William turned from the door and

addressed Nat.

"Do you, sir, know the contents of this letter?" His tone was harsh.

Nat stood up with his usual cheery open smile.

"No indeed, Cousin. We presumed it was natural for your mother to wish to send a word to you. She might have come herself but for her other guests."

"Then this proposal she puts forward is not of your making?"

"Proposal?"

Daniel's stomach contracted. What could that foolish, presumptuous woman have written?

William went on in a level voice, "My mother wishes me to consider seriously" – he checked the letter for the exact words – "the proposition that I should give my daughter to your son in marriage when he graduates from Cambridge University. Do you endorse this?"

Daniel didn't dare to look at Eunice but a suppressed gasp came from that corner. He heard a soothing murmur from his mother before she stepped back to the table. She and his father both began to speak at once.

Bel exclaimed, "You should know, William, that I am no lover of arranged marriages," while Nat was answering mildly, "I am sure we would have no objection if the young people wished it but they scarcely know each other –"

To Daniel's astonishment Eunice jumped up from her seat and screamed across the room, "Daniel said the idea of loving me was preposterous."

She stood for a second open-mouthed at her own extraordinary eruption, then turned and clattered up the steep wooden stair and slammed the door at the top behind her so that the flimsy house shook.

Daniel, appalled, felt all their eyes turn on him.

"I – I did say something like that but those maddening French girls were tormenting me. I didn't mean – it is as Father says – we don't know each other. I have no thoughts of marriage for years to come."

William held up his hand for silence.

"If such words were spoken at all it suggests to me that an inappropriate conversation had already taken place. What is the truth of this?" His face was reddening and his voice rising a pitch. "Has my mother already been plotting this and you, boy, have turned her down? Why then would she persist?" He slapped the letter. "Oh I can well see that a baronet would view marriage with a daughter of this house as preposterous. But that he should tell her to her face –"

Daniel drove his hands desperately through his hair. "Mother! It wasn't as it seems. Oh, sir," to William, "I wouldn't for the world have caused her pain. And I am far from regarding *rank* – why, she is my equal in every respect – if I could only explain to her – will you not call her down?"

"I will not, sir." William took a step closer and his teeth were clenched. "I have striven to keep her away from temptation but she enters that house and all this has followed. I smell a conspiracy of the devil. My mother's deviousness I know well but there has been cruelty here too. Within a few hours of meeting with my daughter's innocence you have trampled on her feelings. God forbid that worse has been done." He shook his head with an expression of agony. "She has not told me all. I see there was more, much more. But why has my mother done this thing now?"

Daniel shrank before him. Although he was taller than William he felt the man grow in stature as he grew in fierceness. Feeble protests that Eunice had overheard something spoken and nothing at all had happened died on his lips. He had never encountered anyone like this. He saw his father lay a hand on William's arm.

"Pray calm yourself, Cousin. I know of nothing that passed between these two young people –"

William shook off his arm and turned his dark brows on him.

"Ay, you indeed know nothing. No, no one knows but these two and God above. And I feel the presence of the Father of Lies more strongly than I do the Lord at this moment."

Bel intervened at his other side with a half-suppressed laugh. "William, you are at risk of being ridiculous. I preferred you when you were seventeen and had nothing to say for yourself."

"Ha! Ridicule I am well used to. It touches me not at all. *You* have not changed. You had nothing of the meekness of womanhood then and have learnt none since. If I am not to be told the truth by your boy here I would wish you to leave this house. But if he has had his evil way with my girl then I call down heaven's curses upon his head."

Bel started to say, "Oh come, Nat, Dan, let us leave this mad house," when the door above opened and Eunice stood in the doorway.

"Father!" Her voice was shrill, "You shall curse no one. Why will you not believe that nothing happened? Oh go all of you! You have nothing to do with us. You can never be a part of our lives. Tell my grandmother so." She made desperate shooing motions with her arms.

Daniel took a step towards the foot of the little stair. His head was on a level with the worn slippers he saw peeping below her dress.

"Please believe me – I never meant –"

William grabbed his arms from behind and propelled him towards the door.

"She has told you to go. Your presence is unwelcome."

"Yes go," she pleaded. "I should never have opened my lips. Just go."

She disappeared inside and closed the door again.

Daniel looked in utter frustration from his father to his mother and then defiantly at William.

"I hope, sir, you have abandoned your wild and horrible imaginings. Do you believe now that we are both innocent? You will not cruelly interrogate your daughter when we are gone?"

William stared him down with eyes like ice and turned to Nathaniel. "You, sir, will tell your son that he comes between father and daughter at peril of his soul. Remove him, I pray. He has his mother's fiery spirit. You, I think, are a peaceable man but peace must sometimes give way before righteous anger and the search for truth. I bid you good-day."

He had now opened the door and there seemed nothing they could do but leave.

Bel however could not resist a word. "You make rods for your own back, Cousin William, but please spare that poor little child. I knew what it was to have a cloud overshadow my youth. It might have broken me down altogether but for the love of this man." She tucked her arm through Nat's. "Do not break your daughter's spirit, William, because you tragically lost the wife you loved."

William's face contorted with anger and Bel propelled them both away, grabbing Daniel's arm with her other hand. He glanced back once to see William's black-clad figure with thunderous face and hand upraised as if in cursing before he turned into the house and shut the door.

They were round the corner into the adjoining lane when Daniel pulled his mother to a stop and burst into a flood of weeping on her shoulder.

"How can we leave her to him?" he choked out. "He is truly mad."

People were stopping in the street and looking at them.

"Is he ill?" A woman coming from a candlestick-maker's with a basket of candles stopped to ask.

Daniel brushed his hand over his eyes and shook his head, shame-faced. They hurried on together until they came out onto Cheapside.

Nathaniel said then, "No, I do not believe William is mad.

He looks upon the bringing up of his one daughter alone as a terrible responsibility. He is a sad, lost man without his wife and has thrown himself into this enforced poverty as a kind of penance. But for that unfortunate letter from his mother he was prepared to welcome us with courtesy though he sees any young man's presence as a threat."

Bel concurred readily with that. "Indeed he was eying Dan with suspicion from the moment he saw us. I sensed him stiffen when Dan went to help her with their wretched curtain. And I know you'll say I was too flippant with him, Nat, and made things worse. I'm afraid I can't tolerate fanatics. They are too free with the Lord's name. I believe God's in His heaven and we can only struggle on here below and do the best we can."

Daniel considered this as he sniffed away his tears of anger and frustration.

"But, Mother, we didn't do our best. He wanted the truth and I was never allowed to tell him exactly how those stupid words she quoted came about. And now she'll think – well, I don't know what she'll think."

"And do you mind so much what she thinks?" His mother was grinning up at him. "Do I sense my boy is a little in love after all?"

Daniel stamped his foot. "No I am not. I don't know what being in love means. I don't want to know. All I've learnt since we came down here is that women are trouble. We've seen London now and I'm ready to go home. I only wish those Rombeau girls were not coming with us." He hunched his shoulders and plodded on, fearing that his parents were exchanging amused glances. The visit had been a disaster and he wished with all his heart it had never happened.

CHAPTER 8

EUNICE was allowed the indulgence of sobbing on her bed for a mere five minutes. They were tears of fury at herself. Why had she shouted out those hurtful words? They had hurt her when they were spoken not because she cared for Daniel at that stage but because they confirmed what she knew too well that she was an object no one would ever care about. Then had come the vision of him at the door of her room and she had believed for a moment that he *did* care. It was a wondrous moment but could never have any consequences for her. His next words, his pursuing her down the stairs, his speaking up in the hallway were drops of balm to her soul even though she had had to rebuff them. Why then, on hearing the contents of her grandmother's letter, had she so stupidly shouted out his earlier remark which she was not supposed to have heard?

The idea of loving me, she told herself, *was* preposterous, he did say it, but of course it was. I had been rude to him. I have never learnt how to speak to people, much less a young man. Did he and his parents really only come to say goodbye? Did they guess what Grandmother wrote? But he doesn't wish it. He has no thought of marriage. They are all sorry for me, that is the beginning and end of it. But they will go away and forget me. Father will for ever be the ogre guarding me and why should they brave an ogre when Daniel Horden is a young man who could have anyone he chose?

She heard her father praying from the moment the door had been shut on the visitors and five minutes later he summoned her down.

She knew there would be more interrogation. She wiped her eyes and descended the stairs. Every word of every speaker in that house of sin as he called it would be drawn out of her. So she had better tell it all and let him make of it what he would. Her own replies too would be laid bare and he would probe what was behind them. "You said you were my possession?" he would repeat. "Why? You are my beloved daughter. That is why you are guarded as the greatest treasure I have."

She stood before him and let the questioning begin and it all unfolded exactly as she had foreseen up to those very words. After that his one commendation was for her rebuff to Daniel spoken in his mother's hallway, words which he had heard with his own ears.

Now her father surprised her by standing up abruptly and pacing about the room. Then he stopped in front of the table as she sat still, wondering if it was all over. He clasped his hands in an attitude of prayer and gazed at her with great intensity.

"I see I have done those three some wrong. It is true that Arabella speaks in haste without thought and her son likewise though his youth excuses him somewhat. But I see now that my wrath was misplaced. The young man spoke the words you so imprudently quoted back to him in a moment of impatience at the folly of others, and you, listening as you should not have been, overheard them. No good ever comes from eavesdropping and now you have caused me to sin. I spoke in anger not knowing all the truth. I must do penance but first I must confess my sin to them and beg pardon. I must write them a letter. That is a hard thing. You know why it is hard? Because of pride. It is pride that must be overcome. And it is doubly hard because of the young man's sin."

She looked up at him startled. "But he didn't –"

"True. Perchance he was foiled by circumstance. Only God can know his heart. I meant the sin of tempting you to disobey me."

She gave the tiniest shrug of her shoulders. That was a kindly impulse, she was thinking, not a sin.

He struck his fists on the table. "Do you not see, Eunice, how one wrong leads to another? Your listening at doors was wrong and telling half the truth was wrong. Both have led me into the sin of anger which leaves me grieved and humbled."

She glanced up again. It had to be said. "I am truly sorry, Father."

"Very well. But I fear that your feelings have been stirred by this young man or why did you call out those words in his presence and in that tone of voice?"

"I don't care about him. I wanted you to know he didn't care about me. You might have thought he did from what he said in Grandfather's hall. Father, you don't always understand other people. You thought his parents were lying just now when they said they were not privy to what Grandmother wrote. But I am sure they weren't."

"I believe that now. And you may be right that I do not always understand other people. Many times I do not wish to. But I do know my mother. I believe she hatches her own little plots and plans and that is why she invited you at the time of their visit. But none of that excuses the partial truths you told me the day I brought you home. When I question you on any matter you must recall every detail that you can. I wish all my words and actions to be based upon a knowledge of the whole truth. This is where I failed today and allowed the sin of anger to rise up in me. Do you understand the gravity of that?"

She wanted to scream, "Be silent. Leave the thing alone now." She murmured softly, "I do. Here is paper." She pushed the writing materials over to him. "When you have written we can forget all about it."

He paused as he drew the paper towards him. His brows met in one line. "Not *forget*, child. Learn. From every sorry happening like this learn a new lesson. I too must learn – learn to seek the truth with diligence before making a judgment."

He sat down, trimmed a pen with his knife and began to write unhesitatingly.

She got up to fulfil her morning task of cleaning their little window and wiping from every surface the soot that daily seeped in from the baker's chimneys.

My father is the most meticulous man in the world, she told herself with every stroke of the cloth. He enrages me, but he doesn't spare himself. He tries himself as much as me. If he does not lash himself physically he does spiritually. Perhaps he is perfect in the sight of God and I am wild and wayward because I can neither control my thoughts or my utterances.

She washed out her cloth in the bucket by the fireplace and taking it up she paused by the door till her father raised his head.

"May I go for fresh water?" He nodded.

She went out and emptied the bucket into the runnel and walked up the street to the conduit fountain. When she came back he had folded and sealed his letter.

"It is written to Cousin Nathaniel but I have put in also a brief note to your grandmother."

Eunice waited to see if he would disclose what he had said but he just went to the door and called Tom Fletcher, the leather-worker's boy.

"Run there and deliver this to the direction written down. When you return you shall have an orange from this bowl and I will give you your writing lesson."

The boy grinned and ran.

Eunice looked after him and wondered if the letter would for ever close the door on that episode.

Nathaniel received the letter when they returned that afternoon from a visit to St James' Park. Taking Bel and Dan with him he walked out of the dining room door onto the terrace. The French party were resting their tired feet in the drawing room above, Clifford had gone to his office and Celia was giving orders to the cook.

"We have some leisure at last from endless company and we will see what that poor man has written. I little expected to hear another word from him."

They sat down on the sun-warmed stone bench and the river glided below.

Nat glanced at the opening sentence and then looked up in surprise.

"Well, it is an apology! Hear what he says. '*Cousin Nathaniel, I repent my late anger. I abhor myself in dust and ashes. I did not wait patiently for the whole truth to be laid before me. Now I believe I have received it from my daughter's lips and I wish to retract what I spoke in haste. I do not now believe that your son took sinful advantage of my daughter. What he might have done if he had had opportunity of course only he and the Lord know*' –"

"Why, the villain," Bel cried. "He calls this a retraction!"

Nat laid a hand on hers. "He doesn't know Daniel as we do. How could he? To say this much must have caused him a great struggle."

Daniel peered over the letter. "I'm glad *you* both believe in my honour. How does he go on?"

"He finishes that sentence with '*but my daughter has told me the rather peculiar circumstances under which he said that the idea of loving her was preposterous. She has repented of eavesdropping, an activity which invariably leads to more wrong, but if the words spoken by your son represent his feelings towards her he will not expect me to reply in the affirmative to my mother's proposal.'"*

Bel leant forward to peer past Nat at Daniel. "They didn't, did they, represent your feelings, Dan. I saw your tears. *They* expressed your feelings a great deal better."

Daniel leapt up and planted himself before her with his back against the stone balustrade. "No they didn't, Mother, and I wish everyone would leave my feelings alone. When I shed tears I was just mad with frustration at the whole foolish visit. I wish it had never happened."

"Very well, my love," she said. "Go on, Nat."

"There is not much more. He says he has enclosed a note for us to give his mother but for our information he has written, *'I have no wish to give my daughter in marriage to your son or anyone else unless the Lord shows me a worthy man and directs me to do so.'"*

Bel shook her head. "There you are. He calls upon the Lord again. He will make no move of his own volition or responsibility and he will not allow his poor child such freedom either. I cannot think he is right. God has given us minds and hearts and a free will."

"Yet waiting upon Him in prayer is also right, Bel. I pray that our son will live a good life and in due course find an excellent woman who will bear him children."

And *I* pray, Daniel thought, that I will do great deeds for my King, show strength and courage and maybe one day meet a pretty girl who has an uncomplicated family with a comfortable little fortune and a cheerful disposition.

His mother had now risen too and put her arm round his

shoulders.

"Maybe William is not as vicious as you feared. It is much for a man like that to recognise his own faults. Do not be too anxious for little Eunice. He will not let her starve and she will almost certainly grow into a better woman than those shallow French brats."

He pulled away from her. "As I said before I want nothing to do with any girls. How long will this dreadful journey home take? Why can't we go back by sea on our own? How long will the French family stay when we get there?"

"Well," she laughed, "I would say six days to the first question. To the second, it is my mother who is paying our fares. Like the new clothes it is her gift to make up for the years she couldn't help me. I just hope she knows what our roads and stage-coaches are like. As for the third question I expect no more than a few weeks. Henrietta's husband will want her home and so will his father, the old Count Rombeau. And when the girls realise there is no hope of either of them becoming Lady Horden they will be more than ready to go."

"Good," said Daniel. "Then I'll go and have a sleep before supper. I am still recovering from that dreadful ball."

CHAPTER 9

“E are all to get out and walk up the hill. The lead horse has gone lame.”

Nathaniel passed on the coachman’s message to the sleepy passengers.

Daniel jumped out readily and held out his hand to the nearest lady who happened to be Madeline.

“These cursed English roads!” she cried. “Just look at the mud. Well I sha’nt get out. What difference would my little weight make?”

Lady Horden rose. “If your grandmother can walk you can. Put on your chopins as your mother is doing.” Daniel looked at these things curiously. They were French galoshes but with higher heels than English ones. Walking in them, he thought, must be difficult.

His mother had already slipped her pattens over her shoes and she and his father were descending at the other side, followed by Henrietta and the eighth inside passenger, a silent gentleman they had picked up at the last stage. The three outside passengers, two French lady’s maids and the man servant had climbed down out of the basket, shaking the wet from their cloaks.

Daniel assisted his grandmother down and then Diana

eagerly held out her hands to him. "*I'm* coming, Dan. *I* don't make a fuss."

She had picked up his mother's way of always addressing him as Dan and by this the second day of their journey Daniel had finally separated the two sisters from the composite giggling pair they had seemed to be in London.

The trials of travel were certainly a test of character. Madeline grumbled at everything while Diana copied Nat's and Bel's cheerfulness and looked often at Daniel to make sure he had noticed.

Now as he took both her hands she jumped into his arms and peered up at his face with her great black eyes shining as if this was a great adventure.

From first setting off from Aldersgate, Daniel had realised there was no escaping intimacy in a coach and sitting opposite to the girls he had begun to observe the differences between them. He had thought them both black haired, but Madeline's was blue-black while Diana's had a hint of red-brown when a sunbeam shone through the coach window. She had a trick too of winding one of her ringlets round her finger as she chatted. It might be nervous excitement but to Daniel it was appealing rather than irritating. Her mother, his Aunt Henrietta, always contriving to appear elegant and unruffled herself, would tell her under her breath and in French to stop fiddling. Daniel grinned sympathetically at her the first time that happened and from that moment she ceased any vestige of teasing him. This sent her sister into a prolonged sulk.

Holding Diana now as he set her on the ground Daniel

decided she was much prettier than her sister, her nose was not as long or her mouth as wide and her surprised eyes with their arched brows were quite charming. She was shorter and slightly plumper than the more angular Madeline. Her generous bosom brushed his doublet and on the excuse of helping her to the grassy verge he lifted her off her feet over the rough stones and muddy ruts in the road. There had been rain all that morning but the sun was out now and a steamy haze was rising from the wet fields. He took her arm in case her chopins slipped on the damp grass.

Glancing back he saw that his father was helping a reluctant Madeline to descend.

"With six horses," she demanded, "why does it matter if one of them is lame?"

"They are taking him from the traces to lead him on the grass," Nat explained, "which means they must remove his paired horse to have the balance right. It will do us good to walk awhile now the rain has stopped."

She snorted. "What is this God-forsaken place? How far have we to walk?"

"We're somewhere south of Peterborough. The man says he can hire a fresh horse at the next village which is only at the top of this rise. There are fifteen miles more to the next staging inn and then we can have a good supper and a rest."

Diana, her arm happily tucked into Daniel's, was prancing along. She too looked back at her sister.

Madeline, picking her way delicately, was still grumbling to Nathaniel. "In France we never took a public coach. We went everywhere in our own carriage which had the latest springs for comfort. This lumbering thing bounces one to pieces. I know not how *Grandmere* will live through it for five more days."

"Lady Horden is behaving with great stoicism," Nathaniel said. "I am very proud of my mother-in-law but it is only what I would expect of the mother of my Bel. See how your Aunt Bel is striding ahead of all of us."

"Why do you call her Bel? I was always told my Aunt's name was Arabella."

"It is, but she likes everything short and quick, names no more than three letters long. Hence I am Nat and Daniel is Dan."

"She had better not call me Mad," Madeline growled.

Diana looked up into Daniel's face and giggled, "It would be a good name for her in that mood, don't you think so?"

Daniel didn't know what to do but grin back at her.

It was the next day that the all too frequent disaster of coach travel befell them. There had been more rain overnight and puddles dotted the broken surface of the road. The coachman drove through most of them in blind faith but one concealing a much deeper rut deceived him.

Their silent companion of the previous day had become voluble after a friendly question from Bel about his destination. He was telling his life history which included, Daniel was excited to find, a spell of service in the navy. Daniel was leaning forward to catch his every word over the rattling of the coach when there was a tremendous lurch, the sound of wood splintering and then the whole contraption began toppling sideways.

There were screams. Daniel heard his mother shout, "We're going right over. Push the rugs and cushions that side." She was doing it as she spoke, inserting a cushion behind Lady Horden's head as they all slithered on top of her mother, grabbing at the benches to soften their impact. The coach settled on its side and after a pause to see that it had stopped moving they began to untangle themselves. The men strove to avoid crushing the ladies' legs with their boots as they reached to push open the door above them.

The coachman's head appeared in the opening. His worried eyes assessed the squirming mass of bodies.

"Is anyone hurt?"

Daniel, the tallest and most agile, hauled himself out and reached down for the nearest waving arm – Diana's. "I think not," he told the man.

The other ladies were still struggling among the swathes of petticoats to find their feet on the side which had now become a floor. The straw on the original floor had slid into a heap hampering their movement and horribly dirtying their dresses.

The coachman set a box below the new roof and when Daniel had dragged Diana up, the stranger pushing her from behind, he passed her to the coachman who helped her to climb down.

"I have no hurt," she called up cheerfully. "Only a tear in my dress but it's no matter."

Daniel remained on top as one by one the other ladies were lifted out and passed down, sadly crumpled but none the worse.

Madeline moaned to Nathaniel as he heaved her up to the opening, "Your elbow crushed me as you fell on top of me. I shall be black and blue. I know it."

"I am sorry. I daresay we will all have a few bruises but there are no bones broken I believe. Let us thank God for that."

When they were all out they saw that the serving-man was crouched by the roadway, white-faced and clutching his ankle. He had jumped from the basket as the coach tipped and turned his foot on one of the road stones. The two maids were sobbing piteously, coated in mud, having clung on till they touched down and then crawled out. Some of the pieces of luggage on top had broken loose from their ropes and were sitting in puddles in the road.

The little group looked at each other with rueful faces. It began to rain.

Two hours later they were sitting round a roaring inn fire. The innkeeper who had sent a rescue party with a carriage and cart and spare horses was eager in his concern for them. Rooms where they could change their soiled, wet clothes were instantly at their disposal. Ale and wine were flowing freely and two fat chickens were roasting on a spit for their supper. He evidently had an eye for a fortune to be made.

A big-bellied man with a permanently florid complexion,

he planted himself before Lady Horden as she sipped her wine. "Now my lady, after your ladyship's dreadful experience you will not be wanting to proceed on your journey in the horrid stage even supposing they can bring up a new wheel on it by the morning. I can hire you the most comfortable coach and a man that is the best driver in the kingdom. There will be a covered cart for your servants and luggage and if the gentlemen are happy to ride there are horses the like of which you will not see at any of the regular staging inns. I will send word ahead that you are to be as well supplied at the next inn. My man knows only the best places."

"Oh Grandmamma, we must do as he says," cried Madeline. "I will never trust myself in another stage again."

"We will consider your offer, my man, if the cost is reasonable, but you see there are five ladies in our party, myself, my two daughters and my granddaughters. Is there room in this coach for all?"

The innkeeper looked crestfallen. "It is a beautiful coach with padded seats and glass windows but – I fear it only seats four in comfort."

"I shall ride," cried Diana. "I can unpack my riding skirt and jacket tonight."

The innkeeper still looked worried. "It is only two horses I can spare besides the two for the coach and one for the cart.

"Then I shall ride behind Dan." Diana clapped her hands at the brilliance of this idea. "You can arrange a saddle for me, Innkeeper, can you not?"

He bowed several times with a large grin across his fire-rosy face.

"Then it is settled. We will enjoy this, won't we, Dan?"

Daniel could see his mother's face where she and his father sat on the settle at a distance from the fire as the evening was warm. She doesn't look pleased, he thought. She would have liked to ride behind me herself but I'm not so certain that hours of riding with mother would be wise. She would want to be at my secret thoughts all the time. He realised he hadn't answered Diana who was peering up into his face with those black brows more arched than ever.

He laughed. "Oh yes, we'll be all right. You don't mind getting wet if it rains, I suppose?"

As it happened the rest of their journey north was dry and fine. The little party proceeded at a brisker pace than the four miles an hour of the heavy coach and though the servants' cart kept getting left behind it soon caught up at the next stopping place.

By the time they were within sight of Newcastle, Daniel was excited at the prospect of showing Diana all the haunts of his youth. If a thought about Eunice entered his head it passed out again as quickly as it had come. She has food and a roof over her head and the Bible to read. That may be all she wants in life. She is such a pale little mouse. Diana now is alive to everything.

Riding down through Gateshead to the bridge over the Tyne, Diana exclaimed at the sight of Newcastle on the opposite bank.

"Oh what a beautiful city! Look at that magnificent

cathedral – I had no notion – what a tease you were to call it a small town!"

Daniel turned his head to grin at her. "It *is* small compared to London or Paris and that is not a cathedral. It's the church of St Nicholas, but you are right, it's a fine building and an impressive town."

Crossing the bridge just ahead of the coach he could hear his mother's animated voice as she told Lady Horden and his Aunt Henrietta, "Now look to the left just after we leave the bridge. You'll see a bench against the wall. That's where I was asleep when Nat rode up. That's when we first met. That's when we fell in love. Look, look, there it is – an old tramp is sitting on it. I can never pass it without thanking God for that bench."

Diana's voice at his ear, murmured, "Oh how delightful! Aunt Arabella is a true romantic, is she not? My poor mother was taken to France to marry my father whom she scarcely knew. There should be true love, don't you think?"

This is dangerous ground, Daniel warned himself. I mustn't be bounced into anything by this girl, good fun as she is. He had already confided in her his ambition to serve in the navy and she had said it was so brave and noble and much more romantic than studying at Cambridge.

When he told her she would meet his Nana Sula and must not be upset by her deformed face she had exclaimed, "Oh Dan, I am much too kind-hearted. If she has loved you from babyhood I shall love her devotedly. What do outward looks matter?"

This seemed to him singularly at odds with the hours she and Madeline had spent on their appearance before evening parties in London. They even wore patches on their faces, a new-fangled fashion which Daniel thought ridiculous, but which was supposed to enhance the beauty of the wearer.

As they rode through the streets of Newcastle, heading for the Pilgrim Gate he managed to avoid answering her question by pointing out the major buildings and the way to his grammar school. After they passed through the Gate into the Liberties and out into the open country his own excitement at nearing home after what seemed an age made him fall silent.

"Not far now," was all he could say, turning his head to meet Diana's eager look and when at last the gates of Horden Hall came in sight he was speechless with emotion but Diana's enthusiasm bubbled over.

"Oh what a grand place! *Ma foi*, is that what you called an ordinary house, you mischievous boy. Look at that sweeping drive and the way the mansion sits against the woodland and whose is that splendid equestrian statue in front?"

"My great-great-grandfather's, Sir Ralph Horden, of King James's time. It's considered rather a clumsy sculpture. Ah!" he exclaimed, "here is Nana Sula running to meet us. She is quite ancient now but still runs everywhere."

His heart lifted at the sight of the scurrying figure, holding up her arms with joy towards him. She had put on the starched white bonnet she wore when strangers were about so that her face was partly shaded. She wore a plain grey dress and pinafore and Diana, dismounting first with the help of the groom, whispered to Daniel.

"Is she a nun?"

"No, but like you she is Catholic."

Diana made a face as if to say, "That matters little to me," but she went forward before Daniel's feet had touched the ground and held out both her hands to the surprised little woman.

"You are Ursula, *Saint* Ursula, Dan tells me, his very special Nana Sula. I am so happy to meet you. I am Diana Rombeau."

Ursula was curtseying low but Diana lifted her up. "No no, please, call me Diana. Dan and I are great friends."

The rest were now gathering and Dan saw his mother hasten to clasp Ursula in her arms.

"Oh Urs, I've missed you so but you would have hated London. It was so hot and we rushed about so every day. Is all well here?"

His father had now joined them escorting the other ladies.

Ursula told him, "Oh sir, the dear Reverend, your father, is not so well or they would have been here to welcome you." She again curtseyed low, concealing her face, before Lady Horden, Henrietta and Madeline. Daniel intercepted the look Madeline gave her sister for paying attention to a servant.

His father said, "I will ride over to the vicarage as soon as our guests are settled in."

Ursula looked up at him then and her poor twisted face was plain to see.

Daniel saw Madeline recoil and take her mother's arm and hurry past her.

"Come, Maman, you are to show me this place you grew up in and I long to take off these travelling clothes."

Bel resumed with an effort, Daniel thought, her office of hostess as they went inside.

"Mother, I have given you your old room and Hen, you have yours where I trespassed and chopped up your linen and lace in my wicked years."

Daniel was tickled that she could bring it up now and that she had fallen into calling her sister Hen. On the journey they seemed to have reached an intimacy they had never had in their younger days.

Diana stood gazing about at the foot of the stairs. "The hall is so big and grand. Oh the magnificent plaster work!"

"You girls have your Uncle Robert's old room."

Bel was leading them up the stairs as she spoke.

"*Sacre Dieu*!" cried Madeline, "I trust he was not laid out there after his fall from his horse? I wouldn't sleep a wink."

Daniel, following, called out, "It is also my room you have been given and I assure you I sleep there like a log."

Diana turned round to him with her eyes wide with concern. "Oh but where are *you* to go, Dan? We are turning you out!"

"I have the little room that was once the chapel and then was Mother's from which she invaded yours, Aunt Henrietta, but I promise you I will do no such evil deeds. The door between has been boarded up long since."

There was some laughter at this but Daniel was aware that his grandmother had been silent from the moment of their arrival. He remembered how she had looked when Madeline and Diana had asked about her memories of Horden Hall. She had gazed into the past and it was steeped in sadness. Now she was moving slowly with a set face towards the room she had shared with Sir John twenty years ago. She had left him then to accompany her daughter to France and never seen him alive again.

Bel had told Daniel often that the departure of her mother and sister had been welcome because they had rarely shown her any affection. In the face of her own overflowing love to him he had found that shocking. Now he watched with some curiosity as his grandmother, very straight-backed, was ushered into the bedchamber where her years of marriage had been spent. Her maid came scampering up the stairs followed by their man, limping badly but with her ladyship's trunk on his back. He set it in the room and retreated for the next load. The maid scuttled in and Daniel heard his grandmother's voice, *"Fermez la porte, Maria."*

The door was shut firmly and Bel looked at Daniel. "My ice mother is a little overcome."

Henrietta's maid, whom she was sharing with her daughters, was bustling about on the landing, making sure the bags went to the right rooms.

Madeline put her head out of their door and said, "Where are your servants, Aunt Arabella, to help our man?"

Bel smiled. "Our groom will be watering the horses so that the hired men can start back this evening. Ursula will be in the kitchen feeding the men and one of the maids will be setting a tray of wine and refreshments for you as soon as you are all ready to partake. The other has been borrowed from the vicarage and is preparing for your supper later. They have made up the beds and carried water to all the rooms so I trust you will find nothing lacking."

Madeline's mouth hung open. "But your own maid, Aunt, to unpack for you and lay out your things?"

Bel held out her hands. "What are these for?"

Diana's head appeared and seeing Daniel pulling their boxes along while the French man-servant took Henrietta's trunk to her room she loudly reprimanded her sister.

"You know well enough that they have the servants they can afford here and we are very grateful to be invited. Thank you, Dan. That is my box and I will have it this side. I see there is not a thing of yours left in here but I shall love to think I am sleeping where you usually sleep." She cast down her eyes and raised them again with her most alluring smile.

"Good," he said. "There will be beer and wine downstairs. I'm thirsty." And he hurried away.

When his mother joined him below in the great hall she was bursting with unspoken words. "That Diana! Why are you letting her flirt with you like this? She is the same silly girl you first thought her when you wanted nothing to do with her or her sister."

"Oh come, Mother. Look at the way she behaved to Ursula."

"Only to please you. You had told her Ursula was your beloved nurse."

"No, I can't believe she was dissembling. She showed her

true kindliness."

Bel stamped her foot. "So you are going to fall headlong into her trap, are you?"

"Indeed I won't for there *is* no trap. I've learnt she is very different from her sister, that is all."

"They are two of a kind. They are both in love with you and I can't blame them for that. If I were their age *I* would be in love with you." She was looking him up and down. "Your beautiful flaxen hair, your bright eyes – the blue green of a smiling sea, your height, your long limbs –"

"Mother, stop it! You are making yourself ridiculous. Madeline loathes me and if Diana loves me," he shrugged his shoulders, "well, it can't be helped."

"Madeline is only cross because you started to take notice of Diana. I told you on our first day in London that they would both be after you."

Their maid brought the tray of drinks from the kitchen.

"Set it in the parlour, Jane."

The parlour, like the small dining-room had been partitioned off from the great hall when the custom of the master and mistress dining at a high table with all the retainers below had finally gone out of fashion. There was also an office to the right of the stairs where the estate records were kept and beyond it Nathaniel's study. The alterations meant that the stairs, the great fireplace and the main doorway were no longer symmetrically placed but the dimensions of the hall were still impressive and the heraldic shield of the Hordens had been moved to a point above the archway that led to the steps to the kitchen, midway between the new parlour and the dining-room.

Daniel felt sure that Diana's admiration on her first entrance had not been feigned and he was now highly irritated with his mother.

No more was said then. The guests came down presently for the refreshments and Nathaniel returned from the village with news of his father. To them he said little but afterwards to Bel and Daniel he confided, "I like not the colour of his skin. It is yellowy and he seems very tired. My mother is fearful since he has rarely suffered any illness. She told me privately that she has no desire to outlive him for she cannot conceive of life without him. If he is not better soon I think we should call a physician to him. He would like to see you, Bel, when you can spare the time but this evening I think *you* should ride over, Daniel, before supper. They long to set eyes on you again, they both said."

Daniel went alone, much to Diana's disappointment.

"I would love to meet your grandparents," she said, "but if your grandfather is ill perhaps –"

"Quite so," was all he said.

CHAPTER 10

RIDING the familiar track to the village Daniel thought he had been a little abrupt with Diana. I mustn't listen to my mother. I'm afraid she's jealous. This is the first young lady with whom I have spent much time and she finds she doesn't like it.

Grandmother Wilson was at the vicarage window as he rode up. It was a straggling Elizabethan house much added to for clergymen with large families and the old couple lived in only a few rooms of it.

"Daniel!" she cried when he dismounted and flung the reins over the gate post. She drew him inside. "Ah how my heart lifts to say that name. I wish you could have met your Uncle Daniel, my sweet boy. I will never get over his cruel death as long as I live and if my Joseph dies I will have no will left to live at all. But come in and see him."

Daniel stooped his head at the low parlour door. Grandfather was reclining on the couch with a rug over his knees though the evening was fine. His skin was parchment-coloured and loose over the bones of his face. Daniel thought he had aged years in their absence.

He took his hand and perched on the edge of the couch beside him.

"Well, you have seen the world, my boy." The voice was weary. "And you have met some fine company I am sure, your dear mother's family whom you never saw before. And they are come back with you, grand French nobility. Your father wonders how they are to be entertained, especially the young ladies who have never seen England before, and in so remote a part as this."

Daniel smiled and pressed the thin flaccid hand.

"Oh I believe they will ride and we may hire a coach and take them about a little – to see the coast at Tynemouth perhaps."

Joseph Wilson looked concerned. "Will your father not get into debt with such expenses as well as the cost of feeding his guests?"

Daniel shrugged his shoulders. Debts came and went with the quality of the harvests and the ability of the tenant farmers to pay their rents.

His grandmother sat on a high-backed chair, hunched like a bird of prey; the most prominent feature was her nose poking out amidst her halo of wild grey hair, still streaked with red.

She broke in, her tone sharp and sarcastic. "Your grandfather is thinking that nothing must put at risk your going up to Cambridge. Dear old Queens' – his college and Nathaniel's."

Joseph regarded her wistfully. "Although your grandmother is eager to help in the village children's schooling she is no lover of long hours of study for young men. But it would break my heart and your father's if we failed to give you the wonderful chance we had to breathe the air of learning and meet with the best minds of the age. But I have been trying to put by a little of my stipend every year – we live very simply –"

Anne Wilson started up from her corner. "Nay, Joseph, promise nothing. If you are ill what have we to pay a physician and if you die, God forbid, I have no roof over my head."

Daniel squirmed at the turn the conversation had taken. "Father wouldn't take a penny from you, sir. I can work. He told me how he was a sizar at first and served wealthy students when he first went up to Queens." The time was not ripe to say he had other ambitions than Cambridge. "Truly, dear Grandfather, I only long to see you well. I will come often but you look tired now and perhaps I should go."

His grandmother laid a hand on his arm. "Nay stay, my Daniel, eh, how I love to say that name! Have a sup of small beer. It's all we have but I have made a cordial for your grandfather of honey and suffused herbs. You may try that after your long travels."

Daniel had the small beer and was asked about the journey and his French relations and managed to make them both laugh over his account of their mishaps.

"Well if they wish to make our acquaintance in a little while," said Anne Wilson, "they can come here, for your grandfather's not fit to walk further than the church. I know I must endure to meet the wife of Sir John Horden who found my boy guilty when he was as innocent as a babe. It's even harder to forgive her for the way her son Robert hounded him to the gallows." She was working herself into a frenzy and now raised her clenched fists. "Robert Horden murdered my boy as sure as if he'd done it with his own hands and am I to have her under my roof?"

"Hush, hush," cried Joseph. "God punished him when he fell from his horse. It will be hard for her too coming back here where husband and son were buried and she far away."

"That was her fault for being a Papist. At least they will not be coming to a service here."

Daniel tried to turn the conversation. "They *are* Papists but I know not that they heard a Mass while they were in London."

"The Catholics may come a little into the open now." Joseph's voice sounded stronger since he had drunk his cordial. "I have heard that the new King wants toleration for all. He is right. Let every man worship according to his own lights, say I. The dear people here are not worried whether I wear a vestment or not and they told no snooping Parliament men when I read from the Prayer Book one Sunday during those harsh years. Now I believe both priests and bishops will come back in and our Nat can take the orders for which he was always intended. Is that your inclination too, Daniel?"

Daniel stood up with a nervous laugh. "I can't say I have felt a calling that way, Grandfather, but of course I'm not quite sixteen yet."

"Ay, you are such a towering lad it is hard to remember how young you are. Well, God bless you. I dare say there will be a good supper at the Hall if you go now."

There was a good supper though they had dined well at an inn in Durham at noon. His aunt insisted they broke open the case of wine and they were as merry as the silence of Lady Horden and the tensions between the girls would allow.

Ursula did not sit with them and Bel told Daniel afterwards she had positively refused.

"There will be time enough for the four of us to be a family again when they are gone. That was what she said. I couldn't press her for she was quite determined."

Daniel escaped the card game that was afterwards proposed by Madeline and went into the kitchen to sit with Nana Sula and tell her much that he hadn't mentioned to his grandparents about the London Hordens.

"You speak with compassion about that poor girl, Eunice. Are you a little in love with her or is it that sweet Diana? She's quite a beauty."

"No, goodness me, Nana Sula. Everyone talks about being in love but I have no thoughts that way. Do not you add to the clamour! To be honest –" he leant close to her and whispered, "What I really want to do is join the navy but say nothing of that yet. Father and Mother assume I am going to Cambridge."

She put her head on one side and a cackle came from her twisted mouth.

"My boy wants adventure. I can understand that."

As always her bright eyes with their laughter-lines radiating were full of a love that he knew was without conditions or reservations of any kind.

He went happily to bed in the narrow room that looked

out of its pointed window onto the statue of Sir Ralph triumphantly brandishing his sword.

"You old villain," he said to him, half aloud, before he turned in. "They may say you're no great work of art, but seeing you riding to battle inspires me more than Cousin Clifford's ledgers or father's or grandfather's hours of study. I know not how things will turn out but thank God the northern night is cooler than London."

He had no sooner curled his long body between the sheets than he was fast asleep.

Eunice Horden sat with a sheet of paper in front of her and her mind in turmoil. It was a week since her cousins had set off for the north but she could not banish Daniel from her thoughts. Her father had been quiet and happy, since penning his letter.

Would I, she asked herself, find peace in my heart if I wrote a letter, not to Cousin Daniel – that would be quite improper – but to his mother, apologising for my foolish outburst which quite spoilt their visit and caused her son obvious distress. Cousin Arabella was a warm happy person. I can't forget how she took my hands and wanted to be friendly. I was cold and unresponsive, I was so shocked to see them at our wretched door, all smiles, and he so tall and his eyes so tender . . . Yes, I must write. I behaved very badly.

If I had written before they left London, she reasoned, they would all have been talking of it in the coach. Now I can take time over it and write carefully and address it to Horden Hall.

They may be at home now. Cousin Arabella may then receive it amongst other letters and read it in seclusion. What she tells her son of its contents I can leave to her. I think she is an honourable woman and she will at least pass on to him that I am sorry.

But is it wrong to write at all? Is it indulging a feeling I should not be feeling? The flesh wars against the spirit, as the Bible tells us. Is this a fleshly desire? Yet Father has always said that repenting for wrong-doing should be followed by reparation if it can be done. His letter was all he could do to put right the unjust things he had said. I too should put right what I said. God has given me this hour or more when Father has gone forth to pray before the Tower for an old Leveller mewed up there. He will be a long time. I can write the letter and entrust it to Tom to take to the post house.

She took up the pen with a prayer on her lips. Dear Lord, if I am doing wrong let this letter be lost on its way.

But how to word it?

She wrote, *'To Mistress Arabella Wilson Horden of Horden Hall in the County of Northumberland.'* That part was simple enough. She remembered her father explaining to her that Arabella was not called plain Mistress Wilson after her husband's name. "I fear there was pride," he said. "The name Horden belongs to the baronetcy and her son must come in as – I believe – the fifth baronet of the Horden dynasty. They put Wilson before it for form's sake."

But now how to continue?

'Pray forgive my presumption in writing to you, dear Cousin

Arabella, but I have been uneasy in my mind since your visit to our humble dwelling.'

That should be 'in my heart' but therein is danger. That is the flesh.

'I spoke rashly and hastily then and for that I am truly sorry. At my grandfather's house your son rightly expressed to others that the word 'love' should not have been mentioned at all. We had scarcely become acquainted. I was very wrong to listen to that conversation. Later when he witnessed my distress at my father's arrival I know he meant only kindness so I grieve that he should have become the object of my father's anger both at my grandfather's and during your visit.

'Pray convey to your son my deep regret that my thoughtless words produced that further wrath on my father's part for which I know he has already apologised in a letter to your husband. Troubled as I have been, I believe I am right to add my own apology.'

Oh how to explain her tone of voice when she had repeated Daniel's words? Was it not plainly the cry of one deeply hurt? That could not be explained away. He had understood it then and wanted to comfort her but she had not let him. Terrified of her father and of her own feelings she had told him to go. Nothing she wrote now could wipe that out. Of course he would have put it all behind him in the excitement of the journey home and the company of the French cousins. Away from London it was inevitable that he would grow much closer to them.

She laid down the pen and buried her face in her hands.

This was a foolish letter. She was needlessly exposing herself to him.

She read through what she had written. No, it must go but just as it was. It was enough. She had said she was sorry.

She took up the pen and added only, *'I pray that you have reached home safely in the care of the good Lord and I wish every blessing in life to you and your family.*

Pray forgive your affectionate but unworthy cousin,

Eunice Horden.'

Sealing it up, she ran next door and finding Tom Fletcher writing out an exercise her father had given him, she said, "The mail coach goes out today. Run with this to the post house. You will have time to finish your work before my father returns. Here is the money for the letter and a penny for you."

The boy loved her and would have done an errand for nothing. He beamed up at her and ran off without a word.

It was only as she walked slowly back inside that she knew she would not be telling her father what she had done and so it must be wrong to have done it. If he counts the sheets of paper he will know one has gone and I will have to lie about it. Oh the Lord, what have I done? She dropped onto her knees before the cold hearth.

I have obeyed my heart. I could not let that strange episode with my beautiful cousin end where it did. The taste of it was bitter. That is all that prompted me. Oh I love him. I believe he has a tender loving heart but it is not directed to me in the way of the love of a man to a woman as mine is to him. There! I have acknowledged it to myself at last. I love him. Perhaps his mother will think more kindly of me if she ever receives my letter. She must have hated me before for causing him a moment's grief. Will she show it to him? Oh how will it make him feel?

Please, Lord, let them forgive me as I begged her.

She must be active before her father came back. She dusted and swept their little home in every corner. She fetched kindling and made up a little fire to cook some fish he had brought from Billingsgate the evening before. She heard Tom come back. He would finish his work and not mention his errand. He was a boy of deep thoughts but very few words.

Her father returned as the fish and a few vegetables were cooking. It smelt good to him, he said, and he commended her diligence. He never counted the sheets of paper. She never told him what she had done. Only when she thought of Daniel her heart beat faster and she feared her father would be able to see into her and discover the strength of her flesh and the weakness of her spirit.

CHAPTER 11

IN the first two weeks of the visit Lady Horden continued to pass like a slow shadow about the Hall and the immediate grounds. Her maid said she was recovering from bruising caused by the overturning of the stage coach but Bel told Daniel, "Her heart is bruised. The place is empty of my father and I do believe she is mourning him at last. When she is her steely self again she will be able to deal with your other grandparents if they are ready to invite her."

Meanwhile Daniel had to take both the girls out riding. He couldn't help enjoying Diana's company more for her sheer delight in every place they explored while Madeline went about under sufferance with dull eyes and pouting lips.

Grandmother Wilson sent word at the end of two weeks that Joseph would like to see the visitors and she thought he could manage them for an hour. She had not been to the Hall herself yet on the excuse that she was nursing him and missed Peggy's help. In fact both Peggy and Ursula had run back and forth between the Hall and the vicarage and Nathaniel had spent time there while Lady Horden was resting and Bel was showing Henrietta the limited repairs made after the Scottish occupation. But at last Daniel, apprehensive of the outcome, escorted the French party on foot the half mile to the vicarage.

Once there he had to gather into the little parlour what stools and chairs there were in different parts of the house so they could sit in a semi-circle before his grandfather's couch. Grandmother had no wine to offer them but she had bought in a flagon of ale and there was a jug of her honey cordial on the table.

Lady Horden declined anything but she led the conversation.

"Pray tell me, Reverend Joseph, how you came to be vicar here? I understood from the English newspapers which were sent to us in France that the office of Vicar was abolished during the dreadful Protectorate."

He smiled wanly. "It was, my lady, and Parliament sent Presbyterian preachers to most parishes but there were never enough. The incumbent here died shortly after we all came north from Yorkshire and there being no one to minister to them the parish invited me to step in quietly and make preaching my principal duty. I have never felt much of a preacher but I did my best and no one bothered us. I wore a plain gown and only administered the sacrament when a few souls asked me to do it secretly."

Daniel saw that Diana was listening to him with her hands clasped on her skirt while Madeline shifted on her stool and her eyes roamed round the room. There was little to see but she looked curiously at a framed picture of a childish painting of a tree beside a bright blue strip of river with some strange animals drinking from the bank.

Anne Wilson saw her looking at it and Daniel knew at

once what was coming – the story of her boy hanged for a crime he did not commit, a crime inadvertently perpetrated by his own mother.

"My Daniel painted it," she said to Madeline when the conversation between Lady Horden and Joseph reached a natural stop. "Not *that* Daniel, *my* boy, his uncle. He grew to nineteen years but remained a child, the sweetest-natured child you could imagine."

"No, Anne," Joseph interrupted, "I do not think our visitors would wish to hear that tale."

"But we know it, Reverend Wilson," Henrietta said, and Daniel stiffened in astonishment. "At least my mother and I do. Arabella wrote to me and told me the whole story. She was so thankful that she had been forgiven and that you were all living in harmony. We were closer in our letters than we had ever been in our youth. You see we both lost other children and that was a bond between us."

Daniel had not heard his aunt speak tenderly of his mother before. It pleased him that she was not just an elegant, fan-rustling vicomtess as he had supposed. But Grandmother Wilson was not pleased to be checked in the narration of her Daniel's story. She got up and stalked about like an eagle frustrated of its prey and when Lady Horden resumed her conversation with Joseph she actually left the room.

Daniel thought he ought to follow her and let her speak of his uncle although he was sure there was not an episode of his childhood he had not heard before. So when Lady Horden began saying to his grandfather, "It seems to me, Reverend

Wilson, that you are accommodating in your views," he slipped from his stool and went after his other grandmother.

He found her in the big square vicarage kitchen with a scrubbing brush in her hand attacking a mark on the table top. She looked up and pursed her lips at him.

"It surprises me that your mother would herself tell that story to anyone. Oh I forgave but I cannot forget. It is a hard thing and the pain never goes away."

For the first time he felt no fear of her. He gently eased the scrubbing brush from her hand. "*That* mark will never go away, Grandmamma. You made it when I was eleven and you were telling me about Uncle Daniel wanting to march with the soldiers. You forgot you were resting the hot iron against the wood."

She cackled suddenly. "Ay, I did." Then she looked up into his face. "I let him go. I thought he could be bold and valiant and his brother too – your father – who was ever in his books. They both had to be men. *I* should have been a man. I would have fought a good fight, but Nat was no fighter and of course Dan copied him – and you know what happened. What have *you* done with your life, you great tall lad?"

"Not much yet but I will, Grandmamma."

"I hope I live to see it. Are they still chattering in there? Those French girls are no beauties. You'll not have an eye to one I hope?"

While Daniel was hesitating how to answer, Diana appeared in the doorway. Her eyes were agog with excitement but all she said was, "Oh Mistress Wilson, forgive me but we think we should be leaving. Your husband is looking weary."

"Very well, child. I will see you to the door. You all walked from the Hall I believe."

"Oh yes, it is so fine and dry underfoot and Dan is our escort."

"Dan? You call him Dan?"

She was bustling into the parlour as she said it and handing Lady Horden her short cloak.

Diana winked at him and murmured, "Wait till I tell you what was spoken of just now."

Daniel bade a hurried farewell to his grandfather who was closing his eyes on the departing guests and followed Diana. She hung back for him, letting the others go out of earshot, and tucked her arm through his.

"Guess what our grandmother asked your grandfather?"

"Nay I don't know. She seemed to be suggesting he was a little too tolerant."

"But it was for a good reason. She went on to ask him his views on mixed marriages?"

"Mixed?" Daniel asked it lightly but his throat had gone dry.

"Between Catholics and Protestants, you silly boy. Now why would she ask that, do you think?"

"I've no notion. What did Grandfather say?"

"Oh he is a sweet man! He said true love can overcome many difficulties. And you needn't pretend to be dim-witted like your poor uncle Daniel. No names were spoken but it was plain enough who everyone had in mind. If Madeline's eyes had been needles I'd have been pricked like a pincushion by now."

The day dimmed for Daniel though the sunbeams were still shining through the trees and dappling the grassy track before them. I am not ready for this, his mind was telling him, though his heart was touched that a bright, smiling girl was walking beside him wanting to marry him. I was warned one of them might be pushed at me but I never thought *love* would be the driving force. Does she really love me? That makes it so dangerous. I don't want to hurt her but –

She clung more tightly to him and peered up into his face. "Dan? Why do you not speak?"

He swallowed hard. "We're mighty young to be talking like this. I mean I am going up to Cambridge you know –"

"Nay, Dan, you told me you were going to rebel against all that. You want to be a great sea captain and serve your king. Of course I would hate you to be away but there is no fighting going on at present. We could be married at once and live in London –"

He looked desperately about him. She was compelling him to walk slowly and the others were far ahead. Why had his mother not told him how to deal with a proposal of marriage directly from the young lady herself? Surely this was not how such things were meant to be.

"You know," he said at last, "it is not grandparents that make matches, but parents. I have no notion if mine would consent to a Catholic. I mean, you know, my father will be ordained in the English church as soon as he can."

She was now very rosy in the face and her black eyes were wildly dilated.

"What is up with you, Dan? You have shown me all this time that you have eyes only for me. If *you* are suddenly finding religion a trouble I will turn. What is the Pope to me? As long as you are no dissenter who wants to do away with Christmas and all jollifications I am happy." She had finally pulled him to a stop and made him face her. "Why are you suddenly all cold and distant?"

What could he say with her great eyes pleading? "Nay I am not sure that we go about it the right way. Your father is in France and he will have much to say on the matter."

She threw back her head and laughed. "Oh if that is all! Why I overheard him say to my mother before we left 'And if you can make up a match with that young baronet for one of them it will be well done.' So you need have no apprehension on that score."

He was truly in a trap. The more tightly she was closing it the more he knew he wanted to escape. Had he really been remiss in showing her attention? He had used no loving words to her but maybe he had done enough. If his mother had known his feelings better than he did himself she should have stopped him.

He knew this was unjust to her and that he needed her help and support. "I think we had better catch up the others," he said. "I am supposed to be escorting your grandmother. She might need my arm to lean on."

He began hurrying forward and she had to break into a

run to keep up with his long strides.

"*Grandmere* has her parasol to lean on. You are being a brute. Something has changed you. What is it?"

"I just wonder if you took their meaning up wrongly when they were speaking of mixed marriages. I think we should be careful of running ahead of them. Old people don't like it you know. They have to arrange these things themselves and I'm sure my father and mother who were not there today –"

"Your *mother*! She is the great romantic. She speaks always of how she loves your father. How could you think for a moment that she would oppose your true love?"

"But my father you see – he is set on my going to Cambridge. I could not hurt him. We will still be young when I graduate and you may not care for me any more at all."

She slapped his arm hard. "You want that to be so because *you* do not care for me now. How can you be so cruel?"

"Nay I do love you." The words came out of their own accord because she looked so piteous. She's right about Mother too, he excused himself quickly. Mother rates love so highly and here is this girl loving me and feeling wounded and angry because I am not responding.

She did smile. She laughed with glee. She flung her arms round his waist and peered up with her eyes glowing like beads and her lips inviting.

He had to kiss her. It was a clumsy push at her moist mouth and then he had taken her hand and they were running after the others.

They caught them up as they reached the Hall. The track

led to the stables and the kitchen, but they were starting to walk round to the front entrance when Bel appeared at the door and called out, "Pray come this way if you are tired, Mother. Ursula has made a refreshing drink from the juice of oranges. Do try some."

Ursula was bobbing in the doorway. She had discarded her bonnet now that the guests were used to her, the day being so warm.

Diana, darting round the others who were slowly adjusting to the change of direction, clasped Ursula in her arms and said in a whisper they could all hear, "Oh Nana Sula, your darling Dan has declared his love for me. Is that not wonderful?"

Daniel at once felt his mother's look as sharp as a sword thrust. He lifted his shoulders and spread his hands but her look only pierced more deeply. He had made a great mistake. He tore his eyes away to see how the others had taken it.

His aunt was beaming; his grandmother lifted her brows in disapproval of such forward, extravagant behaviour but did not seem perturbed. Only Madeline scowled.

Ursula herself was chuckling and patting Diana's hands, unaware yet of Bel's reaction. She led them all into the kitchen.

"Take a sip, my lady, and if you like it I'll bring the tray into the parlour."

Lady Horden graciously pronounced it "very refreshing," and she and Henrietta followed Ursula along the passage and up the steps to the great hall. Diana had now seized Daniel's hand and was skipping after them when Bel called out "Dan, your father wants you in his study. A letter has come."

Madeline behind them hissed, "*She* doesn't want you, Di."

Daniel, hot and cold by turns, excused himself, saw the sisters, breathing fire at each other, disappear into the parlour and himself darted across the hall to the study door, gave a perfunctory knock, slipped in and closed the door quickly behind him.

His father looked up from his desk with a surprised smile. "Who are you running away from? I hadn't time to say 'come in'!"

"I beg your pardon, sir. Mother said you wanted me."

The door was pushed open hard and he had to jump away. Bel appeared.

"I was misleading you," she said. "The letter is to me I'm afraid."

She closed the door firmly and put her back against it.

Nathaniel looked more surprised than ever.

"To what do I owe the honour of this double invasion? Has something happened?"

Bel snorted, "Something has certainly happened. This boy of ours has got himself tangled in the web that that French harpy has been spinning for him. She has just this minute announced to Ursula, 'Nana Sula! Dan has declared his love for me.' 'Nana Sula' indeed and 'Dan'! Who gave her leave to be so free with our pet names?"

Nathaniel looked from Bel to Daniel and back again. Daniel held his breath.

His father said cautiously, "You needn't look so fierce, Bel. Surely we saw it coming. If they really love each other – of course he must take his degree first."

"Oh I would do that, Father. I want to do that." Cambridge would surely put everything else on hold.

"Love each other!" Bel said with scorn. "This child – barely out of his cradle – has no idea of love. And she – why she only wants what every girl is supposed to want, a husband, and before her older sister too! What a triumph!"

Nathaniel got up and motioned Bel to his chair which was the only one in the room. He perched on the desk. Daniel shifted along so that he now blocked the door. He could imagine Diana any moment wanting to burst in upon them. He wasn't quite sure yet whether he was angry with his mother or infinitely relieved.

His mother had picked up the unopened letter lying on the desk and was twisting it in her hands but not looking at it. Her gaze was on his face, assessing him.

His father smiled up at him. "Do you want to be betrothed now and married after Cambridge?" Sensing Bel about to erupt he held up his hand. "Let the lad answer."

"I don't think Mother should call me a child. I mean, I'm old enough to be betrothed. *She* was."

"Don't you quote that at me," she snapped. "I was forced into it. I yielded to buy time. My father was ill and I couldn't hurt him any more. I had no intention of marrying William as you well know and thank the good Lord I didn't. This is nothing like that. I never gave William a second's encouragement. What have you said to that girl that she can construe in such unequivocal words?"

"I'm afraid I said I loved her. Well, at that moment it was hard to see what else I could say."

Bel looked triumphantly at Nathaniel. "Is that the voice of a true love? As I said, she has tricked him into it." She glared at Daniel. "How could you be such a fool? Now I will have to grovel to Hen to save you from this. God knows I don't want you to go away to Cambridge but still less do I want you to make a bad marriage."

"Are you sure it would be so very bad, Mother? She seems fond of me. I think I could get her to do all I wanted."

"What! When she has been at pains to get you to do what *she* wanted and succeeded mightily!"

Nathaniel interposed gently, "Marriage is not the exercise of power by one over the other, Daniel. The man is appointed the head but he must not be a tyrant."

Bel grumbled, "*She* would be the tyrant unless this boy grows into a man."

Daniel planted his feet apart and folded his arms across his chest. The moment had come. "The fact is I *want* to be a man. I don't want to study for three years. I want to join the navy and serve the King."

Bel sat back in the chair and thrust her big jaw up at him. "That you shall not do. What! You were seasick going from the Tyne to London. At least I was with you and could hold your head. How would I live if I thought you were in a storm at sea or attacked by pirates or under Dutch guns – for there will surely be war again till they or we are masters of the oceans." She turned to Nathaniel and clasped his hand that rested on the desk. "Oh Nat, why do we bring children into the world? We lost two after this one and I thought God must suppose I loved Dan too much to have any to spare." All of a sudden she wrapped her arms round her bent head and sobbed.

Daniel had never seen her weep not even when she followed two little coffins to their graves. She gave herself then to comforting him and his father. It was a terrible shock to see her so distraught and to know that somehow it was all his fault.

Abruptly he turned round and opened the door and went out. He heard her start to exclaim, "Where –" but he shut the door and almost ran across the hall and into the parlour. The four faces turned and stared up at him.

He must speak at once or he'd be lost. "I am going to Cambridge soon and I can't think about marriage for a long time. I am very sorry but that is the way of it." He drew breath. The Lord be praised, he thought, Diana has her family about her or I couldn't have done it.

It was bad. Madeline laughed and Diana fell into hysterics. His aunt opened her mouth to speak but then flung her arms round her choking daughter.

Only his grandmother remained stony. She held up her hand to quell the girls' noise but neither was looking at her.

"Sit down, young man. Madeline, Diana be silent." They subsided then, Diana staring with her great eyes at him over her clasped hands. Daniel perched on the window seat as far from the group as he could go.

Lady Horden went on in a clear voice as if addressing an

assembly. "I have never seen a marriage proposal begun in so unseemly a way. There should be no outbursts from the young people. Indeed it is usually better if they have not met till the matter is settled by their elders. The trouble that results otherwise is all too plain to see now. Daniel Horden, I presume you have been speaking with your parents. We will speak with them in due course and try to ignore all that has already taken place. In other words we will start afresh."

She had paused only to let her words sink in but Daniel blurted out, "It might be better not to start at all."

"But you *did* start," Diana shouted at him.

"Peace, child," her grandmother admonished her. "This is the thing I have just deplored. Let all be done in order. Now, daughter, I know that you and Henri had an idea that a match might be made with young Daniel here if you saw there was any attraction between the parties. Myself, I would have preferred an approach by letter while we were still in France to ascertain the needful facts, first, the willingness of the young man's parents that he should conform to Rome." Daniel sat up at that. "Second, the young man's prospects which depend on the revenue from this property, third, the amount of dowry that would be expected. Fourth – but perhaps it should be first – the desirability or otherwise of the marriage of first cousins. I know it is common but I have heard wise men say it is unhealthy. Now if all that had been established there would have been a foundation laid. I made a very tentative move this afternoon in sounding the reverend gentleman on *his* views, speaking only in general terms. If he had felt strongly that husband and wife should be of one faith, as I do, we would have known where we stood. You, Diana, as I have been telling you, behaved most precipitately. I suggest you go to your room and read a good book. You, young man, keep away from her. Henrietta, we will say nothing more on this matter until your sister and brother-in-law wish to discuss it. Now I will take to my bed for my rest before supper."

She rose and Daniel leapt to open the door for her. He wondered what his father and mother were doing or saying. Evidently they had not wanted to see what sort of chaos he was causing among his cousins. He dare not look at Diana though he was aware she was trying to make him. As soon as Lady Horden had gone upstairs he crossed the hall and knocked again at the study door.

They were standing at the window looking out into the wood at the back of the house, with their arms twined round each other.

The letter he had seen before was lying on the desk, its seal now broken. As they turned round he saw the remains of tears on both their faces.

His mother pointed to the letter. "Another one! Well, I have always known I must take a second place one day. You may read it. But tell us first what happened in the parlour."

He told them what had been said though his eyes were drawn to the letter.

Bel's interest in her mother's speech was intense. "So she still believes in arranged marriages! My father was her best prospect seeing she was only the ward of the old Count

Rombeau. So she was carried off to Northumberland, a Catholic to a Protestant house at fifteen years old. Now you see she says husband and wife should be of the same faith. She brought up Henrietta Catholic and when she took her to be wed to the count's grandson the politics of the time let her stay in France. She knows my father pined for her and she has been a little sad here but she has tightened up her heart strings again now and repudiated love. We can be plain with her about Dan, but Henrietta – she will be more difficult. I, the younger sister took over Horden Hall. She resents that even though she is mistress of a French Chateau. That one of her daughters should become Lady Horden is the thing she has hankered after." Now Bel pointed an accusing finger at Daniel. "And that my boy should pay attention to Diana and then throw her over – well, she is going to be very angry."

"Oh Lord! I haven't exactly thrown her over. Maybe in a few years – but she is as angry as her mother now. What can I do? We'll all have to meet round the supper table."

"Do not say 'in a few years'. She is not worthy of you and never will be. I know you are a poor dithering creature at present but you will grow into a good, right-thinking man." She put her arm through Nat's again. "Like your father."

He looked at them both and thought I could never see myself and Diana in a marriage like that. Will I ever be able to equal that sort of love with anyone? At that moment it seemed utterly impossible.

She detached herself briskly and, straightening her spine, made as if to shoulder a musket. "Now to do battle with my sister."

"Must it be a battle?" Nathaniel asked. "Should I not come with you?"

"To keep the peace, my angel? I think not. Hen bullied me all my youth and though we reached a happy truce in our letters I do not find we are as close as sisters should be. I will hold my own but there will be no victory either way. An agreement not to meet again in the flesh might be the safest."

She picked up the letter and handed it to Daniel. "Try this one."

She went out and Daniel looked doubtfully at his father before turning his attention to the letter. "What does she mean, try this one?"

"I think she hoped to lighten the situation with a little jest."

Daniel looked at the signature. "It's from Cousin Eunice!" The tiny figure with the severe hair and mouse-like face rushed before his eyes. The handwriting, small and neat, expressed her perfectly. His eyes flew over the words.

"Has her father made her write this?"

Nathaniel smiled and shook his head. "Your mother interprets it as a love letter to you. Perhaps that is fanciful. I believe Eunice's thinking is governed by her father's teaching and seeing us grieved by his anger, for which she felt partly responsible she needed to put pen to paper as he had done. Do not read too much into it. Your mother will not reply because she is sure William would be vexed at such a correspondence and Eunice would suffer for it."

Daniel nodded slowly. At that moment he felt like the babe

his mother had called him. He needed guidance. Life – and particularly the female variety of it – was too complicated.

He looked down at his father still perched on the desk.

"I've caused a great deal of bother, haven't I?"

"Yes." Nathaniel rose and though he still had to look up at his son he had a dignity and steadiness that Daniel envied. He had not often been in awe of his father but just now he was.

"How can I make amends, sir?"

"By apologising to Diana and her family with true contrition and by not mentioning again to your mother the notion of entering the navy."

"I can do both of those, sir."

"And this autumn go dutifully to Cambridge and be a credit to her and me."

Daniel swallowed. It was a huge sacrifice prompted by his mother's tears. He felt purged even as the vision of a great vessel of the fleet and the officers standing on the quarter deck vanished before his eyes. One day perhaps.

"I *will* go to Cambridge, sir. And oh, thanks be to God, there are no girls there."

CHAPTER 12

The Hordens of the Hall did not have to hire a coach to take their guests to Tynemouth or anywhere else. The French party made one visit to Newcastle with Ursula to show them where a Mass could be heard. Lady Horden said they should not commit themselves to the dangers of travel without absolution first. But after that, much to Daniel's relief, the visit was to end as soon as arrangements could be made for the journey back. Diana refused to speak another word to him while Madeline became quite confidential.

"Di would never have waited three years for you. She hoped to steal a march on me, that's all. But I will marry when we return to France. There is a nobleman only awaiting a settlement. He has large estates and dozens of servants. I could never have stomached this shabby old place and I wager Di would have regretted it after a month or two. You needn't fear that you have broken her heart!"

This was some reassurance but it was an uncomfortable time till they could wave them away. Lady Horden spent an hour in the village visiting her husband's and son's tomb and taking leave of Joseph and Anne Wilson. Daniel who escorted her knew both his grandmothers were glad to part.

"I will not be returning," Lady Horden told him on the

walk back. "I needed to come but this was never a happy place for me. It is well that our families are not to be more closely linked. You are like your mother and I never felt comfortable with her though she was my youngest child. Madeline and Diana are silly girls but I can manage them as their grandmother. I am happier in France. There everyone knows their place and what is correct. In England there has been a loosening of society. I find it unsettling."

"Yes Grandmother," was all he could say but of the four women to whom he bade farewell he had to admire her straight-backed dignity most of all. His aunt allowed herself tears when she embraced his mother.

"Oh Arabella, it has all been unfortunate and I so hoped we would be united as sisters as never before."

Bel kissed her warmly. She was of too loving a nature not to respond to tears, but when the hired coach drove away she gave a skip of glee and turned back into the house with her arms round Nat and Dan.

"Well, my men, I think we are well out of that."

Ursula who had been bobbing in the background said, "Now, my Bel, be not uncharitable. There is good in them all. They attended Mass most devoutly and the priest blessed them for their journey."

Bel flung her arms round her. "Urs, you will make excuses for the devil on Judgment Day. Oh what a joy to have you back at mealtimes! I wondered why I could not digest my food so well. But you do right to chide me. I will heartily love my mother and sister and nieces from now on. I will write affectionate letters when they are back in France. Indeed, if I could do embroidery I would start at once on a pretty cushion for Madeline's wedding present."

Their laughter rang about the great hall. It was good to be on their own again.

The rest of the summer was overshadowed by Joseph's illness and Daniel's preparations for Cambridge. Although he had repudiated the idea of holy orders Daniel found his grandfather still seemed to assume that was the only possible outcome of a Cambridge degree.

Weak and husky of voice Joseph said the same thing on all Daniel's visits. "I seem not to have many books to give you, my boy. Of course I passed them on to your dear father when he went up to Queen's. The few Greek texts and works of theology on that shelf there I do dip into from time to time. They are a comfort though I may not need them much longer. You shall have them when I am gone. Your grandmother would light the fire with them."

"I will want no fires," she snapped. "I'll follow you as quick as I can."

They were not happy visits for Daniel. On his return he would say to his father, "Grandfather is *still* convinced I am to take holy orders. If I must go to university surely I am not obliged to do that?"

One day his mother was present in the study and intervened.

"Our Dan is not for the church and he was never a Greek

scholar like you, Nat, though you did your best to force some into him. But why do you think I am dreading his going away? Not for his beautiful presence about the place of course, nor for his cheery nature, nor for his popularity with everyone about us, oh no, for none of these things." She was clasping her arms round Dan as she spoke. "No, I am facing the fearful prospect of having to do all the estate accounts by myself."

Dan kissed the top of her head. "Oh Mother, you are very good with figures."

"And your young brain is twice as fast." Still holding onto him she looked at Nat. "Have I not heard that they study mathematics at Cambridge and strange new sciences about the properties of light, air, water and such? You brought some paper from Newcastle where I read this and that the King himself is mighty interested in such things."

Dan looked eagerly at his father. "Perhaps I could make some great invention that would come to the King's ears. Oh sir, let me pursue that path, I beg you."

Nat put on a very solemn face and began to shake his head. Seeing Bel about to burst out he laughed. "I think that is the first time in this boy's life that he has shown true enthusiasm for learning of any sort. Daniel, if you will work in that field I will give you my blessing."

Bel transferred her hug to Nat.

Now at last Dan began to look forward to a new phase of life. It would be strange to stand on his own feet and be part of a competitive world of men but he was eager for the chance. He joyfully unpacked all the books his father had given him and rode into Newcastle to see the library at Trinity House on the quayside where there were the latest papers on astronomy and the mathematics of navigation and some reports of studies on the refraction of light. He made copious notes and came back with his head bursting with ideas for experiments.

Nat meanwhile had made inquiries and found that Trinity College might be a more appropriate alma mater for such studies than Queens'. He wrote to his former college friend Lord Branford to see if he knew anyone with influence who might get him entered for Trinity.

The earl wrote back and said his son Henry was entered for Trinity to study mathematics and the physical sciences and he would be delighted to see that Daniel was accepted too. He hoped they would be good friends as he and Nat had been. All this was very comfortable for Nat and Dan but as the day of his departure approached Bel became unusually quiet and tense.

It was his last day at home, his travelling chest was packed and roped and Daniel was checking the closet in his bedchamber to see that the breeches and doublets he had left behind were really not fit to take. He was closing the door when he noticed at his feet a crumpled paper. He picked it up and found it was the letter from Eunice Horden to his mother. He remembered that when she had left the room 'to do battle with her sister' the letter had been lying on his father's desk. His mother had jestingly called it a love letter and he had picked it up and slipped it in his sleeve. It must have fallen out when he hung up his doublet. He had thought of it occasionally since but not finding it had decided his mother had retrieved it. It had been addressed to her and his mind had been too full of other things for him to want to question her about it.

Now he read it again. Love letter? Surely not?

Bel appeared that moment at his open door to see that all was ready.

"What have you there?"

He held it out. "This. You think she wanted you to show it to me?"

"Why, it's Eunice's letter! I thought I had lost it. Oh certainly she did."

"You called it a love letter. Why?"

"Well, she cannot let you go. She is clinging to that brief time she saw you. Poor girl, she has few excitements in her life. It was the tiny gesture of a limpet to see if it could keep hold of a rock."

"Oh. Well, I have cast off one limpet. This is not the time for another."

"No indeed." His mother sat down on the bed and he knew she was trying to laugh to stop tears coming. "I am your strongest limpet – holding on for sixteen years and tomorrow I must let go. Write as often as you can. Keep a journal and send me pages."

She got up and left him quickly.

When he was alone again Daniel smoothed out the crumpled letter and slipped it into his Bible. It hurt him to think that little Eunice had cast it forth and never even known if it had reached its destination. There would be several staging inns on his journey and what more natural than to pass the evening writing to Cousin Celia to tell her he was on his way to Cambridge. She had whispered to him as they took their leave, "You are just the boy I wish I had had. Clifford came down hard on William, pushing him into the business, and he went meekly in at first but of course turned against it in the end. You knew your mind from the beginning and spoke up boldly."

He could insert into the letter to Cousin Celia a message to Eunice.

Next day the parting he dreaded was brief but painful.

"I cannot come to the staging inn in Newcastle," his mother said. "I would have to stand about in the inn yard and every minute of loading up and arguing who goes where would seem an hour. Adam will take you and your luggage on the farm cart. I will give you one hug and then I will run indoors. Your father can wave till you turn out of the gates but I would be running after you and begging you not to go."

She kept her word but he was painfully certain that her tears were bursting out before she had disappeared into the house. Ursula and his father did wave till he saw them only as tiny figures against the solid bulk of the Hall. Great-great-grandfather Sir Ralph was perpetually waving his sword. The top of his head and the tip of his sword were the last things Daniel saw as the morning sun caught them. He gulped with excitement and a little apprehension, but Adam saw him and his luggage safely onto the stage and that at least was managed for him and his journey was underway.

Not at all sure of himself the first night he eschewed the company of the other passengers round the inn fire and, after requesting a candle and writing materials, he retreated to the chamber he was to share with a taciturn lawyer and sat down at a small table.

That was the simple part, assembling what he needed. After that it was hard labour. The need for writing letters had seldom occurred to him. When he had stated that he was going to Cambridge and what he was to study he wondered what else he could say. Then he remembered that Celia had played hostess again to the French relations before they took passage to France and had no doubt heard their version of his unseemly dallying with Diana.

'*I am afraid that I caused offence to my Aunt Henrietta,*" he wrote, "*who thought I had paid too much attention to Diana. The truth is I want to achieve something in the world before I think of marriage. I intend to study hard and make a name for myself before I devote myself to my duties at Horden and I do not think either of my French cousins would wish to be mistress there. It would not be the life of luxury and high society to which they are accustomed.*'

That was surely enough before he came to the real purpose of his letter.

'*And now, honoured cousin, I would beg you to do something for me. When you see your granddaughter, Eunice, pray tell her that my mother received her letter and thanks her for it but thought it wiser not to reply directly in case her father was angry with her for having written. He is your son but I know you feel he has not always pleased you in the way he deals with his daughter. I feel great sympathy for her as her life is very restricted. I have had every advantage that loving parents could give me but even I have felt hemmed in sometimes and unable to enjoy the freedom to pursue my own ambitions. So if you can convey to her that we all wish her well and appreciate the thoughts that led her to write to my mother I would be most grateful.*

'Pray greet Cousin Clifford from me and tell him I was honoured by his invitation to come into his business, although I felt obliged to decline, and believe me, I remain your humble cousin,

Daniel Wilson Horden.'

He read it through and felt he had phrased it very well. Sealing it up and leaving it with the innkeeper to be handed to the mail coach next day he put every thought from his mind but the excitement of being on the threshold of a new life. He did not however throw away Eunice's letter but kept it folded in his Bible. If he did not read that as often as he had promised his father he was no different from most of his fellow students when he was finally installed at Cambridge.

Eunice was surprised to receive a visit from her grandmother in person. Little notes came occasionally which she always felt obliged to show her father but mostly they said no more than that she and grandfather were well and hoped the same of her and her father. She informed them of the departure of the French cousins and pointed out that now they were alone they would be happy to see her and her father any time at their house in the Strand. William always told her to ignore the letters.

"They would take you away from me if they could and teach you to think that wealth and luxury are the things most to be desired in this life."

William was not at home when his mother called on a mild breezy autumn day. She left her coach at the end of the lane and walked through the swirling dust to the little door between Fletcher, the leather-worker's and Thomson, the baker's.

Eunice was happy to see her and embraced her with such eager warmth that it brought tears to Celia's eyes.

She wiped them with her handkerchief and protested that it was the "dreadful dust this wind has blown up."

"Poor Grandmother, pray bathe your eyes." Eunice took a small wooden bowl and filled it from the bucket.

Celia dabbed at her face. "Oh my dear, I would come more often –"

"But for this neighbourhood," Eunice finished for her.

"Indeed, I had scarcely left the coach when a one-legged beggar on the street called to me. I dare not open my purse in case another man in league with him fell upon me. But he cursed me and that frightens me."

"Do not fear him, dear Grandmother. His other leg is tucked beneath him. My father says the curses of a liar have no effect. Come, sit down. You are shaken. I fear I have nothing to offer you till Father returns."

Celia shook her head. "I have brought a little packet of a new substance your Grandfather is now importing from India. You pour boiling water on it and it makes a refreshing drink. They call it tay or tee I believe."

"Shall I make some of it for you?"

Celia looked doubtfully at the empty grate. "Do not trouble now but when you have a fire lit and your kettle boiling try some yourself."

"Father will not allow a fire till the evening except on the coldest of days but for you –"

"Nay, child. I must say what I came for before he returns." And she produced Daniel's letter from her sleeve. "See what this dear young man has written. It is for your eyes I know, though he writ it to me for form's sake."

Eunice's heart was thumping but she took the letter with no outward sign except a blush which she could not control and which she feared her grandmother must have noticed.

She read it through and handed it back. "It was very kind of him to write. I was perhaps foolish to write to his mother but my father was angry with them when he called and I felt myself to blame. I am glad to hear he has gone to Cambridge and is to study subjects that interest him."

Celia turned to her and clasped her hands. "But my dear there is much more between the lines. Why is he so particular to tell you that he has no interest in his French cousins? Why does he say neither of *them* could ever be mistress at Horden Hall?"

Eunice, unable to speak, shook her head.

"Because he knows who would be perfect there. Because he knows whose hand he will be seeking when he has graduated from the University. Oh, dear child, it is what I wished for you even before I saw what a fine, handsome young man he was, those bright intelligent blue-green eyes and that flaxen hair. If I had been your age I would have longed to attract his notice. You must not worry that your father says he wants no alliance for you with that family. When the time comes I will work on him. Does not the Bible honour human love in the Song of Solomon? Does not St Paul say that the relationship of man and wife reflects that of Christ and His Church? Your father loved your mother and cannot deny you that joy in life."

Eunice was holding back sobs. She longed to believe Daniel loved her but her grandmother was seeing too much in the letter and far overrating her own influence over her son. Nor did she understand that the loss of his wife had turned his mind against marriage altogether, as the cause of too much pain.

Celia rose to her feet. "I must be gone before he comes back. Do not mention this to him, just hold yourself in readiness. Your day of happiness will come. I am sure of that. I know well that the less you say the more you are feeling but my bad son has so crushed your spirit that you can hardly confide in me, your own grandmother, the only female relation you have at hand."

Eunice had risen too. "Oh do not call him bad. He strives day by day to do good. He is the soul of truth. He always gives out of our little store to any that are poorer than we are and he is his own hardest task-master if he thinks he has done the slightest wrong to any man."

Even as she said it she knew that if he asked her "Has anyone called?" and she said his mother she would have to relay the whole conversation to him word for word to the best of her memory, and that therefore she would lie and deny that anyone had been.

She handed back the packet of tiny leaves. "Take it Grandmother. He would wish to know whence it came and I can't face the questions."

Celia shook her head till her cheeks wobbled but inserted it into the pocket that was suspended from her waist under her skirts. "You poor love and yet you call him good!" The letter went too.

Eunice seeing it disappear thought how she would have loved to place it beneath her pillow and look at it every night.

From the door she watched anxiously till she saw her Grandmother safely pass the beggar and reach the coach into which her maid helped her. The groom swiftly whipped up and drove it away. Eunice ran back inside, restored the wooden bowl to its place, and left the door ajar so that the rising wind could swirl in and remove any trace of her grandmother's perfume.

"Three years of study," she said to herself. "Then he will ask for my hand. He will be nearing twenty I believe and so will I. That is still young. I have endured eleven imprisoned years. What are three more?" She gave way to hysterical laughter.

Three years would be nothing if she had hope – but she had none. Of course he had no love for her and if he had it would never survive the wonders of his new life. And yet, she thought, there can be no living a life without hope.

I must distract my mind, she determined. Her father had told her lately of a clergyman who had rounded up some of the orphaned children that roamed the streets and had set up a little school for them in the crypt of his church.

"He needs help to teach them, Eunice. I believe the Lord is calling upon you to do this work. He is advanced in years and has a wife who will be at hand so I believe you would be safe with him and I would look in from time to time."

The idea had terrified her. She had seen these children and they pestered passers-by and threw mud and stones at coaches.

"There will be no pay," her father told her. "I myself will try to raise money for their daily dinners which the reverend gentleman says he will provide so that they cease from begging. Consider it the Lord's work."

Yes, she decided, while her heart quailed at the prospect, the Lord has sent this so that my mind will not dwell sinfully on my cousin.

When her father came in she said straight out, "Tell the Reverend Woodhouse I will come tomorrow."

"You have prayed for guidance?"

"Oh yes, Father."

It was yet another lie.

CHAPTER 13

March 1664

BEL took Dan's letter to the bench under the Hall windows. There she was sheltered from the March wind and with the sun shining and Spring in the air she would have been in high spirits – only she was almost afraid to open the letter.

"No," she said aloud. "I must." She couldn't wait for Nat to return from the village church where he had been reading the morning office. "If it's bad news I will do my best to get over it before he comes."

She broke the seal and unfolded the letter. Immediately her eyes flew to the opening sentence and she laughed aloud with relief.

'You will be pleased to know, honoured parents, that yesterday, Ash Wednesday, I received my Bachelor's cap. It was a strange ceremony where an ancient graduate of Trinity dressed up as a jester and sat upon a tripod and read satirical verses. Though I only came midway among the graduates and Henry Branford had almost the lowest marks possible to be made Bachelor we were so happy that we listened to not a word of what was

read out. To tell the truth we are mighty relieved it is all over for we are both tired of study and wish to do something more active. That is not to say we are not grateful to have been sent to Cambridge. They have been happy and fruitful years but now is the time for something new.

'All the talk is that we must soon go to war with the Hollanders who lord it about the seas as if our navy was nothing. I hear that we have sent a fleet against a Dutch trading post in Africa to show them we mean business. Another has gone to New Amsterdam in America to capture the fur trade there. How I would have loved to be on one of those expeditions but Branford's father, who you know to be a good man because he was a friend of yours, Father, has the ear of the King. He can get us entered into the navy as 'volunteers per order' who I understand carry the rank of midshipmen. We will learn the art of navigation and if we show promise we can go on to become lieutenants. This will be an excellent way of putting our scientific knowledge to good use.

'As you know I have longed to serve the King from the very day we saw him enter the city. I have dutifully obtained a degree in obedience to your wishes and would now seek to fulfil my own hopes and ambitions. I am uncertain whether I can make the long journey home to see you before our enlistment but rest assured I am always,

'Your loving son,

'Daniel.'

By the time she had read through to the end Bel's joy had

been swallowed up in shock and misery. When she heard Nat's footsteps as he came to look for her she let her sorrow turn to anger.

"That Branford boy! If you hadn't encouraged them to be friends just because you and his father were friends at Cambridge this would never have happened."

Nat sat heavily down on the bench. "So they have both failed their degrees and I am to blame?"

She flung her arms round him. "Nay, my love, they have graduated but now they want to turn sailors and go to war!" She handed him the letter. "And he's not coming home at all. He's afraid to face us, that's what it is."

Nat read the letter. "He has been awarded a degree – that is something. I knew he was already weary of study when he wrote in his second year of the new brilliant student who had come to Trinity – what was his name? Newton, Isaac Newton. He said the sight of Newton's copious notes took the heart out of him. But that he should think of joining the navy with young Branford –"

"Of course he will be seasick but what is so much worse he will be a target for a canon ball – being taller than all the rest of the ship's crew."

"But we are not at war."

"Not yet. But see what he says –"

Nat sighed deeply. "I have seen and I know not why there is a mood in the country for war when surely we have all suffered enough from men's folly and wickedness."

Bel leant her head against his shoulder. "I can't bear to

speak of battles. I try not to think of them. But now –!" She shook her head as if to shake the subject away. "Did anyone attend your morning office?"

"Only my mother. She says she is ashamed of the many times she failed to hear my father read it in her days of darkness after Dan's death. But she thinks I put too much expression in it. My father always read in a sweet low murmur. She also says my sermons are too vehement for our quiet village. Maybe our Dan thinks so too. He seemed embarrassed by my preaching when he came home for Father's funeral."

"You had only just been ordained. It is your vehemence against strife and bloodshed that he deplores – since he seems happy to go forth and kill people. Oh Nat, can we stop him. He is not yet of age."

Nat looked at the letter again. "I see he is staying at Lord Branford's house in London. You remember we passed it on our way to Cousin Clifford's? The Lord Branford I knew long ago was sent to the Tower by Parliament and died there of an apoplexy. His eldest son was killed in battle. That was why my friend Edward became the earl. I would have liked to meet him again but maybe – now that the boys are good friends –"

"Oh Nat, you're not answering my question. Can we stop him joining the navy? I want Dan here, not with the Branfords and not on board some hateful battleship. *I* want him. I want him at home where he belongs."

"My dearest, he is a man and will have to make his own path. You know how I hate war, particularly because I was briefly a soldier. He will learn."

"You escaped from it quickly, but he won't."

Nat pulled him to face her. "Do you think he is braver than I? You don't know how often I asked myself if I was a coward."

"You were brave to face being called a coward. But that is all nonsense. You were ill with a fever."

"So were many men but they recovered and went on fighting."

"You never wanted to join. You were pushed into it." She sat up suddenly. "Nat, you don't think your mother has been inciting Dan to go to war and be a hero, the hero you and that other Daniel never were. Remember how furious she was when they executed the last King. She wanted to go out and avenge him herself. Has she told Dan to go out and kill this Charles's enemies?"

Nat smiled and shook his head. "The Dutch didn't kill Charles the First."

"Your mother won't mind that. If she has encouraged him –"

"Come, my love, you sound as fierce as she. No, I'm afraid this is something Dan has longed for himself. You remember the day when he said he would like to join the navy –?"

"And I said he should not. Are you overruling me now?"

"He has fulfilled what we demanded of him and now perhaps a spell of a different life will be good for him."

"With a musket bullet through his heart! What about his duty to his estate? Perhaps we should produce another heir just in case. I am not too old you know."

"Oh Bel, I do love you."

"And I you, but I think you still doubt your own courage and want to be brave vicariously through your son."

Nat stood up, his jaw set and his teeth clenched. Bel gazed at him in admiration. "Bel, that is not true. You and I have been tested sorely many times in the days of war and of persecution by the Puritans. We have come through together and I have never doubted *your* courage. But Dan has not been tested yet and he feels the want of it. If we stop him he will come home sulky and morose."

"And if we don't he may not come home at all."

Ursula, trotting round from the kitchen, found her in a sudden paroxysm of sobbing.

"Oh my Bel. That letter was bad news."

"Daniel has graduated but he's going to join the navy." It was choked out in jerks.

"He's alive and well," Ursula said. "So come in and have your dinner."

Nat took her hands in his. "What would we do without you, Ursula?"

"Reverend sir" – since Nat's ordination Ursula had been unable to use any other expression – "Reverend sir, you would do very well. You have each other."

Bel smiled through her tears. "Yes, we are Nat and Bel, one flesh, but not quite complete without Dan."

Ursula cocked her funny little head on one side. "Ah that's what you have to learn, my Bel. Let go and he will come back stronger than ever, wife and children and all."

"Wife! Ah, there is a thought. He must visit Eunice while

he is in London. I know she has never left his heart. Perhaps she can keep him from throwing himself into danger."

Nat drew her up and tucked her arm through his. "That is a wild hope, Bel. I do not believe he ever felt more than sympathy for her situation. Come, let us go in or the boiled beef I believe I can smell will be spoilt."

They went in to dinner. I am the only one, Bel thought, prepared to admit to the dangers my boy may face. Surely, sweet Jesus, you wouldn't let him grow to manhood and then take him from me like the others?

Daniel was delighted to receive letters from home giving him permission to join the navy. It was obvious that his mother was grieving which he was sorry for but he could bear that when he didn't have to see her distress. One duty she said he should fulfil was to pay a call upon Cousins Cifford and Celia. This was easy enough since the Branfords' house was in the same street. In another sentence his mother had written, *'I am sure your heart will tell you to find a way to see Eunice too. I have rare letters from Celia and she said Eunice is teaching orphans in the crypt of St Mary Magdalen's in Milk Street. You may be able to see her without encountering William.'*

The sight of that name fluttered his heart briefly but it produced a rebellious knot in his stomach too. His mother should not presume to know what was in his heart. His way into the navy was now clear ahead. He had escaped the Diana trap by the skin of his teeth – with a little help from his mother he must acknowledge – and this was not the time to fall into another.

As for Cousins Clifford and Celia he knew he should pay them a courtesy visit but had been putting it off. He and Henry, released from obligations of study, were like two rampant puppies. They did everything together and Henry was not interested in calling upon his friend's elderly cousins.

Henry's parents, Lord and Lady Branford, seemed to Daniel young and energetic though Henry said they were ancient – over forty for sure – and it was strange to hear Lord Branford speak warmly of his friendship with Nathaniel Wilson at Cambridge.

"I would never have graduated in theology if your father hadn't helped me through and you say he is now a country vicar which is what he always wanted to be like his father before him. And is his fierce mother still alive? He was anxious about her all the time I knew him."

Daniel felt some pangs of homesickness, thinking of the folk back at Horden.

"She's pretty dashed at the moment because my grandfather died. It's near enough a year but she can't get over it. She couldn't get over my Uncle Daniel's death and now she's plunged in melancholia again. Father spends a lot of time there because of course it's the vicarage and if she's very low he'll stay with her, though she's got a girl lives in. I ought to go home and see them but it's a long way and Mother would want to keep me for months if I went. I don't want to miss my chance here."

Henry, a short, wiry youth, restless and boisterous,

distinguished only by protruding ears, exclaimed, "No, no, you must stay here. Father will get us on board a ship of the line next week. We might be at war with the Dutch by then."

Lord Branford laughed. "Not next week, Henry. The King will delay as long as possible. The fleet is not ready. There is not the money in the coffers for a war. Nor does the King wish England to seem the aggressor. That would put us in ill favour with the French."

Daniel listened in awe to conversations like this. Once more to be near the centre of power, to feel history unfolding around him thrilled his heart. Lord Branford, who had sat in the Lords since his father's death, spoke freely of speaking with members of the government, even with the King himself.

To whet their appetite he arranged for the two young men to be allowed on board one of the ships of the line that was refitting. It was a three-decker carrying a crew of six hundred and fifty men. The spaces on the two lower decks where they would have to sling their hammocks had a headroom of less than six feet. Daniel walked with head and shoulders bent. Henry romped up and down companionways, peering here, there and everywhere till he was rebuked by the master mariner, but Daniel let his imagination play, trying to envisage this huge structure swaying on the ocean, running out its guns in earnest and bringing them to bear on an enemy ship, receiving fire, masts crashing down with spars and sails tangled. It was fearful but exhilarating.

"The next step," Lord Branford said, "is to present you at court so you can offer yourselves for the navy under the King's own patronage. But first, Daniel, you should visit your cousin, the merchant. Keep in with men of wealth. You say he has no male heir?"

"Only a son who abandoned working for him long ago." Somehow he couldn't bring himself to mention Eunice. "But I don't think Cousin Clifford approves of me since I too rejected his offer to come into the business. Still I suppose I must go."

Henry sprang to his feet. "If I come too you will not have to stay long."

"We will go in the morning then when Cousin Celia will be on her own. The merchant will be at his desk with his piles of ledgers and his commodities ceiling-high in his vast warehouses."

"What a dreadful fate you escaped!"

"Indeed. I would have died of suffocation."

So with much merriment they set off on a pleasant April day to walk to the house with the gravelled drive, the stone pillars and C C with H beneath carved above the doorway. To Daniel it seemed a lifetime away that he had crept up to that door ashamed of his soiled clothing.

Now he wore a velvet doublet, which he had purchased from the Branford's London tailor, and a sword hung from a new belt, adding not a little to the debts he had left behind in Cambridge and which he had not yet confessed to his father. He had an idea that things back home were looking up after some better peacetime harvests. Besides his father was now receiving a small stipend for the living of Nether Horden – though he paid most of it over to his mother – but there might, Daniel thought, be the wherewithal to pay his debts.

A footman carried the names of Sir Daniel Wilson Horden and Sir Henry Branford up to the drawing room and they were immediately invited to walk up.

Cousin Celia, plumper than ever in both face and figure, greeted them with delight.

"Well, are you not two fine young gentlemen fresh from the University and bachelors too! Daniel, I swear you have grown another inch. You'll have to bend to give your old cousin a kiss." Daniel pecked her on both cheeks though the flesh felt spongy and distasteful to his lips. "And you are Lord Branford's son! I made Lady Branford's acquaintance at the play not three weeks ago when we were in adjacent boxes. Now you shall stay to dinner. My husband returns prompt twelve o'clock."

Daniel looked at Henry who shrugged his shoulders up to his large ears.

Meeting Clifford was not to be avoided. Celia was already summoning servants to give her orders. Daniel walked over to the doors which stood open onto the balcony and looked down at the terrace below where he had first cornered Eunice. When she had escaped from him and the French cousins had collared him that was when he had uttered the unlucky words "That I should love Eunice is preposterous." He felt a tender pang at the thought of her. He was reluctant to ask after her in case Celia made too much of it. But they had scarcely sat down when Celia, quite undeterred by Henry's presence, clapped her hands and exclaimed, "Did I not say you would be back when you had graduated?"

Daniel could remember no such thing. He half smiled, shaking his head.

"But *I* did. I told Eunice. I said, 'I warrant he'll be back for your hand in marriage as soon as he leaves the University.' And here you are."

Daniel's jaw dropped before he could master himself.

Henry was grinning at him. "You never told me you were betrothed, you sly thing."

"I'm not. I mean nothing has ever been *said*. Well, things have been *said* but not arranged."

Celia was not at all perturbed at his reaction. His confusion seemed in fact to please her. She shook a finger at him.

"Ah but your mother and I knew your feelings and I know Eunice's. Never mind her father. Clifford and I can be too many for him. You'll see."

Daniel looked hopelessly at Henry, wishing he would come to the rescue about their plans for the navy but he just sat there chuckling like a monkey.

"I fear marriage is still a long way off, Cousin Celia," he said at last. "Henry and I hope to be commissioned in the navy soon and who knows what the next few months will bring. There could be war."

"With the Hollanders? Ah, Clifford did tell me there was a loyal vote in the Commons on that very matter. I take little note of these things, Daniel, but I cannot see how that would affect your marrying."

Henry butted in proudly, "My father voted in the Lords to

concur with the Commons' vote but he thinks the King will play for time."

"Then nothing hinders you to be married, Daniel. Your father and mother would be happy for you."

"But Cousin William –?

"He must have his daughter married one day and the way they live she will meet no one else of any suitability."

"I thought – I mean marriage settlements take so much time to arrange and with my family so far away –"

Henry did step in then. "The fact is, Ma'am, my father is taking us to court tomorrow to kiss the King's hand and after that we will be away. There is a young lady in mind for me too but she must wait while Daniel and I do some living first."

Celia folded her arms on her capacious bosom and beamed at them both. "Ah well, as long as these things are understood we know where we stand. So, Daniel, we can be working it out with your father in the meanwhile."

Daniel gave up. Further protestation would sound hurtful but he resolved to make it plain in his next letter home that he was not betrothed, he would not be hemmed in by anyone, and he expected to be allowed the same freedom his parents had had to make their own choice of spouse.

They chatted of other things. Celia was concerned about the effect on the price of silks if trade should be interrupted by hostilities and when Clifford arrived, not too pleased to see his comfortable dinner-time invaded by two young men, he would talk of little but the ships he had at sea and the danger of piracy or attack by the Dutch.

"So you are going into the navy, young cousin?" he said when he finally heard their news. "You know as little of that as you do of business."

"We will learn, sir. And at Cambridge in our mathematical studies we were once shown how the new Mercator's Projection is used in navigation. We are not totally ignorant."

"I'm blessed if I can remember it," Henry giggled, "but as Dan says we can learn."

They were ready to take their leave when Celia said casually to her husband, "We will be writing to Cousin Nathaniel about getting up a match for Eunice with Daniel when he has seen some service."

Clifford bent his thick brows on Daniel. "What, have you declared yourself, young man? Are you after my fortune without being prepared to work for it?"

"No, indeed sir. It was only that your honoured lady believes Eunice has no other –" He didn't know if he was going to say 'chance' or 'choice.' Either way he was in hot water. He finished pathetically. "I mean I haven't said anything yet. It's too soon."

Clifford's thin, tight lips were drawn into a sneer. "I think it *is* too soon. You have proved yourself in nothing yet."

"We have graduated, sir," Henry piped up, "and tomorrow we kiss the King's hand."

Clifford, Daniel was sure, was never likely to get to court. He had been too supportive of the Commonwealth while both Daniel's family and Henry's had suffered for loyalty to the King. He could see Clifford was impressed, much against his own inclination. Perhaps a grandson-in-law in favour with the new regime would not be unwelcome. At all events he just grunted and turned the subject and presently, rather uncomfortably, they took their leave.

As soon as they were outside in the Strand again Henry clapped Daniel on the shoulder and chuckled, "Is this Cousin Eunice some ugly old harridan then that you are trying to escape from?"

Daniel saw her tiny shape and poignant little face in his mind's eye. "No." He found he didn't want to speak of her. His emotions were too tangled up. "I shan't be pushed, that's all."

Henry gave him a quizzical look and said no more. They spent the rest of the walk back discussing how they should dress next day for the momentous occasion. Daniel felt that his tall frame with its long legs looked ridiculous in the short doublet and baggy petticoat breeches with trailing ribbons that were all the fashion but Henry said he would look out of place if he didn't conform.

"That's why you had them made as soon as we came to London."

"I know and a terrible expense they were but when I saw myself in the tailor's mirror I hated the look."

"That's what it must be, however." Henry, whose compact shape was unremarkable except for his ears, was adamant on the point so they set off next morning in Lord Branford's coach, Daniel fiddling self-consciously with the ribbons dangling over his knees and from the waistband.

He could not believe he would actually kiss the King's

hand until they arrived at the Palace of Whitehall and passed though the Holbein Gateway. His mouth dried and his heart began to pound.

They were informed that His Majesty was in the Privy Garden where his precious sundial was being cleaned and they could join him there. Passing through the Palace both Henry and Daniel were the butt of many merry jests from the courtiers.

"If they are for the navy God help us."

"The little fellow had better not turn those ears to the wind or his ship will be carried off course."

"Nay but if t'other's ship loses a mast he can stand in for it himself."

Lord Branford ignored it all and shepherded them along with the occasional bow to an acquaintance. Daniel wanted to be able to describe the palace in his letters home but he found he dare not lift his eyes. A page conducted them by the Stone Gallery and they emerged onto the Privy Garden where Daniel to his astonishment found himself looking down on the figure of the King who was examining his sundial. He had always thought of the King as high above him but he had only seen him on horseback and he felt acute embarrassment at his own height.

Lord Branford waited until the equerry standing at a respectful distance caught the King's attention.

"Earl Branford to present two young gentlemen for your naval volunteers, sire. His son, Sir Henry Branford and Sir Daniel Wilson Horden.

The King looked round and his eyes went up and up till they reached Daniel's.

Daniel, fearfully ashamed, dropped on one knee although he was still some yards away.

The King laughed. "Nay, stand up young man. I have seen you before, that height and that flaxen hair. I believe you are even taller than you were. Where was it?"

Lord Branford pushed him forward. "Answer the King," he hissed.

Daniel swallowed. "By London Bridge, Your Majesty. On the day of your return. I was in the crowd. You did me the great honour of noticing me."

"I remember. How tall are you?"

"Three inches above six feet, I believe, Your Majesty."

"Three inches taller than your King then. We can't have that. Shall we chop off his head or his feet, Branford?"

"Like my son, Henry here, he wishes to serve in your navy, sire, and will need all his parts."

"Very well. They will get their papers."

The King held out his hand towards Henry first and Henry dropped on one knee before reverently kissing it.

Daniel followed suit, before Henry stood up, and then realised he was supposed to wait for the King to extend his hand. He knew he was blushing furiously.

But the King seemed amused by his unfamiliarity with court etiquette.

"Horden?" he said, as he held out his hand and Daniel scarcely dared touch it with his lips. "Where are you from,

Sir Daniel?"

Still on one knee, Daniel answered "Northumberland, Your Majesty, Horden Hall, to the north of Newcastle."

Again the King gestured him to rise.

"Did you suffer in the late wars?"

"Yes, we were overrun by the Scots and sequestered by Parliament, sire."

"You have been restored to your estates?"

"Yes, ire."

"But you are deserting them for the navy?"

Daniel had a horrible feeling that he was being rebuked.

"I can think of no greater honour in life than to serve Your Majesty. My estate is in good hands." He dare not say principally his mother's.

"Very well." The King turned abruptly to Lord Branford. "If the lads know nothing of service at sea they had better start learning at once. Speak to Mr Pepys who will give them their documents of accreditation."

They were dismissed and backed out as far as the Stone Gallery where they were allowed to walk forward again. Daniel, glancing back saw that the King had turned to his sundial again and seemed to be pointing out some place where he was not satisfied with the cleaning.

As they passed through to the gate Daniel again saw nothing of his surroundings so dazed with wonder was he that he had held speech with the King.

Henry said in a huff, "He spoke not one word to me."

His father clapped him on the back. "You kissed hands.

The Branfords are known to the King. My brother was killed at Naseby. Horden was a new name in his ears."

"He remembered me at London Bridge." Daniel found that overwhelming. He couldn't wait to get back to the Branfords' house and write to his mother.

CHAPTER 14

EUNICE looked up from the catechism she was teaching to a motley group of a dozen children. The figure of her grandmother blotted out the light filtering into the crypt from the top of the stone steps.

"Leave that, my dear," Celia said, all smiles. "Reverend Woodhouse has given you permission to speak with me for a few moments."

Eunice rose at once, unable to control a quickening of her heart. Celia's visits always brought word of Cousin Daniel.

"Repeat over what you have learnt," she told the children and came to the foot of the steps out of earshot.

Celia did not look inclined to climb down as there was no rail to hold onto so Eunice mounted to her side. She could hear the children breaking into shouts and fights but there was nothing she could do about that. They were only quelled for short periods under the threat that they would get no dinner if they had not learnt to repeat at least one sentence before noon.

Now that she had her to herself in the shabby space which had once been a side chapel but now held only a worn table and benches for the children's dinner, Celia took both her hands.

"Well, he has come. He called upon us yesterday. He is now a graduate of Cambridge and will soon be an officer in the King's navy. He is taller than ever and twice as handsome. Such a fine figure in a velvet doublet and wearing a sword! This very moment he will be at the Palace of Whitehall kissing the king's hand. Oh my child, how you will be lifted up from all this!"

Eunice saw her casting an eye round the bare stone walls. The day was warm outside but here with the stone flags striking cold through her shoes Celia couldn't stop shivering. Eunice suppressed her usual ready sympathy. Every part of her grandmother's little speech angered her but she took her up on the last point.

"*I* lifted up! I have not asked to be lifted up. The work I do here is a good work. As for kings they are no better than the rest of us."

"Come now, Eunice, that is your father speaking. I know your heart."

Eunice struggled to stop her eyes filling with tears. It was best to be cool and distant. "Are you referring to Cousin Daniel, Ma'am? You have not named the gentleman."

"Now, my girl, be not coy with me. I told you he would come back for you when he graduated."

"But you say he has come back to enter the navy."

"He cannot come for you now but he will when he has served his King. Your grandfather is to write to Cousin Nathaniel and start negotiations. Once a settlement is worked out it will all be official and then you can look forward to a better life than this."

Eunice raised her head and stiffened her slight frame. "I will look forward to nothing, Grandmother. Father tells me to live one day at a time. We can serve God only in this present moment. The past is lost opportunity and the future is unknown."

Celia absolutely stamped her foot. "Oh he has warped your mind! He has turned you stubborn and obstinate. Do you not want marriage and children like ordinary girls?"

"I will never contemplate marriage unless a godly man I can love and honour stands before me – with my father's sanction of course – and desires to wed me. Now I must return to my pupils before they hurt each other."

"Ah you say this now and mighty fine it may sound in your ears but I know better. You'll soon change your note, my girl, when you see him." She looked down into the crypt again. The noise was growing louder. "Do you receive a wage for this work?"

Eunice shook her head. "I get anything left over from their dinners to take home with me."

Celia sighed. "I wager they leave nothing, those little vagabonds. This is not how my granddaughter should be living. Well, it saddens me but I will leave you for now, poor deluded girl."

"I thank you for coming but pray do not write to Cousin Nathaniel about me."

Celia gave her a peck on the forehead. "I think I can write what letters I choose," she muttered as she turned away.

Eunice heard that plain enough as she watched the stout figure waddle away to the care of her maid waiting at the sunlit doorway.

She turned back to the head of the steps but how was she to quell these unruly children when her own thoughts were scampering in her brain like wild beasts?

It was cruel to have dangled this beautiful young man before her again when he was no more than a mirage. She was nothing in his life. Of course he could have come to her if he had wanted to. He could have come today with his cousin but he was engrossed with his new prospects.

This talk of a marriage was not the work of Daniel's parents, she was certain. It was got up by her grandmother, though it was quite possible that Clifford for all his shallow republicanism might be eager for a titled alliance. She had often heard her father bemoan *his* father's hypocrisy before begging the Lord's forgiveness for breaking the fifth commandment.

This was why she had come to admire her father more and more. He was for ever checking himself and confessing the thoughts of his heart. And this was what she must do now. Put her heart in a straight-jacket. She stepped quickly down into the chill crypt and waved the children to sit down again. It was getting near to their dinner time and the Reverend Woodhouse or perhaps even her father of whom they were very afraid would come to hear a sentence of the catechism.

Today they were learning, "to keep my hands from picking and stealing and my tongue from evil speaking, lying and slandering." It was impossible that they could go through life obeying all this when she herself, with all her advantages, still found herself telling lies to her father. She had had to leave out 'honour and succour my father and mother' since they had none, but hearing each in turn mumbling all the other words by rote left her sadly disillusioned with 'the good work' about which she had boasted to her grandmother.

At least, she thought, while they are in here they are not picking and stealing and they can sleep here if they wish which keeps them safe and dry at night but they are not prisoners. Daniel said, "Will no one speak up for Eunice? Do we stand by and let her be taken back to prison?" He believes my life is a prison. He has choices – the university, the navy, his estates. And yet he could speak too, in that letter he wrote, of feeling 'hemmed in'. Are any of us free?

"He said 'pricking', mistress. That's wrong, ain't it?"

She pulled her mind back.

"*Picking*, Johnny. You know what it means. You run past a stall and *pick* off an apple. You don't *prick* it. If you think what the words mean you'll say them right first time. Now, once again."

Would it never be dinner time? She was as hungry as they were.

Daniel and Henry found themselves on board the *Elizabeth* more swiftly than they could have imagined. It was a ship of the line that he had noted on their passage down river but it was only a third rate, at which they were a little disappointed.

Nevertheless it carried sixty guns on two gun decks and the captain assured them that this type of enlarged frigate was the most useful vessel in the navy.

Exciting as it was to be fulfilling his dream Daniel felt quite breathless at the sudden change in day to day living. He and Henry exchanged their spacious bedchambers for the cramped berths under the gangways which the midshipmen shared with the coxswain.

The high-ceilinged dining-room and elegant parlour of the Branford's home, the leisurely dinners with abundant choice of meats, fish and fowl, the free time to play tennis or go the theatre or just sit back and enjoy lively conversation, all this was suddenly at an end. On board the Elizabeth Daniel had to stoop low after several bangs on the head. He and Henry were subjected to ill-cooked food, constant swearing and excessive drinking by the other midshipmen who were younger but had some experience of the sea which they seemed curiously unwilling to share.

Daniel commented to Henry, "They are suspicious of us because we have been to university and they fear we will soon overtake them. Let us do our best to do so."

Captain Wallace, who had seen service in the Dutch wars under Cromwell, was unusual in taking the training of young officers very seriously and they were immediately put to learning all the parts of the vessel with lessons on navigation, seamanship and tactics. They were introduced to the theory and practice of gunnery, but not allowed to touch the guns themselves.

After one week they felt they had been there a lifetime and Daniel couldn't help stabs of homesickness, when he wondered what they were doing in the leafy surroundings of Horden Hall as spring turned into summer. He had little leisure for writing home and no letters from there had yet found their way to him on board.

He was conspicuous not only by his height, which was nothing but a nuisance, but by his swift mastery of the maritime terms and the principles of navigation. To apply his understanding of mathematics to real problems fascinated him. The only area in which Henry excelled him was in climbing the rigging – a feat they were expected to achieve early in their training.

Henry's smaller body and agile limbs took him up like a monkey. Daniel, sent to the masthead, had to endure the gibes of the master seaman who called out, "What ails the lad? He's half way up when he's standing on the deck."

Daniel had not been aware that he had a problem with heights until he reached the yard arm. Sweat soaking him he pressed on up the ratlines though he dare not look down or his hands would be glued to the ropes and he would be unable to move at all. When he reached the masthead he could only think, "Cling on or you're a dead man." To begin the descent he overcame fear such as he had never in his life experienced. When he reached the deck he had to rush to the rail and vomit. He was almost dead with shame when the wind blew some back in his face and everyone who saw it laughed and cheered.

"Keep off the windward side, landlubber," roared the master seaman and hosed him down.

The first time their ship ventured out on exercises to test both ship and crew he expected to feel seasickness before they were clear of the river. To his great relief it didn't come. He decided that his body having stopped growing was at last more stable.

In the early autumn, though there had been no declaration of war, news spread round the ship that the Dutch had been defeated by Admiral Holmes in raids on their trading posts in Guinea and New Amsterdam in America. There was great delight among the crew and impatience to be at sea and involved themselves. By turns the officers had leave to go ashore but in December all were mustered again when news came that there had now been a terrible reversal in Guinea and De Ruyter the Dutch admiral had recaptured all the prizes that Holmes' fleet had taken. The mood was now all for revenge. Although war was not officially declared till January 1665 no one had any doubt that hostilities had commenced and they would soon be called into action.

Daniel at last received a letter from Bel in reply to his first sent from the ship.

'We lapped up your news here like thirsty cats but I cannot pretend that it made me happy. Here we are in Northumberland, remote from the folly of war. How placidly we could look on our lovely winter landscape, serene under a blue sky and delicately whitened from a recent snowfall and could ignore all that is going on in the seas around the southern coasts, but that we

know our precious son is in the midst of it all.

'I dream of battles fought between great ships, splendid in their beauty, but swiftly ravaged by cannon fire. Oh how I wish you could understand the daily torment I suffer from not knowing where you are and what dangers you may be in! Dear Ursula tries her best to keep me cheerful and your father hides his own anxiety so as not to increase mine.

'I never imagined being torn apart like this. I thought myself quite the stoic. Twice I have let my mother and sister go from me with hardly a pang. I never truly loved my brother. I loved my father in his last years and grieved at his death but it was a simple passing pain. Since loving your father – as you know with great passion – we have been through many trials but he was always at hand. Then God sent you into our lives, our first and only surviving child. I don't think I knew how desperately I loved you until you deliberately put yourself in peril of your life.

'I know I should not be writing this. Your father would disapprove and say I am giving you unnecessary pain, but oh, I beg you, dearest Dan, when you have satisfied your longing to serve your King, come back to me, dwell here in safety in your ancestral home and give your poor mother the joy of seeing you daily.

'I may add your Grandmother Wilson says she is only staying alive to hear of some heroic exploit of yours and then she can quietly depart and be with her Joseph and her own beloved Daniel. It makes me tremble to think that you are only a few months older than he was when he met his untimely death – for which I still feel in a small way responsible – and I fear that by

not expressly commanding your presence here after graduation we may be responsible for yours! My head tells me you will return a more mature man but my heart fears for my boy.

'I must mention that we have had a letter purporting to come from Cousin Clifford, though it is in Celia's hand, saying that they would be interested in getting up a marriage between you and Eunice. You said you had paid a call on them. Did you see Eunice herself or William? If you are secretive about it I am sure your deepest feelings are involved. When you were younger you told me everything. How can we answer the cousins if we know not your own thoughts? I have laid bare my heart to you.

'Pray write when you can send letters ashore. They give me joy, although I still shake at the thought of you at a masthead, but at least I know that you were alive and well when you wrote.

'May God bless you and bring you safe home from this foolish and unnecessary fighting so that smiles may again wreath the face of your ever loving Mother,

Bel Wilson Horden.'

It was not a letter to lift the spirits of a serving officer, Dan decided, having thoroughly digested it. He was asked to lay bare the deepest feelings of his heart when he had neither time nor leisure to indulge them. He was fighting for a foolish and unnecessary cause. He was a cruel son to bring his loving mother pain and suffering.

Of course she imagined him in the midst of flying cannon balls when all the fleet had done lately was progress towards the Dutch coast with the idea of blockading it but because of the problem of victualling so many ships at a distance from port they had been forced to withdraw towards the coast of Norfolk. The crews, bored and impatient, were waiting to see what the next orders from on high would produce. War was not after all exciting. Most of the time was spent in petty discomfort among men – apart from Henry Branford – whom he would not have chosen as particular friends.

At last in June word came that a real battle might be imminent. At the same time news of an outbreak of plague in London began to filter through to the fleet. Pockets of plague were so common that little notice was taken. Much more exciting was the prospect of a Dutch fleet with over one hundred ships bearing down upon them.

Daniel gulped at the news. This was what he had enrolled for – to defend his King. The moment was surely coming.

"We have a hundred ships too," he told Henry, "and better guns than theirs."

"They have more warships."

"But we are backed by large merchant men. We will knock them to pieces."

It was light talk but when Daniel saw the Dutch approach from a row of dots on the horizon to a great fleet in line of battle and, looking about, saw all the sea filled with vast ships on both sides, his soul was stirred as it had been when the idea of naval service had first seized him. This was what he had seen in his mind's eye. It was happening all around him. *Elizabeth* was in the centre of the Red Squadron with the Duke of York himself in his flagship, the *Royal Charles*. Here were the splendid ships, awesome in their beauty as his mother had written, but soon to be ravaged by cannon fire. He took his station on deck, his pulse galloping. How did a sea battle begin? He had no notion.

The stately lines of ships first passed by each other warily at a distance but after the English fleet tacked again at closer range the guns opened up. It was the first time Daniel had heard them in anger. He had laughed at the noise of cannon on the day of the King's return but this was incomparably louder, beneath his feet and filling the air above from every direction. The orderly lines on both sides began to break up and the seamen were kept busy trying to maintain station. Daniel and Henry could only stand by to help where a hand was needed.

The hot June day wore on and the Dutch were taking the heavier punishment. In mid-afternoon a tremendous explosion rent the *Eendracht*, one of the Dutch flagships as a cannon ball from the *Royal Sovereign* hit the magazine. Daniel saw the great vessel engulfed in a plume of fire. The sight sickened him. There were hundreds of men aboard her and his mother's words of 'foolish and unnecessary' seemed tame indeed. All around him though was cheering. Confusion quickly seized the rest of the Dutch squadrons as they set sail to escape some one way and some another. The English pursued into the night before orders to shorten sail on the Duke of York's flagship led to a withdrawal of the Red Squadron, to general disappointment.

Rumours flew that the Duke of York himself had been wounded, then that a group with him had been mowed down by a single cannon shot, spattering him with their blood. Daniel had looked up during the battle to see a hole rent in their ship's sail directly above his head. If the elevation of the Dutch gun had been lower he would not be here.

That was my first taste of action, he thought, trying to seek comfort in sleep which his long legs always made difficult. I am alive but I did nothing of any consequence. He closed his eyes but could still see a great ship burning like a candle on the ocean.

Eunice emerged from the crypt of St Mary Magdalen to break into an instant sweat as the midday heat wrapped round her. Immediately she could hear the distant rumble of guns.

"What is it?" she asked a street pedlar.

"Eh, there's a great sea battle going on off Lowestoft they say. Folks have been running down to the river all morning to hear it louder."

"Are all our ships involved?"

"Nay, I know not, but 'tis likely. They say the Dutch are in full strength. Now, mistress," as she began to move away, "look at this bunch of ribbons for a penny. You'll not get better than that anywhere."

She shook her head. Apart from tying up her hair and lacing the front of her bodice she had no use for ribbons and Father would have frowned at the bright colours of the bunch the man was holding out.

She hurried off but had to slow down as she breathed in the hot smoky air. Despite the warmth people had their fires lit to cook their bit of fish or a few eggs for their dinners. All the time she was asking herself, "Is Daniel in the midst of this fighting? Dear God, protect him."

Glancing down a narrow lane her eye was caught by a glaring red cross painted on a door. Above was scrawled also in red the words, 'Lord have mercy on us.' So the plague had reached to here. There had been cases since May in St Giles in the Fields but now they were appearing closer to home. It struck her that death was not only lurking out there where those sullen booms were sounding but here all around where thousands of people were at risk of its silent progress.

She found her father laying out on two wooden plates some cress to which she added from her basket the cheese and rye bread she had been given by the Reverend Woodhouse. The jug of milk he filled daily from the dairy was on the table.

She wiped her brow with a clean rag and he silently poured her a mug which she drank at a gulp.

"Slowly, slowly," he said. "Everything in moderation."

She wanted to scream at him that it was a furnace out there and she was dying of thirst. All she said was, "The plague is in the alley leading to Foster Lane."

He nodded. "Judgment has come upon the city. From the King downwards there has been evil debauchery and out in the sea men are killing each other at this very moment."

She bit her lip to hold back angry tears. "Why, Father? And why do the innocent suffer with the guilty." But Daniel, she thought, is not innocent. He has gone into this with his eyes open. He has been caught up in the mad fervour which calls itself patriotism. But the plague was different. If it was God's punishment why were little children dying?

"That house I saw with the cross, Father. There may be babies there. Why should they die?"

William looked her in the eye as if wondering at her ignorant question.

"They are born for eternal life. What matters it then if their span here is short?"

"Oh Father, you grieved when Mother and my baby brother died together."

Pain and fury crossed his narrow face. "I had not found the strait gate then. I lacked the Lord's strength to uphold me."

"Will you not weep if I catch the plague and die? Our Lord wept over Lazarus."

"Of course I will weep, child. Life here and now can never be constant happiness. Man is born to trouble as the sparks fly upwards. This earth is our testing ground. If the just never suffered the wicked would attempt goodness only to save themselves punishment. But the Lord will uphold me as He will uphold you should I go first. Let us sit down and ask his blessing on this food."

Eunice washed her hands and sat down. Conversations with her father always ended like this. He put her down with what to him were self-evident truths. When she examined them in the quiet of her own chamber they still had the ring of truth but there was a warmth and a wideness lacking. It might be the tone of his voice but whatever it was the sayings were cold and hard and left her unsatisfied.

CHAPTER 15

It was two days before the city was filled with the news of a great English victory at sea. Despite the threat of plague and the continuing hot weather, bonfires were lit in the streets and there was a general air of rejoicing.

Eunice wondered if her grandparents had heard any news of Daniel. She dared not go and ask or her curiosity would be exaggerated into a passion for him. But it *was* a passion, she had to admit. His image in her room at that house and again here at home at the foot of the wooden stair was as bright as ever. Whatever had happened to him afterwards she knew he had not been indifferent to her in those moments and it was to them she clung. Meanwhile the plague spread as the summer advanced.

The horrible cry of 'Bring out your dead' was heard at night as the carts went round the streets with bells and lanterns collecting the corpses. Many were unidentified and space in church graveyards was quickly used up and plague pits dug so that the bodies could be disposed of as quickly as possible. There were no more celebrations.

The Reverend Woodhouse closed the crypt and decided to send the children into the country where he had a cousin with a farm. "He will teach them to bring the hay in. It will strengthen their bodies and perhaps their minds too."

"Aren't you coming with us?" they called out to Eunice as they clambered onto the wagon sent to fetch them.

"I keep house for my father."

"You'll catch the plague."

"Then you must pray for me." She waved them off, knowing she would miss them. Uncouth as they were she had grown fond of them.

She had spoken cheerfully to them but there was a chill apprehension always in the pit of her stomach as the hot weather helped the disease to flourish. She was horrified when she realised that houses with the red cross sign were to be boarded up for at least a month so that no infected person could escape and carry the disease further. The coffin makers and apothecaries grew rich though there were few remedies that had much effect. The plague nurses used vinegar to disinfect but were more interested in looting from the dead and dying and they too stashed away small fortunes during these desperate months.

Eunice had heard nothing from her grandparents till Tom Fletcher told her he had passed the house in the Strand on an errand and had learnt from a neighbour's servant that the Hordens had fled into the country early in June and the business was being run by a manager. Trade was slack because of the fear of interception of merchantmen by Dutch ships at sea. There had been no more big battles. The fleets were stalking each other in the northern waters and prizes were taken on both sides but there was widespread confidence that we were slowly beating the Dutch.

Eunice was grateful for any scraps of news but nothing in her experience enabled her to picture Daniel in a sea battle. This was frustrating as it left her imagination too much scope. As for her grandparents she was glad they were out of London but a little hurt that they had sent no word of their going. The number of deaths increased through August and it was not only the wealthy who fled London. Many shops shut including Thompsons', the Baker next door. Eunice had to trail further through the dusty streets to find bread.

It was a day in September when the weekly numbers of deaths was at seven thousand that her father came in one day from preaching at Billingsgate his usual message of the need for prayer and repentance.

He sat down at the table, his face more than usually sallow. His hair which he had lately allowed to grow hung limp about it. In silence he began to take off the shabby black coat he always wore, which reached to his knees and partly hid his threadbare breeches. Eunice, frightened by his manner went to help him.

"Touch me not," he cried. "Keep your distance."

She shrank back and watched in horror as he stripped off his shirt also and lifting his arm revealed a blotchy swelling under it.

"As I thought. I have sneezed and my head has been aching all morning. You must leave this house. You must report to the authorities that it is a plague house and you must not come back to it. Go to your grandparents." He looked round at her then with a ghastly smile. "I never thought to say that to you but they are your only kin that will lodge you and I pray God you have learnt enough to be submissive to them but not to engage in their service of Mammon. Go, this minute."

"I cannot. They are out of town and I know not where they have gone. But if you think I would leave you in your illness you know me very little. In this for the first time I will not obey you."

He staggered to his feet and stared at her long and hard. She stared back, her lips compressed and her eyes pricking with tears. Holding onto the table he seemed to accept she was immoveable.

"Then you will be utterly alone when I am gone," he choked out.

"No. You may recover. Many have. I have learnt what must be done. Can you get up to your bed? You must have every blanket we have to cover you and raise a great perspiration."

As he began to move he was violently sick and almost fell to the ground. She grabbed his arm although he tried to pull it from her grasp and guiding him round the vomit she walked him to the foot of the little wooden stair. He caught hold of the rail and dragged himself up, she with a hand on his bare back to support him. Somehow he tottered to his bed and fell back onto it.

It was the first time in her life she had ever seen him helpless. She hauled one blanket from beneath him and pulled it over him as he struggled to aid her by rolling onto his side. He seemed to have no strength left and she could only marvel at the will-power that had got him home when he already knew he was smitten.

She now ran into her own small chamber and took the blankets off her bed and piled them over him. Although she had never had the money to lay in any remedies herself she knew that Mistress Fletcher, the leather worker's wife, had a whole shelf of jars and bottles that she swore contained all that was needful.

Without thinking of the consequences she ran next door and cried out in the doorway, "Pray give me what I need, Mistress Fletcher. My father has the plague."

The woman screamed out, "What! *He* is punished when he has breathed curses on all us sinners! Stay away from me, Eunice. Keep clear of my house," and she rushed on her and pushed the door shut in her face.

Eunice was shocked. She had known this woman for most of her life. She backed slowly off looking up and down the street but already her cry had been noted and people were scurrying into their houses and barring their doors.

She went back inside and cleaned up the floor as best she could. It needed to be done and for the moment she was too stunned at what had happened to think what else she should be doing.

When she had finished she heard an urgent tapping at the window and ran to pull back the sacking. Tom was outside.

"Quick, Eunice," he mouthed and held up a bottle and a small earthenware pot.

She opened the window. "Oh Tom, what have you brought

me? Don't touch my hands as I take them."

"That's vinegar," he said. "Your father should drink some and you as well but also wipe it on every place your father touched. This is an ointment for the plague sore. It may help. Mother has plenty of both. I pray she won't miss them."

"Tom, you are a good, brave boy. God bless you."

"But oh Eunice, you will get it if you nurse him. I could run for one of the plague nurses."

"Never, I wouldn't trust them near him. I believe they are in league with the coffin makers and will let no one live."

There was a shout from his father's shop. "Come away from there, Tom."

"I must go. But knock thrice on the wall if you need help."

"You can do one thing. Notify the parish examiner of our plague state."

"I will." He ran.

Eunice took a clean rag and wiped vinegar onto her own hands and then the door handle, the table and the banister rail and everywhere she could think that her father's hands might have touched.

Next, clutching the pot of ointment, she scampered up the stairs to look at her father. He was rolling about under the pile of blankets and seemed delirious. She must turn back the covers again and treat the plague spot. The ointment had a strange pungent smell. When she uncovered him to reach the spot he thrashed so much it was almost impossible to hold him down and apply the greasy substance to the lurid swelling. Some went on the bedding and some on his chest but she managed to get a blob of it in the right place and smooth it over. She didn't dare to rub it hard but he was already groaning so that she couldn't tell if it burned or soothed him.

She covered him up and ran down to wash her hands and coat them again with vinegar. She heard Tom at the window again. He was holding up a mug. When she opened the window he said, "Mother was sorry and has sent this. She said he must drink something but cold water would be bad. It's a posset of sack. She said I must put it on the ledge and run back and not touch you."

"God bless her and you, Tom."

"I've notified the examiner and they will send a man to paint the cross and no one must go in or out for a month. They nail a plank across the door."

To Eunice it sounded like a death sentence. Her father would die and she would follow a few days later. Then the dreadful carts would come and their bodies would be taken away at night and flung into one of the plague pits.

This body is nothing but dust, she repeated as she carried up the posset of sack to her father. A new body will be given us at the resurrection. I must not be afraid.

But she *was* afraid. She was shaking so much that a little of the precious liquid spilled from the mug before she could get it to her father's lips. He rolled his head away from it. In a panic now she set it on the small table by the bed and dragged him into a sitting posture. "You must take this, Father," she yelled at him. "Drink!"

His eyes opened and for a second he seemed to be there in

their dark depths.

"Drink!"

He seized it from her then and tossed it off. Immediately he fell back onto his pillow and though his eyes were open consciousness had vanished again.

She dropped to her knees. "Don't die. Don't leave me. What if I live! I will go mad in here. Father, we are to be shut up for a month. How can I endure that?"

She gabbled on to him because there was no one else but she knew he was taking nothing in. What can I do for him now? Oh God, tell me what I am to do.

She ran down the stairs again, half expecting to see her father sitting at the table with his Bible open. She could ask him what to do. He had always told her and nearly always she had obeyed him. He would know what she had to do.

The bench was empty. It was he on the bed upstairs, the wild, thrashing body. How could he have been reduced to that when he was always so in control, so certain of everything!

She heard a cry or a shout from him and clambered back up and stood fearfully in the doorway of his room. He was sitting bolt upright, glaring at her.

"You have given me strong drink. You know I do not touch it."

"Oh Father, it was medicine. It will do you good."

"Do me good to break my oath? Do me good to sin when I am dying?"

The covers had slipped down and she saw dark spots on his chest. Pity turned to anger. How dare he berate her if he was dying! Was that the last word she would have from him – a reproof?

"I was *told* to give it you," she yelled at him. "You don't have to die if you will do what is wise. Drink what I give you and keep under the covers. You have to sweat it out. I have heard that from the few who recover."

"Ay, few indeed. Bring me my Bible but don't come near. You can reach from the doorway to set it on the table and I can pull it towards me. I must make my peace with God. He is calling me home."

The speaking exhausted him and he slipped back onto the pillows. She took a step towards him to pull the covers up but he croaked out, "Keep your distance." A skeletal hand appeared and drew the blankets up to his chin.

"I will set a mug of vinegar there too with the Bible. Sip it when you can."

She ran down again. It was unnatural to be giving him orders but it was beginning to come more easily since his outburst. Could it be that the return of consciousness meant that he would recover?

She brought the Bible and the vinegar and set them down. His eyes were closed but he muttered, "They gave me gall and vinegar to drink. Ah my Lord, your sufferings were worse than this."

She slipped into her own room. A horrifying feeling came over her that she didn't want him to recover. He had oppressed her life so long. She would be free at last. At once she fell to her knees by her bed and gabbled prayers that he would live.

That night she didn't go to bed. She had no blankets but the warmth of the day had seeped into these small upper rooms with their ceilings so low that even she could put up a hand and touch them. Her father had to stoop when he came up here. Would he ever stoop again?

For hours he lay groaning and restless. She didn't think he had touched the vinegar so she moistened a cloth in it and touched his lips and tried to squeeze some into his mouth but he rolled his head aside and she backed away and wiped her own hands with it and went back to her room. She sat on the stool by her bed and tried to pray.

The day was bright when she woke to find herself curled on the floor. She started up wondering what hour it was. The sun was high in the sky. She peeped into her father's room. His eyes were wide open and fastened on her. Was he dead? She had seen the dead look like this.

But then he spoke. "The spot is hardened. That is a bad sign. I may not have long. You must pack up and leave this house. It is not safe for you to stay in it. Go to your grandmother's."

"They have fled and I may not leave here for a month."

He had forgotten what she had told him yesterday, a man who remembered every detail of a conversation for months, even years afterwards.

"God is telling you to go. He speaks through me, your father. You do not have to pay heed to any other man's word. You are still healthy. You have a life to live."

His speech was coming in painful jerks but his manner was of great urgency. He does care for me, she thought. He has always loved me in his own way.

"Swear to me that you will leave this house," he gasped out. "Do not touch the Bible but from where you are standing hold your hand towards it. Swear that you will go."

She did as he told her. "I swear that I will go."

I have not said when, she thought. And she noticed he hadn't moved the Bible all night – or the drink. His lips looked dry and cracked.

"Drink the vinegar," she ordered him. He reached it but his hand was unsteady and he spilled some. When she leapt forward to grab it his eyes were so piercing that she shrank back.

"Keep away. You have sworn to go, now go."

She saw him raise his head and drink some, his face distorting at the bitterness of it, but his eyes never left hers. "Go," he said again, setting the mug down and dropping back but still directing all the old fierceness of his authority at her. "Go."

She scurried back into her own room and shut the door. Of course she couldn't leave him *now* but she had sworn. That was a real oath, she reminded herself, though I didn't mean it when I said the words. But it was done before God on the Bible and I will be cursed if I fail to keep it.

She pulled from under her bed the worn leather bag that was all she had brought from the old home after her mother's death. Into it she piled her few clothes and her one pair of shoes she seldom wore as she was always in clogs on the filthy streets round about. The cloth slippers she was wearing in the house she would put in last although they were almost worn through. She had one coarse woollen winter cloak which she must take though the weather was so warm at present. She took from her small drawer her mother's miniature and her purse with a few pence in it. Her father might have money in the pocket of his black coat but she would not touch that.

Going downstairs to look about for provisions she saw there was a jug outside on the window ledge. It was set to the side so she could open one casement and reach it. It contained milk so Tom must have been to the dairy that morning to fetch it with their own supply.

She emptied the bucket of kindling into the grate and made a fire. She would cook some porridge and try to make her father eat. When it was ready she carried it up but found him delirious. She could not force food into him in that state and if she tried she risked the return of his fury. He thought she had gone.

She ate the porridge herself and drank some milk and felt invigorated. She was alive and wanted to go on living. As the afternoon wore on she began to hear unusual noises from the leather-worker's shop. Presently there was the sound of wheels and peeping from the window she saw a cart outside and Mistress Fletcher and Tom carrying out boxes from the shop door. Bundles of clothes and bedding followed and then baskets of provisions. They were leaving. Was it because of her father's sickness?

Most of the wealthy had long since escaped into the country and many shops had shut. She remembered Mistress

Fletcher saying she had a sister whose husband ran a small-holding south of the river. Was she going there and would Tom stay to help his father in the shop? She wished Tom would come to her window and tell her what was happening.

Every half hour she ran up to look at her father. His face looked more sunken and ashen as the day drew towards evening. In her heart she was railing against God for everything – his sickness, her helplessness as a nurse, her lifelong fear of his anger and his persistence in living. Some people she had witnessed with her own eyes fell down dead while they were walking in the street.

These thoughts filled her with sickening guilt and she could only creep back to the window and, shaded by the sacking, keep one eye on what was happening next door. What she saw – and heard – this time was Giles Fletcher himself nailing up the window shutters and boarding up his shop. They were all going then and she would be even more bereft.

As she looked she heard a ghastly rattling cry from upstairs. Stumbling in her haste she clattered up and stared into the room. Her father had arched his back and was struggling to breathe. Even while she looked his face contorted and he fell back with a small grunt and she knew life had gone.

"Oh God," she sobbed, "I did nothing to help him." She ought to hold him in her arms now and pray his soul to heaven but she couldn't do it. His "Go, go" was still in her ears. The fear of the plague that had gripped all London had taken hold of her. She seized the bundle she had prepared. She dare not touch anything from his room if she was to have a hope of escaping the infection from which so far miraculously she felt free.

Downstairs she put on her clogs, drank the rest of the milk and gathered into a basket the few remaining provisions from the shelf. At least he had touched nothing there since he had come in sick two days ago.

Setting down her burdens at the door she lifted the latch and pushed hard. It did not yield. She seized the poker and hammered at it.

Giles Fletcher's voice sounded outside. "You cannot come out, the door is sealed up."

"My father is dead."

"We'll tell the coffin-maker. Stay where you are."

She heard his footsteps going away. She heard Tom's voice protesting something. He sounded high up. He must be already on the cart. Then his father's voice geed-up the horse and she heard the clip-clop of his hooves.

They were going, the only friends she had.

She pushed one of the benches against the window, shouting, "Tom, don't leave me here."

She was small enough to get through. She leant out first and lowered the basket as far as she could before letting go. Then she realised there were other noises in the street – a party of revellers rolling by singing a bawdy song. One of them snatched up the basket. "Thank you for our supper, m'lady," he shouted.

One of the others yelled, "It's a plague house. Are you mad?" and dashed it from his hand. The contents rolled in the dirt.

Eunice, sitting on the sill, was squeezing feet first through the aperture so she could drag her bundle through after her. “How dare you?” she screamed.

One of the drunks turned round and pulled on her legs so that her skirt rode up round her hips. “Oh ho, my pretty, what have you there” and he put up his hand to touch her. A friend yanked him away yelling, “She has the plague, you fool. Run.”

Eunice, horribly scraped, landed on her feet and the bundle she was clutching followed in a rush hitting her on the shoulder. She was ashamed and sobbing. Father was right about men. They all wanted their wicked way with women. She pulled down her skirt and looked to see if the drunks had reached the corner of the lane. They had met the dead-cart there with its doleful bell and swaying lantern. She heard them shout, “There's a plague house breaking out,” and the officers came on at a run.

“You, girl, plague girl, stop in the King's name.”

Eunice shouted, “I am well. There is a body inside,” and she fled the other way, up to the top of their lane which looked like a dead end but gave onto a narrow alley between two houses. She would double back on her pursuers.

Though it was still only dusk it was utterly dark in the alley and she tripped and fell over a corpse. There was another and another. She sprang onto them and over them. The stench was unbelievable. This was what London had come to, unburied bodies shoved up alleyways and back lanes. At the end of the alley she turned right onto a street of little shops all shut up. Running down it she came out onto Cheapside and saw progressing slowly in the distance the Fletchers' piled up cart. Tom and his mother were sitting among the baggage with the father driving.

"Tom!" she shrieked, realising it was the noise of the drunks that had prevented him from hearing her at the house. "Don't leave me behind."

The boy looked round. She was catching them up.

"It's Eunice," he called to his father. "Won't you stop?"

His mother looked round. "Do you want to give us all the plague? Why do you think we are getting out of London? If you are a Christian keep away."

His father was trying to whip up the poor horse but he could go no faster.

But Eunice had stopped. Her father had urged her to go because he was selfless and should she endanger others' lives?

"Go home," Mistress Fletcher said again. "Stay there and if you are clear they will let you out. That's what the laws are for, child, to stop it spreading."

Tom's face shone with tears in the light of the lantern he was holding. Eunice bowed her head and turned back.

She began to walk towards the foot of their lane when she heard the dead cart again. "Bring out your dead!" She slipped behind a projecting doorway and saw the cart emerge and turn the other way. There was another body on it wrapped in a coarse shroud. Her father? The two officers who had begun to chase her had evidently decided it was a waste of time. She could go back now unseen.

When she reached her house door she saw the plank had been removed and very roughly knocked back. The red cross was still on the door and the dreaded writing, 'Lord have mercy' scrawled above it. I could probably rip the plank off with my bare hands, she thought.

She couldn't do it. The notion of going inside where the plague was lurking and the officers would come again and seal the door for four more weeks appalled her. I am free, she told herself. God's heaven is above me. I am alive. I can walk where I will in the world. I made an oath that I would go and go I will.

She saw her scattered food on the stinking road, the loaf, the cheese, the bag of oatmeal. God had fed Elijah in the desert. She kicked the basket aside, slung her bundle over her shoulder and began walking.

CHAPTER 16

BEL took her letter from Dan when she went to visit her mother-in-law, Anne Wilson, on a balmy evening in late September. She never went by the shortcut she took to the village as a child, following the marks she had cut on the trees in the wood behind Horden Hall. Since its association with the night of the rick-burning she had kept clear of that way and the ensuing years had made the undergrowth so dense that it would be impossible to get through. As she followed the longer, open route she was telling herself that when Dan began to do his duty by his estates one of the tasks he must tackle would be the care of his neglected woods.

She strode freely down the track already leaf strewn from the first autumn gale and reached the plank bridge over the Horden Burn. Beyond it lay the Turner's farm on the left and the haystack, plentifully crammed with hay, on the right. "Pray God it may never again be fired by such carelessness as mine that night," she said half-aloud.

She was not surprised that her thoughts were occupied with that night's disaster. She was making this visit to the vicarage by herself, something she couldn't remember doing before. Nat spent many hours with his mother since his father Joseph's death, and Bel sometimes went with him but today was a Saturday and Nat was preparing a Michaelmas sermon about angels.

"I will be an angel and take Dan's letter to share with your mother as he asked us to do," she said.

Nat had looked up with a smile. "Good. Tell me how she seems today. Dr Harlow is afraid her heart is weak but she will scarcely let him examine her."

The church with its squat Saxon tower stood among trees just before the track reached the village but Bel turned aside into the gate of the ivy-strewn vicarage.

She hadn't sent word that she was coming but the Turner's daughter, Peggy, who opened the door said her mistress would be very happy to see her and took her into the parlour.

Anne had shrunk into a little old woman since Joseph's death though she was still not seventy. Her promise not to outlive him had not been fulfilled. "I can't help living," she said often, "though I know not what good I am to anyone."

Bel found her pacing the room with a pamphlet in her hand, trying to read though her eyes were not good and the evening light was partly blocked by the ivy outside.

Noticing Bel's entrance she threw the paper on the floor. "It's all nonsense."

Bel picked it up. "What is it, Mother Anne?" This was how she liked to be addressed. Bel saw it was an issue of *Mercurius Politicus* from May 1655 and was open at an advertisement for the Countess of Kent's Powder which was supposed to be a cordial for everything from colic to the plague.

"This was a Puritan pamphlet. I'm surprised you have it

in the house."

Her mother-in-law cackled. "Joseph had it off a pedlar selling pots of the powder. I remember his surprise that those republicans should let a noble woman's name sully their pages. I was only reading it to make me cross. I'll get Peggy to light the fire with it if it turns cold tonight and I'm still living."

Bel put it in the log basket by the empty grate. It was useless to ask Anne why she wanted to be cross. Her moods were quite unpredictable.

Her mother-in-law sat down in the basket chair by the window where Joseph had always sat and motioned Bel to the stool by the small table.

"Well, it's not often I see you on your own, daughter Bel," was her greeting. She sounded breathless and Bel was surprised by the high colour in her cheeks.

"Have you been exerting yourself?" she asked.

"I've been to my Daniel's grave and I hurried back."

"You didn't know I was coming?"

"No, but I was excited. I thought, I'll meet him soon. He'll be with his father and he'll look up and say, 'Here's Mother come now.' Feel how my heart's racing at the thought." And she beckoned Bel over to her and laid her hand against her flaccid bosom.

Bel could feel little but she smiled and nodded.

"I've brought you a letter from *my* Daniel. He asks me to share it with Grandmother Wilson."

"Very well, you may read it to me. My eyes are blurred tonight."

"He greets us as '*Honoured and much loved parents*'".

"Very proper."

"And begins '*We have been harrying the Dutch merchant ships and taken many prizes so I have at last been paid.*'"

"That will please him. The young can never have too much money."

"Ah but he says, '*One day I shall repay you for all you have done for me.*' He has good intentions, my Dan, even if he can't always carry them out. He goes on, trying to reassure me. '*They have not been very serious battles so you need not be anxious for me. It is much more dangerous in London we hear with this terrible plague. My friend Henry's family have gone into the country and they let me know that Cousins Clifford and Celia have gone too although they didn't know where. I hope they have not pestered you or William about a match between Eunice and me. It will never happen but I hope they took her with them to the country.*' He does care for her still whatever he says." When Anne made no comment she went on reading. "'*Everyone says that the plague is much worse in those narrow little streets where she and her father live because people are so crowded together.*

'I know all about being crowded together in a ship but at least we have no plague here and are surrounded by the great salt sea and pure air. I have grown quite used to life aboard a ship of the line but believe me I do think much about home and especially I remember the Christmases we had at the Hall in Cromwell's time when we were not supposed to celebrate it but all was done secretly yet with the knowledge and contrivance of

the whole village."

Bel broke off to say, "You remember those times, don't you, Mother Anne?" But Anne's face was passive. She seemed far away. Bel went on reading because she loved to speak Dan's words though the longing for him was making it harder to keep her voice steady. "He says, '*I thought that was so exciting, wondering if a heavy knock would come on the doors which were all locked, but it never did and we had holly and ivy and mistletoe and even music and dancing and no one in the village ever betrayed us. It makes me homesick thinking about my very happy boyhood. Note, I say homesick for I have never been seasick yet.*

'Alas, I will not be at home this Christmas for though we will have leave there will not be leisure to go all that way and the muster could be called at any time since we know not what the Dutch will be up to next.'"

Bel stopped abruptly, her voice breaking.

"Is that it?" Anne looked up surprised.

"Not quite. But oh, sweet Mother Anne, I can't bear him to be in danger. I can't bear not to have him home for Christmas. He never missed while he was at university though we could ill afford the coach fare. And now I know not *when* we will see him. To be honest with you the pain of his absence is eating me up."

"Ah! Eating you up!"

Anne's face had become bright and eager. Her eyes glistened. The red spots glowed over her high cheekbones. With her sharp eagle nose she had the look of a bird of prey spotting a vole.

Bel was puzzled by this sudden animation. "What is it, Mother Anne?"

She was sitting bolt upright with an air of triumph. ""Now, Bel Horden, you have hit it. You are sharing not just his letter with me but my pain. Eating me up. Those are the very words. That's what my pain did and still does. I just wish it would hurry up and devour the last remains of life. But it will not kill *you.* You have hope your boy will come back. Mine never did. You know your Dan has seized on the dream he craved. My Daniel was seized by cruel hands and led where he would not. Yours will receive praise and honour for what he does, mine received death and dishonour for what another did."

Bel sank to her knees beside Anne's chair. "Oh don't go on, Mother Anne. I have been thoughtless in speaking of my puny longings. My suffering is but any mother's anxiety. Yours has been a hundred times greater and I am still guilty."

"Forget your guilt." In her excitement Anne rose up, her hands gesturing in a wild dismissive motion. "Your guilt was a little cloud and I blew it away myself years ago when I called you an innocent child. But I have been eaten away ever since with anger at the injustice to that poor boy. I looked again today at the stone we put up in the wood at his poor little burial place. 'Daniel Wilson done to death in his innocence, mourned for ever by his sorrowing parents.' I should only have put *mother* for I felt Joseph got over it and I am sure Nathaniel did."

Bel stood up too and looked down on the fiery little figure.

"Oh you're wrong there. Nat and his father grieved inwardly. Nat still does but his love for God gives him peace. He can thank God for his brother's life and sweet innocence."

"Ah well that is what I haven't been able to do. I have never thanked God. I have berated Him in my heart for letting it happen." Anne was panting now and Bel became alarmed.

"Pray sit down," she urged her.

"No. This is what I wanted. This is why I ran home from his grave after one last look. This is why I looked about for something foolish to read. To excite me, provoke me. I am so glad you came. I have had an ache in my arm for a while and I so wanted it to get worse. Now it is a knife here." She pressed her hand on her side. "Tell your Dan how much his letter helped me. It was all I needed. Ah!"

She seized Bel's hands in a ferocious grip, falling against her so suddenly that Bel, calling out for Peggy, could hardly stand.

Peggy came running in and together they lowered her into the chair. There was one more convulsive movement and then her grip relaxed. A little sigh came and a smile spread over her face, so beatific on those sharp features that Bel looked at the terrified Peggy and smiled even as the girl broke into sobs.

"Oh no! Is she dead? Oh poor soul. As quick as that!" She stared at the face as if expecting it to come to life. Then she looked anxiously at Bel. "I should have told you, my lady, how odd she's been today. She was so tired this morning she could hardly eat her dinner but afterwards she said she was going to walk to Master Daniel's grave and *run* back. I thought it was said in jest. She says strange things sometimes. I begged to go with her but she wouldn't let me. You know how determined she is."

"I do indeed. It would have made no difference. Will you run to the Hall and tell the reverend? I'd like to stay by her till he comes. And we must tell Doctor Harlow who has been treating her."

"When she'd let him, my lady. He came but mostly she sent him packing."

Peggy ran. Bel knelt down on the floor again and looked in bewilderment on the dead body. She had seen many deaths, more grisly and horrible than this, but she had never been conversing with someone the moment before they were struck down and the suddenness was a fearful shock.

"Where are you, Anne Wilson?" she said aloud to the inanimate parchment face. She looked about the room as if she expected to see her standing there, ready with a harsh laugh and one of her barbed replies.

It was a struggle to repeat a prayer and as she did so she couldn't help reflecting on the way her mother-in-law had gone. The injustice her Daniel had suffered had corroded her mind all these years and left her believing that no one had mourned him as she had done.

But was it not cruel, Bel thought, to dismiss my cloud of guilt so lightly? She never knew how it dominated my life until she 'blew it away' as she put it. I married her son and was happy and she and Joseph came to help us with our little school and we were all in harmony, I believed. Poor soul to let herself brood so long.

She stood up and went to fetch a sheet from the bed in the adjoining room. This was where the old woman had slept after her husband's death. She wouldn't stay in the marital bed upstairs. She said she couldn't bear the empty space beside her. I would be like that if I lost Nat, Bel thought, as she drew the sheet over her. And what will I be if I lose my Daniel? Oh God, you must, you must protect him! Death can come so easily. The heart fails or a bullet smashes into it and life has gone in a moment." She turned and ran from the room.

She was sitting on a stool in the kitchen with her elbows on the table and her head in her hands, sobbing uncontrollably when she heard Nat arrive with Doctor Harlow and Peggy. They went first to the parlour and she could hear Nat telling Peggy to wait in the hallway for any orders the doctor might give her.

Then very quickly he came to find her and clasped his arms about her and murmured, "My darling, what a shock for you. Don't grieve. Mother wished to go when Father died. She would have wanted it swift like that following her final goodbye to her Daniel. Peggy told me about that as we came along. Don't weep, my precious."

Bel was too honest to pretend. "I'm not crying for her. I'm crying for Dan."

Nat pulled up a stool and sat down by her. "Dan? But he was fit and well when he wrote his letter."

"Yes, *then*. But what may have happened since? Your mother sent off her Daniel and he never came back. Why should the same not happen to us?"

Nat had taken hold of her hands but he released them now and stood up. "Bel, this is an odd time to be obsessed with such worries. I have just lost my mother, my remaining parent –"

She stood up too and gave him a brief hug. "I know. I'm sorry, but the first day I met you you told me she hadn't loved you as a child." He was about to protest but she put her hand over his mouth. "All I can think of is that she let her Daniel go to war against her husband's wishes. And now you have let our Dan go to war against mine! She was punished by his death and now we will be punished by our Dan's."

She sank down again and broke into renewed sobs. The doctor, a small, round man with an air of his own importance, came into the room.

"I was going to ask my lady about Mistress Wilson's last moments but it can wait."

Bel shook her head and brushed her hands across her eyes. "No, I can tell you. I can tell you she hastened her own death –"

"What?" said Nat. "She swallowed something?"

"Did you see her take some pills?" the doctor asked.

Bel gave an hysterical laugh. "She would have liked to do that the day her husband died but she knew right from wrong and refrained. No, she worked herself up into a state of excitement today. She boasted that she had run back from visiting Daniel's grave and then she used my presence to get herself into one of her passionate outbursts. She thanked me for coming and helping her to do that. So she got her way in the end."

Doctor Harlow nodded solemnly. "Exertion and excitement could indeed have finally snapped the thread of life. Her heart was in a fragile state. You are upset, my lady, very naturally, and I could prescribe a soothing cordial –"

"No thank you. I want nothing in life but my son back from the wars and that, I'm afraid, is beyond your prescription."

"I'm afraid it is."

Doctor Harlow bowed and withdrew with Nat to make the necessary arrangements. Peggy slipped back into the kitchen.

"I know it's not the time to mention it, my lady, but what will happen to me now?"

Bel smiled at the girl's round cherubic face. Even when solemn and worried as she was now it was all dimples.

"Well, this is still the vicarage and you are still the vicarage maid and the Reverend Nathaniel will remain the vicar for as long as he's able to. He won't often stay the night but he will probably keep books and papers here now and maybe write his sermons here. Who knows what a few years may bring? He and I may be coming to live here all the time if Sir Daniel marries. It would be right and proper for the baronet and his bride to live at the Hall."

And I won't grudge him the love of a good woman, she said in her heart. I won't feel one pang of jealousy if I can just have him safe a mere half mile away.

"Oh my lady, is Sir Daniel betrothed then?" Peggy asked.

Bel came down with a bump from the happy picture she

had just seen in her mind's eye. "No, Peggy, he is still at sea fighting the Dutch."

Peggy clasped her hands before her face. "Oh how exciting that must be! But oh my lady, he'll be sad to hear about his grandmother and not able to come to her funeral. He used to come here often and when the old reverend wanted to give him books he sometimes took them to please him and then handed them to me at the door and said to put them back on the shelf because his grandfather liked those ones and would miss them. He was very thoughtful that way."

"Was! Don't you dare say 'was', girl"

"Oh I'm sorry, my lady, I didn't mean no harm. It's just it's a long time since he was here."

Bel gave her a hug to conceal the tears she felt rising again. A long time! It was certainly that.

"You're a dear thing, Peggy. Now put clean sheets on the bed in there so she can be laid out, poor old Mother Anne. God bless her and you for your patience with her odd moods."

"Oh thank you, my lady, and for keeping me on. When it's all clean and tidy here and the reverend doesn't want me will I be allowed to run to the farm and help Mother sometimes?"

"Of course you will. She is blessed in having you so near." Bel was still fighting tears. Everything conspired to remind her of Dan's absence.

When she and Nat walked back to the Hall together in the warm twilight she could still scarcely refrain from speaking of Daniel rather than Anne.

"I have more sympathy with your mother now than I ever

did and it's too late. Sometimes I hated her talking endlessly of her Daniel. But we were at one just now a few moments before she died. His sad fate has been eating her up. Those were just the words I used to her about Dan's absence when I'd read her his letter."

Nat stood still on the track and made her face him. "Bel, this must not be. You must seek a calmer spirit. The Bel I married was full of hope and joy in the midst of poverty and homelessness. Your spirits lifted mine. I was doubtful and cautious but you inspired me."

"But I was never calm. I was always passionate. Were you not afraid I would wear you out as your wild mother did your father?"

"Yes, briefly. But then you were full of plans for our little school and I knew that as long as you had a purpose and great activity you would put all that energy to good use. And you always have."

"Oh I can keep busy. Ursula and I will make pies and puddings and sweetmeats for the funeral and then Peggy and I will clean the vicarage out from top to bottom and I will get a plasterer to fill in all the cracks and I will dig the garden and tidy it up for winter and all the time my mind will run on Dan. What is he doing this moment? Where is he? Is he in danger? No, Nat, don't ask me to straightjacket my thoughts for I cannot."

She marched on fast and he had to quicken his pace to catch her up.

He grasped her arm to check her. "Can you not thank God

that Daniel is not in London in the midst of the plague?"

"If I think of that I worry about poor little Eunice if Clifford and Celia have not taken her into the country with them." She looked up at him with a wry smile. "I'm sorry, Nat. I lacked love as a child and thought I could never give it but since I found it I want it to surround me always. To give it and receive it. I could love Eunice if she would let me. If she was here I would fold her in my arms and make love bloom in her, for me, for you, for Daniel. But they are all scattered."

"And my mother, whom you did try to love though she made it hard, has just gone from us. Will you mourn her at all?"

She stood still in the lane and embraced him. She drew his face down and kissed him. "I do already. I want her back so I can love her more than I ever did. But I will not be restored till the living one that I love is with me again. Only I will try not to weep because it distresses you and Ursula."

"That's my Bel," was all he said and they walked on together with their arms twined round each other.

CHAPTER 17

EUNICE had not walked two hundred yards before the enormity of what had happened struck her like a blow. Her father, to whom she had deferred all her life, was dead and she had allowed him to be carted away to a common burial ground, where there would be no memorial. she would never know which of the pits he had been thrown into, and she had spoken no prayer over him.

Crushed with guilt and sorrow she had to put out a hand to a house wall or she would have sunk to her knees. There was not a soul in sight but she could hear the shouts and singing of revellers in the distance. The world was a hostile place but she had sinned grievously and deserved punishment. Night was coming on. She might be free but she was alone and friendless.

She made herself walk on and presently the huge bulk of St Paul's loomed ahead of her. Fearful of the danger from drunken men she decided she must find a dark corner to hide for the night. There would be shelter in the portico at the western door if it should rain and though her father had often denounced the cathedral and its worship as profane and idolatrous she felt some comfort in being close to a building dedicated to God. She climbed the steps and passed under the colonnade. Then she opened up her bundle, drew out her cloak, wrapped it round her and curled up on the paving stones close to a pillar.

The great doors were fast bolted now but she knew they would be unfastened at daybreak and swarms of people would set up their little stalls in Paul's Walk as the nave of the cathedral was generally called. There would be water-carriers, fruit-sellers and a variety of other provision merchants as well as many booksellers. She had with her a copy of Dent's *Plain Man's Guide to Heaven* which she hoped to sell to buy provisions for a day or two till she could find work somewhere. Apart from her father's big Bible which she had left by his bed and her own smaller one she had brought in her bundle it was the only book her father had allowed in the house and she had popped it in among her clothes with one mug she used herself, a small knife and spoon and a wooden plate. Now she was glad it might prove useful.

Sleep eluded her for a long time. Although she was in complete darkness she was afraid of the searchers roaming the city who might come upon her and guess she had escaped from a plague house. She could hear sometimes far off and sometimes alarmingly near the bell of a dead cart. Worst of all were her own thoughts. No one must ever know that she had walked out and left her father to the scavengers of corpses. *God* knows, she told herself, and in His great mercy He has forgiven me.

It was the world of her grandparents before whom she would stand ashamed. They would also berate her for her folly in leaving the only home she had and exposing herself to dangers on the streets. Before she fell asleep she resolved to take on a new identity. The alliterative syllables of Patience Porter came into her head, she didn't know why, unless it was because her father always urged her to be patient.

Patience will be a different character, she decided. She will do what Father always preached, live one day at a time, doing whatever lawful task is put upon her, having no romantic longings, no dreams, no lustful thoughts of a tall, flaxen-haired god.

Why then, she wondered, as she left the cathedral behind her next morning, equipped with a small loaf, a few ounces of cheese, two apples and a bottle of ale, did she turn her feet in the direction of the river. The river meant ships and although she knew no big ships could come as far up as this she might follow the river till she came to some docks. She had no idea how far Deptford and Woolwich were but she had heard them mentioned as places for fitting out and repairing naval craft. She had not totally shed Eunice Horden and it was she who was drawn to any spot where it was just possible she might see Daniel. Patience Porter was to look for some work as a maid or shop girl where she could earn an honest living, meekly serve her master or mistress, read her Bible, think holy thoughts and never look beyond the next day.

Refreshed with a small breakfast of a mug of milk and an orange she set off walking, telling herself this was a new life and nothing in the past was ever to trouble her mind again.

It was nearly Christmas at Horden Hall and Bel with the help of Ursula, hopping up and down ladders like a happy little bird, was decorating the great hall with boughs of holly.

Adam, the groom, came from the kitchen with some letters.

Bel, almost snatching them from him, glanced swiftly through and saw nothing in Dan's writing, but there was one from Celia. At once she imagined it was bad news of Daniel and she darted into Nat's study and flung it on the desk before him.

"You open it. I dare not."

Nat broke the seal and began to read, "My dear Cousins, I have to tell you sad news." His voice faltered and Bel shrieked and clasped her head in her hands.

"No, no, no!"

He was glancing down the page. "No, it is not Dan. It is Clifford."

"Oh." She had sunk into a chair, white as death. "*Clifford*!" She breathed deeply. "Clifford! I care not one iota what happens to Clifford."

Ursula was hovering anxiously at the door which she had left open. Nat beckoned her in. Neither of them had a closer friend than Ursula.

She put her arms round Bel's neck. "My Bel is not chiming charitably but she has had a shock."

Bel kissed her cheek. "Rebuke me all you wish but if he has gone I am only sorry for Celia."

Nat had been reading on. "Well he has not *gone* but he has had a seizure which has left him scarcely able to speak or move. News came that Dutch warships had captured several merchant ships in which he had a large financial interest. I don't think Celia understands how much it will affect his business. Her letter is rather rambling. They had only just returned to London believing the plague to be much declined and Clifford had been growing more and more anxious about the manager whom he had left in day to day charge. Then this news broke." He turned the page. "Wait, there is more here. Oh, that is bad indeed. Not Dan. No, I see Dan mentioned further on. She has seen him. He had leave before this all happened and has gone back to his ship but she says he was well and cheerful."

Bel reached her hand for the letter. "Let me see. How dare she see him well and cheerful when *I* cannot!"

But Nat drew back the letter. "No, Bel. Be satisfied that our boy is alive and well, for here *is* sad news which will grieve you. She believes both William and Eunice have been carried off by the plague."

"Eunice too? Oh that is horrible. Ursula, I am a poor worm. I have not prayed earnestly enough. I have not imagined this plague or how consuming it has been, far away as we are from it. But, Nat, why does she say 'she believes'? Does she not know for certain?"

"I will read what she says. '*A lad called Tom came to our door a few days ago when I was still all in a worry about Clifford with the doctor coming and going and the manager wanting orders and I could hardly attend to this young man. He said he was the son of the leather-worker who lived next door to our son and granddaughter. So of course I enquired how they were and he tells me his family left for the country the very day after William was laid low with the plague. They were terrified that it had got so close and indeed it was in September which was the worst time for deaths since the awful scourge began. Eunice called out to them that her father had died. To tell you the truth the boy broke down in tears then and said he had wanted his father to take her with them but he and his mother were determined she should stay in the house the prescribed time which was a month. He was quite distraught that they had left her to her fate. But now they had returned he tried to find out what had happened and questioned one of the searchers, the men who find out the plague houses and seal them up and then come back to let out the living when the time is over. The man he spoke to said he remembered coming back to that house and there was certainly no one in so he presumed all bodies had been taken away. It wasn't he who had taken them. The crew of that dead-cart had both died of the plague themselves. So I am in a dreadful state you can believe with husband terribly ill and son and granddaughter gone and she no more than twenty years old and with her life ahead of her and as I hoped and prayed a happy marriage to your Daniel.*

'My poor William prophesied dire punishment on the city and the court for all the wickedness and profanity he said was going on and he included his parents in that for he hated us to be prosperous and now we may not be wealthy at all with such disasters falling about our ears and yet he didn't predict his own death or his poor innocent daughter's.

'I am in such a state you must forgive me for not having

mentioned yet your last letter, Arabella, in which you told me your sad news of your mother-in-law's death. Of course I send my sympathy to you and Cousin Nathaniel but the old lady had run her course and death at that age is natural. Clifford is a good deal younger than she was I believe and he has rarely ailed anything.' It is here," Nat said, "that she mentions Daniel but he knows nothing of it yet. She says she leaves it to us to tell him about Eunice if we think fit. She wouldn't know how to get word to him and she thinks it would be cruel to tell him when he may be ordered to sea any moment. Here you may read it all through yourself now, Bel."

Bel took the letter. "I will tell him nothing about Eunice till we know with more certainty what happened to her. Have there not been proper records kept of the names of the dead? Of course Celia is too troubled at present to make inquiries but I would like to go to London myself and find out more. This lad, Tom. I would like to question him more particularly about that day they left London. William's death seems certain if Eunice called out that he was dead, although even that is no proof. William might have been insensible and recovered later and they might both have escaped the city." She shook her head. "I can't imagine William succumbing to the plague. He would fight it as he fought the devil with the whole armour of God. Yes, I would like to go to London, Nat, and comfort poor Celia. Ursula and I could set out as soon as Christmas is over though I scarcely feel in a festive mood for that."

Nat folded his arms and looked at her very steadily. "So you propose going without me –"

"You should not leave the parish and someone must be here to keep things running smoothly."

"What you are hoping is that you will have a chance to see Dan. If his ship is still in dock you will certainly force your way on board."

"Well of course I would."

"I am sorry, Bel, but no one is making that journey in mid-winter. I absolutely forbid it. Maybe when the summer comes we will all go. You know you can trust Sam Turner to keep his eye on the estate. I have taken no time away from my parish and many vicars do so frequently. The Bishop will understand the family circumstances and there are now several young men coming forward for ordination who could be placed as curates where help is needed."

"But summer is so far away. It will be much harder to trace what happened."

"Nevertheless a winter journey is not to be considered. There is no sense in hazarding life and limb on such a quest. Where would be the gain if more deaths or injuries or sickness were the outcome?"

Bel thought she had never seen Nat's mild grey eyes so steely, nor his gentle face so determined. It was good that he was stronger and more assertive than his father Joseph but that didn't mean she would submit.

She got up with compressed lips and Ursula said, "Come, my pretty, back to the greenery."

For now she agreed and returned to the pile of holly, fir and mistletoe on the wooden floor of the hall to pick out the best pieces to decorate the Horden crest. I do not believe Eunice is dead, she kept saying to herself. If Daniel does care for her deep in his heart I will not have him thwarted of his bride. She may not have the beauty or stature expected of the lady of Horden Hall but if he wants her he must have her. Please God keep her alive and safe for him.

Patience Porter was the new maid at the home of a rope-maker in Woolwich. It had taken Eunice four days to walk from St Paul's Cathedral and she had survived the hazard of being seized by drunken sailors in Shoreditch after she had crossed London Bridge the first day. She escaped by screaming at them that she had the plague. After she had used up her provisions two days later hunger drove her to offer her services to an old barrow-man whose barrow had been tipped over by some mischievous youths. Luckily the market area had just been strewn with fresh straw and his fruit was not spoiled. When she had quickly righted the barrow and picked up all the fruit he wordlessly handed her some apples, oranges and a bag of figs. At intervals she would come to a conduit and fill her mug for a drink.

When she reached Woolwich in the middle of a fine autumn afternoon she was thrilled to see ships in the docks. Not knowing what they were she asked a waterman, sitting smoking his pipe on a low wall.

"Yon's a small frigate," he said, "and the bigger one is a ship of the line but only a fourth-rate."

"Do you get larger vessels in here?"

"Not of the first and second rate. But we built the *Mary* here, when it was called the *Speaker*. She's a third rate. The King changed many of the names from the Protector's time. Had the new ones painted on before he'd been a day on the throne." He took his pipe out of his mouth and spat on the ground. Eunice sensed a fellow republican but just smiled in the hope he would talk more for she wanted to lap up all the information she could. "Ay," he said, "if it's great ships you want to see, mistress, you'll need to go on to Chatham. Nay, I forget, we had the *Royal James* in here three or four years back and a great trouble it was to get her in, I can tell you. Just the head of her and then shored her up to wait for the tide. Is your man a seaman then?"

She blushed, but remembering who she was, she shook her head. "I'm looking for work. I'm the only one left in my family from the plague. I came here to get away from it."

"Ay, it's a place to keep away from is London just now." He eyed her up and down. "What sort o' work can a little mite like you do?"

"Oh, shop work. I can read and write and add up. But I'll do anything –sweeping, scrubbing, washing. I'm strong."

He grinned. "There's Harrison, the rope-maker. His wife lost her maid the other day. She's not found anyone yet to take her place." He grinned again and Eunice was not too sure what the grin signified.

"Can you point me out the house? Is it far?"

With the stem of his pipe he indicated a sign on a long low building a little way inland and Eunice read Harrison, Rope-maker. "That's the ropery and very handy it is too, for down there is the ropeyard where they stores everything for the rigging of every blessed ship that comes in here. So he does all right, does Billy Harrison."

"And does he live next door to his long shed?"

"Bless you, no, girl. Mistress Harrison has grander ideas than that, but if you go along to the ropery and say Jack sent you he'll take you home with him when he quits work."

"I thank you." Eunice followed a cart track to the long shed, sorry to leave the river where a fresh easterly breeze carried what she supposed must be the smell of the sea. As she approached she saw the big wooden doors standing open and a rattling and banging of machinery coming from within. Several men were working at different benches, turning wooden handles which twisted three strands of rope into one thicker one. The ropes stretched the whole length of the shed and she stood for a few minutes watching the process fascinated.

A shaggy, thick-set man approached her. "What do you want here?" he demanded.

"Mr Harrison?"

"That's myself."

She waved her hand toward the dockside. "A man called Jack told me your wife needs a maid. I am from London looking for work."

He backed a little from her. "You've not been near the plague have you?"

Eunice, answering for Patience, shook her head but the

lying gesture dug into her conscience. What would her father have said?

"What's your name?"

"Patience Porter."

His grim, hairy face relaxed into a grin like the waterman's.

"Patience you may need, girl. Well, you're small. Can you work hard?"

"Certainly I can." Eunice was beginning to feel apprehensive but she was very hungry and the thought of food and a bed which surely she would be given made her determined to endure anything. She had seen on a milestone at the outskirts of Woolwich how far it was to Chatham and felt she could not go another step today.

Mr Harrison took her arm then and drew her out to the centre of the cart track and pointed to a church. "My house is forty paces to the east of that church. It stands on its own and has a porch with cherry trees either side. Go round to the back door and knock. I reckon she'll take you on."

He was turning back into the shed when she asked, "What will I earn if you please, sir?"

"You'll get your keep. If she likes you maybe three shillings a week."

Eunice nodded and giving him a little bob to show Patience's submissive nature she set her tired legs to follow a cobbled lane towards the church.

The house was easily found and to Eunice looked spacious compared with the hovel she and her father had lived in for most of her life. It was next door to the vicarage and suggested that Billy Harrison for all his uncouth appearance had some status in the town of Woolwich.

Seeing a path to the rear she turned down it and found a small gate in the wall leading to the back door. Beside the door was a large buck-basket full of dirty linen.

She knocked and presently a woman put her head round suspiciously. "Yes?"

"Mistress Harrison?"

"Ye-es."

Eunice could hardly see more than a sliver of the face with black ringlets and one dark eye.

"I understand you are looking for a maid. Your husband said I could come."

The door was opened further and a hand shot out and pulled her in.

The woman was about fifty but her hair was dressed like a young girl's, tied in ribbons either side of her head so the curls dangled forward round her face which was made up very pink and white. Her dress was youthful too, low cut with her bosom pushed up and her waist pinched in.

She fixed her eye on the bundle Eunice lowered from her shoulder.

"What's in there?"

"All I have in the world."

"Are there bugs in it? I will have no fleas or bed bugs in my house." Eunice began to open the bag to show her but she stopped her. "Leave it outside. You will be sleeping in the stable loft. You saw a basket of washing by the door. Do it."

"You are taking me on?"

"Do the washing and we'll see."

Eunice looked round the room which was a large square kitchen but she saw no buck-tub. Mistress Harrison pulled her across the room and shoved her at a door to a washroom where a large buck-tub stood with an under-buck ready below the tap and a worn table and scrubbing brush for obstinate stains. To do a big wash like this was a long process and Eunice doubted whether she had the strength.

"Where do I draw water?"

"We have our own well. Out there behind the stable. Take your bag up the ladder at the back and you'll find your room."

This suggested she was staying so Eunice went outside again, saw the well and the stable and clambered up the ladder to the little room above. There was a truckle bed with very thin bedding but she didn't stop to look about. At least it was better than sleeping on the streets. Dropping her bag onto the bed she climbed down again, drew a bucket of water and carried it in. Mrs Harrison had disappeared.

She drew in the buck basket of washing and sorted it into piles, personal linen, stockings, bed linen and towels. While the water was heating she looked round the kitchen. Father would not have approved. He insisted on their tiny house being cleaned daily. Here the shelves for pots and pans had not been cleaned for some days and the floor needed sweeping. Nothing she supposed had been done since the other maid had left. Hanging from a hook in a corner were several rope ends. She wondered what they were for but she supposed a rope-maker would have lengths to cut off and would bring them home for tying up boxes or bundles.

When the water was hot she knew she would not be able to lift the boiler so she took some out with the copper jug and replenished it from the bucket.

Now she got to work with the washing. There was a poss-stick and the wooden table-top to scrub things on if necessary so she was hard at work when Mrs Harrison came back.

"You'll suit me. What shall I call you?"

"My name is Patience Porter."

"One of these Puritans eh? With a name like that?"

"I was brought up that way."

"Can you use a flat-iron on Mr Harrison's shirts."

"Yes, Ma'am."

"Can I trust you with my lace collars?"

"I haven't been used to lace but I would be very careful. May I ask you something, Mistress?"

The woman brought her brows together and her doll-like face took on a sinister look. "What?"

"I am very hungry since I haven't eaten for many hours. If I could have just a crust of bread so that I will have the strength to finish this work –?"

To her astonishment the woman snatched down a length of rope from the hook and struck her across the shoulders.

"You get supper when supper is made. That's just to let you know I don't stand uppishness."

Eunice was not much hurt but she quickly realised why the last maid had gone and why both the waterman and Harrison himself had been grinning.

She turned back to the washing without a word. Patience, she resolved, will do nothing to give this woman another excuse to use that rope.

This, she soon found, as one day of drudgery succeeded another, was not so easy. Mrs Harrison would not spoil her hands, which she tended as carefully as her face, with any work at all, so Eunice had to cook as well as everything else. Not sure how to prepare some dishes, especially beef joints or venison pasties, which she and her father had never been able to afford, she received many strokes of the rope. Mrs Harrison gave few instructions beforehand but waited for her to make mistakes.

Never mind, she told herself after the first week, she doesn't hit very hard and Patience Porter is learning useful skills. Mrs Harrison must have been a good cook before Mr Harrison's income rose to respectable heights and she gave up work. When I overcook a chicken she tells me she will be able to afford a proper cook soon and I will be relegated to general maid. Still, I am well-fed. I can eat up the left-overs when she's not looking.

The master was a surprise. He dominated his ropery but at home his wife ruled. He seemed to find her adorable, calling her pet names and bending to her will in all household matters.

To Eunice he was merely indifferent. Once or twice he winced when he saw his wife strike her but he said nothing. Only as winter came on and the little room above the stable became bitter cold he did say one frosty morning when Eunice came down trembling with fingers so dead she couldn't make the fire, "You won't leave, will you? You're the first one she's liked."

"Could I have another blanket?" she felt bold enough to say.

Glancing round to make sure his wife had not come downstairs yet he said, "I'll bring something from the shed tonight." What he brought were three large sacks. Two she piled on top of herself at night and the third she hung over the ill fitting door. There was no window and the only daylight that came in was from the gap between the top of the door and the thatched roof of the stable.

The only time she had outside the house to gather news of what was happening in the world was when she was sent on errands to market. Listening to peoples' conversations she learnt that elements of the fleet had been out in the Baltic and the Channel harrying Dutch merchantmen and trying to keep their navy bottled up in port. There was talk too, in January, of a declaration of war by the French.

Her friend, Jack, with whom she sometimes had a brief conversation, shook his head at the news.

"Ay, the French fleet will come up the Channel and we will be squeezed between them and the Hollanders. I doubt if we have the ships or the men to beat them both. The old Armada days are in the past when we drove the Spanish off the seas altogether."

At first this frightened her but when nothing happened on

the French part such talk died down. As the days lengthened however, she began to see recruiting posters for seamen for the spring campaigns against the Dutch and she realised the war was entering a new phase of activity. She saw the press officers come ashore and seize men off the streets, leaving wives and families running weeping to the quayside. She burned at the cruel injustice of it.

Most days though were uneventful and if she had been quick with her purchases she would walk to the dockside and gaze eastward and try to imagine what the open sea was like. Rarely did she turn her eyes westward towards the pall of smoke that marked London. When the wind was in the west the stench of the place drifted down river to her.

London was a different life. London was Father and the strange, intense, moral scrutiny with which he watched over himself and her. Sometimes she wept for him at night, her tears wetting the cover she pulled up round her and bringing out its peculiar damp sack smell. Sometimes she wept for herself and the scrutiny of a different kind that Mrs Harrison exercised over her. Sometimes she wept for Daniel in a sudden passion of longing that one day she would set eyes on him again. At such times she knew that being Patience Porter was a meaningless charade.

When spring comes, she resolved, I will not be afraid to risk sleeping in the open at night and I will leave this place and make my way to Chatham. He must not see me but if I could see him embarking or disembarking, just feast my eyes on him, I would be satisfied that he is still living. Perhaps

Chatham is a bigger place than this and I could get better work teaching in a school.

From time to time she wondered if her grandparents were back at home in the Strand and whether they had ever sought her. She could go back to London and ask them to take her in. There she was most likely to see Daniel when he had leave and called upon them but that would be to walk into another kind of imprisonment. Her grandparents wanted to manipulate her life. They would plunge her into the cruel situation of being rejected by Daniel as his bride. Here she had a kind of freedom when she remembered to be Patience Porter, unemotional, concentrating only on the next task to perform to the best of her ability. In reading her Bible and praying for a quiet mind she achieved intermittently a modest contentment. A day in which she had not once been struck by the rope end was a goal achieved.

CHAPTER 18

DANIEL was very conscious of the renewed activity in the spring. Since France had declared war there was apprehension that a French fleet might come upon them in the Channel. The fleet went out on manoeuvres, the ship's complement was increased and he found himself promoted to lieutenant which gave him great delight. He was saddened by news from home of the death of Grandmother Wilson. She would have been glad, he thought, to know I am making a success of a naval career, something my father and uncle never did as soldiers. Another letter told him Cousin Clifford was ill but this touched him very little, so engrossed was he in fulfilling his new duties. His promotion had come ahead of Henry's which he attributed to his impressing the captain with his study of navigation.

Following the captain's lead he began to take an interest too in the men as human beings rather than the amorphous mass of bodies they had seemed at first. He hated to see floggings which still went on as most of the officers believed extreme harshness was the only way to maintain discipline. They were wary of the captain's methods, as he was of undermining their authority by commuting the punishments they handed out. But Daniel guilelessly listened to the men's troubles and offered to write to wives and families on their behalf particularly if they had been pressed and no compensation paid.

It was at the end of May that the fleet was divided into two, Prince Rupert sailing to intercept the expected French fleet and Albemarle having command of fifty-six ships in the Downs. On the 31st orders came for them to sail north towards Harwich off the Thames estuary and early the next morning they were rounding the Long Sand Head when the cry went up "A sail, leeward, a sail!" But almost immediately more and more sail were in sight and it became obvious that the whole Dutch fleet was bearing down upon them.

"They know we are at half strength here," Henry muttered to Daniel. "Why did our scout boats not warn us of their coming? The admiral could put in to the Thames for safety till Prince Rupert's ships can be summoned."

"No, the signal is up from the flag-ship to engage the enemy."

It was the first time they were going into action greatly outnumbered. What was worse the wind was heeling the ship over so far that the captain gave orders for the gun-ports on the lower deck to be closed. The firepower of the English guns, usually superior, would be greatly reduced.

Daniel was keyed up with apprehension and excitement in equal measure. It was very different from his fear when he climbed alone to the masthead, fingers almost glued to the rigging. The enemy was at a distance and the whole ship and all her crew were equally in danger. Death might come leaping from the mouths of those guns at any moment.

In fact as they passed and repassed the Dutch ships in line all that day the *Elizabeth* somehow escaped the heavy mauling which some of the fleet suffered. By evening two or three ships had to withdraw, no longer fit for service, but the *Elizabeth,* in the middle of the line, was ordered to tack northwards as the Flanders coast was in sight. The ships in the van were left behind and disaster overtook some of them in the night.

Daniel could see from the deck that several were trapped among the enemy and attacked by fire ships. These, the most dreaded sight to all sailors, could be seen creeping like flaming dragons over the water towards their prey. Somehow clever seamanship and firepower enabled some of the English ships to sink them or evade them and fight their way out but in the morning news flew round the fleet that Vice-Admiral Sir William Berkley of the White had been killed and his flagship seized.

The second day of fighting began with fifty English ships against seventy-seven Dutch. Daniel had snatched two hours sleep when they were hove-to and the guns of the distant fight were silent. When he came on deck even the early morning was hot and the temperature increased during the day to sweltering. His shirt, unchanged from the day before, was soon wet with sweat.

The orders were to run down on the Dutch ships and haul up into line when they were close. The Dutch tried to keep their line and for a while the two fleets were passing and repassing as they had done the day before, but soon individual ships were tacking to escape capture or to bring guns to bear on isolated enemy ships. At one stage the Dutch Admiral Tromp was cornered among the English fleet and Admiral de Ruyter took part of his squadron in to rescue him. With his superior numbers he could leave the rest to cover him till he and Tromp had made good their retreat. Daniel had been told that this Tromp was the son of the admiral that he had thrown overboard in his childhood game with home-made boats and stick men. It sickened him now in the bleak reality of war to recall the gleeful brutality of youth.

By nightfall Albemarle had only twenty-eight ships still capable of fight. Daniel and Henry, deafened by the guns, were still standing on their damaged but serviceable third rate.

"We are ordered to the rear," Daniel told Henry. "The admiral must want to use the first rates as a line of defence. They can fire their stern-chasers to harry the Dutch if they attack."

Henry scowled. "I want to be up and at 'em for the damage they did yesterday."

"You are to check the lead. These are shallow waters. I don't trust the charts and the tide is falling so be sure we are in clear water. I am to take charge of the lower gun-deck."

"If we are in the rear you will have nothing to do. We can't fire on our own ships."

"Well we will see how the day turns out. I can't see that the Dutch will let us keep this formation for long. They have enough ships to be in amongst us soon enough."

Daniel allowed his gun-crew some ship's biscuits and a mug of beer at noon and shortly afterwards signals flew round the fleet that Prince Rupert's squadron was in sight in the west. A cheer went up. At last they would be nearer the Dutch in numbers.

The renewed cheerfulness of spirits was short-lived for what Daniel had feared happened. An uncharted shoal lay in the path of the *Royal Prince,* the flagship of Admiral Ayscue and she ran aground later in the afternoon. The Dutch were quickly aware of this and sent fire-ships towards her. Daniel saw the outcome. She lowered her flag and surrendered. Both admiral and crew were taken prisoner and the ship itself burnt. Daniel was deeply moved by the sight. The *Royal Prince* was one of the ships that he had first seen lying in the Thames when he had been inspired to serve in the navy. Its immense height had struck him as awesome and he knew now it had a complement of eight-hundred men. To see it a horrible roaring mass of flame appalled him. It was hard to imagine how Ayscue and his men, now prisoners of the Dutch, must be feeling at the loss of their beautiful ship and their own liberty at a stroke.

I think I would die rather than be taken prisoner, he thought, and yet life is precious. I suppose there will be an exchange of prisoners when this horrible war is over.

Not for the first time he realised he was classifying war as horrible. There had been moments of exhilaration when he saw masts and rigging crashing down on a Dutch ship following a salvo from his own guns and there had been a surge in morale when Prince Rupert's squadron had appeared on the western horizon but most of the two days' fighting had been a hellish blend of noise, smoke and the shrieks of the wounded.

And it was not over. The two fleets regrouped to lick their wounds and be ready to fight again on a fourth day. There was plenty of repair work to be done on their own ship though it had come off well so far. What with the hammering and the groans of the wounded there was little sleep to be had in the short hours of the June night.

On June 4th Daniel found himself on deck again and a bleary-eyed Henry joined him to peer round at what they could see of the other ships of their fleet and at a distance the Dutch.

"The captain says we have about fifty left in the two squadrons combined," he told Henry, "and the Dutch have seventy."

"God in heaven, we are still heavily outnumbered."

"But we have more discipline. The captain says the Dutch are split because the *Royal Prince* surrendered to Tromp. It was *his* prize but de Ruyter ordered the fire-ships to go on and destroy her. Even if she was disabled when she ran aground she could have been towed away when the tide refloated her. So the two admirals will be at odds with each other which gives us a chance to exploit their differences. There could be confused orders from them."

"Well there will be no hanging back today, no sheltering behind the first-rates. We will all be needed."

Daniel nodded, slapped his friend on the back and went down to his gun-deck. He checked the ammunition that was left. The initial allowance of forty rounds a gun was greatly depleted. It would not see out another day's fierce fighting. He swallowed hard, briefly remembered his mother and prayed she did not yet know what was going on here. As they were ordered into line and advanced towards the Dutch fleet he put her swiftly out of his thoughts.

The day began with early passes in line firing as the guns bore but soon individual squadrons and gradually individual ships were fighting their own duels.

It was well into the afternoon when Daniel came on deck to report to the captain that the ammunition was exhausted. The captain was watching the manoeuvres of one of the larger Dutch ships which, sensing by the silence, the *Elizabeth's* helplessness, was passing across their bows to rake them stem to stern. It was within musket range and some sailors were aloft ready to fire. Others lined the foredeck, muskets primed. As they discharged their weapons the first salvo came.

Daniel was aware that Henry had found a musket from somewhere and was also taking aim. Next moment from the corner of his eye he saw Henry's musket flung up into the air and crash to the deck. He turned his head as the trunk of his friend fell backwards. A thing rolled away across the deck, round with protruding ears and eyes wide in astonishment.

The sight made a momentary impact on Daniel's brain but was overwhelmed by more thunderous noise and a splinter was torn from the foremast immediately above the captain's head. He was yelling a warning at two seamen as the yard of the foresail was torn from the rigging and hung above them before crashing to the deck. They flung themselves out of the way but now the captain himself was in danger as another cannon-shot struck the foremast. Daniel flung himself at him and propelled him clear just as the mast split and fell, ripping sail and rigging with it and enveloping them on the deck. Daniel could hear the shrill screaming of a boy who must be trapped under the mast. "I am alive," he told himself and found he still had his arms about the captain's waist.

"Sir, are you hurt?" He freed his knife from his belt and slashed at the sail.

The captain rolled over and their faces were within a few inches of each other. The captain was bleeding from a deep scratch on his forehead but seemed unaware of it. "Thanks to you, lieutenant, I am unhurt. And you?"

"Likewise sir." He enlarged the slit he had made and scrambled upright and helped the captain to his feet. When he put his weight on his right leg Daniel became aware of a searing pain in the side of his calf just above the ankle bone. He looked down and saw six inches of a splinter of wood protruding through his stocking which was rapidly turning from white to red. The sight made him feel sick and faint but he thought, it's only a flesh wound. What of that boy who was screaming? What of the ship itself? What of Henry?

The big Dutch vessel had moved on to wreak further havoc among the smaller English ships but it had left devastation behind.

Daniel saw the boy soon enough, the mast crushing his chest. He was dead. There were men crawling about, bleeding but struggling to free themselves from sheets and sails. Daniel tried to step out to help them but some rope tugged on the splinter in his leg and he almost screamed out. In fury he reached down and dragged the splinter out, aghast at its length.

The acute pain lessened though he was aware of leaving a trail of blood. But with his knife ripping the sail he was able to help several men to their feet and set them to carry the wounded below.

Seeing another place where there was a bulge in the sail and a stain of blood he slashed another hole and Henry's eyes looked up at him. Except they were not looking. There was vacancy. Enlarging the hole he found only the gaping bloody neck and no body. And then he knew he had seen it happen. He had seen the head with its protruding ears bouncing over the deck into this corner.

He staggered to the side and vomited. The noise of the guns roared in his ears and then shrank to a thin buzzing as his vision blurred and he subsided to the deck.

He became aware of someone lifting his head and putting a cup to his lips. He drank greedily, realising it was not beer but good quality wine. His eyes cleared and he saw to his astonishment that he was in the captain's cabin. His right leg was heavily bandaged and throbbed fiercely but the wine revived him and he sat up himself and looked about. It was the captain, his head bound up, who had been helping him to drink.

"Sir," Daniel exclaimed, "you administering to me!"

"Why not, man? I owe you my life. Besides below-decks is thick with the wounded everywhere and the surgeon and his mates are sorely overstretched."

Daniel became aware from the squeaking and groaning of the timbers that the ship was underway.

"Is the battle over? Where are we heading?"

"We are under tow, limping into Sheerness."

"Did we lose?"

The Captain shook his head. "No one won. Losses have been terrible on both sides. Yes, we had to withdraw and no doubt the Dutch – what's left of 'em – will go home and celebrate a great victory. But you will all be laid off while repairs are carried out. Go home to Northumberland, Lieutenant, and get that leg healed before you report for duty again."

"I'll soon be fit, sir. Branford and I will stay with his family in London. It takes a mighty long time to get to Northumberland and back if the muster is called."

The captain's face clouded. "Branford? I thought you knew. We found you close to his –"

Daniel clasped his hands over his face, shutting his eyes, but he couldn't shut out the image. "Oh God, sir," he mumbled at last, "how can I tell his mother and father?"

"Let us hope the casualty lists are printed before you see Lord and Lady Branford but I fear they run into many thousands. Tell them he died in an act of great courage. He snatched a fallen seaman's musket and aimed at the Dutch commander before he was struck."

Daniel wept.

"You enlisted at the same time but I believe you were already old friends."

"From Cambridge, sir. And *his* father and *my* father were friends in their time at the University."

The captain patted his arm and moved the wine bottle and glass within his reach. "Rest, lad. I must on deck."

Daniel lay back on the pillow. Henry was dead. The Captain had spoken the word Northumberland which sounded sweet to his ears. If he could get back there would his mother ever let him return to the navy? Surely this wound would heal quickly. His leg was not broken. He was a fit man compared to many he could hear now moaning or screaming under the surgeon's knife as crushed limbs were amputated. But did he want to come back? Did he want again the hell he had already been through these last four days? Was that cowardly? He had entered under the King's own sponsorship. He had longed to serve him but in what way was the king served by losing so many good ships and men – for what? And Henry his friend was dead. They had knelt together in the King's presence and received their commission from him. But would the seas be any safer for Henry's death? Would trade prosper?

Daniel sat up and poured himself another glass of the captain's best wine. He wanted oblivion but it was a long time coming. At last, unaware that the captain had come quietly back and laid down on cushions on the deck beside the bed, he fell asleep.

CHAPTER 19

"WELL, I hope you are satisfied, Reverend Nathaniel Wilson Horden. He is wounded. He has written from Cousin Celia's where he is staying."

Bel had run all the way to the vicarage on the hot late June day with her letter in her hand. Nat had visited a sick parishioner and was sitting on the bench outside in the sunshine preparatory to walking home to the Hall for his dinner.

The vicarage garden was full of the scent of roses which rambled up the walls of the house since he had himself ripped out the ivy and encouraged the neglected roses to climb. He smiled and made room for her on the bench.

"So I get called by my full name instead of the usual Nat and you are laughing as you say it so I take it he is not seriously hurt and you are mightily relieved that for the moment he is out of the war."

She sat down panting. "Oh Nat, I am, but of course he is making light of it to spare us anxiety. It is his right leg and he can walk about with a stick. Maybe he has lost it altogether and the stick is a crutch." She handed him the letter.

He looked it over rapidly. "But this is tragic. Henry Branford is dead. What must my old friend Edward and his wife be feeling and you are all smiles because our Dan is safe. Do you care more about that than their grief?"

Bel stuck out her chin. "Yes, if I am honest. And so would any mother. I can feel Lady Branford's agony only too well but if you are asking me whether I would rather Dan had been killed and Henry spared then no, I would not. He says Henry was mowed down right next to him. Do you see then how close our Dan was to death? Have I not been right to worry all these months? But now that is not the point. You see that he has been told of William's death and Eunice's disappearance. He will be restless and anxious on that account and will want to go searching for her. I must go to him at once."

Nat looked back at the letter. "What he says is, '*Unwittingly I have come from one scene of death and destruction to another. Poor Cousin Celia is stricken by her husband's illness and also the loss of her son and granddaughter to the horrible plague. I do not think any of us at sea realised how awful that was and what a swathe it has cut through the population of London. I grieve for little Eunice. They say no one knows where her body is or I would go and strew some flowers on her grave.*' Does that sound as if he believes her to be still alive?"

"Well, *I* have a feeling here" – she laid her hand on her heart – "that she is alive somewhere. I want to question that leather-worker's boy who was the last to see her. Anyway, what say you, my husband? Do we go to London and bring our boy home?"

"He writes of returning to his ship when it is seaworthy again –"

"Never, if I can prevent it."

Nat got up with a sigh and took her hand. "Well, we will go but we had better send word ahead by the post which will be quicker than we could make it."

"If we had good horses at every stage and rode the whole way I wager we could do it as fast as the post."

"We haven't and we have arrangements to make before we can go. Come let us have our dinner. Ursula always has it ready by noon."

Eunice had seen Daniel. Jack, the waterman, had kept her informed as news of the battle filtered back.

"Eh, there's many a good ship lost and the Lord knows how many good men dead and wounded."

"Where will they bring the wounded? Is there a hospital in Chatham?"

"Not what you'd call a regular hospital. They billets them all over the place and is supposed to pay for their keep but I never heard of anyone getting paid for nursing a sick sailor yet."

"Will all the ships be brought into Chatham?"

"Nay, we may get the third rates here. If there's as many battered to bits as I hear they'll need every dockyard there is in the river."

Eunice inquired if there was any way of finding out which ship an officer was serving in but she was told the lists would be at the Navy Office in Seething Lane, back in the City. If she could have broken her vow to be Patience Porter she would have walked all that way back. As Eunice Horden she was ready to throw up her position at the Harrisons at any moment but she waited, torn between the two roles, and was rewarded one morning by hearing Mr Harrison tell his wife that two third rates were coming in and they would need "Miles of new rope. Thou shalt have a new summer dress, my lovely."

Mrs Harrison had a dressmaker in the town and as soon as he had gone to work she ordered Eunice to guard the house with her life and have dinner on the table at noon. She was going to choose her material for the dress and another for the petticoat and she would be "some time about it."

Eunice watched her go and after five minutes tidying up to be sure her mistress didn't come back for something she had forgotten she slipped out of the back door, locking it behind her and placing the key under a flower pot by the step. She ran towards the river by a route that didn't take her past the rope-works.

Her waterman was not there but there was great bustle in the dockyard and looking down river she saw the sorry sight of two ships of the line being towed towards the docks. Both had masts and rigging destroyed and many gun-ports smashed. Keeping hidden behind a shed she watched the slow process of them being eased alongside the quay and the gangplanks lowered. First came the *Mary* which she remembered the waterman telling her had been built here. Many wounded were carried off but she couldn't discern most of their faces so swathed in bandages they were. Officers supervised the exodus and she looked hard at them but none had Daniel's height. The *Elizabeth* docked further along the quay so she scuttled by, dodging behind the many small buildings to a place where she could peep from behind bales of straw on the quayside and watch the entry port at close quarters.

Again wounded men were the first to be carried off, then came some walking wounded. She scanned the officers she could see on deck but none were Daniel. She was just about to turn away, thinking of the beating she would get if the dinner were not on the table, when she saw a flaxen head emerge from below decks.

It was he.

She knew him instantly and her throat contracted so she could hardly breathe. As he came up slowly she saw he had his hat in his hand and was holding out the other to the man she guessed must be the captain. They shook hands and the captain gestured to a seaman who came running up with a crutch which Daniel tucked under his right arm. Then he put on his hat and limped to the gangway.

He is hurt, she thought. He has suffered pain. That sweet boy is now a man.

She noticed several coaches drawn up in the roadway behind her. She dodged round the straw bales as Daniel passed and she watched him climb with some difficulty into one of them followed by two other officers who seemed fit and healthy. Presumably many would be laid off while their ship was refitting. She studied his profile and thought he looked drawn and exhausted. He certainly winced with pain as he climbed in. The coach drew away.

"Where will they be going?" she asked the driver of the next one.

"London, of course, mistress."

She ran back to the Harrisons' house. Why did I leave London? she asked herself. I am not Patience. I could go back. I could see if Grandfather and Grandmother are in their house in the Strand. She let herself in, thankful that her mistress had not yet returned, but aware that she had barely half an hour to make dinner.

Oh father, she thought, you kept my lustful thoughts at bay. What am I to do without you? That man there has forgotten my existence. He is nothing in my life. Oh yes, Daniel Horden's parents might be happy to wed their son to me for Grandfather's wealth and my grandparents would encourage it to keep their business within the family but I could never be forced upon an unwilling man. She couldn't banish from her mind the vehemence with which he had said, "The idea of being in love with Eunice is preposterous."

Let him remain a man whom she might – if God willed it –see occasionally at a distance. But was it God's will? She had walked far to put herself in a place where chance might throw him in her way and it had been some months before chance had obliged. Eunice had done wrong as usual and Patience, trying to perform her daily tasks dutifully, would suffer for it.

She had to make up the fire before she could boil the piece of beef in its cloth that had been selected for dinner. She half filled the brass cauldron and swung it round over the flames, dropping in the beef before the water had boiled and adding plenty of salt and pepper. There were still ten minutes before the Harrisons would be back so she threw in carelessly chopped turnip and onions, in her haste forgetting to place them in their net so they could be easily extracted. There was no time to make one of the complicated sauces Mrs Harrison favoured but she put some flour in a pan and spooning out some of the broth she thickened it and added a sprinkling of herbs from the jars on the larder shelf. She was still stirring this over the fire to stop it from going lumpy when she heard Mr Harrison come in.

"What, your mistress is from home?" he exclaimed looking about him.

"She went shopping, sir."

Eunice knew her face was red and moist from the heat, her hair had escaped from its pins and hung damply over her forehead.

He was wiping his own brow from the noon heat outside and didn't stay in the kitchen but walked through to the adjoining room where they always dined.

"The table is not set," she heard him shout.

Standing the pan on the hearth she scurried in and began laying the cloth and napkins and a knife each when she heard Mrs Harrison come in. She went first into the front parlour presumably to lay down her purchases but then came straight on to the kitchen where she must have tested the beef with a skewer because she screeched out. "The meat is not cooked. What have you been doing, girl?"

Patience walked meekly back into the kitchen and answered truthfully, "I went out to see the ships come in and was late back."

"You will be whipped," Harrison said, following her, "and this time you have deserved it. The house is never to be left empty."

He looked quite pale with anxiety and ran out and up the stairs right to the attics. He must hide his savings up there, Eunice thought. I should have thought of a good excuse but Patience is more truthful than I.

Mrs Harrison was standing in the middle of the kitchen with a bunch of rope ends in her hand. "You wicked, disobedient girl!" She began to lay about Eunice's head and shoulders with all the strength of her arm. "I thought I had found a good girl at last but you are as bad as the rest of them."

Eunice ducked and weaved to stop the ropes from stinging her face.

"Please, Mrs Harrison. I am truly sorry. Pray stop hitting me. The beef will be cooked soon and there are vegetables boiled with it. But I will leave at once."

She slipped under her arm and made for the back door.

Mrs Harrison lowered the ropes. "What? Now!" She looked down at her own hands and brushed from their smooth plump backs bits of hairy rope.

Mr Harrison clattered downstairs again his face relieved and his colour returning. "All is well, my dear."

"She speaks of leaving us, Bill. I haven't told her to go. I don't want her to go. See my beautiful hands and I have brought the silks I have chosen for the dress and petticoat to show you."

"You will be the loveliest lady in Woolwich," he said. "And if you don't beat Patience again she will stay."

Eunice was standing with her hand on the door latch.

"But she must never leave the house unguarded again," he added hastily.

Mrs Harrison hung up the rope ends. She frowned at Eunice. "They will stay there as a warning." She stalked out of the room. "Come and look at these silks," she told her husband.

So I am to stay, Eunice thought, and when I go errands I can have a quick look to see how his ship is coming on for he will surely come back to it when it is ready for sea. She found a clean rag and wiped her neck where she could feel blood trickling down. If her dress was marked she would have to change it and try to sponge out the stain. She only had one other, plain grey like this, and two shifts. Would her small wages ever enable her to buy more clothing?

She prodded the beef. It was nearly done.

Daniel received his mother's letter with mixed feelings, joy that he would see her and his father soon, fear of what they would make him do. He had seen such horrible injuries on other men that his own seemed negligible. It was never going to be enough to justify him quitting the navy. But the image of Henry's head rolling across the deck would not leave him.

He had endured a painful morning with Lord and Lady

Branford trying to avoid giving them the details of his death. "Where was he hit? Did he suffer long?"

He could hardly speak of it without weeping himself but he could assure them his death was instantaneous and he was commended for his bravery.

Although Cousin Celia had been pleased to see him when he had first presented himself at their door he was aware of a change in the atmosphere of the house which was not due only to the master's being bedridden. Before there had always been an air of unlimited wealth. There were more servants than work to keep them busy. Now there was a lady's maid for Celia and two chambermaids, but only one footman to answer the door and run errands. In the kitchen there was certainly a cook and Daniel supposed two or three kitchen maids. There was still a coach and two horses and a groom but Celia went out very seldom. She spoke little to Daniel of their affairs but he suspected that she was concerned at the proposed visit of his father and mother. How long would they stay and would it be hard to keep up appearances before them?

Although she urged him to spend time with Clifford Daniel went into that room with great reluctance. The first time had been a shock. To see the intimidating merchant lying propped up on pillows unable to utter coherent sentences was a horrid embarrassment.

As soon as he entered the room he found Clifford's eyes fixed on him and it was obvious that he was trying to rebuke him. His right fist came up and he seemed to be wagging a forefinger at him. Sounds came from his lips.

"Why 'avy 'ot 'ave my 'ip?"

When Daniel looked to Celia, who had accompanied him, for help in deciphering this, she said, "Don't be alarmed that he looks angry. It is not with you."

Clifford however was still gesturing fiercely at him and repeating the same sounds.

"I think he's trying to ask you why the navy didn't save his ships – from the Dutch you see. There was much merchandise aboard, some that came from the West Indies."

Now Clifford was nodding and still directing angry looks at Daniel.

"Tell him about the battle. Tell him all the news you can. He's hungry for information."

So Daniel described everything that had happened since he had joined the navy apart from Henry's death, but when he got up to go Clifford tried to grab him and hold him back.

It was the same every time he looked in on the invalid. Clifford always wanted more news even when nothing was happening but the fleets refitting and rearming.

"Will he get any better?" he asked Celia but she shook her head sadly.

"The doctor says it's very unlikely. If he had been going to recover from the seizure it would have happened by now. I can't tell you how wretched it makes me seeing him so helpless. He is always asking for Richard Corcoran to come and talk about the business. We left him in charge when we went into the country you know but when I send messengers it is only one of the under-managers who comes very reluctantly and can tell him little of the state of things. They are frightened to see him like this, that's the truth of it. I suppose the war has disrupted everything and they know not where the merchant vessels are. I'm sure *I* don't know so I just keep telling him it'll all come right when the fighting stops and he mustn't worry. Of course that just makes him more frantic than ever. I wonder when your dear parents will get here."

To escape from this sad household Daniel, disobeying doctor's orders, took short walks usually heading towards Whitehall so as not to pass the Branford's mansion. But one day he thought he would walk into the City and look at the little house where William and Eunice had lived. He found it easily enough. The door was standing open and a young man was sitting at the old deal table which had been moved nearer the door for the light. He was stitching pieces of leather together with a fierce looking needle.

He looked up startled when Daniel appeared in the doorway.

"Oh sir. You are of the Horden family." He jumped up and putting down his work, came round the table and bowed. "I remember seeing you call here, sir, in the old time before the plague." He went on breathless with apologies. "Pray don't think we are doing wrong in using this place. If ever anyone comes to claim it we will move out at once. If we had left it vagabonds would have broken in at night and slept here, taken it over no doubt. Many houses left empty by the plague have gone that way. Of course when we got back here my mother made me scrub it all out and burn the clothes and bedding on a bonfire. The preacher's Bible is still here if you want it, sir."

"No no, I came out of curiosity to look at the place. He was second cousin to my mother. I was at sea when the plague struck and didn't hear till much later that both he and his daughter had perished. Please carry on with your work."

The youth bowed again and ducked back to his place. When Daniel leant against the doorpost as if he wanted to say more the boy looked up again.

"It was never official, sir, that Mistress Eunice perished but I fear it was so. There was bodies carried by with names chalked on the shrouds but some was just 'Boy child from Fetter Lane' or 'Old Woman from Milk Street'. No one could say who they was, sir."

Daniel had a fearful picture of Eunice's dainty body stuffed into a sack and dumped on a cart to be trundled to the nearest plague pit.

"What's your name, lad?"

"Tom Fletcher, sir."

"Tell me how it was, Tom. Her father died first? Is that right?"

The boy described exactly what he had seen that night.

"You think she went back to the house, fell ill and died there."

Tom nodded. He had tears in his eyes.

"We carried on our business south of the river where my mother's sister lives and the Baker moved away too and most of the lane did or died where they stayed. There weren't people around to know if she came back."

"I thank you, Tom." Daniel held out a shilling to him but he shook his head.

"Preacher William was a good man. He taught me to read and write and she – she was always kind to me. I miss them."

Daniel inclined his head. I do, he thought, not William much, but it is very grievous to come here and not see her little timid face and those deep searching eyes. There was so much hidden passion in that small body waiting to be released from the cage of her upbringing.

To hide his own tears he turned sharply away and unthinkingly put all his weight on his injured leg. A tearing pain shot through it and he couldn't help an audible gasp. Feeling faint he hung over his stick for a moment to recover himself.

"Are you all right, sir?" The boy was at the door looking up into his face.

He smiled down at him. "War wound. I haven't walked as far since I got it."

"I can run for a hackney from the Stand."

"Thank you, but I should walk. I'll never get fit if I sit too much." He waved a hand and saw the lad return to his work.

As he walked he felt a wetness in the bandage over which he had stretched his white stocking that morning. When he was out of sight round the corner he looked down and saw a stain creeping over the stocking and spreading down his leg.

Damnation, he muttered, the wound has opened up when I thought it was knitting well the last time it was dressed.

Nevertheless he walked back and at last reached the house

with the walnut tree. He was exhausted from the pain and the effort but as he turned in at the gate the front door opened and his mother came running towards him.

He almost fell with the violence of her embrace.

She was sobbing and laughing. "Oh Dan. It's really you. Let me hug you to pieces."

"Let me get inside and sit down."

"Of course you are hurt. I'm a fool! Oh look at your poor leg. Why have you been walking on it? Lean on me. Nat, Nat, he's here. Come and help," she shouted.

Then his father was there too at his other side and together they propelled him into the hallway and onto the velvet sofa that sat against the panelled wall.

They were all in tears at the joy of reunion.

Cousin Celia came wobbling from the kitchen where she had been checking that the dinner was ready.

"Oh good, good, he is back and the dinner isn't spoiled. Why would you go out walking so long and not be here to greet your parents?"

Mother Bel intervened at once in his defence. Oh it was wonderful to be in her presence again. It was a true restoration.

"He didn't know we would be here today, Celia. We lay not far from London last night and came on early. But look at his poor leg!"

Celia threw up her hands. "The doctor said he should still be resting it. Wherever have you been, you bad boy?"

Celia, Daniel noticed, had become more like a grandmother to him these last days.

"I went to look at William's house."

"Ha! He means Eunice's. Poor lad he is mourning her sadly, Arabella. But we must get that leg dressed again. I'll tell cook to hold dinner."

Daniel stood up, gritting his teeth at the pain. "Pray don't. It can get no worse if I am sitting at table and I'm hungry. Something smells very good."

As they went in Bel kept her arm twined about his waist. She couldn't stop looking up at his face.

"You've aged, my little Dan," she whispered, "and I've aged missing you. We must go home soon. You can't walk about in a coach so we'll be sure you are resting that leg."

"But my ship –"

She reached up and laid her finger against his lips.

"No more ship now I've got you back. I want you at Horden Hall." She nodded towards Celia at the dining-room door giving orders to the maid while they took their places at the table. "She is not happy with us here. I could tell at once. We've been up and seen Clifford and he too is distressed at our presence. We will go as soon as it can be arranged."

Daniel was concentrating too hard on showing no outward sign of the pain in his leg to argue with her.

CHAPTER 20

EUNICE, relying on her waterman's gossip, learnt that there had been another battle on St James Day in early August when the English had been successful and had later raided and destroyed 'hundreds' – so he said – of Dutch Merchantmen in a great bonfire of ships off the Zuyder Zee. She had seen with her own eyes that the *Elizabeth* was still under repair in Woolwich Dock so Daniel, she thanked God, could not have been involved.

Mrs Harrison had been much more forbearing with the rope ends since the last incident and Eunice had tried not to prolong her outings to a suspicious length. There was no danger of her arousing anger one day in late August when she had been sent to buy a long list of provisions at the market because Mrs Harrison had her dressmaker in fitting yet another new dress she had had made.

So Eunice was happy to linger when she heard two prosperous-looking gentlemen sitting at tables outside an alehouse discussing the state of the war.

She asked for a glass of small beer and sat at the next table.

The younger and smarter of the men slapped his pewter mug on the table. "What I say is the Dutch are as weary as we are of all this loss of trade. They'll not have the will to launch another attack for a long time."

The older man in a long wig shook his head. "Ah but they'll pick off our merchantmen where they can to avenge their losses at the islands of Vlie and Terscelling. Merchants are fearful of trusting their goods to the sea now which is bad for trade. If they don't get their stuff out how can they buy more?"

"They will, they will. You are an old doom-monger. There's talk of peace terms. The big merchants in the City are ready to bet on that and will vie with each other to be the first to launch out again."

"Nay, I'm not so sure of that. There's many frightened by what happened to Horden."

Eunice started at the name and listened intently.

"Horden? His trade is mainly in the West Indies is it not?"

"It was. Have you not heard? He lost several cargoes in succession to Dutch action. He'd gone into the country to escape the plague and left the business to his manager Richard Corcoran. *He* speculated to reclaim their losses and now that has gone wrong too. They say he's vanished with what's left of the fortune and poor old Horden has died of shock."

"Clifford Horden dead? That *will* alarm the City. If a big business like Horden's can disappear who is safe?"

"Well, that's what I'm saying."

Eunice drank off her glass and slipped away. Her mind was hardly on the purchases she had to make. Grandfather was dead! As she went from stall to stall and her two baskets became heavier and heavier she was repeating to herself,

"Grandfather dead!" It wasn't until she was trailing back to the Harrisons' house, weighed down with her purchases, that she began to apply her mind to the loss and what it meant for her.

Going in the back door she could hear voices in the front parlour so the dressmaker was still there. She began to unpack, refilling herb jars from the packets she had bought, replenishing the empty earthenware crocks with butter and cheese in the larder and hanging up the shoulder of lamb on its hook. The fresh local apples she had bought she kept out on the table for today's pudding.

She hung the empty baskets on pegs in the wash room out of the way of rats and began the preparations for dinner. All the time she was saying to herself, Grandmother is alone now. She has lost her son and her husband and must believe I too am dead. It is possible that Daniel is staying with her but I think he will be recovering at home in Northumberland. His mother will want him there. She always looked at him with such love and pride. But poor Grandmother! I have been selfish in running away. I know why she and Grandfather didn't try to take us into the country with them. They knew Father would not desert what he saw as God's work for him in London and that I would never leave him. Dear God, I left him when he was dead and for that I will always feel guilty. But since then I have pursued what Eunice wanted whilst trying to live a lie as Patience Porter. That must stop. Grandmother needs me. I must care for her in her old age. I must give her the love that Grandfather only showed her sparingly and my poor father not at all.

She stirred the broth in the cauldron, round and round unnecessarily when she should have started on the apple pie she was to make. Upon hearing Mrs Harrison showing her dressmaker out, she began to peel the apples.

When her mistress looked into the kitchen Eunice said at once straight out, "Mistress Harrison, I am afraid I must leave you. I am needed in London by my grandmother. I will work my week but then I must go."

Mrs Harrison's mouth hung open. "How did you hear that? You have had no letters. You are making this up. You have never mentioned a grandmother."

Eunice realised she could be in very great trouble if she revealed she had been working under a false name. One lie led to another as her father had always said. But the lie popped out easily enough.

"A messenger came seeking me and saw me shopping. I must go to my grandmother. She has no one but me. I needed to earn my own bread but now she is alone I must look after her."

"Let her come and live in Woolwich so you can keep an eye on her."

"She wouldn't leave London. She has a house there. I must go to her."

Mrs Harrison was glaring round at the kitchen and the dinner preparations. "Where is the pastry for the tart?"

"It's not made yet, Ma'am."

"And Mr Harrison will be here any minute! You are

hopeless, girl. As I have always said, I must get a cook-maid. You are dismissed. You can go at once."

She stormed out of the room and went to the front door to look for her husband.

Eunice, or perhaps it was still Patience, quietly went on with her preparations. There wasn't time to make pastry so she stewed the apples with some cloves and put them in a dish decorated with cherries.

She heard the master come in and remonstrate with his wife.

"My precious, she cannot leave till you have found someone else. Think of your lovely hands. I will put bills up and in the newspaper that you need help and if Patience will write some lines that she is leaving of her own accord and this has always been a happy place that will bring the girls in."

This Eunice knew she would have to do. She excused herself for the deception with the thought that she had had some contentment in her own soul and had perhaps taught her mistress that beating did not produce the best servants. Still her conscience troubled her that evening when she put her name to this declaration as 'Patience Porter'.

Four days later on September the third a gangly girl, taller than Eunice, but looking no more than fourteen was taken on. The rope ends had disappeared and Mrs Harrison, her hair frizzed into the tightest ringlets and wearing her new rose pink gown and cherry-blossom petticoat, welcomed her with smiles.

To Patience she gave a curt farewell nod and Eunice,

shedding her alias, walked out of the house, carrying the bundle she had set out with and in her purse enough money from her saved wages to get to London by river.

It was early on a Monday morning and she was surprised to see an unusual number of boats coming down river and disembarking at the stairs. They were filled not only with people but many household goods, furniture and chests of clothes and musical instruments.

"What is happening?" she asked Jack the waterman who had got himself a skiff and was preparing to leave with a man she now knew to be his son.

He spat on the ground as he usually did before answering. "When there's work to be done even an old 'un must make a killing."

"If you are going upriver have you room for me," she asked, "as far as London."

"Is it the burnt part you want or the rest?"

"What do you mean?"

"Are you the only soul that doesn't know London took fire yesterday morning and it's spreading fast. Folks are getting their goods out to friends and relations that live in these parts. Come down in if you're coming but the City is burnt to the waterline at the bridge."

Eunice, sure he must be exaggerating since fires in London were common enough, clung on to the rail and descended the slippery steps. "I am going to the Strand. Can you get me to Milford Stairs?"

He took her hand and jumped her into the boat, an

unusual courtesy, the watermen being notoriously surly.

"Sit you there under the hood. When we're turned around you'll have shelter from that east wind, and don't you fret, the flames won't have got as far west'ard as Milford Stairs."

Several other passengers squeezed in and the old man and his son pushed off and were soon rowing vigorously.

Eunice sat clutching her shawl about her more with excitement than cold for the morning was sunny again after a long dry spell. She didn't expect to see Daniel at the end of this day but there was a sliver of hope that she might. She could do so without embarrassment since she had such good reason to visit her grandmother. She would meet him coolly and give him her hand without a tremor. But even as she thought of it she quivered and pressed her hands together over the string of her bundle which she carried on her lap.

"Not cold are you?" The old boatman was at the oars nearest to her and grinned up into her face. "Take a turn here and you'd be warm enough."

"I am not cold I thank you."

She decided to look about her at the busy river and put aside all thoughts of the end of her journey. It was such a joy to be out of the Harrisons' house with no chores to do that day. Even under the boat's hood she could feel the fresh air coming from the sea and not the stifling heat from a kitchen fire. She took gulps of it and gave thanks that Patience Porter was no more.

As they neared London she was shocked to see a vast cloud of reddish smoke shrouding the City. This was no common fire. The other passengers were all speaking of it. Some had come to see if friends and relations were safe or in need of help to get away. What will be the fate of our little house? she wondered. I would like Father's Bible from it. How he treasured it!

Rounding the next bend in the river they could see the Tower and behind it a great mass of flame reaching up into the sky.

"What are they doing to stop it?" she cried.

One of the passengers said, "I heard they pulled down some houses to make a clearance but they did it too near the fire and it burnt through the debris before they could shift it. The timbers are brittle dry with all the sunshine we've had. There needs to be some order taken and things managed better or the whole city will go – even beyond the walls."

The skiff passed some stairs where people were waving and calling out. The fire could be seen and heard behind them for the roaring and crackling was now fearsomely loud.

"We'll pick 'em up on the way back," the old waterman said, "but we can't take much baggage."

They now shot through the arches under London bridge and set down one or two at each of the stairs till Eunice was the only one left. She was so horrified at the extent and fury of the fire that she could hardly think of the coming encounter with her grandmother. But by the time they had reached Milford Stairs they had left the fire behind. She fumbled in her purse for what seemed an exorbitant fare.

"It's a mighty long row from Woolwich," the old waterman

said, seeing her alarm and hesitation.

His son looked round and growled, "If she has friends in The Strand she can afford it." It was the first thing he'd said the whole trip.

Eunice frowned at him but didn't stop to haggle. She was glad to get out with only a few splashes of wet and mud on her skirt and, negotiating the steps, she climbed the narrow alley to the roadway of The Strand. Even here the sky was darkened by the thick pall of smoke but surely the fire itself was quite far away. The sight of it though as they had passed had been so horrific that it loomed in her mind's eye like a great pursuing monster devouring all in its path. Fear made her set off almost at a run towards her grandmother's house. Would she feel safe, even when she was inside, so swift was the speed of its travel?

When she reached the house it looked as it had always looked, comfortable and sedate. She saw it with new eyes since her father's death. Before that the sight of it had always been coloured by his disapproval, a 'temple to Mammon' he had often called it. Now it was hiding death and suffering and loss.

As she ran up to the front door her heart expanded with love and longing for her grandmother.

A sharp-featured woman in cap and apron whom she didn't remember opened the door to her knock.

"If you're peddling things we don't want 'em."

Eunice realised that in her very worn dress, shabby shawl and with a bundle over her shoulder she must not resent this greeting.

She put out a hand as the woman was closing the door. “Mrs Celia Horden will want to see me. I am her granddaughter.”

“No you’re not then for she’s dead. I know your sort, talk your way in and then it’s what you can pick up quick. I’d like to know what’s in your bundle from other folks’ houses.”

Eunice lowered her bundle. “I’ll show you. Perhaps you will recognise your mistress’s handwriting.”

The woman, still very suspicious, peered at the Bible she drew out. But before Eunice could open at the fly leaf to show that Celia had indeed given it to her as a child, she jumped back inside and yelled, “Robert! Guard the back door. There could be men breaking in while this girl’s keeping me talking at the front.”

“No truly –” Eunice began and then saw behind her the round figure of her grandmother hovering on the stairs.

“What is the trouble, Betty?”

“Grandmamma!” Eunice called.

“Oh dear Lord, it’s the child’s own voice!” Celia almost tumbled down the stairs, clutching at the banister to check her descent.

Betty stood aside, muttering that she was only doing her duty and how was she to recognise folks as was supposed to be dead and gone.

Eunice slipped her Bible back into the top of her bundle and letting it fall within the door, ran into her grandmother’s arms.

Celia was at first speechless with sobs. At last she held her away to look into her face. "Oh my little one, where have you come from? Have you dropped from heaven?"

"I came when I heard by chance about grandfather. I am so very sorry."

"Well you shall come up and see him. That'll be a sight to revive him if anything will. Betty, bring refreshments up to the parlour."

"What sort, Ma'am?"

"Oh anything. What there is." And Celia seized Eunice's hand and began drawing her upstairs.

Revive Grandfather, Eunice thought. Is she mad? Has she kept him here and not buried him yet?

The best bedchamber was on the same landing as the parlour and looked out over the river. It was to this that Celia hurried her and opening the door called out, "Now, Clifford, look at this!"

The bed curtains were only partially drawn and Grandfather, a shrunken version of his old self with a lopsided face, was propped against pillows.

His eyes darted round and fixed on Eunice and became animated with delight and astonishment.

Eunice had to curb her own surprise. She mustn't report what rumours had been saying and yet as she went near and had to bend and kiss him she thought he was not more than half alive. He gabbled sounds which she couldn't decipher and the arm that flapped about to hold her seemed scarcely to belong to him.

"Oh Grandpapa, I am so sorry to see you like this."

Celia interpreted his exclamations. "He wants to know where you've been all this while and so do I. Did your father recover too?" She looked quite frightened at the thought. Eunice guessed that she had grown used to the idea that her fearsome son would no longer berate her for her worldliness.

Eunice shook her head. "Father died of the plague and they would have shut me up in the house for a month. I couldn't bear the thought of it. I ran away. I got as far as Woolwich and found work as a housemaid. I heard someone speak of the Horden business and that you were – ill, Grandpapa." She could see he was taking in what she said. His mind was still there in that miserable skull.

He was trying to ask questions. He seemed to be saying something, a name over and over again.

"He wants Richard Corcoran to come and report to him." Celia said this softly, then out loud to him as if he were deaf. "*Eunice* can't make him come if *I* can't, Clifford." She dropped her voice again. "Be careful what you tell him. He wants to know exactly what you heard."

Eunice was in a dilemma. Evidently he knew only part of what had been going on but then how could she be sure that what she had heard was not false rumours too, like his death.

"Something about merchant ships captured by the Dutch." He groaned and frowned as if in pain.

"Ay that's what brought this on," her grandmother said.

And then Betty called from the landing. "There's refreshments in the parlour." They could hear her feet stomping downstairs again.

"She's a terrible rough woman, but come along. You must have missed your dinner so we'll see what she's found for you."

She led the way out and Eunice squeezed her grandfather's hand and had to follow, though his eyes were begging her to stay.

On a tray on the walnut table was a motley collection of food. There were slices of bread and butter, a slab of cheese, a sprig of mint, two oranges and a jug of chocolate from which steam was rising. Eunice had smelt this new drink at the Harrisons where she had been taught how to make it but had never been allowed it herself.

Celia picked up the mint between her finger and thumb and looked at it closely. "She has just picked this. We have some tubs of herbs at the back door but look at it. She hasn't washed it."

Eunice looked. It was blackened with ash. "It's from the fire. Oh Grandmamma, it was terrible to see as we came along the river."

Celia put her hands up to her face. "Is it coming nearer? I heard it was just among the old houses near the bridge. Oh quickly, child, fill your plate and eat up. Do you think we will have to move?"

"No, Grandmamma. It is a long way off. You eat too. You look tired."

Celia sank into a chair. "Pour me a glass of chocolate. I don't know how to tell you what dreadful news I have had today. And I dare not tell *him*. We are ruined. His lawyer came to say he is working out what debts are still owing. I wouldn't let him in to see your grandfather." She took the glass from her and sipped it with sighs of relief.

Eunice felt sure that 'ruined' was an exaggeration. No family with a house like this could be ruined. She had known what it was like to live from hand to mouth and you didn't have servants. She helped herself to the food. It was wonderful to be told to have as much as she liked and she was hungry. She sat on one of the two straight-backed seats at the table and poured herself some chocolate too.

Celia was watching her. "So you see, poor darling, that I can't look after you, much as I would have wanted to. The business is no more. I have been told that Corcoran disappeared with the last penny and I know not what is to become of your grandfather and me."

Eunice paused with a piece of bread half way to her mouth. "I didn't come to be a burden, Grandmamma. I came to see if I could help. I can work. I thought I would like to go back and get Father's Bible from our house – if it is still standing. When I've done that I will look for work."

Celia's little eyes became cunning. "If it's housework you want I can get rid of that woman out there. I never liked her and since she got wind of our troubles she has grown surlier by the day."

"Of course I will help you but is there no redress, if you have been robbed by this Corcoran?"

"The lawyer says the man will be out of the country by now. An under-manager came but he was frightened to tell Clifford he had gone. Worse, that he had taken with him the contents of the strong box in the office. Only Corcoran and your grandfather had keys to that. Of course he knows I am keeping things back from him. I dare hardly go in to see him for the questions he is trying so hard to say. He is tearing himself to bits worrying and not being able to do anything." She finished her chocolate and began to cry, her hands flopped in her lap, her little features puckered up, crowded by her flabby cheeks which she was making no effort to wipe.

Eunice was full of pity. She got up and gave her a kiss but Celia waved her back to the table shaking her head as if to say kisses were no remedy for despair.

Eunice sat down again and held back the question she most wanted to ask. Had Daniel stayed here? Instead she ate all she could from the tray and then remembered guiltily that she had not said grace before it and it was the largest meal she had had for months. She looked up and smiled at Celia.

"Thank you for that, Grandmamma, and I thank the Lord too for his goodness in providing the materials for such a feast."

Celia sat up. "I don't know about thanking the Lord. He has hit us with one blow after another. The plague which took your father and thousands more and the war which has destroyed innocent ships on the sea and sent my poor husband into a fit from which he'll never recover and now He has sent a destroying fire to take away what little we have left. Don't come preaching to me, girl, like your father did. No doubt he would say we deserved to be punished but what did we ever do wrong? Your grandfather gave work to hundreds of men in his warehouses, in the docks, in ships at sea. Why should we be cursed for that? And if we're all to be punished for the wickedness of the court as William always said was lewd and licentious – well, *we* served the Protector when we had him and were obedient to the lawful parliament and never wanted the King back." She sniffed. "And now I suppose because of that we'll get no compensation for losses in a war the King chose to wage with the Hollanders. I know Daniel said the Dutch started it but I'm not so sure of that."

She had talked herself to a standstill and she had spoken his name. Eunice didn't have to broach it first.

"Did Cousin Daniel come here then?" She asked it as casually as she could.

Celia leapt upon it. "Ay and we all but lost him too so his mother writes and that would have been the end of all the family I told her for I didn't know I still had you."

Eunice gasped, "He only had a leg wound didn't he?" The words were out before she realised the implications

"How could you know that?"

Eunice had to describe seeing him come ashore at Woolwich.

"Why did you not speak to him?" Celia almost screeched it. "It would have given him such joy. Do you not see? We had to tell him you had caught the plague from your father. He was heart-broken and if you had only accosted him we would have known you were alive. Then of course he would have insisted on bringing you to London with him and you could have been married from here and cheered us all up. Instead of which his mother would take him back home before he was fit to travel and he got a horrible infection in his leg which laid him low for weeks. You see what a trouble you caused, you foolish girl."

Eunice could find no words to answer her. She was too engrossed in asking questions of herself. Was I foolish to hide round those bales of straw when it would have been so natural to greet my cousin and inquire after his health? Did I never suppose I would be mourned? Was he really heart-broken? So wretched that his mother took him home for country air, a change of scene, to forget all about me, and then he nearly died – which it seems is all my fault?

Celia got to her feet and shook her by the shoulders. "Have I not told you from the beginning that he was smitten by you? And then you go and disappear so he thinks you dead, he and all of us? Look what you've put us through by your obstinacy."

Eunice was only too ready to think the worst of herself. Everything in her time with her father had humbled her but she felt a flame of anger rising up now.

"Yes, Grandmamma, you told me he was smitten as you put it but what evidence did I ever have? You said he would seek me out when he left university. He never did. Some girls get love letters. I didn't. I was hardly at the fringe of his life whatever you say. So why would I thrust myself forward?" She checked herself. She could see the astonishment in her grandmother's face at this outburst. "Forgive me, Grandmamma. I am sorry that I let you think me dead but when I ran from Father's house you were living in the country and I didn't know where. I had to make a living somehow –"

Celia shook her head. Tears were welling up again. "We should have let you know. Oh it has all been a sad tangle and now if ever you and your cousin meet again your grandfather and I have no dowry to give you so we might as well be burnt in our beds and go to heaven like the old martyrs for there's nothing left on earth for us now."

Eunice rose with a smile. "There is, Grandmamma. I am young and strong and can look after you. You have a lovely house here and I am sure the fire will burn out only the small, huddled streets. I will take the tray down to the kitchen to save Betty's legs." She paused as she took it up. "Just tell me, you said Daniel was very ill. Is he well now? Have you heard lately from Cousin Arabella? Is he returning to his ship soon?"

"Oh he is well enough I believe but there is no action afoot at present. And she says she will never let him go again. But young men are foolish. *He* is – if he has let you think he doesn't care for you. You are a good girl I am sure but my sad misguided son was a harsh taskmaster to you. Well, take the tray and I will look in on your poor grandfather till supper time. We have a nurse that the physician sent but she sleeps in the daytime unless I need her. She is a big fat silent woman who's drinking her way through our beer cellar, but she's strong. She can lift and turn your grandfather which I can't. Tell Suzy the chambermaid to make up a bed for you where you please. There are more rooms than we will ever need for I can't see us ever having visitors again."

Eunice carried the tray downstairs, every step reminding

her of the last time she was in this house and Daniel had followed her down and pleaded with her father for her in the hallway.

Suzy was a pleasant-mannered girl whom she remembered from her last visit.

"I will sleep in the little dressing-room," she told her, "next to the bedchamber the French young ladies had. Do you remember? Is there still a bed in there?"

"Oh yes, but Mistress will want you to have the grand bedroom I'm sure, now you've come back."

"She said I could choose and I'm not used to grand bedrooms. The little one will be much grander than I have had lately. I'll help you make the bed up."

The thought of clean linen sheets and down pillows after the scratchy sacking, the thin mattress, the scampering mice and the draughts of her stable loft, was very alluring. Ah, the temptations of ease and pleasing the flesh, her father would have said. I am afraid Patience Porter was in every way a nobler character than I, she reflected, as she and Suzy prepared the bed. When Suzy came up later with a brass jug of warm water and asked what else she would like she felt she had also left behind the stoical Eunice Horden of her youth.

CHAPTER 21

EUNICE stood gazing out of her window trying to decide what time it was. There was a white disk in the dark sky but she could hear the servants getting up. With a sick fear in her stomach she realised that it was actually another fine September morning. The lurid purplish darkness was the pall of smoke that had turned the newly risen sun into a moon. As she looked flakes of burnt paper and cloth floated by on the wind. Down below, the terrace was blackened with ash. So it seemed that no efforts had managed to stop the fire in the night and it must be much closer.

Would she find that the poor little house in which she had lived most of her life had been engulfed? Were they secure here or should they be thinking of moving to safety?

She dressed quickly in her second dress which was as threadbare as the one she had worn yesterday but cleaner.

Running down to the kitchen she found Betty building a fire in the hearth and the man Robert bringing in a bucket of coals so that the oven could be heated for the breakfasts.

"Eh, you're early, Missy. Master never wants his breakfast before eight and Mistress lies abed till then or later."

"I will go out and find what the news is about the fire. I'll be back soon."

"Take care then. The street's been full of carts and pack-horses and people with great burdens all night. The noise came up to the front attics and I've scarce had a wink of sleep." He reluctantly opened the back door for her and she scuttled past the coach house and out to the street.

He had not exaggerated. The Strand was like a river clogged with the debris of a flood. To pass in the opposite direction she must squeeze by the walls and hedges and from time to time voices shouted at her.

"You're going the wrong way, girl."

"The fire's coming."

"Ay, it's taken half Cheapside already."

Panic gripped her. Their own little alley between Milk Street and St Lawrence Lane was just off Cheapside to the north. Obstinacy made her push on. If it was creeping from the south-east the fire might not have reached there yet.

When she came in sight of St Paul's the great bulk of the cathedral was silhouetted against a wall of flame which seemed about to swallow it up.

"How close is it to the other side?" she asked a verger who was trundling a wheel barrow of silver plate out of the west door. She saw he was only one amongst a mass of other staff, from sextons to canons who were carrying out goods to a row of covered carts collected in the precincts.

"Near enough."

She ran on and came out into Wood Street. That was still untouched but the noise of the fire was now so loud that she desperately wanted to turn tail. Only a longing to see the place before it perished, and perhaps retrieve her father's Bible as the only memento of him she would ever have, kept her moving fearfully forward.

As she turned into the top of Milk Street she saw a horse and cart come out of their alley. Tom was sitting on the horse and his father and mother were walking by the cart with hands up to the pile of furniture and goods to steady it as the wheels lurched on the cobbles.

Tom had seen her.

"It's Eunice! It is! Look."

The scene was so like the last time she had seen them that the terrible day of her father's death came rushing back.

As she came up to the Fletcher family they all shouted at once.

"We thought you were dead."

"Where are you going?"

"Don't go back there!"

She only answered, "Is my house still there?"

"Yes but the fire has reached St Lawrence. It's leaping houses. It's not safe."

She shook her head and darted into the alley. Yes, there were flames in the roofs at the far end. The air was full of flying debris some of it still alight. The sound was like a howling tempest of wind but she could see their tiny house, the sack still hanging in the window. Would the door be nailed up? The heat was now fearsome.

No, the door was ajar. She was inside and dodging round the table which inexplicably was up close to the door.

Looking neither to right nor left she scampered up the stairs and turning into her father's bedroom snatched up the Bible. She kept her eyes from the bed in case his skeleton was lying there. There was a jug with the dried remains of vinegar in it. She took nothing but the Bible and almost fell down the stairs in her haste.

Glancing to her left as she emerged from the alley she saw a house in the tiny passage by which she had escaped the drunken revellers totter in a mass of flame and crash to the ground. Burning timbers shot along nearly to her feet as she raced the other way. Then she heard screams behind her. She stopped and looked back. A woman was emerging from the last house at the corner of their alley. Eunice knew her. She had been denounced many times by her father for being in league with the devil. She told fortunes in a little tent at the market and was reputed to have money hidden in her house. Now she was dragging out a strong box but the house that had just fallen was a flaming mass right in front of her. Eunice looked in horror. The woman turned to run back inside but her own house was now alight, the upper storey so close to the burning ones across the alley that it had caught in a moment. Eunice took two steps in that direction but the narrow way was full of burning debris.

"Dear God," she prayed, "I am helpless. Please let it be quick."

It was. Even as she looked the upper storey of the house collapsed and the woman was buried. Eunice heard or imagined she heard screaming and then she was running for her own life, terrified that fire would catch at her skirts. She didn't stop till she was below the north cathedral wall where she patted her hair and all round her clothes to make sure she was not scorched anywhere. She sank to the ground and covered her eyes from the sight she had just seen.

A man yelled at her, "You could have been killed. More houses are to be pulled down and there isn't time to wait for fools who have stayed too long. Look there." She saw a body of workmen running with ladders, axes and grappling irons to a row of houses in Old Change. "It's not as quick as gunpowder but they hook up on the timber struts and get them down in a jiffy. You don't want to be underneath when they fall, do you?"

She shook her head and looked up at the cathedral wall. "No fire could touch this place surely?"

"No one believes so for there's a mass of people bringing their goods inside. But I say the Dutch or the French are spreading the fire. There's one arm of it heading north to Aldersgate and another west along the river and how could that be if there wasn't some treachery at work?"

Eunice just shook her head and, clutching the big Bible, hurried on. Her grandmother must be sick with worry for her.

As she emerged into Fleet Street she saw the Fletchers' cart ahead and Tom looking anxiously round. When he saw her he raised a hand in obvious delight. She stirred herself to wave back. She was sure he had wanted to go back to seek her but his parents would have forbidden him. The likeness to the last disaster was uncanny but the warm affection he showed comforted her a little.

They were not turning into The Strand. She saw them continue from Fleet Street up Drury Lane probably heading for St Giles' Fields with most of the other fugitives, looking for open areas where they could be safe for a while. They were lucky to have got out in the nick of time but now what would happen to all these refugees she couldn't imagine, their houses and shops and livelihoods all destroyed.

She turned along The Strand and was surprised to see people here too already bringing out goods from their mansions. One elegant lady was looking up and down the street with her maid and three young children by her all dressed for a journey. Behind the group were piles of roped chests and boxes and the family coach was being brought round from their coach house. They were not going to risk waiting too long to save their wealth like that poor wretch back there.

The lady was grumbling, "We cannot go and leave all this here. Why are the carts not come? I sent for them an hour ago."

The maid was almost in tears. "Oh my lady, they say there are no more carts to be had if you offer thirty pounds for one. The box of plate could go in the coach with all the clothes. It would stand the jolting."

"I am not leaving my Delftware or Italian glass to the thieves. We must get a lighter and send the goods by river and the footmen accompanying them must be armed with pistols."

Eunice heard no more as she walked past, slowed down by the press of people. Her father would have made a sermon out of the incident. Thank God, I am not encumbered by any treasures, she reflected. Now that I have this Bible there is nothing else I value.

When she reached the house she found Celia up and in a state of great anxiety.

"How could you go out, Eunice? The sky is raining fire they say. Neighbours are packing up. The Earl of Branford has gone with his lady. Their coach went by ten minutes ago. Can it be that it will come as far as this?"

"They are tearing down whole streets in its path and there are fire-posts at intervals where officers seem to be deciding on the best strategy. I cannot think they will let it reach here. It is not at St Paul's yet and surely that will be saved."

Celia was hardly listening. "How can I move your grandfather? I woke the nurse but she is half drunk. We still have our coach and horses but I know not if we could get him inside. If he was strapped to a mattress Robert and the coachman might be able –" Then she wrung her hands and collapsed on the bottom stair and wept.

Eunice saw that one calamity on another was too much for her. She raised her up and took her back upstairs and led her into Clifford's room where Betty had brought up a bowl of porridge.

"There, help to feed Grandfather before this goes cold."

She was rewarded by seeing her grandmother pick up the spoon and put it to his mouth. I don't believe he knows anything about the fire, she thought, and I hope Grandmother has the sense not to worry him.

She took herself up the next stair to her own little room at the back and drawing back the bed curtains she sat down with her father's Bible. She was shaking more than ever now from her ordeal. She tried to focus on the fly-leaf of the Bible but the sight of the flaming house burying the woman reared between her and the page. She shut her eyes and prayed for it to leave her.

When she opened them she read, through tears, the words written in a careful boyish hand "William Horden, his book to be treasured all my life long."

She began to turn the pages and read the notes he had written in the margins. The flaming picture was coming back. Desperately she felt for the pages and finding a marker sticking out further on she turned to it and opened it and saw, blinking her eyes again, that she was very near the end in the Book of Revelation. Her father had underlined some words and written in the margin in large letters 'Very soon.' The words were 'The merchants that were made rich by her . . . stood afar off and cried out as they looked upon the smoke of her burning saying 'What city is like the great city?"

Eunice fell on her knees by the bed "Oh father, did you see this coming? Plague and then fire? You were indeed a prophet." She prayed then that the fire would be stayed and that it would have a purifying effect on people's hearts and lives, an end to corruption and all that a devotion to riches brought with it.

Rising, she knew for certain that she had been called here to be a comfort to her grandparents and she spent the rest of the day with a cheerful outward front, fulfilling every whim of Celia's. She helped Betty carry several empty crates from the cellar and packed into them all the valuables Celia brought to her, wrapping her three prize Chinese vases in pieces of fine linen, padding the silver cutlery with old woollen rags so they wouldn't rattle and give away their presence to handlers. She folded small rugs about the best mirrors and pictures.

"Let us not take anything out of Grandfather's room," she suggested, "in case he becomes anxious."

Celia, apparently deriving much comfort from all this activity, demurred at this since there were two portraits of herself and Clifford on the walls and several of the very best silver candlesticks on the side table.

Eunice reassured her. "We will have plenty of time for them. If we keep a watch at the front gate we will know if the fire reaches the far end of The Strand so we will have due warning."

She said this to reassure herself too. Having been so close to the conflagration and felt the force of the wind and the terror of the heat she could not quell a deep-down sense of panic just waiting to burst out.

Later in the day they heard from passers by the horrific news that the fire had after all engulfed St Paul's. No amount of clearing around it had had any effect since burning embers had been blown onto the roof and set fire to timbers that had been used to replace holes in the lead. The huge building had burned from the top down and though the walls appeared to be standing the place was an incandescent mass, all the lead melted into St Faith's below and the mortar burnt out between the stones.

Eunice who heard this from one of the servants felt sick to her stomach. She wanted to keep it from her grandmother but before nightfall Celia went on the terrace herself to look eastward. She couldn't see the cathedral from there but the curve of the river showed her that fire was beginning to attack the buildings of the Temple close to the water's edge.

"Eunice," she cried coming in in a panic. "If it has come so far what about the cathedral?"

Eunice was obliged to tell her then that the fire had not only consumed St Paul's but had leapt the Fleet River and attacked Ludgate Hill too.

"Then we are doomed indeed. My wretched son will be laughing in his grave."

"Nay, Grandmamma, he may have foretold destruction but he was a compassionate man and wished no ill to any who repented before God."

"Well I will not take my clothes off this night. I have not been enough of a praying woman and will spend the time on my knees by Clifford's bed."

"Will that not distress him?"

"I will draw the curtains around him. He calls out in the night sometimes and the nurse goes to him but I will do so myself tonight for it is very likely to be our last."

But it was about eleven o'clock that night that the miracle

happened. The wind dropped. Eunice went to her window and listened to the change. She looked down river to the Temple. Some buildings behind the Inner Temple were still burning, but as a static, containable bonfire. The wild flames hurrying westward were stilled. I think we are safe, she murmured to herself. Thank God.

She lay down on top of her bed and fell asleep.

In the morning she found her grandmother curled into a plump ball on the rug by her husband's bed. The nurse had been in and covered her with a blanket.

That day there was an air of great relief in the house, but when Celia woke she would not authorise unpacking any of the goods that had been set aside yesterday. It was plain that buildings at the Temple were still burning and there were reports that a light southerly breeze had now arisen and would drive the fire towards Holborn. Several times loud explosions were heard which frightened them all.

Eunice, now the calmest among them, said she would go into the street and find out what had caused them. She found some people who had left their homes cautiously returning with their carts still laden. One man said he and his family had slept under the cart all night in the fields and had sent his son forward at daybreak who had found their house at the top of Fetter Lane unburnt.

"The Duke of York is there himself," he told Eunice, "and he has sailors and dockworkers blowing up houses with gunpowder. That's what you heard. But he has also rounded up everyone in sight to clear even more space to stop the fire.

They say it is still raging in Cripplegate and will go right to the wall. We are going slowly till we know if he has spared our house from the general demolition."

"Would you think The Strand is now safe?" Eunice asked him.

"If the Dutch and the French do not come up river and start all up again." He seemed to be grinning when he said this so she took it lightly. Still there were rumours on every side that the great fire had been no accident. If it wasn't foreigners responsible it was home-grown traitors.

Eunice went back inside and spoke cheerfully to her grandmother. But Celia was shaking with a new fear. "Your grandfather has guessed something terrible has been going on. I took away the silver candlesticks and he noticed and wanted to know why. I had to tell him that there had been a great fire and all the City was burnt down to the river. So he tried to sit up and babbled about his warehouses and of course they are gone. He became very agitated and now he has fallen back in a fit. I had to fetch the nurse. She says he has had another seizure and I should send for Doctor Rowe but what will have happened to him who can tell. He lived in Monkwell Street near the Barber Surgeons Hall."

"I will go and see if his house has been spared and bring him if I can." Eunice longed to be doing something useful.

"Oh, child, that is a long way and you could be in danger from fires breaking out again."

But Eunice insisted and set off. She soon found she must bear north but she was not allowed up Fetter Lane where the fire had been stayed half way up it by demolition of a wide swathe of houses. All the burnt area was still full of smouldering fires and the ground was too hot to walk on. The pall of hot stinking air made it almost impossible to breathe. Picking her way among debris where workmen were beginning to clear passages through the exploded houses she was able to skirt the burnt ground and get out with much relief into Moorfields.

She was not surprised to find it full of refugees from the fire. Some had rigged up makeshift tents and shelters and there were men from the trained bands taking water and provisions around on the King's orders she was told. Venturing back in through the walls further along she saw that the Barber Surgeons Hall was still standing though with black scorch marks up its walls. It seemed the fire had been stayed here too. She asked a gentleman inspecting the premises if he knew aught of Doctor Rowe.

"His house was one that was pulled down before the fire. He went off with some of his goods and I have no notion where he has gone."

"Are you a physician, sir?"

He acknowledged it with a little bow.

"Could you come to my grandfather? He has been ill for a long time after a seizure and can scarcely speak nor move but hearing that his warehouses had all been destroyed he has had another – so the hired nurse says who has been helping my grandmother look after him and –"

The gentleman interrupted her. "If he has had another fit

that will be fatal. I am needed to treat the hundreds injured in the fire. Go back and you will find your grandfather dead."

Eunice could scarcely credit the callous way he said this. She made no reply but turned and began the long walk back. Now that she was sure how to go she looked about before passing through the gates again and surveyed the desolation of the whole burnt area. It was astonishing to see right down to the river over the blackened ground with its stumps of church towers. Down there on the waterfront warehouses that must have held barrels of oil and other combustibles were still burning fiercely. Were any of those grandfather's? She didn't know. How could she tell one street from another now? Where was the old alley she had only just escaped from yesterday? What would the Fletchers do? Where would they set up a business that young Tom could work at the rest of his life? Gazing over the wreck of so many futures it seemed to her that the world had come to a full stop. The heart of London had been ripped out and how could it ever revive?

The thought reminded her of her grandfather and spurred her into motion again. It was a tedious way and she was tired but she walked quickly once outside the wall again and returned through Holborn which seemed largely to have escaped because of the open spaces created.

She found her grandmother arguing on the doorstep with a stout woman in blue serge gown and a very grubby white cap who she supposed must be the nurse she had not yet encountered.

"No I will not lay him out till I am paid and if I don't get what I'm owed I'll fetch the nearest constable." The woman's voice was slurred and she was supporting herself with a hand on the doorpost but her tone was determined.

Celia saw Eunice and cried out, "He is gone. Not ten minutes after you left. I would have sent Robert after you but I had no notion which way you would go if you could find the place at all. And now what can I do here? There is no more money in the house."

Eunice came up to them and looked at the nurse with her gentlest smile. "Surely you can see this is not the time to be making such a disturbance?"

"You pay me then."

"How much do you say you are owed?"

"Two pounds for the weeks I have been here. It should be more for the heavy work it was."

Celia clasped her hands in horror. "She has been well fed, has slept hours of the day and been in liquor most of the time. Our food and our liquor."

Eunice laid her hand on her grandmother's arm. "If she will wait here I will see what I have left after my fare from Woolwich."

She ran upstairs and took her purse from the drawer of the bedside cabinet. There were three shillings in it and a few pence.

Coming down again she found the nurse in the same belligerent posture, chin jutted out at Celia who looked ready to drop.

Eunice handed over the money. "That is all I have and I

worked very hard for it. Now pray leave us in peace."

The woman took it into her grubby hand, saw how much there was and spat on the ground. "I'll be back for the rest." She lurched away, the leather bag she carried bouncing on her large hips.

"What was in the bag I wonder," Celia said as she closed the front door. "It looks fatter than when she came."

Eunice put her arms round her. "Sit down a moment, Grandmamma. She is gone and you are well rid of her. Let me fetch you a glass of wine."

"What am I to do? I am a widow. You won't leave me now, will you, child?"

"Of course I won't."

"Oh promise me, promise me faithfully. I am so alone. I have never in my life been so alone."

"I do promise. Before God, I promise. He sent me to you for this very thing."

Celia was still all of a quiver so Eunice fetched her the wine. She was loath to encourage her to find solace in that after all her father had taught her about the evils of drink but it brought a temporary revival. Her grandmother got up and turned to her and took her hands.

"That's better, dear girl. I shall not grieve for him. The life he was leading was no life at all. The day I lost him was when he had his first seizure. He could not bear the helplessness nor I to see him like that. Is the horrible fire out now?"

"Not out but not coming this way. Shall we unpack the treasures?"

"Not yet. How can I tell what we may have to part with for some ready cash? I told you I could find none in the house. But I have sent Robert for the lawyer. He lives out in Bow Street so he will have been safe. He will tell me what to do now I'm a widow. Eh that word! It has a black sound to it and black is what I must put on."

The lawyer came in the early afternoon, a big bluff man whose manner to Celia was not as kind or respectful as Eunice expected. He was accompanied by a law student carrying all the ledgers and other documents which the under manager had brought to Clifford on his return from the country after the plague – the news that had triggered his first seizure. At least this action had saved them from the fire.

It was quickly evident that the lawyer had studied them since taking them away at his last visit but he had also brought a pile of letters he had been sent himself since rumours of Clifford's death had excited the commercial world.

These letters he spread out first over the dining-table. He slapped a hand on them. "Creditors – every last one. Your husband trusted Richard Corcoran, Mrs Horden, but he always had his own hand on the tiller so to speak until lately. Corcoran thought he could do better by greater boldness. On his own initiative he bought a large consignment of spices and cocoa beans which would have made a great profit if they had ever arrived. They were seized by the Dutch. Frightened by the loss he tried to put it right with another outlay which also came to grief. Knowing his master would soon be home he took from the strong room enough to cover his own pay and to get himself to France – but that was all there was. The under-managers and the men are still owed several months' wages."

Celia clasped her head in her hands. "And my people here have not been paid since my poor husband's first seizure! The very nurse who was supposed to care for him demanded two pounds and dear Eunice here had only three shillings to give her. What money Clifford had on him when we came back from the country has gone in daily expenses and I know the butcher's bill has not been paid because he came himself having lost his shop to the fire and wants all owing to him so he can start up again somewhere. Did I not tell you we were ruined, Eunice?" She burst into tears.

"Now then, Mrs Horden, you are not going to Newgate Prison, not yet for I believe it has burnt down too. I saw several chests and boxes in the hallway. Had you been planning to run away from the fire? No doubt they are full of valuables. I can get a good price for them from foreign visitors. There are many have come to gloat over the City and pick up what bargains they can. Then there is this house. With thousands of homes destroyed – including some of the grandest like Dorset House – good mansions such as this will be much sought after."

Celia looked wide-eyed at Eunice. "But where would we live? You are not saying I will have nothing left at all."

"That *is* what I am saying. I doubt if even that will cover the debts but we will hope creditors will be prepared to wait. These are difficult times for everyone. The Lords in Council may issue grants for rebuilding to those totally ruined by the fire but that will not help *you*."

Eunice looked him in the eye. "Can you not temper your tone, sir? My poor grandmother cannot take any more blows than she has already suffered."

"Alas, the truth *is* unpalatable, my dear young lady."

"What then do you advise us to do, sir?"

"There must be friends or family who would take you in."

Celia shook her head. "We have acquaintances in London. Lord and Lady Branford who live further east along the Strand must have a dozen rooms they never use but they have just lost their son in the navy and anyway have run away to their country place from the fire. Clifford made enemies rather than friends in the days of his success."

"*Your* family, Mrs Horden?"

Eunice realised she had never known any relations on her grandmother's side.

Celia shook her head. "My parents died soon after I was married and my brother was only fifteen when he was drowned in the river at Eton in some silly schoolboy prank. You are going to say I must have inherited some wealth. I did but it helped Clifford with his business and now this is how I am to be rewarded – a pauper in my old age. I have no family. I have nowhere to –" She stopped suddenly and seized Eunice's arm. "The cousins! They owe us a favour. They came here expecting hospitality which we gave them gladly and their French relations too."

Eunice swallowed hard. The lawyer stuck his head forward.

"Who are these people, Mrs Horden?"

"*Clifford's* cousins, the Northumberland Hordens. Why, Eunice here is practically engaged to Sir Daniel."

Eunice felt her cheeks flame up. "That I am not. We could never beg *them* for help. They are poor too."

The lawyer however became very interested. "But landed gentry? Is it a baronetcy?"

"Oh yes, yes," cried Celia. "They *were* poor but the husband has a stipend as the vicar and their land will have recovered from the ravages of the late wars and they are kind, generous-hearted people. We will go to Northumberland. It may be a wild uncivilised place but I am sick of London. London is verily a cursed city." Then she looked as suddenly downcast again. "We cannot write to them. The post office was burnt down and are there any coaches going out of London and how can we pay for the journey?"

The lawyer chuckled and held up his hand. "The post office is to be temporarily located in Covent Garden and many stage coaches were driven out in advance of the fire and will certainly be plying for business. As to your last question I have one other piece of business to state which is happier news. Mrs Horden, you know that your husband made a will before you went into the country. Because of the plague he thought it a wise precaution. Did he show it to you?"

"No. Everything was to come to me, he said."

"But he had already been adding to an annuity he had set aside" – he looked at Eunice – "for his granddaughter. These are his words." He unfolded a parchment and read from it.

"'Inasmuch as my son William has cut himself off from me and chosen voluntary poverty with no forethought for the daughter who is certain to outlive him I wish to provide for her, Eunice Horden, a sum that will bring her in thirty pounds a year for life.' Now with my help in drawing up this provision that sum is safe from creditors. They cannot touch it and when his death has been officially attested I can pay out the first thirty pounds as soon as you wish to claim it."

Eunice sat speechless, astounded.

Celia rose and flung her arms round her neck. "Dear child, we are saved."

The lawyer snapped, "You appreciate this is *her* money."

Eunice glared at him. "Of course it is at my grandmother's disposal. She should have had all my grandfather's wealth but for these unhappy circumstances. Now we do not need to be under an obligation to anyone. We can rent a small property and I can also work and support her."

Celia held up her hands and her little eyes gleamed like beads in the folds of her podgy face. "I am going to Northumberland and you promised faithfully before God never to leave me."

Now the lawyer chuckled. "Your granddaughter is not obliged to pay your fare. And I'm afraid you still owe me my fee."

Celia pulled at a ring on her finger and with difficulty wrenched it over the swollen knuckles. "Take that. It is worth forty guineas at least. Give me change out of it for both our fares for we cannot owe you that much in fees."

He looked at it critically. Then he reached into his own pocket and drew out a little purse from which he counted twelve gold sovereigns and laid them on the table.

"I will consider myself paid though there will still be much to do before your husband's affairs are tidied up. I take it you will want your servants here paid off since you will not be able to take them with you wherever you go."

He began gathering up the papers and summoned his student who had been sitting in the hallway awaiting orders. "Put these back in the document box and call a hackney if you can find one."

When the young man had gone he beamed at Eunice and her grandmother.

"I will be sending a dealer to value the house and its contents but now, ladies, you are free to sort out your destiny between you. Send for me as you need me but at all events let me know when and where you go."

He bowed himself out.

"Well!" Celia swept up the sovereigns. Her small mouth between the plump cheeks was positively grinning. "Now you shall not escape your Daniel, my girl. We will go as soon as it can be arranged."

Eunice saw how she had fallen into a trap. Oh it would be pain and humiliation to go begging to Horden Hall. She did not for a moment believe that Daniel loved her. How would it look to him? She imagined herself saying, "Here I am, homeless, so you will have to marry me." But no, she reminded herself. I can go as an independent woman. If

Cousin Arabella befriends Grandmother I will have done my duty by taking her there. I can settle nearby perhaps – I have no concept of villages and country houses – but with thirty pounds a year surely I can support myself.

Next moment she was asking herself, what would Father say? He would warn me of the sin of pride now that money has been dangled before my eyes. Life is service to others. I must remember only Grandmother's desolation and her need of love, not her cunning or her skill in manipulating events.

Under it all a part of her was singing, I will set eyes on Daniel again.

"Grandmamma," she said out loud. "Are there any clothes in the house I can alter for my use? My own dresses are sadly worn."

"Of course, but we must both be in black though it will not set you off so well for your man. I have two mourning gowns for myself in fine wool which I wore when we heard William and you were both gone but as time had already passed I did not wear them long. For your tiny figure I can surely find some material. You are quick with your needle I know. Come with me and we will look into the dressing room and equip ourselves for the North. We must travel soon before winter sets in or we will never arrive."

CHAPTER 22

BEL tapped at the door of Daniel's bedchamber and looked in. It was flooded with the light of another fine autumn morning but his bed curtains were drawn and no sound came from behind them.

"Dan, we mustn't waste another good day. The oat fields have been cut and I am ready to help with every man and boy we can bring in. You used to love that."

She paused but there was no reply. "Don't pretend you're not strong enough yet for we both know that's nonsense. You'll only get back to full health by activity. Your leg is perfectly well and the doctor says it only needs exercise."

There was still silence so complete that she suddenly thought she was talking to emptiness. He must after all have got up and gone out without showing his face at breakfast.

She stepped to the bed and pulled back the curtain.

He was there, flat on his back and glaring up at her.

"Is there no such thing as privacy?" His voice had that flat dull sound that she had come to dread. It was as if an imposter had taken the place of the warm, laughing, impulsive boy she had once loved.

"Oh Dan, please. Come out of this mood. I can't bear this. It is almost worse than your absence. Nay" – she sat on the bed and gazed at him – "it *is* worse. That was a clean sharp pain. You were out at sea, you were in danger, but you were still my boy. Now it is like having a stranger in the house. You walk about like a shadow."

"If you get off the bed I'll get up – if that's what you want."

She was near to tears which she knew he hated. She stood up and went out without another word.

Nat had gone to the church to say the morning office but Ursula was in the kitchen. She ran down to her.

"Oh Urs, what am I to do with him?" She saw Ursula was kneading bread on the kitchen table top. She grabbed a lump of dough from her and began pounding it with all her might. "That's what I want to do with him."

Ursula's brilliant blue eyes were alight with love. "Well, my Bel. *You* should understand him if anyone does. He has a cloud."

Bel stopped pounding and dug her fingers deeply into the dough as she stared across the table at Ursula. Then she shook her head. "When I had my cloud I was still as wild and impulsive as before. It made me wretched and cross and sad but I was still alive. He might as well be dead. No, no, I don't mean that but you have seen it – something has died inside him." She drew out her fingers and licked them.

"I *have* seen it." Ursula flattened the dough, incorporated Bel's lump back into it and folded it together again to pound it some more. "It's something that happened at sea, I think, in the battle."

"I thought so but then I remember how he was when we

were reunited at Cousin Celia's house. He was my boy, loving, glad to see us. Of course he was quiet. I realise now how much pain he was in. And he suffered on the journey here but without complaining once. He didn't want to talk about the battle or how he got the wound but that I understood. He was grieving for his friend. But it was after he recovered from the fever that he fell into this sullen mood just when he should have been back to his old bouncy self – riding, walking, finding a hundred things to do."

"Have you and the Reverend forbidden him to rejoin his ship?"

"We didn't need to. His Captain sent him a short letter telling him to recover fully. There was no likelihood anyway of a fresh muster soon. I said 'Thank God for that' and Dan just nodded. He knows how we long for this peace treaty that's talked about. I thought he did too. Didn't you hear him say when you came running out to the coach to greet him that it was a joy to see you and Horden again. I hoped then that he had had enough of the navy."

"He did, bless his heart." Urusla set the dough to rise near the fire. "Well, if it is not a cloud hovering over him like yours all those years then it's inside him. He has made the passage from boy to man but somewhere he's taken a wrong turning." She wiped her floury hands on her apron and beamed at Bel.

"He has indeed but how do we get him back again?"

Daniel sauntered into the room from the stable-yard carrying a bundle of letters. "Anything to eat, Ursula?"

"What's wrong with Nana Sula?" She cocked her twisted

little face at him, her eyes twinkling.

"A bit childish now I suppose." He held out two letters to Bel. "The post-boy just gave me these. The rest are for Father."

"I always give postie a mug of ale," Ursula said going to the back door. "Has he gone?"

"Yes, I scolded him for waiting till he had a bundle to bring. I told him they might be important."

Ursula gave him a sad look but said nothing.

"This is from France," Bel said, perching on a stool and opening the seal. "Well, well, my sister is to become a grandmother. Madeline is to present her count with an heir. Poor Diana is still husbandless, she tells me. I think I detect a note of reproach." She looked up. "Where are you going with that?"

Ursula had handed Daniel a plate with two slices of ham, the heel of the old loaf and a hunk of cheese. He was heading out of the kitchen with it.

"To eat it somewhere quiet."

"You are not taking it to your bedchamber to scatter crumbs there. Sit and eat it here and be pleasant."

He shrugged his shoulders and took another stool and began to eat.

Bel went on telling Ursula what was in the letter. "The old Count Rombeau is in failing health. Henrietta will become a comtesse when he goes, that will please her. She will outrank our mother." She turned to the other letter. "This is Cousin Celia's hand."

"Why not read it to yourself?" Daniel said. "Why should

Ursula be interested?"

Bel held in her anger with difficulty. She glanced down the letter. "Well, this *does* concern Ursula because Celia is coming to stay so a room will have to be prepared for her and another for her lady's maid. She doesn't say how long – goodness me! I think she means for ever."

"What about Clifford?" Dan asked.

That was something. A spark of interest. "Clifford sadly had another seizure and is dead. It seems that great fire we had news of in London has destroyed his warehouses and the shock was too much. Why, this letter is more than two weeks old! She speaks of setting off soon. She could be here any day. Well, she must have Henrietta's old room and the maid can sleep in the old chapel. We could reopen the connecting door between. That is a task you could do, Dan. Adam has enough to do without little things like that."

"I might take myself away somewhere. I can't abide Cousin Celia. She never leaves me in peace."

Bel slapped the letter. "I am no admirer of Cousin Celia myself but apparently she is ruined – or so she says. I know she is devious and manipulating but she must be desperate to want to travel up here and leave her London home to the creditors. So I have to believe she is truly in trouble. I must show compassion. I have been homeless too, when the Scots army walked in here and threw us out at half an hour's notice. Ursula remembers that only too well."

Ursula nodded. "The great snow was just melting and we were plunging through slush." Bel saw how she was sending beams of hopeful love at Dan from her bright eyes. "But we were together and the Lord brought us safe to your father. And you, my Daniel, wouldn't be here at all if that hadn't happened. Be glad then to overflow with love to this cousin. If you think badly of her now you can be sure both she and you will be all the better for a strong dose of love."

Daniel had been eating quickly to clear his plate. Now he got up abruptly and pushed the empty plate at Ursula. Bel could have sworn he was choking with tears. He left the room in a hurry.

Bel went round the table and hugged Ursula. "I do believe you pierced that hard crust he has grown. God bless you, my guardian angel."

Ursula chuckled. "Funny sort of angel. But I believe the dough is also growing and we don't want a hard crust on *that* yet. I'll give it another knead in a minute and then I'll come and prepare for our visitors."

Bel was longing to get out in the fields on this lovely autumn day but she must turn her mind to the very sparse linen cupboard. They had just enough to replenish the beds they were using. Would she have to ride into Newcastle and order new sheets? However confidently she had spoken to Daniel she was dismayed at the prospect of Celia and her lady's maid in her house for an indefinite stay. Dan was right, she thought. She will be all over us, mealtimes, outings, village occasions. She will want to improve our lives, make us join the best of Newcastle society, spend money we haven't got. And if she drives Dan away I will never forgive her.

She got up reluctantly.

"I'd leave him be for a little while," Ursula said. "He won't run away."

Bel nodded. Nat would be back soon and he would bring his calm, rational mind to bear on the strange news.

Eunice helped Celia into the stage-coach at the newly appointed staging inn at Aldgate, the fire having burnt out the traditional post for north-bound journeys. She was still uneasy in her mind that they were setting off without a reply from Horden Hall that they were welcome. If it hadn't been for her annuity money which gave her some independence of action she would not have agreed to go so soon. At least if Cousins Nathaniel and Arabella were from home and Daniel returned to his ship she could surely rent some small place for herself and her grandmother in Newcastle. Apart from her brief sojourn in Woolwich she had never been outside London and it was impossible to picture a remote northern town or the countryside about it. The adventure would have excited her as a new experience but it was so tangled in her joy and dread at the thought of seeing Daniel that she hardly knew what she was feeling as she climbed into the stage-coach after her grandmother.

Celia at least was calmer than she had been the last three weeks. Now that they had left the Strand behind them she could no longer witness the stripping of her luxurious home where she had complacently enjoyed wealth and comfort for so many years. She had seen the boxes of her treasured goods taken away to pay the many debts to tradesmen and to the merchants who had had dealings with the business. The house itself would now be sold and the lawyer had not let her expect anything left once the remaining debts were cleared.

As they departed that morning she looked up at the house with the initials over the door. The walnuts were ripe on the tree.

"Someone in days to come will wonder whose initials those were," she moaned softly.

Eunice guided her towards the hackney that had been summoned to take them to the staging inn. "Try to look forward, Grandmamma."

Robert and Suzy, the only servants who had stayed to the end to clean the house, the stable, the coach house and the terrace, carried out their bags.

"Now don't you worry about us, Ma'am," Suzy said seeing Celia's tears. "When Robert and I are wed we'll have one of the two-storey houses that are to be built for the lesser sort. We've been to see the pictures of them and they are to be in brick or stone. The King himself says there are to be no more houses all of wood, so I'll not be frightened of fire again."

Eunice couldn't help seeing again the picture of the old fortune-teller's house collapsing on top of her. It had frequently haunted her sleep in fearful dreams. Sometimes she was herself the victim and woke in a sweat as the burning timbers engulfed her. She was only glad that apparently she didn't scream out. Neither Grandmother nor the servants had ever heard anything.

Now at last as the stage began to roll forward Celia smiled and turning to Eunice whispered, "You remember the last time I came to that dreadful little house where your father imprisoned you so long? Did I not say to you then 'your day of happiness will come?' Well, we are embarked on the quest for it now and I verily believe it will be there awaiting us at the end of this journey."

She leant back and folded her arms across her bosom and shut her eyes with the confident smile still on her face. Very soon, despite the jolting she was fast asleep.

Eunice was thankful. She wanted no more talk on those lines. She longed for sleep herself. Every day she had been at Celia's beck and call and she was quite worn out. The lawyer had said they could pack what was reasonable of their personal belongings but jewellery of any kind must be set aside to be valued. Celia told Eunice to wrap a pearl necklace in some linen handkerchiefs and when she objected Celia flew into a rage. "It's my wretched son speaking through you. These people are robbing us. Are we not to save something from their plundering?" Eunice was sure she packed it herself later. She was only thankful that she herself had so little.

Between the sorting out and packing up she had made herself a bodice and skirt from some yards of black drape Celia had found at the bottom of a linen chest. "I think it was hung about the house when Clifford's sister died, but you must have it for your mourning dress. If it makes two and a little cape you will do very well."

Eunice had only time to stitch one outfit before Celia

sickened at the sight of strange men assessing her house and goods and suddenly announced that they would set off as soon as their places could be reserved in the coach. Wearing the new black dress Eunice had studied herself in the only mirror left in the house. She decided black made her look horribly pale. If only she had a higher colour and flaxen hair like Daniel's she might not look so drab. She had allowed her hair to grow longer but refused to put curl papers in. She didn't scrape it back the way her father had insisted so it hung limply about her face and no amount of brushing saved it from its mousy dullness.

Well, they were on their way and Daniel might be at the end of the journey. She leant back too in the coach and shut her eyes and was glad that she did not see the burning old lady but Daniel's image as he had stood before her chamber door, arms outspread like her guardian angel.

Daniel set himself to walk to the village forgetting that he would certainly meet his father on the way back from reading the morning office. He had angrily brushed aside the tears that Ursula's little speech had provoked. At least she hadn't mentioned God. What sort of a God was it that sent plague and fire to carry off innocents like Eunice? It was harder to blame God for Henry's death. God hadn't ordered the English and the Dutch to go to war.

But where was God, he had asked himself in the long convalescence from his fever, where was God when I stood on the deck with Henry beside me and a cannon ball carried off his head. Inches away, I was left alive. Life – death. It happened in the fraction of a second. What is life then that it can vanish in a moment? His eyes stared up at me but he had gone. Where? Nothingness? He was not particularly devout. He was not thoughtful. He lived in the moment. He laughed readily. Things happened. He responded much as he was expected to do. He was cheerful, friendly. He enjoyed his food and drink. He loved his parents. When I asked him if he wanted a girl of his own, to marry and have a family he laughed and said 'Oh yes. I daresay it will all happen.' He would never *make* things happen. And then one moment he was speaking to me and the next he was dead. Just like that. So what did his life mean? Why was he given life to have it snatched away? Do any of us have lives that mean anything at all?

Why am I walking along this particular grassy track that I know so well? Why am I alive? They tell me I was near death when my very minor wound went bad on me? If I'd died would I have gone somewhere and seen Henry, laughing, with his head back on his body? Would there have been the Wilson grandparents and Eunice and William? Now Clifford's joined them all. That great mass of the dead?

"Why, Dan, it's good to see you out walking." His father stopped in front of him. "Are you heading for the farm or the village? Perhaps you wanted to talk to Sam Turner about the harvest."

"Oh." He stood still. "I was just walking. Cousin Celia is coming to live with us. I suppose I was walking to get away from the news. Some letters came. Madeline is with child and

Diana can't get a husband. I think I'm meant to feel sorry for her."

"Well! You feel something about Cousin Celia. You don't want her to visit. I'm surprised she would come all this way. Is Clifford better then? I take it she wouldn't come alone."

"Oh he's died and she's destitute. It's no visit. It's what I said. She's coming to live with us." He looked down into his father's eyes for a moment and saw only surprise and concern. "I suppose you'll put up with it."

"Nay, Daniel, I hope I'll do better than that. If it is as you say we will welcome her and show her every kindness. But I must see her letter and learn a little more of this. You say your mother has heard from France too?"

"And there are letters for you. One has the seal of the Bishop of Durham. Maybe he'll increase your stipend so we can afford Cousin Celia. She eats well."

His father's face showed a flush of excitement. "Ah, the Bishop. I sent him a paper I wrote on the Book of Job. I hope this is his response. I wrote it while you were ill. I was moved by your suffering. You called often for your friend, Henry, when you were delirious. I wish you could talk about him. Remember I was his father's friend too. I loved him. I understand your sorrow."

Daniel shook his head. "Lord Edward Branford is still alive. You can go and see him if you want."

His father reached out a hand to his arm. "Oh, Daniel, it *is* the loss of your friend –"

But Daniel wasn't ready for that. He shrugged his shoulders

– a gesture he knew exasperated them all – and hurried on, leaving his father standing. I know he is looking sadly after me, he thought. I can feel it. Why is he so sure of everything? He has just recited the morning office. Was it a recitation or a genuine prayer to Someone? I see no sense in it or in these tired dandelions by the track or the leaves that are starting to flutter down. Autumn, winter, spring – what do they mean? Death and resurrection?

He walked fast till he came in sight of Turner's farm but then, not wanting to meet anyone he turned abruptly back. Men were working in the fields. He didn't want them to see him so he struck off by the footpath that followed the Horden Burn. Here he was hidden among trees. He kept walking. He knew all the footpaths. He would pass an angler's hut and there might be fishermen at the places where the burn ran into deeper pools. Everyone knew him of course even from a distance with his distinctive flaxen hair and he had walked out without a hat not intending to go anywhere. They think I am someone. "There's young Sir Daniel. He must be recovered. It's good to see him out." And really I'm nothing. Everything is nothing.

When he came to a junction of footpaths he took the one that would bring him out onto the Great North Road, the highway that stretched south to Newcastle, eventually to London, and north to Edinburgh. He turned south. The day was warm and he was now very thirsty. There were plenty of inns in Newcastle where he could refresh himself and he was less likely to be recognised there.

His thoughts were going wild now. If there was no God why had he lived so restricted a life till now? He had been held back by his father's example of one woman for life. He had been restrained in the consumption of drink. Though he had incurred debts at the University they were modest compared to many students. He hadn't gambled. I've been almost as much of a Puritan as Cousin William, he thought. That brought his mind back to Eunice.

Where was the meaning in *her* life? She had hardly been allowed to live. She had emotions like everyone else but they were so suppressed she could hardly be said to be alive. And now she was dead. It must be so. How could she have escaped the plague when she had nursed her father who died of it? He called up pictures of her in his head, peeping from the curtain of the bed at her grandmother's, terrified because there was a man in her room. Then that strange look when he had suggested she should never go back to her father. She *wanted* to be liberated. She saw for a second a golden future, with me? He wondered. She couldn't have been drawn to me – she hardly knew me. But at her father's when she fled to her room and reappeared to beg him not to curse me – ? What a waste of so much passion within that tiny body and then for the horrible plague to attack her and for her to die alone, her friends and neighbours fled. It sickens me to think of it. But what difference does any of it make if there is no meaning in anything?

He had reached the liberties without the town wall and from the heights he could look down at all the roofs, the new handsome Guildhall, the elegant spire of St Nicholas, the river beyond with a myriad of boats on its surface and beyond that the rising land with the small town of Gateshead on its slopes.

He walked in by the Pilgrim Gate and reached the staging inn at Barras Bridge where he was suddenly overcome by exhaustion. He had not walked so far for more than a year probably. There was a bench in shade beyond the bow window to the right of the front door. He sank down onto it and a waiter appeared immediately to know what he would drink.

"None of your light ales, man. I'll have your strongest beer."

A stout old man at the other end of the bench moved nearer to draw him into conversation so he leant his head against the wall and closed his eyes.

The beer came and he drank it thirstily and ordered another. He realised the forecourt of the inn was filling up with people. Some had baggage with them. It was the coaching inn so they must be expecting the stage. Some stood around outside while others went in to wait and refresh themselves for the journey. There was an air of excitement and expectation. They all had a purpose in their lives. They were thinking only of the imminent future when they would be on their way somewhere, nervous of the hazards of the journey, anxious that they had forgotten nothing, perhaps dreading the goodbyes.

He sipped his third mug more slowly, ignoring some remark from the old man. Lethargy was stealing over him. It was pleasant. He closed his eyes again.

CHAPTER 23

EUNICE had been enthralled by the journey. She had had no idea what open countryside was like, that there could be miles between human settlements, yet there were always people travelling somewhere. She peered out whenever the coach passed walkers or horses pulling farm carts or pedlars on laden donkeys. Sometimes riders passed them. Once a masked rider galloped up brandishing a pistol and brought the coach to a standstill.

Eunice looked out and told him, "We lost everything in the fire. We are fugitives from London."

The postillion begged the other passengers to find something however small and two handed over some silver. The highwayman touched his hat and galloped off.

The armed guard, who had done nothing at all, peered in at the window. "It's the best way. If I had used my weapon it could have turned ugly."

They proceeded calmly on their way. Celia who had seemed about to have hysterics subsided again.

The final stage of the journey began with an old peasant woman being ordered on top. She told everyone in the inn yard that she was travelling to live with her son in Newcastle. She had been turned out of her cottage unable to pay the rent since the death of her husband.

Eunice tapped Celia on the back as she was climbing inside. "Grandmamma, you don't mind if she comes in beside you, do you. I can sit on top. It's a beautiful day. I shall see so much more which I would truly enjoy."

Celia nodded reluctantly, drawing in her skirts when she sat down so as not to catch the fleas the old woman would surely be carrying.

Eunice happily climbed on top. It felt very high up and there was only a wooden handle by her side to grasp onto. The basket behind was full of baggage but there was a strong farmer's boy beside her who said he would 'catch hold of her' if the jolting threatened to send her flying. She had seen so much more of life since her father's death that she had lost much of the nervousness of men that her father had instilled into her. She didn't see how this lad could 'have his evil way with her' on top of a coach so she just smiled at him and thanked him.

She unpinned her little black hat and let the balmy wind ruffle her hair. It was a great relief to be away from the chatter of the inside passengers whose grumbles at every stage had sounded so trivial. Now she could begin to think about their arrival and a sudden worry came into her mind. She hadn't seen her Grandmother's letter. She remembered Celia saying "I told them I was destitute but said nothing of your annuity." But what if she had spoken of a marriage? Long ago she had threatened to write proposing it. Eunice groaned inwardly. Nathaniel and Arabella are too kind not to be happy I'm alive but Daniel may already be betrothed. If he is not they will still be embarrassed. I heard Arabella say she is not in favour of arranged marriages. She must have her boy free to make up his mind. Does this explain their silence? Oh I pray God they never got the letter and there are no preparations made for us at all.

A jolt of the coach made her grab the handle. The young man held onto her other arm and they had a brief laugh together. The moment made her realise the physical proximity to Daniel that she would soon be experiencing. I must keep very aloof. Oh maybe it will be better if he has already rejoined his ship!

Up and down her thoughts bounced with the jerking of the coach. She was thrusting herself into a situation of extreme joy or extreme suffering. To be close to him and unwanted would be hell.

They halted in Durham to set down passengers. Eunice from her elevated perch could see the Cathedral on its raised peninsula above the river. The sight thrilled her despite the scorn her father had always poured on the cost of erecting magnificent buildings to the glory of God. "What does He desire but humble hearts?" She had once dared to point out that God had allowed Solomon to build a glorious temple to His name, not just allowed, encouraged it. Her father answered, "We are under the new covenant in His Son. In His kingdom will be no temple because the Lamb is the light thereof." He had an answer for everything, she remembered.

It was early afternoon when they approached Newcastle.

As the coach crested the hill above Gateshead she could see the town ahead across the river. It spread sideways beyond its walls into the country to the east and west. Along the waterfront was a row of tall houses with pointed gables. In the centre it was dominated by the spire of another beautiful church. On the east side it was cleft by a deep valley and beyond to the north the land rose to woods and fields. Somewhere that way was Horden Hall. Her heart began to thump with excitement.

The coach horses struggled upwards and then the street levelled out and was lined by a handsome stone terrace. She hadn't expected to see a town with an air of such prosperity. She thought nowhere so far from London could look so sure of itself, so proud of its own identity.

Now they were turning into an inn yard. The clattering and jolting ceased. The horses tossed their heads, impatient for the moment of release. Grooms appeared and the coach door was opened. Eunice knew that from here they would have to hire other transport for the last stage of their journey so she prepared to get down. She glanced below and her eyes fell on a flaxen-haired young man slumped on a bench in front of the inn.

She caught her breath. Could it be – ? It was. She swallowed hard. She stared at him. Had he come to meet the coach and fallen asleep waiting? Then they must have got her grandmother's letter. But he didn't know when they would arrive. Had he come every day since getting the letter to see the London coach come in in case they were on it? Was that believable?

She saw her grandmother scrambling out and hurrying into the inn. She would be desperate to relieve herself. At each stopping place she had had the same problem. She had certainly not seen Daniel because he was hidden from her view by the bow window. The farmer's boy was holding out his hands to help her down. She allowed him to clutch her waist because the iron steps were awkward but the moment she was down he relinquished her with a little bow. She thanked him and gave orders to the hovering serving-man that their baggage should be carried into the inn. She put on her hat again. Then with her throat dry and the blood throbbing in her cheeks she walked round the bow window and sat down beside Daniel.

The little voice repeating his name, "Cousin Daniel," crept through into his sluggish brain. He shuffled into a more upright position and turned his head towards the sound. His eyes seemed to open with difficulty. He must be still dreaming. Eunice was sitting there. He closed his eyes again. The voice repeated, "Cousin Daniel."

He tried again. She was still there. This was annoying. He thought he was awake now. A great racket of voices and stamping of hooves and rattling of harness assailed his ears. He couldn't be at home in bed. He made his eyes open. Eunice was smiling at him. This was madness. You couldn't die and go to heaven in an inn yard. But he *was* in an inn yard. His muscles were sore. He remembered a long walk. His head was sore too and his mouth leathery inside. He sat up properly and said to this being, "I don't think I'm very well. I am seeing ghosts." But it was only one ghost. There were all sorts of ordinary every day people about such as surrounded a stage coach when it was changing horses.

"No. You have been deeply asleep, Cousin. It is I, Eunice. Did you not receive my grandmother's letter that we were coming?"

Grandmother? He had two grandmothers. One was dead and one was in France.

"Your Cousin Celia wrote a letter," she was explaining quietly.

The name Celia brought back something that had happened not so long ago. He was in the kitchen at home with Mother and Nana Sula. He had been cross at the thought of Celia coming and had stalked out.

"There was a letter from Cousin Celia," he said aloud to see what his voice sounded like.

But this was Eunice talking to him. Eunice hadn't been part of anything except a vivid dream he had been having. She had died of the plague.

"Forgive me but I think you have been drinking too much," she said now.

He shook his head and winced. He pressed his hands over his forehead and then looked squarely at this figure who was talking to him. She was all in black. The little mouse-like face he remembered was peeping out from under a small black hat. Her smile was tentative and a little anxious.

"You died of the plague," was all he could think of to say.

Now she laughed. Had he ever seen her laugh before? He didn't know she could laugh.

"You *have* been drinking! If you have seen Grandmother's letter then you knew we were coming."

At last he seemed to be in a real world. He could answer that. "She wrote that she was bringing her lady's maid."

"Oh!" Her face looked shocked.

"But you *are* Eunice. How? Why? Oh glory be! You are *real*. You're alive!"

He swung round and grasped her hands.

Now her eyes were shining and her cheeks glowing.

She began to explain how she had escaped after her father's death but then broke off to exclaim, "Why would my grandmother do such a thing – letting you think – saying I was her lady's maid? Of course I'm happy to serve her as such but to tell your mother –!"

He saw Cousin Celia appear round the bow window of the inn. Eunice quickly drew her hands from his but Celia absolutely skipped with glee on seeing him. As he rose shakily Eunice stood up too and just touched his arm to steady him. Then she faced her grandmother.

"You didn't say I was coming too."

Daniel was surprised at the asperity in her tone. He began, slowly because his faculties were hardly functioning yet, to see that this was a new Eunice. This is Eunice without her father, he told himself.

Celia was not in the least put out. "Oh it was to be a

surprise, a lovely, lovely surprise. And here he is come to meet us. Well I never." She embraced him and pulled his face down to kiss him on both cheeks. She glanced sideways at Eunice. "I didn't know where you'd got to, you naughty girl, leaving me like that, but now I see there was a much greater attraction. So we will not have to hire a vehicle, Daniel. Which is your coach?" There were several drawn up which had come to meet the stage. "You told the man to put our baggage in the inn, Eunice, did you not and now it may be mixed up with everyone else's."

Daniel, swaying a little, realised he had to take charge of this situation though he hardly felt able to walk safely.

"We don't have a coach. I'll see what they can let us have here." Holding onto the doorpost he stepped inside and waved to the serving-man who had brought his beer. "Have you any sort of vehicle we can hire to get us home to Horden Hall. It's only four miles."

He could hear Cousin Celia behind him muttering, "Not have a coach. Landed gentry and not have a coach. How did he get here himself?"

He turned round as the man went to inquire. "I walked. We have horses. We usually ride but I walked, a long way round. I just happened to be here." To his own ears his speech sounded odd.

It seemed there was an open carriage that could be fetched but they had better come in and eat something while it was being got ready. Daniel had no idea what time it was. He had brought no watch with him nor, he found to his dismay, any money. Nevertheless he gestured the ladies inside and found them seats vacated by the stage coach passengers going on north. He ordered them slices of a chicken he could see on the spit which looked well-roasted. It came with some boiled beef, a dish of eggs and chopped onions.

Celia asked if they had chocolate to drink rather than ale, but this puzzled the inn servants. They had never heard of such a thing.

"Ah it will soon be all the rage in London. The best coffee houses are serving it regularly."

Daniel was pleased to see that Eunice ate well. She was not quite such a slight figure as she had been. He sensed her observing everything he did so he helped himself too, with no idea when he had last eaten, and began to feel better for it. His headache was disappearing but he still found it hard to grip hold of the situation. When was it he had first heard of Celia coming? What would they all be doing at home when he finally arrived there with the visitors? He had no idea.

He asked Eunice to finish telling her tale but she demurred. "It is enough for now that God has been good to preserve me from both plague and fire and happily reunited me with Grandmother. If we may stay a little with you till we can fend for ourselves we will be most grateful. When we meet your kind parents I am sure there will be much to tell on both sides."

Well, he thought, she can converse like a mature young lady. She doesn't run into a corner and hide. But she attributes her preservation to God. Does she also credit Him with her father's death and her grandfather's? Her grandfather's! Of course, this is why they are both in black. I have said not a word to Cousin Celia about her loss. What will she think of me?

He began an awkward speech about his sorrow at her bereavement but she interrupted him.

"You saw him, Daniel. He tried to question you about the navy and why his ships were lost. He was a broken man and it tormented him that he couldn't make himself understood. Death came as a happy release in the end."

Daniel was pleased to see the serving-man approaching. "The open carriage is outside, sir, and I've stowed the bags under the seats. Perhaps you would like to make sure they are all there." They went outside and Celia and Eunice confirmed that nothing had been left behind. "It's five shillings for the hire, sir, since you need our man to drive and bring it back and it's two shillings for the dinner and ninepence for your beer, sir, for you had three pots."

Daniel felt desperately in his pockets, knowing he had no purse on him. "My father will pay when we get home. I'm Sir Daniel Wilson Horden. You can trust me."

Eunice had produced a purse from within the pocket inside her skirt. "Let me, Daniel."

He shook his head, feeling himself blushing.

"Well then, here is something for you," she said to the man, "for looking after us so well." She handed him sixpence and he gave a delighted chuckle. Her confident manner amazed Daniel.

"That was too much," Celia said when they were on their way. "A penny would have done very well."

"I prefer to be generous if I can. My father was when we had little ourselves."

Out in the open Daniel's head cleared some more. The mood he had been in, what his mother had said, what Nana Sula had said, the meeting with his father all fell into place. They would be wondering where he had gone. And surely they had only received Cousin Celia's letter that morning! Yet here he was bringing her and, of all people, the long lost Eunice. Yes, and all that that meant came back to him in force – his mother's insistence that Eunice loved him, her 'love letter' as his mother had called it, which he had carried about with him till he believed her dead, and especially Celia's determination to bring them together. Now she had brought her.

He was of course delighted to see her alive. He did feel a little excitement that she was sitting so quietly and demurely beside him, looking about her with great interest at the places they past as they drove out through the Pilgrim Gate. Is she not too composed to be in love with me? Mother thought *I* loved *her*. Mother could be wrong. On board ship he had often thought of 'little Eunice' with tenderness but supposed she had passed out of his life. Now suddenly she was here and practically planted in his lap. The only thing he knew for sure was that he could never behave to his parents in front of her as he had done that morning. She had already looked askance at him for being drunk.

He told himself, I *was* drunk and I'm ashamed of it, but

could I live with her the rest of my life? Could I have with her the marriage Father and Mother have had? I am not in love as they are. I can't see where my life is going. I feel like wreaking vengeance on the Dutch for Henry's death but I know that we have killed thousands of their sons. I seem to have little heart for the care of Horden Hall and its estates. Mother has her finger on its pulse of life with more enthusiasm than I ever could.

"Nothing to say, Cousin Daniel?" Celia snapped. "I asked you if you have fully recovered from your wound."

"I beg your pardon. Yes, indeed, I thank you."

Celia chuckled, oblivious of their driver. "Ah, I know you are in a heaven of delight at the return of your long-lost love."

He felt Eunice quiver and he knew he was blushing hotly himself, with anger, not love. Fortunately he was distracted by them reaching the junction of the two tracks one leading to the village and one to the Hall.

"Keep to the right hand," he ordered the driver. Thank God they were nearly there but what mischief this woman would make if she was permanently among them he could hardly bear to think.

In his confusion he began to gabble to Eunice about the state of the woods which were now visible ahead of them. "They are all ours but in a neglected state. We haven't had the men to clear them and encourage the best trees to flourish."

"But to own whole forests!" she exclaimed. "Now you are well what a grand work for you to do. In London I would have thought it a delight to have a blade of grass outside our little house. May I walk in your woods, Cousin? I have never done such a thing in my life."

"Of course you may. I will clear some of the paths." Why had he not thought of that before? Wielding an axe might have dissipated his black moods. "Now" – he pointed – "you can see the first glimpse of the Hall. As we come round this bend, there are the gates ahead."

In the sunshine the solid grey stone rectangle of the Hall with its pillared porch, its ornamental brick chimneys and the flamboyant equestrian statue outside did, he thought, look rather grand. He felt a little pride which he swotted down quickly when he thought of the house Eunice had lived in most of her life.

"Oh!" she exclaimed. "I never imagined anything so magnificent."

"Wait till you get nearer. You'll see it's sadly in need of repair. We keep a bucket in one of the attics where the roof's leaking. Ah, here are my father and mother running out and Ursula. You saw Ursula, Cousin Celia, I believe on your long ago visit. Eunice, she is an angel but terribly deformed. Don't be shocked."

Celia was shaking her head. "It was her face made your Uncle Robert's horse rear up. That's what killed him. I was there. It was very dreadful. So she's still with you, is she?"

They were now recognised by the excited group outside the house and Daniel could only glare at Celia as they drew up in front. No one should live at Horden Hall who did not love Ursula.

He jumped out and lifted Eunice down. She was trembling and quite pale with nervousness he could see, but much lighter than he remembered Diana Rombeau.

"Look what I've brought you, Mother."

Bel was in tears of ecstasy. He could see that. She couldn't speak. His father's sweet kindly face was brimming with joy too and Ursula was absolutely bouncing up and down, her bright eyes lit up.

Celia was forgotten. The driver handed her down and unloaded the baggage.

The air was full of unspoken questions but just now, Daniel thought, I am aware of nothing but the love my parents are showering on Eunice. His own eyes filled with tears as his mother at last released her from her enveloping hug.

He needed that too. "Mother." He flung his arms round her as if he too had been away a long time, which was truly how it felt.

"Cousin Celia," his father said, when he too had kissed and embraced Eunice, "you are most welcome. I fear you catch us on the hop. Your letter only came to hand this morning. We have no idea how Daniel came to fetch you. We didn't know where he was. We waited dinner a while. I am afraid it has now been eaten but Ursula here is a wonder at producing refreshments in a hurry."

Eunice had not spoken at all. Daniel saw she was too overcome at the warmth of her welcome. They all began to move towards the house, Celia explaining that they had eaten in Newcastle. Then Eunice looked up at him and murmured,

"May I be presented to Ursula?"

Daniel reached out and grabbed Ursula who was trotting after them.

"Meet my cousin, Mistress Horden."

Eunice stopped still and held out her hand. "Eunice, please."

Ursula gave a little curtsey. Daniel was amused to see they were the same height. They looked into each other's eyes and then Ursula clasped Eunice's hand.

"We are friends already," she said.

CHAPTER 24

EUNICE stood at the pointed window of the former chapel room, looking out at the statue of Sir Ralph in the soft glow of the autumn sunset. She had refused to be housed in any other room when Bel protested that this had been chosen for Celia's lady's maid and their man had opened up the connecting door to Celia's room.

"Then I can fulfil that function perfectly from here," Eunice had told her. "I have lately been only a kitchen maid."

Bel had laughed and agreed. Bel was fresh air after Celia. There was no fussing and she must remember to call her Bel and the Reverend Nat.

Eunice had unpacked her own things while Bel was with her and a cheerful plump maid called Peggy had helped Celia settle in "for now," Bel said, "because you must come down and sit in the sunshine. We are all waiting to hear your story."

So she and Bel and Nat had sat on the bench below the Hall window with Daniel on the grass at their feet and she had told her tale.

They were engrossed and asked questions but it was nothing like the fearful interrogations her father had conducted. She could withhold her reasons for heading to a town with dockyards. They accepted she was escaping from

London's plague-ridden streets. She never mentioned Patience Porter though she made them smile with her account of Mr and Mrs Harrison's household. She touched lightly on the rope ends that had hung in the kitchen. She kept quiet about seeing Daniel disembark even when he exclaimed that he had come ashore there and if only he had known he would have rescued her from them. She was able to report truly how she had overheard talk of the death of her grandfather and had hurried to London. But when it came to the Great Fire she spared them the worst horror she had seen.

"Our little house was consumed and all the streets from there to the river. We were packing up in The Strand when it was at last stayed. And that was when the lawyer came and told poor grandmother of the state of her affairs."

At this point she wanted to be open about her own annuity but feared it would sound as if she were saying, "See, Daniel would not be marrying a pauper."

She had watched him as she talked. He was absorbed and then abstracted, digging little holes in the grass with a stick he had found. He is not in love with me, she told herself now as she gazed out at the statue. Whereas I, yes, I am *in* love with him, I know. But I must not *love* him. I do not know at all what sort of a man he is. He was certainly drunk when I met him. He had left his parents with no idea of where he was. He could have been helping in the fields, Bel told me, for he is fit enough but she didn't know why he had walked to Newcastle.

"The truth is," Bel said, "he has not been himself since his illness. We must give him time."

A little time, Eunice reflected, is what I will need to discover his real nature. If I then truly love him it will be sad for me. Maybe I will have to go away. Maybe I will have to take Grandmother away if she upsets their happy household. I will have to find a place for us both in Newcastle and earn a little and support her.

Meanwhile, she thought, as she stepped to the bedside, I am here, in his house, which I never dreamt I would ever be. There is food and shelter and I can work in any way I can to help that sweet soul, Ursula, who is full of laughter. I am most blest. I will learn to laugh too.

Bel lay with her arms round Nat and her lips close to his ear.

"You are right that Dan is better than he was but he is not whole yet."

"Is that not because he is unsure of his feelings towards Eunice? Celia is so determined to bounce them together and Dan is not prepared to be bounced."

She kissed his nose. "You put that so well, my darling, and you are right, but there is something deeper than that."

"He is still troubled by his friend's death. I was near to uncovering something when I met him on the way home from the church but he left me suddenly as if he couldn't bear to speak of it."

She kissed his cheek. "Right again, but I still believe there is something more. On Sundays you are at the altar, not sitting beside him as I am, and I have sensed discomfort, rebellion even. He was wayward in his attention as a boy but this is the questioning of a man. He speaks the responses under protest. I can feel it. Oh it was wonderful to have him hug me today as if he knew how much he has hurt us all lately. Some sort of restoration took place when he found Eunice at the inn. It was more than the pleasure of seeing her alive. He was among people again. He had to speak, arrange things, make decisions. He needed that. He had so isolated himself since his illness. I do not think he will fall back into his shadow existence but he is still troubled. We must tread carefully. We must make no assumptions about him and Eunice, which will not be easy with Celia around, but –"

He laid a finger on her lips. "But, my Bel, if it is his *faith* he has lost surely I as both his father and pastor should speak with him."

She rolled over onto her back and thought about this. "I'm not sure, Nat. If he approached you, yes, of course. Let us see what the next days and weeks bring. It may happen of itself because Eunice is here, or she may make it worse."

Nat raised himself on one elbow and looked down at her.

"How worse?"

"Because this is a new Eunice, or at least the Eunice she always was till she was squashed into a timid worm by her father. Look at how coolly and calmly she told her story and yet she had at her feet the young man of her dreams. She has amazing self-control. She is years older than our poor Dan in maturity."

"But why then would her steadfastness make Daniel's doubts and troubles worse?"

"Just because she is so steadfast. She has been through horrid experiences and kept her faith. She cannot conceive of denying it and will tell him so when they really start to converse. I think he will be a little frightened of her, a little intimidated, which is not a good prelude to love."

"Do you want him to love her?"

"Oh I do. I could give him to *her* if I have to give him to anyone. And I will have to give him to another woman I know but if I gave him to Eunice I would never lose him. She is not predatory. Strong as she is she is of a humble spirit."

Nat lay down again. "Well, we will see what happens between them but I believe you are right about handling Dan carefully. I wish they might have one day the marriage that you and I have had."

"And still have," she said and next moment they were in a passionate embrace.

Bel soon found that Celia was making herself thoroughly at home. She wanted breakfast in her bedroom so Eunice brought it up to her. Then she would dress with Eunice's help and come down to the parlour about ten o'clock expecting Bel to sit with her and chat. At first because she was so newly come Bel obliged but after a week or two it became intolerably irksome. One October morning when the sun was shining outside and Celia had commented yet again on the impossibility of running a place as big as this with so few servants Bel decided to be very direct with her.

"Cousin, you have been used to a lady's maid but Eunice

is acting that part very well. We had another maid as well as Peggy when Nat's parents were living at the vicarage but she left to be married and Peggy helps here now as well as cleaning the vicarage. We live simply. Adam is a good man now he has learnt more than how to groom horses. He makes the fires and chops wood but Dan or Nat will chop wood if he is on an errand. There is a certain amount of work that any household requires and none of us is ashamed to turn our hand to anything. We have had to do it. It may be we will grow more prosperous. Already the tenants are paying their rents more regularly and we can sell the produce of our land. The farmhands from the home farm and the other farms help us and each other when fields are to be sown or harvested. It may be a different society from London life but I'm sure you will learn to love it."

"Oh I know you seem to manage, but I don't at all understand about the ugly woman, Ursula. She is your cook-maid, I suppose, and yet you told her to sit with us at dinner the first day when she was leaving the room. That is unheard of and it seemed to me she was very reluctant to do so."

Bel remembered very well the little scene she had had with Ursula afterwards.

"I didn't sit at table, Bel, when you had the French family."

"Ah but they were merely here for a visit. We may be encumbered with Celia for the rest of her life and I will not let her disrupt our arrangements. Peggy and Adam would be embarrassed if I asked them to sit down with us but you have been a friend from my childhood."

"Mistress Celia is not happy looking at me across the table."

"Then Mistress Celia must get used to it. That's an order."

Ursula made her first and last little act of rebellion. She stuck her hands on her hips and planted her feet apart. "Bel, you said we were old friends. You don't give orders to friends. If I am to take orders I am a servant and will stay in the kitchen."

"Oh you cunning, adorable angel. Then I will say, dear friend, I will be sad and hurt if you do not sit with the family at meals."

Ursula made one of her submissive little curtseys, her eyes twinkling with mischief. "Put like that, I can't refuse." And so, having served dinner, she would now slip into her place and eat it and be the first to rise and clear away. She had not chatted at all at table since the arrival of their guests but that, Bel hoped, would change.

So, struggling to put on her most patient smile, she told Celia now, "Then I will explain about Ursula. God sent her into the world with that deformity of face to test all those with whom she has any dealings. He also gave her the most cheerful loving disposition and the blessed gift of contentment. She expects nothing from life or people so we give her everything, all the love of which we are capable. She is the dearest friend I have and is the most important part of our family."

"But she does the cooking!"

"Well, I would do the cooking if I was half as good as she is. I do what I can under her advice. And now of course we have an extra pair of hands in Eunice. I found her helping with the washing yesterday."

"Oh well, look at the life she has led. I wonder how she will ever manage to be the lady of the manor."

"Very well, if it is Horden Hall of which she is the lady."

"If! Do you not expect it, Arabella? Is it not obvious they will marry?"

"I will expect it when they find it obvious themselves and not before."

Celia now became the impatient one. She rose from her chair and walked about the parlour. "Well! I must have words with Eunice. She doesn't do nearly enough to make herself attractive to a young man. What can we do about her hair?"

"Nothing, I beg, Cousin. I would wish Dan to look beyond the outward person to the soul within."

Celia stopped beside a portrait of a handsome lady in the ball gown of Queen Elizabeth's time. "I have it. We should give a ball to celebrate her coming back to us so miraculously and also of course your Daniel's recovery. Then I would see that she dressed up properly. Maybe you always have a harvest ball. I have learnt that country people like to link their festivities with those sorts of things."

Bel laughed. "I have never known a ball here all my life. That wicked old man out there on his horse, the husband of the lady in the portrait, gave balls a plenty and his descendants have had to pay his debts. My father put on a harvest supper for the tenants when he was in funds but we have never copied the splendid functions held by the coal merchants of

Newcastle. That is where the wealth is in this part of the world. Besides," she added, "you and Eunice are still in mourning for your poor husband."

Celia waved her podgy arms about. "True, true, but I thought you who pay so little attention to what is proper might have disregarded that."

Bel chuckled. "Dear Celia, pray wear your mourning as long or as short a time as you see fit. This is your home now and Nat and I want you to feel free to do as you please, come and go as you please and be as happy as you can."

To her shock and dismay Celia's puffy face crumpled and she burst into a flood of tears and sank back into her chair. Bel was beside her at once ready to enfold her in her arms but she waved her away.

"What did I say?" Bel had a guilty feeling she had been teasing her.

"How can I do as I please?" The words choked out between sobs. "I have no money. It would please me to go shopping in Newcastle but how would I get there and how would I buy anything? Eunice has money but I don't like to ask her even though it's what my own husband left her and what did I get? – only his debts."

Bel stood still beside her chair. This was a surprise. Eunice – an heiress? Had not Clifford's whole estate been swallowed up in the failure of his business ventures?

Celia gulped a little and looked up at her. "I shouldn't have said that if she has not told you."

Bel shook her head. "There is no harm done. I can ask

her myself. But you" – she knelt down by her chair and put her hand on her arm – "I should have considered how you must be feeling. I have been homeless myself but I was young and could work. I will talk to Nat. You must have some independence. Please don't cry."

Celia clasped her hand. "You are a strange girl, Arabella, but I believe you have a heart of gold."

Bel laughed. "If I am still a girl with a grown-up son I am happy indeed but pray call me Bel. Everyone does. Cheer up and I will see what can be done. I wonder where the young people are?"

Daniel, armed with an axe was hacking at the tangle of brambles that blocked his way into the woods from the stable-yard. He had seen Eunice in the kitchen with Ursula preparing dinner and had made sure she knew what he intended to do.

"If I could make a path direct through to the church it would be a useful short-cut for my father."

She had smiled her approval but said nothing.

He had been at it an hour or two and had felled some self-sown sycamore saplings and made an opening a few yards in. A quarter of a mile, which he reckoned it would be, was going to take a long time. He wanted to see instant results.

He was wiping his brow when Eunice appeared behind him with a mug of ale.

"Ursula thought you would be thirsty."

He took it and drank it off.

"Another?" she asked and there was a meaningful look in

her eyes.

He set down the axe and grinned at her. "You heard the boy at the inn say I had had three pots of beer." She nodded. "He was right and it was the strongest they had. Do you think I make a habit of indulgence like that?"

She spread out her hands. "I don't know. I only know how you seemed when I woke you."

"Yes, and I remember how I felt and I didn't like it. I saw plenty of drunkenness on board ship and it made me wary. That day, when you came, I didn't want to be wary. I just wanted to forget."

"Forget what?" The way she asked it told him she really wanted to know but he couldn't speak of Henry's death, much less the turmoil in his own mind.

"Oh just things. Everything if you like. I'd better get on with this work."

She looked down at the scattered strands of blackberries he had flung out behind him.

"You have cut them off at the level of the soil. They will grow again. If you tell me where there is a spade I will fetch it."

He cocked his head on one side and looked down at her little determined figure. "You hadn't even a blade of grass in your little lane. What do you know about brambles?"

"I remember a place in the Moorfields where Father and I sometimes walked in autumn. We picked the blackberries if they were ripe but he also preached a little sermon about them. He said if they choked up a garden you had to do more than cut them back because they would come again stronger than ever, like sin. Every scrap of root must be dug up just as we try to eradicate even the smallest temptations to sin."

"I can imagine him saying it. Well, you may bring me a spade from the shed beyond the stables if you wish but spare me the sermon. I will do my best with the roots. This task is going to be a great one if I have to dig up every weed." She began to trot away. "Will it not be too heavy for you? You are such a little thing. It'll be nearly as big as you."

She smiled over her shoulder and walked off.

What swift, light steps, he thought. I love the way she moves. He waited idle till he saw her coming back with the spade on her shoulder like a farm worker. She set it down by him and pointed to where a thick stem poked up a few inches from the earth.

He drove in the spade and upturned a wiry mass of roots. She pointed to another emergent stem.

"What a taskmaster you would be!" he chuckled and to his surprise she chuckled too.

"I was acting just the way Mrs Harrison used to do when she was pointing out specks of soot on the mantle above the fireplace." She smiled up at him and added, "The dinner will be ready in half an hour," and walked off again to disappear in at the kitchen door.

He wanted her back. He wanted that roguish little smile. Never had he imagined from his brief meetings with her in those old days that she could smile like that. Ah, but she had preached to him. She could never escape her father's influence. He dug up one more bramble and then resumed his vigorous hacking with the axe.

Bel found Nat in the study. "Two things," she said, sitting down on his desk and displacing some of his papers. "Celia has just told me Eunice has money. Somehow Clifford left her something which she can keep. I must find out how much. But the other thing is that Celia is completely without any money at all and she would like to go shopping in Newcastle."

Nat laid down his pen and sat back in his chair. "Number two thing we already knew surely, so she can *not* go shopping in Newcastle. Number one thing. How do you propose to find out?"

"Ask Eunice of course. But think again about number two thing for a moment. Celia has never in her life wanted money. She was in tears just now as if it had only just struck her that she can do nothing for herself at all. The power to snap her fingers and servants would come running, the freedom to call for her coach and go to her dressmakers for a new silk or a collar in the best Florentine lace. None of these things can ever happen to her again. She cannot even order a little treat for supper."

"Yes, I'm sorry for her but life is hard and she will have to get used to it. As to Eunice, do you really think you can ask her directly?"

"Yes. She is a direct sort of girl and she knows I am too. But about Celia, I was wondering. Could we possibly make her a small monthly allowance? She could have some choice then, spend it on trifles or save it up if she wants a new gown."

"I fear it would be wasted but I suppose I could spare her a quarter of my stipend, say, a round figure of a pound a month. Now may I continue my work? That paper on Job that I sent to the Bishop, he likes it and will help me to have it published, but he has made some suggestions where I might amplify certain points."

"Oh my darling, and I interrupted you. You work so hard in the parish for only fifty pounds a year and write learned treaties too. And what do I do?"

"Just run this vast estate for our indolent son."

"Ah but there you are wrong, Nat. Before I came to you I spoke to Eunice and Ursula in the kitchen about the dinner and they tell me Dan is in the wood hacking a short cut to church for you."

"I'm delighted to hear it."

Bel saw him return to his paper on Job with renewed zest.

She went back to Celia in the parlour and found her slumped in her chair with her double chin on her chest. Her flabby cheeks were pale and there were still tears glistening on them. How comfortable we could be, Beth thought, if she quietly slipped away to her Maker. *He* would know how to manage her.

Celia opened her eyes and sat up.

"Oh Arabella, you startled me. Have I been asleep?"

"A few minutes. And it's *Bel.*"

"I'll never get used to that, it's so abbreviated. You said you were going to speak to Nathaniel."

"Nat. I did. He would like you to have an allowance of a

pound a month."

"Oh!" Bel could see her thinking of the jewellery she had had to sell and how impossible it would be ever to replace it on a pound a month.

"Do you realise, Celia, that we are now a household of eight persons and a pound a month is just about a quarter of a clergyman's stipend?"

"Oh no, I never understood money. What do you pay that Ursula?"

"Nothing. She is family. She has never wanted money. If I see her dress or aprons looking shabby I buy her some material or more likely find some old curtains and she clothes herself anew."

"You are trying to make me ashamed."

"No truly. Ursula has been used to a different life. Nat would like you to have what I said. We can manage. Dan may even get some back pay from the navy. Apparently they are always in arrears but I dread him hearing of a new muster in the spring. Let us pray for peace, Cousin, and meanwhile be happy."

She stooped down and gave her a peck on the cheek.

Eunice came in and said dinner was ready.

"Daniel says he is very hungry," she added. Her smile and flushed cheeks told Bel all she wanted to know.

It was after dinner when Daniel had gone back to his work that Eunice found herself alone with Bel in the dining-room folding the linen cloth that had been used on the table.

"It will serve another meal," Bel said, laying it on the side table.

"Cousin Arabella," Eunice began in what sounded in her own ears as an unnecessarily portentous tone.

Bel faced her. "Bel, please. What is it?"

"I want to tell you something."

Bel drew her to the window seat, her face alight with excitement. Oh, thought Eunice, she believes it is something about Daniel.

She broached it quickly, "If I stay here, Bel, I would like to contribute to the household expenses. Or I could take Grandmother away and find ourselves a little place in Newcastle. I might be able to teach in a school. You have been so kind to us but I'm afraid Grandmother is a trial to you."

Bel took her hand and patted it. "Trials are good for us, but tell me how –"

"It was Grandfather. He left me an annuity of thirty pounds a year. I have never had such wealth." It was said at last and with much relief.

Bel, who seemed to have been holding her breath, drew a long sigh and then smiled into her eyes. "My dear, it is not a great sum. Keep it for your own needs but pray, don't think of leaving us. How would we manage without you?"

"But I have always had work to do with the poor. I taught orphans for a while before the plague drove them away. The life here – it is so happy and comfortable –"

"Ah, comfort is sinful is it not? That is the legacy your father left you."

Eunice felt tears rising. "Do you all despise my father?"

Bel was shocked. "Despise! Never. Well, yes, I might have done when I was forced to be betrothed to him. He was so shy, so silent, so overawed by *his* father. Now I can understand how a fanatical sect could get hold of him and transform his whole view of life, turning him against all that his father stood for, the getting of wealth, the living in luxury. No, he found his voice all right and he held to his principles. I could not despise him though I might have found it hard to love him."

"He loved my mother."

"Do you remember your mother?"

"Oh yes, I was five when she died – and my baby brother. Father was a broken man for a while. Then he began to go to these meetings and he came to believe that we must seek hardship in this life as a test, relieve it where we can and preach repentance."

Bel smiled. "My Nat would agree that life is a testing time which is why he is so courteous to your grandmother however much of a trial she may be. I am more impatient because I want to truly love her and sometimes it's hard. What we are sure of is that God is infinite love – as he said in his Sunday homily."

Eunice thought for a little. Bel was still holding her hand. "I had never been to a service with the sacrament and such short preaching. You call it a homily. There was deep matter in it but no fear. I don't understand why my father spoke against so many things – bishops, vestments, even the sacrament. He loved me I know but he never hugged me. I see you all the time, touching, loving. You hug Ursula many times a day. You hugged me when I arrived as I have never been hugged in my life. It was a wonderful thing."

She realised she couldn't stop the tears now. They flowed and Bel held onto her and wept too.

At last Bel drew back her head. "No more talk of leaving us? I have an idea what you and I can do today. We will get Adam to harness up one of the horses to our old cart. It's a ramshackle thing but it will suit our purpose. We will load it with the logs from Dan's tree-cutting and go round the village to the poorest people."

Eunice jumped up. "Oh yes, that would make me very happy." She hesitated. "But I would still like to contribute –"

"Well, we will speak of that another time. You will need clothes when you come out of that gloomy black which I think you should do at Christmas. You are young and that is long enough mourning for a grandfather." She was laughing as she said it, with an arm round Eunice's shoulders as they walked through to the kitchen.

Bel told Ursula what they were going to do and then they passed into the stable yard to find Adam.

CHAPTER 25

BEL thought life was going along calmly with Celia till Daniel's twenty-second birthday loomed in October. Celia exclaimed one day in the middle of dinner, "This young man here tells me he was on board ship for his last birthday. That means the baronet, Sir Daniel Wilson Horden, has never had a coming of age party. What, no ceremony for the heir of this great estate? It must be rectified at once."

Dan mumbled into his dinner, "I don't want a party."

Ursula, who rarely spoke at meals with Celia there, lifted her head. She said softly with her bright eyes fixed on his face, "Will you finish your path by Christmas? *Then* you might like a party."

He met her look and Bel saw with a stab of jealousy that a special spark of understanding passed between them. She instantly crushed down the jealousy and rejoiced.

Dan said, "When I reach the church eh?"

Ursula nodded. The deepening fan of lines at the corner of her eyes and the wide grimace of her twisted mouth showed she was smiling her broadest.

Bel realised Nat was trying to catch her eye. He was shaking his head, oblivious of the significance of what had just passed.

"I'm afraid we haven't the funds for a party at present,

Celia. I would wish to do something for the whole village at Christmas but –"

Celia clapped her hands. "At Christmas then. I have some pearls I saved from the grasping lawyers. One of those wealthy coal owners might like to give them to his wife at Christmas. If I just have enough for a new gown for Eunice you can have the rest for the party."

She beamed round at them all, her little eyes almost disappearing behind the mounds of her cheeks.

Nat shook his head again. "We couldn't touch that."

Bel saw a real shadow of disappointment fall across Celia's face. She reached a hand out and clasped hers where it had flopped to the table.

"No, you *shall* give us a party, Celia. Last Christmas was so sad for us without Dan. Let it be a Twelfth Night party. Nat's spiritual duties will be over by then."

The shadow was gone in a moment. "That will give us more time and who knows," Celia was looking from Dan to Eunice, "there may be more to celebrate by then."

Instantly she had spoilt Bel's pleasure as she sensed the embarrassment of the young couple.

Nat had not missed that and Bel could tell from his expression that it angered him but he kept up his unfailing courtesy. "Well, Celia, it is most handsome of you and we are grateful."

Celia wagged her finger at Dan. "Now, young man, you shall come of age properly whatever you say."

There were times in the next weeks when Bel wished

she had not been so ready to accept Celia's idea. Celia could talk of little else and her ideas for musicians, decorations and the food and drink to be ordered made them wonder if the pearls would stretch so far. She hired a coach to take them into Newcastle to a jeweller's and insisted on Eunice accompanying her.

"You shall choose the material for your dress. Oh how I would have loved to dress my little girls who died. Now I have a daughter again. What fun this will be!"

Eunice confided to Bel that she would be pleased to take advantage of Celia's experience in these matters but would pay for her own dress. When they returned Celia said it must be a secret till Twelfth Night and Eunice told Bel, "I will sew it in my room to humour her but it will be no great surprise – just a dress."

"But the first evening gown you have ever worn so you are allowed to be a little excited."

Dan pressed on doggedly with the work he had set himself, rain or shine. As he extended the path further into the wood there were places where he could move faster because it was too dark for much undergrowth but he was ruthless in removing dead branches and closely set saplings and Bel and Eunice or sometimes Eunice alone, now she had become familiar with the village people, kept them supplied with logs and kindling. The pile for the Hall's own use grew in the tool-shed.

Bel was closely observing Dan's changes of mood. Mostly he seemed quiet and she was sure he was avoiding being alone with Eunice. Bel blamed Celia's little hints and teasing. "She will drive them apart," she said to Nat. "Dan has a rich vein of obstinacy in him. I have tried to explain this to Celia but she just laughs and says they are bound to come together living in the same house. Poor Eunice suffers worst because she is seriously in love with him. Oh she keeps her composure outwardly but it must be a torment for her."

"It's a pity then that he has not been summoned back to his ship."

"Don't say that. I couldn't bear to lose him again. Surely the peace negotiations will be concluded soon and then the navy will not *want* him back. They can't pay so many in peacetime."

"Being away however might make him realise what a treasure Eunice is."

Bel shook her head. "Too high a price for me to pay."

One thing Bel had insisted on was that the village who were invited en masse to the party should have some part in the preparations so instead of ordering costly hanging decorations she and Eunice visited the school with some old paper bills and dried up tubs of paint and suggested the children could cut the paper into triangles like little flags and paint over the writing in different colours. The children had a lovely messy time pounding the paints into powders and mixing them with oil and brushing them onto the flags. They spread these out on the schoolroom floor to dry. Old lengths of ribbon were gathered together from every household, slotted through a corner of each flag and tied together to make long streamers. On the afternoon before the party two of the older children brought them to the Hall in a clean sack.

"I can't put them up till I've finished my path," Daniel said, but he hacked through the last branches and beds of nettles as the short winter daylight faded. Then he brought in from the barn the ladder he had used for putting up holly and mistletoe on Christmas Eve.

"You're tired," Bel said. "Do them in the morning."

"No, I'm happy, Mother. I'll do them after supper."

She looked into his face then, wondering at the excitement in his voice.

He grinned down at her. "Nana Sula was right. I had to make that path. Those last yards I could see the low light shining through the church tower windows. It was good, that light." He gave her a spontaneous hug and she hid her tears of joy against his chest.

Later when she had a moment alone with Nat, she told him, "You have your short-cut to the church and we have our son back."

"God be praised," he said.

There was a light-hearted atmosphere at supper in the small dining-room which Bel could see puzzled Celia. Eunice had caught the meaning of it though Dan had said no more to her than, "I've finished the path."

Celia looked from one face to another. Ursula's ugliness was radiant. "Well, parties should happen more often at Horden Hall," she said. "It's put you all in a good mood. I'm glad I suggested it." But she obviously felt left out of something she didn't understand and her little eyes darted about like angry flies.

When the meal was over Dan and Adam carried the old deal table from the curtained off corner into the centre of the hall and set two candlesticks on it to illuminate the proceedings. Then Daniel tipped out the contents of the sack onto the floor and Eunice crouched down and began very carefully untangling it all as he set the ladder against the wall above the great doors. There was a brass rail for a curtain to keep out draughts there but the curtain had long since become threadbare and had not been replaced.

Bel was intrigued to see Dan and Eunice working together and kept her distance.

"There are two separate lengths which should reach across," Eunice called up to him. "If you attach one to each end of the rail I think the other ends can be tied round the banisters near the top of the stairs. Here, I've freed one end." She carried it over to him and held it up. He took it from her hand and climbed up till he could fasten it round the rail.

Bel could see he was looking at Eunice with new eyes. Always she had noted Eunice's intense awareness of his proximity but now she could see it in his manner with her too. It's as I hoped, she thought, love spills over in all directions like a flood.

As Daniel drew the ribbon over the rail and tied it Eunice crouched down to separate the rest of that line from the other one.

Bel had left Celia dozing in the small parlour but it was at this moment that she came out to see what was going on.

She trotted over to Eunice exclaiming, “Why are you stooping like that? Here, get it all up off the floor,” and she grabbed the whole bundle and dumped it on the table.

Eunice jumped up too, exclaiming, “Don’t tangle it again.”

Between them somehow – and Bel was sure it was Celia’s flapping arms – one of the candlesticks was knocked over.

It fell among the paper and ribbons and there was an instant flare up. From it fire began to run from one flag to another up the ribbon towards Daniel. Eunice screamed as the ribbon burnt through and flaming flags fell against him. He flapped his hands at it and it was almost instantly extinguished. He jumped down and swept the little fire from the table top onto the floor where he stamped it out. Eunice righted the candlestick which was blackening the table top and in a moment there was nothing but ash and scorch marks left.

Bel had started to run to the kitchen for water but seeing it extinguished she came back, shaking her head, devastated at the thought of the children’s work so quickly destroyed.

Eunice was white and shaking. “Oh Daniel, your hands!” she gasped out.

“No damage.” He held them out. “They are like leather after all the work I have been doing.”

Bel could see Eunice was deeply shocked by the incident. She vanished into the kitchen and came back with a broom and shovel but she was still trembling as she tried to clear up the mess. Ursula followed her with a bucket and a scrubbing brush.

"We'll soon have it cleaned up but whatever will we say to the children?"

"We'll have to tell them the truth," Bel said.

Celia had retreated, squealing, at the blaze. Now she came back to the middle of the room with an air of defiance. "Well, they were tawdry things. The hall will look better with just the greenery. Come it is late, Eunice. Help me to bed."

Leaving Ursula to finish the clearing up she seized Eunice's hand and marched her up the stairs.

Bel saw Eunice look back at Dan. He met her eyes for a moment, smiled and shrugged his shoulders before carrying the ladder away.

Eunice's hands were still trembling as she struggled to undo Celia's lacings. She could pay no attention to her chatter and when she was allowed to retreat into her own little room all she could see in her mind's eye was the sudden burst of fire and its rapid ascent towards the figure of Daniel.

She said her prayers and lay down but the picture wouldn't go away. It was the more horrible because for the first time she had felt a bond with Daniel. I am not just in love. I could love and respect him and he does feel something for me. And then fire had leapt up at him – between them. Was it an omen of doom? She could hear her father's voice preaching of the fires of hell. She was afraid to sleep in case she had one of her nightmares of the Great Fire but at last weariness must have overtaken her because the next thing she knew she woke screaming. A burning roof was about to collapse on Daniel's head. His glorious flaxen locks were already alight.

She clutched her own head as she sat up, gasping in bed.

Did I scream out loud? she asked herself. She drew back her bed curtains and listened hopefully for complete silence. No, there were swift footsteps outside and her door opened. The tall figure of Daniel in his night shirt stood there, just lit by pale moonshine. He looked about him.

"What is it? What happened?"

"Oh, I'm sorry, I'm sorry." She pulled the bedcovers up round her. "I've woken everyone. Oh it was a horrible nightmare."

He listened at the door. There was no more sound anywhere.

"No one else heard. I was awake myself. Your grandmother in the next room must sleep like a log." He shut the door and came and sat on the edge of the bed

Eunice was trying to collect herself. Her father would have been appalled. She had a man in her bedroom and neither of them were properly clothed. But still she could see the image in her dream. She put out her hand and just touched his hair.

"You're all right. You were on fire. Oh it was horrible."

Now she was seeing the house collapsing on the old woman. That was real. That had actually happened.

"What? It was that silly little fire in the hall? It was over in a second or two. You're still shaking."

"It's not the first nightmare I've had about fire. You don't know what it was like in London."

"Tell me."

She shook her head. "You must go."

"Well, I won't because you may dream again. Tell me and it may go away."

Oh how she wanted to keep him there, whole and entire! So she began little by little to describe her frantic visit to their old home to fetch her father's Bible. When she reached the part where she could do nothing but watch as the flaming timbers crashed down on the old woman she was in tears.

"I don't think it will ever leave me but I have never shrieked out before. Only in *this* dream it was *you*." She stopped abruptly fully aware now of their position. She was confiding to this man whom she loved – in her bedroom in the middle of the night. And letting him see her raw emotion, uncontrolled.

In the faint moonlight she could make out his profile. He looked thoughtful, frowning a little. It was very cold and she felt him shiver.

"You must go," she said again. "I am so very sorry."

But he didn't go. "Lie down and keep warm," he said. "I'll put something round me." He got up and fumbled in her small closet and found her winter cloak.

"But – but – this is improper," she murmured, loving to see him wrap it round his shoulders.

"Never mind proper or improper. You've told me your nightmare. I shall tell you mine. Maybe we'll both be free then."

He began to talk very fast and low. She lifted her head to be sure she could hear every word. He spoke of the naval battle that had gone on for four terrible days. He described his friend Henry, carefree, a joker, a slight athletic figure, his only remarkable feature his protruding ears.

"I had come up from the gun deck to report to the captain that there was no more ammunition. Henry was there and when a sailor fell at his feet he seized the man's musket and lifted it to fire but instead the musket was flung back so he fired in the air. I looked round and Henry was a headless corpse falling backward. His head with those ears rolled away across the deck. I will never forget the look of astonishment in his wide open eyes."

"Oh." She could see it too.

"The strange thing was," he went on and she knew that for the moment he was oblivious of her, "everything happened so quickly then that I couldn't hold in my mind that he was dead. The mast was falling and the captain was in danger. I thrust him away and then we were all enveloped in sails and rigging. I was hit with a great splinter off the deck. I had to free others, a boy was screaming. I tore the splinter from my leg so I could crawl out and I freed some who were not much hurt and then I found this thing under the sail and when I cut a hole the thing was Henry's head again all bloody and staring at me. I didn't know where he'd gone and there he was looking at me as if to say 'couldn't you have saved me too?'"

Eunice heard him sob. They were wrenching deep sobs. She struggled to sit up but he was sitting on her legs. She murmured some words of sympathy but he seemed far away, bowed over, his head in his hands.

"It should have been me," he said then. "I'd have been spared all this living."

"No, Daniel." She must break through to him. She struggled to free her legs and he became aware of her movements. He shifted and turned to look at her.

She sat up fully. "Daniel, God has given you life. Be grateful."

"Oh I will, Eunice, if you'll help me"

He had forgotten to keep his voice down. The moon was bright now. It must have sailed suddenly into open sky. They could see each other. He took hold of her hand.

There was a click and a creaking sound. Eunice saw the connecting door opening. Her grandmother stood there.

"Well!"

Daniel jumped up. He put a hand to his head and looked down at Celia.

"I came in because she screamed." He looked at Eunice for confirmation.

She nodded. "I had a nightmare."

"Well!" Her grandmother seemed to be wearing a triumphant smile. "Well, my boy, you'll have to marry her now."

"No," cried Eunice, "you don't understand. I was shrieking out."

"I heard voices talking, no screams. I must say I'm surprised at you, girl. What would your father have said?"

Daniel shed the cloak from his shoulders. "Look, Cousin. You are quite mistaken. She did scream. I calmed her down.

Nothing happened. We began talking."

"Began talking – in the middle of the night!"

"Yes." He sounded angry. "Yes. My God, she's as pure as driven snow. Don't you dare to scold her. I'm going back to bed."

He walked out onto the landing and shut the door.

"Well!" Celia said again, "He can't escape now whatever story he tells his parents. You've got him now, my girl." She rubbed her hands together. "I'll catch my death if I stay up." She turned to go.

"Grandmother, you shall not speak of this. He had no evil intentions. He came out of anxiety and kindness."

"And what would have been his next move? You are a young woman and available and I won't let him trifle with you like that. Have you not a lock on the door?"

Eunice clenched her teeth. She thought she had never felt anger for anyone in her whole life as she did now for her grandmother.

Celia wagged her finger at her as she retreated into her own room.

"You can be sure neither of you have heard the last of this."

Eunice lay a long time, flat on her back, wide awake.

It had been a wonderful, beautiful pain having him so close, his hand clasping hers. But how much did it mean? Her grandmother had distorted and trivialised it all. She would never understand that both she and he had been reduced to tears over recollected tragedies that were nothing to do with love for each other. Eunice went over in her head everything that had passed. He had used her name once at the moment when he pleaded for her help. That was a tender, precious plea but it was not a declaration of love. When Celia had said, "You'll have to marry her now," he had not eagerly endorsed that. In fact she had jumped in herself with her emphatic "No." Nothing had happened that put him under any obligation – that was all I meant, she convinced herself, but would he take it as a harsh rebuttal?

It was cruel, she thought, coming after the wonderful frame of mind he was in at supper when he had finished his path. But it was I to whom he told the tale of his friend's death. He said he had never spoken of it to anyone else. Was it only because *I* had confided in *him*? That thoughtful look was provoked by his wondering whether to tell me or not. We might begin to be close to each other if only Grandmother... I must put him to the test. I must leave and find my own place. It is too painful to be under the same roof. With this resolution she fell asleep.

CHAPTER 26

DANIEL was unable to sleep any more. He knew he must speak to his mother before Celia did. He paced his room. He crept downstairs and revived the embers of the kitchen fire. He fed it some sticks from the basket and watched them catch light. He recalled Eunice's story of the fire.

I was a callous brute, he told himself. I made no comment on her sufferings, showed no sympathy. I launched into my own nightmare and I could feel how moved she was for me. She is a special character and I believe I could be in love with her now. I once thought I couldn't face being married to a saint. But she is vulnerable. She is not the forbiddingly self-composed being I imagined. I think she loves me – but she may not know it yet. She was swift with her negative when Celia spoke of my marrying her.

After watching the fire for a while he lit a candle from it and carried it back up to his room. He opened his Bible at John's gospel. I know this is the truth, he told himself, as she does. There is a bond. He looked out at the moonlit woods.

At seven o'clock when the moon had slipped down behind the trees he dressed himself and listened for his mother and father getting up.

As soon as he heard them he popped out of his room and

waylaid them on the stairs.

"Mother, I must speak with you a minute."

She was only too delighted, he could tell, as she followed him into his room and sat down on his bed and beamed expectantly at him.

He perched on the clothes chest opposite her. "You won't smile when I tell you what's happened. Celia found me in Eunice's room in the middle of the night."

She didn't smile. She stared for a moment with raised eyebrows. Then she put her hand up to her mouth and laughed. "I wish I'd seen her face."

"But, Mother, she says I'll have to marry Eunice now."

"Why not? No, I withdraw that. You are to be as free as I was. Can you tell me *why* you went into her room in the middle of the night?"

He told it all, including the account of the death of Henry which he had never yet divulged. Again he wept but they were gentler tears. The horror was not so sharp.

Of course her arms were round him. He had expected it and let them stay.

She said, "So she has had her horror too, poor girl. Take a lesson in bravery from her. If it hadn't been for that sad little fire yesterday we would never have known what she had to endure."

"But that's the trouble. She is so much better than I in every way. I would fear a sermon from her whenever I came short."

"Well, we have seen a new Eunice since her father's death. She has had to adapt swiftly to life and that shows me she always will. But the new Eunice will bubble with new joy when she knows she has a good man's love for life."

"But will that be me? I am so unsure of myself. You spoke of her bravery. Mine has gone. I was so sure about the navy but now I see the fighting as all madness. It is a different world from the day I waved to the King on London Bridge or when I knelt before him in the privy garden and he spoke graciously to me. Now I know that fighting for him is all mired in blood, politics and money. We don't want peace but we can't afford to make war."

"Oh, Dan, your talk is darting here there and everywhere. You have not slept. Let us get the party over this evening and then make time for Eunice. Talk with her honestly. She admires directness. If you are not ready for marriage tell her you want to know her better. If you want to propose but doubt her reply simply ask her?"

She stopped and listened.

They could hear Ursula's scampering footsteps on the stairs and then she tapped on Celia's door. "I've brought your breakfast, Mistress Horden. Eunice asked me to."

"Ah the worm has turned." His mother was chuckling again. "Are we seeing yet another Eunice? Eunice the rebel."

They listened till they heard Ursula come out and then they emerged and followed her.

She looked round at the bottom of the stairs and grinned her comical lopsided grin. "What have you been up to, Daniel? Eunice has walked into Newcastle to find another home. She said, 'It's not right for me to be under the same roof as Daniel.'

But she wasn't cross."

He looked at his mother. "What does she think? I'll invade her room again?"

"No, you dolt," Bel said. "She's thinking of her own feelings for once. It's too harrowing to have you so near."

"Well, are we still having a party?" Ursula asked. "You finished your path, Daniel."

Bel gave a little skip. "He did indeed. Yes, the village expects a party. We must have a party. I'll help you make some sweetmeats for the children to comfort them for the loss of their flags."

Daniel grabbed her arm as she was dancing to the kitchen. "Oh come, Mother, what do I do *now* about Eunice?"

"What do you do? Well, ask yourself. You could do nothing at all or – of course – you could ride after her."

He stood still as his mother and Ursula went blithely on. Doing nothing did not fit his mood at all.

"Nana Sula," he shouted after them, "tell Adam to saddle my horse."

He dashed back up to his room for his riding boots and a cloak and hat.

Till he was outside he hadn't realised what a sparkling January morning it was. A white frost had succeeded the cold moonlit night and a cloudless sky shed a brittle light over fields and woods. No one was about and indeed he saw no figure at all till he spotted her, a briskly moving speck heading for the junction with the highroad. In all this wide landscape he saw his hopes gathered in that little dot. All he could think was, “I want her. She is mine if I don’t blunder.” But he would blunder. He had no idea what he would say. He spurred forward.

Eunice heard the hooves when she reckoned she had covered two miles. She knew who it must be before she looked round. What she was unsure of was whether she was glad or sorry. He doesn’t know his own feelings, she had been telling herself, over and over again as she walked. Maybe he loves me as a cousin but is not *in love* with me as a woman. Now, she thought, his coming after me may only lead to more torment and confusion, the very things I want to escape. He may propose on impulse as he has rushed to mount his horse on impulse. So what do I do?

She stood still by the roadside, watching him grow from a small mounted figure to his rosy-faced, long-legged self, drawing rein and looking down at her and about to speak – what words would come out?

“Wherever do you think you’re going?”

She smiled, feeling sure he hadn’t known himself what he would say, as she stared calmly up at him.

“I left a message for your mother.”

He flung himself off his horse. “I know, but dash it – you can’t just go off like that.”

“Why not? I only want to make inquiries for two rooms, for me and my grandmother. She is testing your parents’ patience sorely.” She gave him another smile. “And I yours perhaps.”

"Mine? No, why would you say that?"

He is out of his depth, she thought. Am I being that horrid creature I have always despised – a tease? I should be straightforward and honest with him. He is a sweet, confused boy and I love him to distraction, but he is not quite the complete man that I could honour as a husband. Not yet.

"Look, Cousin Daniel," she said, aware of the rutted roadway, whitened in strips with the night's frost, the crisp grass, the steamy breath of the horse, the surrounding fields and woods, "let us speak openly. My grandmother is constantly dropping hints that we are going to marry. That is very uncomfortable for us both. Your mother and father are too wise to do such a thing but we know they would be happy." She held up her hand as he seemed about to break in. "So it is neither pleasant nor seemly for us to be together any longer under the same roof."

"D'you mean if we were it would be?" He lifted his hat and scratched his head. "I haven't put that very well."

"Quite clearly enough."

"Well, how about it then? I mean, perhaps we should. Dash it all. It would solve everything then. It would keep Mother and Father happy and silence old Celia."

She stood very still, controlling the shivering that was trying to take hold of her. She compressed her lips and looked him in the eye. "You call that a proposal of marriage? If that is the proposal what would the marriage be like?" She turned to walk on.

"No, please." He grabbed her arm. "I'm sorry. I don't know

how it is but I can't seem to make any sense today. Last night was good. For the first time we really spoke together. If only Celia hadn't come in –"

"But she did and she said you'd have to marry me and that's the only reason we're having this conversation now." She tugged her arm away. "But I've known for a while that I must go away so think no more of it. Just let me be. Go home, Daniel."

"Let me take you into Newcastle then. Come up in front of me."

She laughed. "I've never ridden a horse in my life. I enjoy walking."

"But you'll come back? What about the party?"

"Oh I'll have to be at the party to wear my new dress. Grandmother would never forgive me."

He still stood irresolute. "I couldn't sleep after I left you last night. That tale of the fire. I never showed any sympathy. I just told you *my* tale and you were so kind. You must think me a clumsy oaf or worse, a brute."

"We did well to speak of those things. We should not hide them when they trouble us. Now let me go, Daniel."

"I feel I've been a complete fool."

She shook her head and walked off, turning once to see him mount his horse. He looked after her till she waved and then he turned his horse's head and rode back.

Oh yes, she said to herself, a fool, a clumsy oaf perhaps, but not a brute and in fact I love you more than ever.

"She wouldn't come, Mother."

Daniel found her and Ursula in the midst of pie-making. Bel looked up briefly.

"She has a strong will."

"Yes, I don't know if I could manage her if she *was* my wife."

"Did you propose marriage?"

"Not exactly."

"That was how you proposed to Diana. If you ever do propose marriage to Eunice it must be in earnest. *Then* you will find her melting in your arms."

"Will I really?"

"Now away with you unless you want to cut out the pastry for seventy pies."

He spent the rest of the morning avoiding Celia by working in the tool-shed, leaving the tools he'd used in the wood all clean and shiny.

Eunice came back exactly at noon, the invariable dinner hour.

"I was fortunate to be given a lift on a farm-cart for most of the way," she declared after she'd brushed straw from her dress and washed her hands.

When they sat down at table she addressed her grandmother. "There are two rooms and a sitting-room above the dressmaker's, very clean and comfortable. You will be happier with the bustle of a town and shops and many pleasant places of recreation where you can walk and see life. I said I would bring you to see the place tomorrow, or the next day if you are tired from the party. The rent is manageable as the dressmaker is reducing it if I help her six or seven hours a week."

Bel was intrigued by the struggle going on in Celia's face. Initial anger was being replaced by cunning.

"Well, I will look at it if you haven't changed your mind by then. We all know why you are doing this – after last night's goings on."

Nathaniel spoke up. "This is not our wish, you understand, but we will not oppose it. Perhaps it will be a temporary arrangement." Bel saw he was looking at Daniel but Dan was keeping his eyes down, evidently determined to take no part in this. It was an uncomfortable meal.

The party was to begin at six with music and dancing first and the supper at seven. Old benches had been brought in from the barn where they had been stored since the last gathering for the restoration of the king. That had necessarily been a frugal affair, planned to coincide with the French family's visit but in the end held later because of their rather abrupt departure.

Bel expected Celia to exact some revenge on Eunice for her high-handed arrangements so she wondered what plot was hatching when Celia whisked her granddaughter away an hour beforehand to get her ready.

The arrival of the children would have been a sad business when they had to be told of the loss of all their flags but the sweetmeats laid out for them on the long table soon cheered them up. The musicians quickly got everyone onto their feet when enough people had arrived to make up sets for the old country dances. The memory of them had been kept alive by the occasional clandestine parties during the years of austerity and Bel and Nat led out the villagers in an opening eightsome reel.

"Why is Eunice not here yet?" Dan asked his mother after he had partnered their own maid Peggy.

"She'll come when Celia lets her. Ah here they are now."

Dan looked up as Celia, still in her mourning dress, led Eunice to the top of the stairs where they were in sight of everyone.

"Oh, she looks lovely," Dan exclaimed.

The plain black dress she had worn every day had been replaced by one in pale green silk with an ivory petticoat decorated in green leaves. The light colour made her hair look darker and glossier, fashioned as it was with ribbons of light green and slightly waved round her face. Celia was making a signal of some kind to the leader of the musicians and a special flourish was played which drew everyone's attention to their entrance.

In the silence when it ended Celia called out in her most imperious tones, "Now, good people of Horden, give a special welcome to the future mistress of Horden Hall."

Bel saw Eunice shrink back and try to beat a retreat but Celia was holding her firmly and an unseemly tug of war would have ensued.

"Sir Daniel," Celia went on, "pray step forward and receive your bride-to-be."

Bel turned her eyes on him and met his.

"What can I do? I'll not have her humiliated like this," he muttered and amid cheering and clapping he bounded up the stairs and grabbed Eunice's free hand. Her cheeks were flaming red and her eyes bright with tears of shame.

"This is not my doing," she hissed at him. "You must tell them it is not so."

Celia was wearing a victor's smile which infuriated Bel as she watched. How would her poor inexperienced boy deal with this?

Daniel led Eunice down one step away from Celia who lurked like a black witch behind. He faced the people. Bel's heart pounded and her mouth dried for him.

"Good friends," he said, "my well-meaning cousin has run a little ahead of events. The truth is I have not yet *asked* the lady." He looked down at Eunice with his warmest smile. There was general good-natured laughter at that. "This I hope to do as soon as I feel certain to be accepted. I mean to say," he addressed a group of the young farm hands who were standing together, "a fellow doesn't want to be refused, does he?" There was hearty laughter and cheering from that quarter. "In six month's time when I hope to have shown myself worthy of this very special prize I will attempt to gain it. Then we will have another party, a summer party to celebrate. Meanwhile on with the dancing and, if she is willing, Eunice and I will lead it off."

He brought her down the stairs into the hall and the musicians struck up again.

Bel looked at Nat with tears in her eyes.

"Was that not well done? Our little boy truly carried off the toughest task he has ever had to deal with."

Nat nodded and glanced at the figure of Celia who was disappearing back to her room. "She thought to create a *fait accompli* but it is she who has been put out of countenance."

"And Eunice can dance." Bel was watching her. "She has natural rhythm. How light she is on her feet!"

Nat looked. "She is quick-brained too. She is watching what everyone is doing and keeping step."

"Oh to think what she has been deprived of for so much of her life, music, singing, laughter!"

"And pretty dresses to make the most of herself."

Bel looked up at him and grinned. "You men! I don't want Dan to fall in love with only her outside now. He must love and want her deep down as I did you."

"Will she hold to this going to Newcastle, do you think?"

"More than ever, I'd say, now that she has been given hope. She'll know he'll yearn to see her around as he has these last weeks. That was the danger of her living here, that she would become a commonplace feature of his life. Now he must make an effort to see her and spend time with her. He has to find out that he can't do without her." She squeezed his hand. "I must go and help Ursula and Peggy with the supper."

When Celia didn't reappear Bel herself took a tray up to her room. She could see she had been crying and was instantly sorry for her but Celia swiftly repelled her sympathy.

She waved the tray onto the bedside table. "Of course I

never intended to be present. Parties are not for those still in mourning. I just wanted to give the child courage to go down. I can sit quietly alone up here in this very room where my poor dear Clifford was with me on that visit so very many years ago. I look at the empty space where he lay." She dabbed her eyes with her handkerchief.

Bel was perfectly sure that the tears had been for her own humiliation just now. There had never been much sign of grieving for her husband from the moment of her arrival.

"I can sit with you if you like," Bel offered reluctantly. "They are all busy eating down below."

"Not a pretty sight I'm sure with the manners of peasantry. I never imagined you would have no real society here."

Bel perched brightly on the end of the bed. "You will encounter some in Newcastle when you go which should cheer you up."

"In rooms above a dressmaker's? If Eunice chooses to go there, are you telling me I have to go too?"

Bel felt a tightening of her stomach. "No indeed but it seemed a pleasant way for you to have some independence and Eunice has been so devoted to you. We couldn't spare Peggy to be a true lady's maid, I'm afraid, when Eunice goes."

Celia had not been able to resist picking at the supper tray and now she looked at Bel with her mouth full and mumbled, "Why can't you stop her? She'll be a silly obstinate girl if she lets Daniel slip through her fingers. He'll try in six months indeed! He's just trying to escape. He thought she was a great heiress and now he knows it's a paltry thirty pounds a year –

though that's more than I get." She swallowed her food with difficulty as a sob rose in her throat.

Bel thought, I won't let her anger me. She is cast on a bleak shore in her old age, dependent on others whom she can't bring herself to love because she really has only ever loved herself.

"I believe and trust Dan and Eunice will come together but it must be in their own time. Nat and I may be unusual in paying no regard to the finances of the case but I assure you Dan is in the same mould. He is impulsive but not calculating."

"Oh he's impulsive certainly. Your sister told me he proposed to her Diana one minute and backed out of it the next. *My* plan was to pin him down this time but he wriggled out of it again."

Bel got up to forestall the retort that rose to her lips. "I must rejoin the party. You are free to go or stay, Cousin. Nat will of course continue the small sum he gives you." She slipped out with as warm a smile as she could raise and ran down to the hall where the level of noise was increasing as the store of beers and ales diminished. She found Nat but Dan and Eunice were not in the hall. "Where are they?" she asked.

"Eunice went to help wash mugs for the next sitting. I think half of *Upper* Horden have invited themselves. Dan followed her. We may not have to wait six months for a resolution."

Bel sat down by him and slid her arm round his shoulders. "If she believes he has recovered his faith. They need to be of one mind there. But Celia, I fear, will stay here whatever happens."

CHAPTER 27

In the event, Bel was wrong. Three days after the party both Celia and Eunice moved into the rooms above the dressmaker's.

"I expected her to come," Eunice candidly told Bel. "She could have absolved me of my promise never to leave her now she has been so welcomed here but she couldn't bear to think of the free life I would have without her."

"She is a limpet round your neck."

Eunice smiled. "I don't mind. She took me in when I was homeless –"

"Yes, to serve her needs in everything."

"Well, I am not used to freedom. I will always impose some yoke upon myself, some obligation."

Bel hugged her. "If it is as Dan's wife and the mother of his children I will rejoice. There I have said it but you must both be sure."

Eunice nodded. Bel could see she was too full to speak.

After that Dan found many excuses to ride into Newcastle. He said his interest in scientific studies had been reawakened and he was examining work on more efficient ploughs and the study of soil types in the Tyne valley and new pumps for drainage of boggy land. A little group was meeting in

Newcastle to carry out experiments and share practical experience. "That he also calls at rooms above a dressmaker's shop is quite coincidental," Bel told Nat. "I expect they walk out briefly together and discuss theology. She is enjoying so much your preparing her for confirmation. Politics is not so safe a subject. She may not have shed William's republicanism yet."

Nat kissed her on her laughing lips. "You think they have nothing else to say to each other?"

Early in February Dan came into the study where Nat was reading to her a paper he had written on Isaiah. She saw Dan was carrying a letter and his face showed relief and secret excitement.

"It's from Captain Wallace."

"But you are not in the navy now," Bel cried. The ghastly months of his absence rushed back like a black wave. He was looking happy to be summoned. Did he wish to escape them all again, including Eunice?

"I have never given up my commission. I promised to serve the King."

"It was a boy's dream. You are a man now."

Nathaniel held out his hand for the letter and read it silently. He shook his head at Bel. "You are rushing into unnecessary panic. This is to tell Daniel that the King has given orders that there is to be no refitting of the navy this year. Ships and men are laid off. This is the case even though the peace negotiations have not yet come to any resolution."

Dan perched his long body on the desk

"Does this mean you are safely out of the navy?" Bel asked.

"No, the picture may change."

"But you could resign. What about your sixth month promise to Eunice?"

"She has recognised that I made it to spare her a very painful public moment. I will ride over after dinner and tell her what's happened. She is very open and honest."

When he had gone, Bel looked at Nat. "Perhaps Eunice is too open and honest. If she had been more mysterious, more alluring he might have been newly married to her and then I think he could have told his captain his navy days were over. 'I have married a wife, sir, and therefore I cannot come.'"

When Daniel knocked at the dressmaker's door it was Eunice who opened it.

"I would like you to come for a little walk," he said simply. "Is it convenient now?"

She smiled. Her light brown eyes looked darker and more sparkly than usual.

"Yes, Grandmother has become so friendly with Mistress Foster, the dressmaker, that they are spending hours together these days. Come in while I fetch my cloak."

She indicated a room on the left and ran up the stairs which led straight up from the front door. Daniel found his heart beating fast as he watched her retreating figure. How neatly and swiftly she moved!

He waited in the room which must be where Mistress Foster took prospective customers on a first visit. There was a long sofa under the window facing shelves full of rolls of material and a table piled with pattern books.

Eunice was back very quickly like a little pixie under her hooded green cloak.

"I just told them I was going out and they hardly looked up."

He drew her arm through his and they set out. He was so excited he couldn't speak as he saw her look up into his face with wonder as if she sensed something momentous in his manner. But she chatted on about her grandmother, perhaps to keep the tension at bay.

"It's quite comical. *I* was to help the dressmaker but it's turning out that Grandmother is spending more time sewing with her than I am. I never had a chance to do more than plain sewing but Grandmother is really skilful and though her eyes are not as good as they were she is enjoying doing really fine lacework in the daylight hours. Mistress Foster has a commission for a wedding-dress and they will not entrust me with it at all." She looked about her. "Where are we heading?"

"Down to the river. Is that all right?"

"Perfectly. It's quite a warm afternoon for February. Are your parents well and dear Ursula?"

"Very well, I thank you." It was impossible to talk. He held her closely.

They were descending the steep lane down to the quayside. The river and the bridge to Gateshead were now in sight. There was craft of all sorts plying too and fro.

She looked up into his face. "You've come to show me the

different boats?"

"No, I want you to come and sit with me on a bench along by the wall. It's not too cold to sit a minute? We are in the full sunshine."

She laughed lightly. "No, it's quite warm. Is there something special about that bench?"

"Yes. I'll tell you presently."

"There are children climbing about on it."

He frowned. "So there are. I hope they are not soiling it."

As soon as they were near enough he called out, "You boys, the bench is for weary folk to sit on. Will it please you to give place to this lady and go and play elsewhere." He fished a sixpence from his pocket and threw it a little distance from the bench. "You are to share it. An apple or a bun each."

They rushed for it and the quickest snatched it up. The others, surrounding him, shouted, "It's for all of us." He nodded and they all scampered off along the quay, one of them turning to call out, "Thank you sir," to Daniel.

Eunice peered up at him from under her hood. "That was well done, Daniel."

They sat down and she threw back her hood and turned her face to the sun.

"It's almost springtime."

He swallowed hard. The moment had come. He turned to face her and took both her hands.

"Eunice, I want to tell you something I did when I was a little boy. I caught a moth that was fluttering on the kitchen window at home. I thought I would make a pet of it and put it in a little box. I could hear it fluttering inside and I took it up to my room and set it on the shelf where I kept my few books. Then I forgot about it. It was half hidden by a book leaning against it. When I next looked the moth was dead and I felt very guilty." He paused.

"Oh," she said, "that was sad."

"But I didn't learn from it because that little moth was you and I did it all over again. When I learnt you had almost certainly died of the plague I felt guilty."

She looked at him with wide eyes. "Why? It was not your fault?"

"I thought of that moth. I told my mother when we were admiring the gardens of the Baker's Hall. I said I couldn't stop thinking of you and how you were like that little moth, fluttering for your life in that prison. Then we went to see you and your father before we left London."

"Oh!" she cried, "don't speak of that. I behaved so badly."

He shook his head. "You wrote that letter to my mother. I kept it a long time after I wrote back to your grandmother. I wanted you to know we had received it. I thought of you often, but then came university and my friendship with Henry and I had it fixed in my mind that women were trouble – after my experiences with the French cousins – and I wanted to join the navy. There was such excitement when we came to London. Henry and I kissed the King's hand. I could have come to see you before we went on board ship but I didn't. I was neglectful as I was with that poor little moth and your grandmother kept talking of marriage and I wasn't ready for that. Then of course you died. Or I thought you had. I felt something precious had slipped from me and I was very sad."

Her eyes filled with tears. "I was remiss in not trying to contact anyone. I thought I was quite alone when father died. I had no money till I found some work and then it was a pittance."

"That was dreadful. Let's not think of the past then. I have had today a letter from my Captain of the *Elizabeth* that there is to be no refitting of the navy this year, no fresh manoeuvres. I am free and if I am called upon at a new muster I will resign my commission because, I trust, I will have something more important to do." He realised he was still clasping her hands. They had warmed up under her gloves from the warmth of his grasp. He drew a deep breath. "Eunice, I love you. Before God, I do. The six months is not up but I cannot wait any longer. I didn't know how much I would miss you when you left the Hall but we have had some good walks since and I believe you know me better. I ask you now, will you accept me as your husband. Can you ever love me enough for that?"

Tears were running down her cheeks. She choked out, "Oh Daniel, I have been in love with you from the moment you stood in my room at Grandmother's and spread out your arms like a guardian angel."

He was astonished. "But we had scarcely spoken two words together!"

"I know. I said 'in love.' I promised myself I would never marry unless a devout man I could love and respect came to me and asked for my hand." She looked him steadfastly in the eye. "Now it has happened. Oh Daniel, I will, I will marry you."

She drew her hands from his and clasped him round the waist and positively melted into his arms. He thought of his mother's words. How understanding she was! Oblivious of passers-by he drew her close and kissed her on the lips. She didn't withdraw. This was indeed a new, a passionate Eunice.

A group of youths walked by and the sound of their jeering laughter finally reached them. They separated, both blushing hotly, then their eyes met and they laughed aloud from sheer joy.

"Come, my darling one. We must tell the world," he said.

He took her hand and they stood up. She turned to look back at the bench.

"You chose this spot. Why?"

"It was where my mother and father first met, where she claims they both fell instantly in love though many months passed before they met again. And you are in green as she was. Father always thought of her as his Spring maiden. If you and I can have a marriage like theirs I will indeed rejoice."

She nodded. "You have her warm impulsive nature and I will help you to learn his greater caution and gentle wisdom. I thank God I can be their daughter now."

They walked slowly up The Side again, too happy for speech

At the dressmaker's house she said, "You must come in. Grandmother is entitled to be the first to know that what she urged so often has truly come to pass."

She led him up the stairs to the sewing-room. The two ladies were working under the south facing windows where the light was excellent. There was a fire in the hearth although the afternoon sun had also warmed the room.

Eunice went in first and walked straight up to Celia and kissed her. Daniel hesitated in the doorway till he heard the words, "My betrothed is at the door."

Celia looked round and jumped up with a shriek to throw a white sheet over the work she and the dressmaker were doing. "Mercy on us, he mustn't see it then."

When it was safely covered she said, "Well young cousin, you've done it at last." She clapped her podgy hands and cried, "Look round, Nellie Foster, there's the bridegroom himself, Sir Daniel Wilson Horden."

Nellie, who was as thin as Celia was plump, grinned round at him. "Ay, lad. I knew the first time I opened the door to you what was coming."

Eunice peeped under a corner of the sheet. "Why do you cover this? It is for some unknown customer."

"No, you silly girl. It is for you. Have I not said for years that your day of happiness would come? You all thought old Celia was a nuisance with her predictions but Nellie and I were determined to be ready when it happened. We already had all your measurements. When is the day? We are nearly ready for it now."

Eunice looked up at Daniel. "You promised the village a summer party."

He stepped up to her and clasped her hand. "If I can wait

till then."

Celia now stretched up her arms to him. "My grandson-in-law!"

He kissed her on both cheeks. "Well, Grandmamma, you have always been a step ahead of us." Mischievously he reached to the sheet.

She screamed, "No, don't you look. It's unlucky." Then she cocked her head on one side. "Am I the first to know?" She was delighted to find she was. "Well, off you go home and tell your parents. Eunice shall stay here and try this on. Did you come on horseback?"

"I walked."

"Well, she can't walk there and back here. It would be nightfall. She must stay here till you're wed you know. It wouldn't be proper else."

Eunice looked at him wistfully. "I will come to the door with you."

A long kiss took place before the street door was opened and Daniel, bursting with joy; almost ran the four miles home to make his announcement.

A week before the wedding Eunice walked over from Newcastle with a bundle of newspapers.

"You will be saddened by this, Daniel."

She handed them over.

He was about to scold her for walking on a June day that was chilled by a sea-fret, when his eye caught the words: 'Devastation in the Medway.'

Sitting down on the window seat in the parlour with his arm round Eunice he read the shocking news that the Dutch fleet had come up the Thames, broken the chain at Chatham and fired many of the English fleet, the *Elizabeth* among them.

He had already written to Captain Wallace that his duties to improve his estate and the obligation to be with his new bride compelled him to resign his commission in the navy.

"But is this not a sign, my dearest, that I was *meant* to finish with the navy? England may sometime be a great sea power again but it will hardly come in our day." He read on. "My God, they have towed away the *Royal Charles* and we have sunk many of our smaller ships to block the river but some were carrying vital stores. Meanwhile the King is dallying with the Lady Castlemaine. I am sickened by all this."

She murmured, her head on his shoulder, "Thank God for our lives here."

He looked down at her piquant little face, more rounded now and utterly serene. "I know you want this estate to serve our community. Mother has built it up by her frugality and I shall set some of the returning pressed men to work in the woods. If forestry is productive it will pay us back a hundred-fold."

"Daniel, we must keep a role for your mother. She is still vigorous and she can teach me so much."

"Of course we will but she and Father want to live in the vicarage from now on. He is to devote his spare hours to writing learned works. His paper on Job was well-received and he has sent one on Isaiah to the bishop. He is as excited about his future as I am."

"And they must have Ursula. I could never separate her from your mother, much as I love her."

"Oh she will be back and forth along my new path as long as she can walk. She doesn't know her age but I'm sure she is over seventy. We will keep Peggy and Adam here. One day we may set up our own coach."

"But I must learn to ride first. Horses are the finest of God's creatures and I shan't be afraid of them."

"But what about your grandmother? It was she who made you come and how can I not be grateful now that she did?"

Eunice gave him an excited smile. "She told me this morning that Nellie Foster has begged her not to leave her. They are both lonely widows and with Grandmother's help Nellie can earn a better living. Of course Grandmother made much to me of 'going down in the world' but she said, 'Nellie needs me and in the Hall or vicarage I would only be in the way with nothing to do.' I hope you don't mind but I offered her twenty of my thirty pounds a month for her lifetime. I should have asked you first."

"Dearest one, to be free of your charming grandmother I would have happily sacrificed it all."

Eunice broke into laughter and a long kiss followed.

"I never imagined you could laugh like that," he said at last.

"Neither did I," she chuckled.

EPILOGUE

On the wedding day the village had the promised party on the lawns in front of the Hall. There was dancing and singing and playing on instruments. Vicar Nathaniel made a speech, Mistress Arabella Wilson Horden, who refused to be called anything but Bel, spoke for a few happy sentences and Mistress Celia Horden of London told everyone that they would remember from Twelfth Night that it was she who had brought the young couple together. Only the timeless Ursula didn't speak. She was too busy running up and down seeing that everyone was fed and happy.

Nether Horden felt the world was right at last. A baronet and his bride were in the Hall, the vicar and his wife were in the vicarage. The home farm was prospering under the tenancy of Sam Turner and rents had been held down at last year's level. There was June sunshine on the wedding day with tables laden with all kinds of meats; several barrels of beer stood in a stately row under the Hall windows, ready to be tapped, and small boys climbed unscolded over the statue of wicked old Sir Ralph Horden.

What more could an English village desire?